2/10/17
7.99

"We hardly know each other. I'm not quite certain what to expect from you."

"Expect to be grateful you're in my bed, and that our chamber is far from my father's so he can't hear you crying out in pleasure."

"You are so blasted arro—"

His mouth slashed across hers as he hauled her up against him. Cloth provided no barrier against the heat seeping from his body into hers, as though he were already beginning to claim her, as though every aspect of him would penetrate her before the night was done.

The past two years had taught her to separate her mind from the physical, had tutored her in the wisdom of not caring, of dispensing with emotion, of holding herself apart from the reality of what was actually happening.

But Locksley knocked down her barriers as though she'd built them of twigs. He wasn't content to simply take. He wanted to possess. She felt it in the thrumming of his pulse at his throat where she laid her fingers, in the vibration of his chest as he growled and took the kiss so deep that she felt as though he were mining for her soul . . .

By Lorraine Heath

Lorraine Heath

The
Viscount
And The Vixen

AVON BOOKS

An Imprint of HarperCollinsPublishers

THE VISCOUNT AND THE VIXEN. Copyright © 2016 by Jan Nowasky. All rights reserved. Printed in the United States of America. No part of this book may be used or reproduced in any manner whatsoever without written permission except in the case of brief quotations embodied in critical articles and reviews. For information, address HarperCollins Publishers, 195 Broadway, New York, NY 10007.

First Avon Books mass market printing: December 2016

ISBN 978-0-06239105-6

Avon Trademark Reg. U.S. Pat. Off. and in Other Countries, Marca Registrada, Hecho en U.S.A.
Avon, Avon Books, and the Avon logo are trademarks of HarperCollins Publishers.
HarperCollins® is a registered trademark of HarperCollins Publishers.

16 17 18 19 20   QGM   10 9 8 7 6 5 4 3 2 1

For Jill Barnett

Who, twenty years ago, provided me with my first unsolicited author endorsement, whose kindness and encouragement helped this fledgling writer believe that maybe, just maybe, I could write stories that readers might enjoy. Thank you.

Chapter 1

Havisham Hall, Devonshire
Spring 1882

KILLIAN St. John, Viscount Locksley, strode past the silent sentinel standing in the hallway without giving the oak inlaid clock much thought. He'd been six when he'd first learned that the hands were supposed to move, that the clock's purpose was to mark the passage of time. But with the death of Locke's mother's, for his father at least, time had come to an abrupt standstill.

When a child doesn't know any differently, he accepts what he knows as the absolute truth for how things are done. He had believed the only rooms that servants of any household ever tidied were the ones in use. At Havisham Hall they straightened the bedchamber in which he slept, the small dining room in which he ate, the chambers occupied by his father, and the library in which his father sometimes worked at his desk. The remaining rooms were mysteries shrouded behind locked doors.

Or they had been before the Duke of Ashebury and the Earl of Greyling, along with their wives, were killed in a horrific railway accident in 1858. Shortly afterward their young sons had been brought to Havisham Hall to become the wards of his father. With their arrival so, too, had arrived all manner of knowledge, including the confirmation that his father was stark raving mad.

Now Locke entered the small dining room and came to an abrupt halt at the sight of his sire sitting at the head of the table, reading the newspaper that the butler dutifully ironed each morning. Normally the older man took his meals in his chambers. More astonishing, his usually disheveled white hair had been trimmed and brushed, his face shaven, and his clothes pressed. Locke couldn't recall another time when his father had taken such care with his appearance. On the rare occasion when he wandered out of his sanctuary, he more closely resembled a scraggly scarecrow.

With Locke's arrival, the butler poured coffee into a delicate bone china cup before departing to retrieve his plate. As customarily he was the only one to dine in this room, he kept his meals simple and small. No sideboards with assorted offerings from which to choose. Just a plate bearing whatever fare Cook was of a mind to prepare brought up from the kitchens.

His father had yet to notice him, but then the lord of the manor tended to spend much of his day and night absorbed in his own private world where memories of happier times flourished.

"Well, this is a pleasant surprise," Locke said as he took his seat, striving to shake off his lingering concerns over the estate's dwindling finances. His apprehensions had roused him before dawn and resulted in his sequestering himself in the library for more than two hours searching for an answer that continued to elude him. He'd decided sustenance was needed to sharpen his mind. "What prompted your change in routine?"

His father turned the inked page, rattled his newspaper, then straightened it with a snap of his wrist. "Thought it best to get up and moving about before my bride arrived."

His cup halfway to his mouth, Locke slammed his eyes closed. His father's memories had become increasingly foggy of late, but surely he was not sitting there awaiting his mother's arrival; surely he didn't believe it was his wedding day. Opening his eyes, returning the cup to its saucer, Locke studied this odd fellow whom he loved in spite of all his eccentricities. He looked like any other lord beginning his day. Unlike any other lord, however, he believed his dead wife haunted the moors.

The butler returned and set the plate heaped with eggs, ham, tomatoes, and toast in front of Locke. Before he could return to his station at the wall, Locke looked up at him. "Gilbert, did you assist my father in dressing this morning?"

"Yes, m'lord. As he has no valet, I was more than honored to handle the duties." He leaned down and whispered, "He insisted upon bathing as well, m'lord, and it's not even Saturday." He raised his white bushy eyebrows as though that was grand news indeed, then straightened his spine, seeming rather proud of the fact that he had bathed the marquess midweek.

"Do you know why he went to such bother?"

"Yes, m'lord. He's getting married this afternoon. Mrs. Dorset is preparing the wedding feast as we speak and Mrs. Barnaby was up early cleaning the front parlor, since the vows are to be exchanged there. It's a splendid day indeed, to once again have a lady taking up residence within Havisham."

Only there was no lady except in his father's twisted and demented mind. "Has she a name?"

"I'm rather certain she does, m'lord. Most do."

Locke had long ago learned that patience was required when dealing with the few staff members who had remained through the years. Positions were never replaced with newcomers, but as deaths or retirements occurred so others had moved up in rank. Nevertheless, perhaps it was time to consider hiring a younger butler, except it was difficult to envision Havisham Hall without Gilbert at the helm. He'd been the under-butler before taking over when the previous butler passed in his sleep nearly twenty years ago. Besides, few were better suited to working with and accepting the strangeness that went on within these walls. "Would you happen to know what it is?" *Madeline Connor, perhaps? My mother?*

"If you want to know about my bride," his father snapped, folding up his newspaper and slapping it down on the table, "why don't you ask me? I'm sitting right here."

Because he didn't relish the sorrow that would overtake his father when he realized the truth of the matter: his bride had been gone for thirty years now. She'd perished the night she'd fought so valiantly to bring his only child into the world.

"When does she arrive?" he asked indulgently, out of the corner of his eye watching Gilbert retreat to his corner.

"Around two. The wedding will take place at four." He lifted his hand, wiggled his gnarled fingers. "I wanted to give her a bit of time to get to know me."

Odd that. His parents had met as children, fancied each other from the start, at least according to his father. He arched a brow. "So you don't know her?"

He lifted a slender shoulder. "We've corresponded."

It occurred to Locke there could be something remarkably more upsetting than his father believing he was residing thirty-odd years in the past and on the cusp of marrying Locke's mother. "Pray tell, what is her name?"

"Mrs. Portia Gadstone."

Locke couldn't help but stare. This development was worse, far worse, than he'd anticipated. "A widow, I presume."

"No, Locke, I'm taking to wife a woman who already has a husband. Think, boy. Of course she's a widow. I don't have time for skittish girls who require patience and educating. I want a woman who knows her way well around a man's body."

He could scarce believe that he was having this ridiculous conversation with his father. "If sexual gratification is what you're seeking, I can bring you a woman from the village. Why go to all the bother of marriage?"

"I need an heir."

Although it was unseemly for a lord to drop his jaw, Locke did so anyway. "I'm your heir."

"With no plans to marry."

"I never claimed I wouldn't marry." He insisted he would never love. Knowing his father had descended into lunacy after losing the love of his life, he had no desire whatsoever to give any woman his heart and risk traveling the same path.

"So where is she, this woman you will wed?" his father asked, looking around as though he expected her to materialize in a corner at any second. "You reached your thirtieth year two months ago. I was married at twenty-six, a father at thirty. Yet you're still out sowing wild oats."

Not as much as he once had, and if he took his responsibilities any more seriously he was likely to go mad as well. "I will marry. Eventually."

"I can't take that chance. I require another heir. I'll be

damned if I'm going to let my greedy cousin Robbie and then his drunkard of a son inherit. I'll not have my title traveling down *that* branch of our family tree, I promise you. And neither is Havisham Hall. You'll inherit first, yes, but when you draw your last, your brother, at least thirty-some-odd years your junior depending upon the fertility of this girl's womb, will be around to step in. Hopefully he won't have your aversion to marriage and will already have the next heir lined up."

His father was breathing heavily as though he'd run around the room while delivering his diatribe. Locke came to his feet. "Father, are you ill?"

He waved his hand. "I'm tired, Locke, I'm simply tired, but I must secure my legacy. I should have married before now, provided a spare. But I was encumbered by grief." He sank against the back of the chair as though little strength remained to him. "Your mother, bless her, should have gone on to her just reward instead of waiting around here for me."

Statements such as that one always tore at Locke, made dealing with his sire that much more challenging. His mother wasn't out on the moors waiting. His father simply refused to let her go.

"I will marry, Father. I will provide an heir. I won't let your titles or your estates go to Cousin Robbie. I simply have to find the right woman first." A woman with a churlish disposition he could never, ever love.

"Mrs. Portia Gadstone could be the one, Locke. I daresay, if you like her when we meet her, I shall be a gentleman, step aside, and give you my blessing to marry her this very afternoon."

As though Locke were open to that happening. Unfortunately for Mrs. Gadstone, when she arrived, he would be showing her right back out the door.

The Marquess of Marsden is in need of a strong, healthy, fertile woman to provide an heir. Send queries care of this publication.

$\mathcal{A}$s the coach bounced over the rough road, Portia Gadstone folded up the advert she had clipped from the newspaper and slipped it back into her reticule. Turning her attention to the bleak countryside she reflected that it wasn't nearly as bleak as her life. Agreeing without compunction or remorse to marry a man whom all of London knew to have lost his sanity pretty much said it all.

Her life was in shambles, she was penniless, and she had nowhere else to turn.

But marriage to the marquess suited her plans beautifully. Havisham was a large estate in Devonshire at the edge of Dartmoor. Isolated. No one ever visited. The marquess never left. It was unlikely that anyone would think to look for her there. But if they did, she would be a marchioness, a woman who had gained power—power she was willing to wield if necessary, to protect herself and all she loved.

The marquess had sent her funds for her journey, but fearing discovery of her escape, she'd purchased neither railway nor coach ticket, opting instead to travel in a mail coach. The driver, a big burly fellow, was kind enough, didn't bother her, and hopefully, after delivering her to her destination, would forget he'd ever set eyes on her.

Reaching into her reticule she removed a hard peppermint sweet from a paper sack and popped it into her mouth. She'd been traveling for far too long, was tired and hungry, but nothing good ever came of complaining. Best to just get on with the task no matter how unpleasant it might be, and she was fairly certain that today would be filled with naught but unpleasantness. But she would push through and ensure the marquess never regretted taking her to wife.

As they rounded a curve, she saw the monstrous building—black as Satan's soul, with towers, turrets, and spires reaching for the heavens—looming before her, growing larger each time the horses' hooves hit the ground. It could be no other than Havisham Hall. A chill skittered down her spine. If she had any other choice—

Only she didn't.

With her marriage to the marquess she would step into the aristocratic circle. Marchioness of Marsden. She would garner respect simply because of her position at his side. And the child she delivered to him would be safe, under his protection.

No one would dare harm the child. No one would dare hurt her.

Ever again.

STANDING at an upper-floor window, gazing out on the drive, Locke laughed aloud at the scene below him. She'd arrived in a mail coach. A mail coach, for God's sake. Could this farce get any more ludicrous?

He couldn't get a good impression of her. She seemed rather small, petite. Ample curves. She wore black. That didn't bode particularly well for the success of a marriage. A ridiculously large black hat covered her head, a veil draped over her face. He thought she might have dark hair. Difficult to tell.

The burly driver struggled to get a large trunk down from the top of the coach and set it at the woman's feet. He tipped his hat, climbed back up to his seat, and was gone. No one tarried at Havisham.

She spun on her heel and began marching with purpose toward the residence. Locke dashed down the stairs. He had to put an end to this madness posthaste.

A banging echoed through the foyer just as he reached it. She was certainly determined to make use of the knocker. He swung open the door. She'd lifted the veil, and he found himself staring into the most unusual shade of eyes he'd ever seen. The color reminded him of whiskey, full of temptation, intoxicating, and threatening to bring a man to ruin.

"I'm here to marry his Lordship," she said in a throaty voice that caused everything below his waist to come to immediate attention. Damn it all to hell. Instead of securing a village wench for his father, he should consider securing one for himself. Obviously he'd gone too long without a woman if it took merely her voice to get a rise out of him. "Fetch my trunk."

Straightening, he drew himself up to his full height, which had him fairly towering over her. "You presume me to be the footman?"

She gave him a slow once-over that caused his skin to tighten as though her fingers were trailing along wherever her eyes touched. When her perusal was complete, she turned up her pert little button of a nose. "Butler, footman, it doesn't matter to me. Trunk needs to be brought in. Bring it in."

"You also presume that Lord Marsden is going to give you one look and still wish to marry you?"

"I have a contract with him. He'll be marrying me or he'll pay a pretty penny."

His father might have mentioned that little fact. Obviously Locke had misjudged all the trouble his father could stir up from within his chambers. He'd thought he did little more than gaze longingly out the window, hoping to catch a glimpse of his love frolicking over the moors.

"My dear," his father announced, suddenly at Locke's side, taking her hand and pressing a kiss to it, even as he managed to artfully skirt her past Locke and into the foyer. "It's such a pleasure to meet you."

Lowering herself into a graceful deep curtsy, she smiled up at his father as though he were the answer to every childish wish she'd ever made. "My lord, I'm delighted to be here, more than I can say."

Locke narrowed his eyes. Why would anyone on God's earth take any delight whatsoever in being delivered to hell's small corner of the world? And yet there was an intriguing honesty to her tone that he couldn't deny. Was she that good of an actress?

"Locke, fetch her trunk, then join us in the parlor."

His father appeared absolutely besotted. Not good, not good at all if Locke had any hope whatsoever of squelching this arrangement. "I'll join you in the parlor first. The trunk is perfectly safe where it is. No one is going to wander off with it, and I'll be damned if I'm going to miss a single word of this conversation."

"You're rather impertinent for a servant," she chastised, with enough edge to indicate she was securing her position as mistress in the manor and reminding him of his place within it.

"I would agree—if I were a servant. As I'm apparently to become your son before the afternoon is done, allow me to introduce myself: Killian St. John, Viscount Locksley, at your service." He mockingly made a sweeping bow. She had to be as mad as his father. Or a woman intent on taking advantage of another's madness. He'd wager on the latter. There was a calculating sharpness in those eyes. He didn't trust them—or her—one whit.

Again she curtsied deeply, elegantly, but for him there was no smile, no emotion whatsoever. The swiftness with which she'd donned her armor fascinated him, more so because she'd accurately judged him a threat. She was no fool, this one. "It's a pleasure, my lord."

Oh, he very much doubted it would turn out to be that.

"This way, my dear. We have very little time to get acquainted before the nuptials." His father led her into the parlor, situated her in a plush chair near the fireplace. Dust rose up as she settled onto the plump cushion. So much for the housekeeper's cleaning abilities.

His father took the chair opposite hers. Locke dropped onto the sofa, sitting on the far end so as to procure the best angle for observing her. She was young, couldn't be much older than twenty-five. Her clothing was well made, in excellent condition. No fraying, no tatters.

She lifted her arms, reaching for her hatpin, and her pert breasts lifted as well. They were the perfect size to fill the palms of his hands. Those very same hands could span her waist, close around it, draw her up against him. Why the devil was he noticing things that had no bearing on his strategy?

She swept the hat from her head, and his breath caught. Her hair was a fiery red that rivaled the flames in a hearth for brilliance. The strands appeared heavy, abundant, and in danger of tumbling down at any moment. He wondered exactly how many pins he'd have to remove to make it do just that. Not many, he'd wager. Two, three at the most.

Shifting to ease the discomfort of his body reacting as though he hadn't been near a woman since he'd left the classroom, he draped his arm along the back of the sofa, striving for a nonchalance he wasn't feeling. He didn't care about her hair, her eyes, or her figure. Or those plump, full lips the shade of rubies. He cared about her motives. Why would a woman as young and enticing as she was be willing to marry a man as old and decrepit as his father? She had to have young bucks fawning over her. She drew attention. So what did she hope to gain here that she couldn't gain elsewhere?

"Now, my dear—" his father began, leaning forward.

"Here we are, m'lord!" Mrs. Barnaby sang out as she bustled in, carrying a tea service. Her hair, more white than black, was pulled back in her usual tight bun, her black dress pressed to perfection. "Tea and cakes, just as you requested." After setting the tray on the small table that rested between the two chairs, she straightened, cocked her head to the side as she studied their guest, her brow furrowing. "She is rather young, m'lord."

"An old woman isn't going to give me an heir now is she, Mrs. Barnaby?"

"I suppose there is that." She gave a little curtsy, her arthritic knees creaking as she did so. "Welcome to Havisham, Mrs. Gadstone. Shall I pour the tea?"

"No, I'll see to it, thank you."

"Oh." Mrs. Barnaby's shoulders slumped. She was obviously crestfallen to be dismissed before hearing anything of note she could share below stairs.

"That'll be all, Mrs. Barnaby," his father said gently.

Heaving a huge sigh, she turned to go. Locke held out his hand. "I'll have the keys, Mrs. Barnaby."

She slapped her hand over the large ring dangling from her ample waist as though he'd asked for the Crown Jewels and she was determined to guard them with her life. "They're my responsibility."

"I may have a need for them. I'll return them to you later." His need depended on how this conversation went.

With a mulish expression, she reluctantly handed them over before marching from the room with righteous indignation shimmering off her in waves. He didn't know why she clung to them so tenaciously when they were more ornament than use. He supposed because they heralded her vaunted position in the household, one she'd acquired because she'd stuck around when many of the parlor maids had gone in search of greener pastures. Or ones less haunted.

Returning his attention to Mrs. Gadstone, he watched in fascination as she slowly peeled off a black kidskin glove as though she reveled in exposing something forbidden. Quarter inch by frustrating quarter inch. Yet he seemed unable to look away as her smooth unblemished hand was revealed. No scars. No calluses. No freckles. She took the same care with uncovering the other, and he fought against envisioning those small, perfect, silken-looking hands gliding leisurely over his bare chest. With care, she set the gloves primly in her lap as though completely unaware of the effect her slow unveiling could have on a man. Although he would wager half his future fortune that she knew precisely what she was about.

"Lord Marsden, how do you prefer your tea?"

Her raspy voice shimmied down his spine, settled in his groin, damn it all. She sounded like a recently sated woman.

"An abundance of sugar, if you please."

Locke watched as she poured, added several cubes, stirred, and offered the teacup and saucer along with a tender smile to the marquess, who smiled back as though grateful for the offering when in fact he detested tea.

"And how do you prefer your tea, Lord Locksley?"

"Surely as my mother, you should call me Locke."

Her gaze came to bear on his, her eyes as sharp as a finely honed rapier. God, she was willing to slice him to ribbons. He'd like to see her try. "I am not yet your mother, Lord Locksley, am I? Have I done something to offend you?"

Leaning forward, he dug his elbows into his thighs. "I'm simply striving to determine why a woman as young and lovely as yourself would be willing to lie on her back so a man as shriveled as my father can slide on top of her."

"Locke!" his father bellowed. "You've gone too far. Get the hell out."

"It's quite all right, my lord," she said calmly, never taking her challenging gaze from Locke's, not flinching, not blushing, not so much as arching a thinly shaped eyebrow at him. "I don't see that your father's preferred position for coupling is really any of your concern. Perhaps he will take me standing while coming in at me from behind. Or on my knees. Or upside down. But I assure you, he will not be shriveled." Then she slowly lowered those damned whiskey eyes to his lap, and he cursed his cock's betrayal. With startling detail, images of him with her in all those positions had flown through his mind. He'd grown so hard and aching that he couldn't have gotten up and walked out if he wanted.

And she bloody well knew it.

"Tea. My lord."

"No." The word came out strangled. It seemed every facet of his body was intent on betraying him.

Her luscious lips turned up into a smug, triumphant smile. She turned to his father. "May I interest you in a tea cake, Lord Marsden?"

Despite the innocence of her words, all he wanted to do was drag her up against him, claim her mouth as his own, and see if it tasted as tart as it sounded.

Chapter 2

"Bravo!" Marsden exclaimed, clapping, his green eyes lively. "I daresay, Mrs. Gadstone, you certainly set my son in his place. Well done!"

"Please, you must call me Portia."

While standing up to Locksley had gained her some favor with Marsden, it still took everything within Portia to keep her hand from shaking as she handed the marquess a cake. Tremors were cascading through her like a never-ending waterfall. It wasn't just righteous indignation that was causing her to tremble. It was a strange and unwanted attraction to Viscount Locksley that was igniting every damned nerve ending she possessed.

Although she had never met him, she'd heard enough stories about him, listened as women waxed on about his good looks, that she'd known who he was the moment he opened the door. She'd been unprepared for the magnetism that his incredible emerald eyes had sparked within her or the desire that had hit her with such force that she'd nearly spun on her heel and gone racing after the coach. His hair, black as midnight, longer than was fashionable, served to make the brilliant hue of his eyes stand out all the more. She'd never in her life had such an immediate visceral reaction to any man. That she found him so incredibly alluring was distracting beyond measure, entirely unacceptable, and remarkably dangerous.

In spite of the rude and off-putting manner in which he was doing it, she knew he was striving to protect his father and couldn't help but respect and admire him for it. Unfortunately for him she had someone to protect as well and she was going to do it at any cost, with any means available to her. Her mind, her body, her soul. She would use them all, in any manner required—no matter how unpleasant or unsavory—to accomplish her goal.

Out of the corner of her eye, she watched as he reached a large hand inside his jacket and withdrew something from a breast pocket. A newspaper clipping that he began to unfold. Based on its size, she knew exactly how it would read. It seemed he was preparing to fire the next volley in this silently declared clash of wills. She shored up her defenses.

"Do you find the countryside to your liking, Mrs. Gadstone?" the marquess asked kindly. She would have liked to have known him when he was younger. She suspected he'd been quite the charmer.

"Strong," Locksley declared before she could answer.

Unlike his son, who was sadly lacking in charm. Although one wouldn't know it based upon all the tittering about him the females of London did. He'd swept half of them off their feet and into his bed if stories were to be believed.

Marsden sighed with obvious annoyance. "I shared my advert so you would know the qualifications I sought, not so you could use it against Mrs. Gadstone. She and I have already corresponded several times. I know she meets all the requirements I seek in a woman to provide me with an heir."

"Surely then there can be no objection to my reassuring myself." His narrowed gaze landed on her like a weighty thing that could crush a weaker woman. "Strong," he repeated. "You must forgive my impudence, Mrs. Gadstone, but you don't look as though you have the strength to shove that chair from one side of the room to the other."

"I do, however, have the strength to call in a footman to do it for me."

"How many households have you visited where the head housekeeper serves the tea?" He held up the keys he'd procured earlier and gave them a little shake, their tinkling echoing between them. "Our indoor staff includes only the butler, the cook, and the housekeeper."

"Surely you have the means to provide for more staff."

"We do, but my father is more comfortable with the staff we have."

She smiled tenderly at Marsden. "Then I shall be so as well."

"Hire as many as you like."

Locksley's jaw clenched, and she fought to keep her expression neutral. It seemed he wasn't only engaged in a battle of wills with her. There was a sharpness to Marsden that belied the rumors claiming he was mad. Already his protectiveness of her reassured her that she'd made the correct decision in answering his advertisement.

"Healthy," Locksley barked.

This time, she didn't hold back the smugness. "I have never been ill a day in my life."

"Even as a child?"

"Even as a child. I was never colicky. Never fevered. I still have all my teeth, so they're healthy as well. Would you care to count them?" Regretting that last offer when his eyes darkened as though he'd count them by running his tongue over them, she waited with bated breath for his retort, grateful when he merely clucked his tongue and gave his head a small shake.

"I'll take your word for it."

She was actually surprised that he would take her word for anything. As he studied her, she waited, dreading the last one, hoping he might spare her—

"Fertile?"

Bastard. Here was the tricky part.

"There was a son. A dear sweet thing. He died before his first year."

Locksley flinched, his eyes filling with regret as though he wished he hadn't asked as much as she did. "I'm sorry for your loss. It was not my intent to cause you pain."

At least he possessed some compassion, even if he was putting her through her paces. She should stop here but she'd come too far to leave any doubt as to her suitability. While she was marrying the marquess, it was evident that his son would play a large part in their lives, and he was the heir apparent. She would be providing the spare. It was imperative that she and Locksley not constantly be at odds.

"The boy was healthy and strong. He died through no fault of his own. The woman who was supposed to see to his care . . . was negligent." She turned to Marsden. "I will hire neither a nanny nor a governess to oversee your son's care. I will tend to him myself. He shall grow to maturity, good and noble, deserving of your family name."

"I never doubted it, my dear." He raised an eyebrow at his son. "Finished with your inquest? We have only an hour before the vicar arrives."

She wondered how he knew that without looking at his watch. The clock on the mantel was obviously broken. It had shown the time as forty-three minutes past eleven when she walked in, continued to reflect the same hour and minutes even though she felt as though an eternity of interminable seconds had ticked by.

"I'd like a few moments alone with Mrs. Gadstone to ensure she understands exactly what it is to which she is agreeing."

"As I mentioned, she and I have already corresponded. I've told her everything."

"I'm sure you have. But sometimes a different perspective can cause enlightenment."

"I don't want you chasing her off."

His gaze slid over to her. "She doesn't strike me as someone who is easily chased off."

Was that respect she heard in his voice? Or a challenge?

Picking up the ring of keys, he unfolded his long, lean body. "Allow me to show you what will become your new home, Mrs. Gadstone. I swear to you that I shall behave as a proper gentleman."

She didn't want time alone with him, and it wasn't because she feared he'd misbehave. She was relatively certain he wouldn't. Her concern was that he was too handsome by half, too tempting, too masculine. She knew from the gossips that he did not live a life of complete leisure, but was prone to traveling in barbaric, challenging parts of the world. He was broad of shoulder and muscled, but not overly so. There was a sleekness to his form. She could envision him slicing through water, galloping over the moors, hefting an ax to chop wood with equal measure.

She should decline, assure him it wasn't necessary. Her mind was made up. As though deducing the path of her thoughts, he angled his chin down slightly, his gaze penetrating. A challenge. Drat him!

Slowly she tugged on her gloves. If he offered his arm, she was going to want the extra layer of material separating her skin from his. Rising to her feet, she took a deep fortifying breath. "I would be delighted to have you give me a tour of the place."

"You don't have to go with him," Marsden said.

"Not to worry. I'm sure he'll behave. And I do want your son and I to become fast friends." She looked at the son from whom she knew she was best served keeping her distance. "Shall we be off?"

He walked over and extended his arm. Swallowing hard, she placed her hand on his forearm. She'd been wrong. The kidskin offered no protection whatsoever from the heat of his flesh, firmness of his muscles, and raw masculinity that radiated through him. If she didn't think he would dub her spineless, she'd step back and tell him that she'd changed her mind. But the one thing she could claim with certainty was that she'd never been a coward.

She could hold her own against him, keep a distance between them.

The problem was, she wasn't certain she wanted to.

WHEN she placed her hand on his arm, his body reacted as though she'd placed her entire naked form against his. What the devil was the matter with him to have such a strong reaction to her nearness? Blast it all, he would be going to the village this very night. He could not stay in this residence, envisioning her in his father's bed—

He clenched his back teeth together until his jaw ached. He was not traveling that path in his mind.

Leading her into the hallway, he cursed each breath that filled his nostrils, his lungs, with her jasmine fragrance. No common rose scent for her. Nothing about her was common. But still he couldn't fathom why she would marry an old man when she could have a young swain.

"I wish to apologize for my insensitivity in questioning your fertility. I didn't mean to bring forth such devastating memories." The pain glazing over her eyes as she talked about her son had hit him like a punch to the gut. If he could have gone back and cut out his tongue before he began his asinine inquisition he would have.

"The boy is never far from my thoughts, Lord Locksley. His death haunts me and guides my actions. Which you see is to your benefit as it makes me empathetic to your cause. I know you are striving to protect your father from someone who would take advantage of him. I assure you that I wish him no harm."

"Still, Mrs. Gadstone, I am flummoxed as to why you would not seek out love but would be willing to marry a man who is at least thirty-five years your senior."

"I've known love, my lord. It provided little security. Now I am in want of security."

"How long were you married?"

"We were together for two years."

"How did he die?"

She sighed. "Illness. He took a fever."

"Again, my condolences. How long ago?"

"Six months." She peered up at him, a slight lifting to her lips. "You should ask your father to let you read our correspondence. All your questions would be answered."

He doubted that. He suspected a lifetime would not be long enough to get the answers to the myriad questions he had about her.

"Are all the clocks in the residence broken?" she asked as they passed a tall one standing in the hallway.

He began escorting her up a set of stairs. "As far as I know none of them are. They were all simply stopped at the hour of my birth and the moment of my mother's passing." Half an hour was all the time she'd been given to hold him, all the time he'd been given to know her love.

"How did your mother die?"

"I killed her." At the top of the stairs, he turned and faced her, surprised to see horror etched over her finely formed features. Apparently his father's correspondence to her didn't answer all questions. "During childbirth. Why do you think he named me Killian?"

Her eyes widened slightly. "I'm sure it's only coincidence. He wouldn't be that deliberately cruel to a child, to label him a killer."

"I'm not certain cruelty was his intent. He merely wanted to ensure that neither of us would ever forget. I believe it's important that you understand what life here at Havisham Hall entails. Let's begin here, shall we?" Sorting through the keys on the ring, he found the one he required, slipped it into the lock, turned it, and swung open the door. He swept the cobwebs away before extending his arm toward the massive room, with its mirrored walls that stood two floors tall. "The grand salon. They hosted a magnificent ball here the Christmas before my mother died."

PORTIA hesitated only a second before stepping over the threshold and onto the landing that led to the stairs descending into the musty-scented room. Cautiously, expecting the dull floor to give way beneath her feet with each step, she walked to the railing. She wanted to wrap her hands around it, allow it to provide some sort of support, but it was covered in a thick layer of dust. As far as she could see, everything was adorned in powdery film, decorated with lacy cobwebs. At the grimy windows that lined one wall, the faded red draperies were drawn back, revealing dust motes waltzing in the afternoon sunlight that filtered in to touch the vases filled with withered and dried stalks of flowers, their blooms long gone.

"On our way here, we passed several rooms with closed doors. Are they all neglected such as this one?" she asked softly, almost reverently. The setting seemed to call for quiet.

"Yes. After my mother passed, my father ordered that nothing be touched, that everything in the residence be left just as it was when she died."

Trying to fathom what sort of impact growing up in a house like this might have on a lad, she looked over her shoulder at him. He stood tall and erect, his face reflecting no sadness, no happiness, no joy, no sorrow. He was accustomed to this bizarre attempt to keep everything as it was. "But nothing stays the same, nothing goes unchanged."

"No, it does not."

"You're grown now. I have the impression you're the one managing things. Why don't you have the rooms tidied up, restored to what they were?"

"Because it would upset my father, just as hiring additional staff, having new faces walking through the residence, would unsettle him."

So he lived in this dreary house filled with its empty memories. For his father. She couldn't help but believe that he was a man capable of great love, great compassion. She had a fleeting thought that if she confessed all to him, he would make it right. What a silly lass she was to think he would look at her with anything other than disgust. No, she was on her own in this matter, had to see to her own needs, protect what was hers.

"You can't compete with her, Mrs. Gadstone. My mother."

"I have no intention of trying. I know what your father requires, what he wants of me. I accept what the limitations of our relationship shall be."

"Why are you willing to settle for so little?"

Because it was her only opportunity to gain so much. "The son I give him will be a lord."

"He will be the spare. He will not inherit until I die."

In truth, she doubted he would ever inherit. Locksley would marry, gain his own heir. "Still, he will be Lord Whatever-We-Name-Him St. John. He will move about in the right circles, have opportunities, marry well. As for myself, I will be a marchioness, also move about in the right circles, and be very well provided for. He has promised me a dower house." She looked over the railing. "May we go down?"

"If you like."

It wasn't so much that she liked, it was more that she needed to distract herself from the doubts that had begun to surface. If there was another way to save herself, she couldn't see it.

He offered his arm; she nearly refused it, except she was averse to using the dusty and cobwebby banister. As he began leading her down the stairs covered in the faded red carpeting, she didn't like noticing how sturdy he was, how strong. Or that he smelled of sandalwood tinged with oranges.

Once they reached the center of the room, she reclaimed her hand, turned in a slow circle, and imagined all this room had once been with an orchestra playing in the balcony, guests waltzing, Lord and Lady Marsden entertaining.

"What will you do after he's gone?" she asked quietly.

"Pardon?"

Twisting around to face him, she realized by his blank expression that while he might consider his father old and *shriveled*, he hadn't truly accepted that he was in the winter of his years, would not be here forever. "When your father dies, will you restore this manor to its magnificence?"

"I hadn't given it any thought."

He truly hadn't. She could see it in his eyes, and she liked him for it. What must it have been like to grow up here, alone—

Only he hadn't been alone. "The Duke of Ashebury and the Earl of Greyling were wards of your father, lived here when they were children."

"That's correct."

"They refer to all of you as the Hellions of Havisham."

He arched a dark brow, his gaze intensified as though he could see straight into her soul and read every story etched there. "It seems you already move about in the right circles."

Damn it. She wasn't being as cautious as she should be when speaking with him. "I read the gossip sheets." Needing to distract him, she gave her full attention to the wall of windows, the glass doors that led outside. "May we go out onto the terrace?"

"I insist. It's part of the tour."

He led the way, flicked a bolt, and swung open the door. "After you."

She stepped onto the stone veranda, wandered over to the wrought-iron railing, and stared at what had obviously long ago been gardens but had since been reclaimed by nature. Still here and there remained evidence that great care had once been taken with it. "No gardener."

"No. Our outside staff is comprised of a head groomsman who also serves as coachman, and a couple of stable lads."

"A pity. I so enjoy gardens and flowers. Does your father never leave the residence then?"

"Was the answer not provided in his correspondence?"

She shifted her gaze over to him. "I didn't think to ask."

Crossing his arms over his chest, he leaned his hip against the railing, painting quite the picture of raw masculinity. "I wonder what else you might not have thought to ask."

"I was striving to make conversation, my lord. I don't care whether he goes out. I obtained the answers to the questions that mattered to me."

"Perhaps I should read your correspondence. I'd like to know what questions mattered to you."

"I'm an open book, my lord."

"I very much doubt that."

"You are a suspicious sort."

"Am I wrong?"

No, he wasn't. She had secrets she would keep carefully guarded from him, from his father. She doubted the marquess would mind, but she suspected his son would care a great deal. Marsden merely wanted an heir. Locksley wanted to understand her. "I assume you go to London for the Season."

She would welcome the months he was away.

"Occasionally. Not as often as I should. I don't like leaving my father alone. Although it appears he can get into as much mischief when I'm here as he can when I'm gone."

"With me about, you won't be leaving him alone. You can go to London as much as you like. I've also heard you enjoy traveling. Where do you plan to venture off to next?"

"I haven't journeyed anywhere in a couple of years now. Have no plans to in the near future."

"But again, with me here, you're free to do whatever you wish, go wherever you want."

"Why am I left with the impression that you're striving to be rid of me?"

Because she was and he was no fool. Still, she knew

the value of a good bluff. "I'm simply trying to be a suitable *mother* to you. Give you some freedom. Lessen your burdens."

Unfolding his arms, he stepped forward and touched his thumb to her lips, before very slowly outlining them, his gaze homed in on her mouth. Heat slammed into her. While he was only caressing the edges, it felt as though he was tracing his thumb along the very essence of her.

"I have to confess, Mrs. Gadstone, that I'm going to have a very difficult time viewing you as my mother."

"You promised to behave." Sounding breathless, her voice raspy, every aspect of her body attuned to his, she cursed him for his ability to stir to life what she was striving so hard to keep banked.

"So I did. But you are not yet wed. It seems like we should at least have a taste of each other before you are."

He moved in. Her hand shot up to the center of his chest, his firm hard chest. Beneath her fingers she could feel the steady thudding of his heart, the tension riffling through him. "No."

His eyes became heavy lidded, slumberous. "Afraid you'll like it too much?"

Terrified that she would indeed be enamored of it. Although he was no doubt testing her loyalty. "I'm betrothed to your father."

He angled his head slightly. "Betrothed is a bit of a stretch, isn't it? You answered an advert. It's not as though he caught sight of you across a ballroom floor, became ensnared by your beauty, and courted you. Before today, you'd never met."

"Still, we are to marry."

"What can it hurt to simply have a sample?" In spite of her hand pushing on him, he managed to lean in until his breath skimmed over her cheek. "He'll never know."

"I'll know."

"So you are afraid. I'd wager you're as aware of me as I am of you."

"You'd lose that wager."

"Prove it." His lips, soft and warm, landed at the corner of her mouth. "Prove you're not drawn to me, that there is naught between us." He pressed his lips to the other corner. "Surely your resolve to marry my father will not be undone by one kiss."

It was dangerous, so very dangerous. She needed to shove him away, knew it was the wise course, but her strength seemed to leave her while he nibbled on her lower lip. Her eyes slid closed as the heat swamped her. His tenderness took her off guard. It had been so long since anyone had shown her any tenderness, since anyone had enticed her with a light lapping at the seam of her mouth. She couldn't prevent the moan from escaping, and in the sound he must have heard her surrender, because the gentleness receded and his mouth came down on hers, hot and hard, hungry and greedy. She should push him aside, kick him, step on his foot, but the awareness had been shimmering between them since he'd opened the door. He was young and virile. Where was the harm in one last kiss of youth, of being held in strong, sturdy arms, of having her breasts flattened against a firm, broad chest? Everything within her screamed that she should run. But his mouth was working its delicious, glorious magic.

And she melted against him.

Chapter 3

*I*T was the very worst mistake he'd made in his life. Worse than the time he'd angered a tribal warlord by flirting with his daughter or gone swimming in the Nile and nearly become a crocodile's main course or misjudged the weather and gotten caught in a snowstorm in the Himalayas.

He knew he'd made a grave error in judgment, egging her on until she finally opened her mouth to him and welcomed his assault. If he'd thought for one minute that his father held sincere affection for this woman, if he thought he viewed her as anything other than a means to an end, he wouldn't have indulged, he would have kept his distance, would have been true to his word to remain a gentleman.

But those luscious lips that spouted such tart rejoinders, that tipped up only slightly when she smiled, that promised pleasure would be found within her arms, were simply too tempting for any mortal man to resist. He'd merely wanted a taste, one little taste, and then he could move on to a tavern wench this evening.

Only now he knew that was going to be nigh on impossible. She tasted of peppermint, and he suspected if he riffled through her reticule that he'd find a little stash of the hard sweets. She'd no doubt sucked on one just as she was now sucking on his tongue, driving him to distraction, causing him to clamp his arms around her all the tighter. She was bold, daring, as adventurous as he. His father wanted a woman who knew her way around a man's body.

He had a feeling that Mrs. Portia Gadstone could turn a man inside out, wring him dry, and have him gratefully asking for more.

Tearing his mouth from hers, he stared down at her. Her eyes were heated, her breaths shallow. Shoving on his shoulders, she stepped back, leaned against the railing, and met his gaze head on as though she'd done nothing of which to be ashamed.

"I hope you enjoyed your taste, my lord. Once I'm wed to your father, there will be no more sampling of the goods."

So cool, so calm, but the flush in her cheeks gave her away. She had not been as unaffected by the kiss as she was striving to appear. What had caused her to learn to shield her emotions like that? What had transpired to make her so wary of revealing how she truly felt?

She gave nothing away, this one. He doubted he'd learn anything about her by reading the correspondence, at least nothing that went below the surface. Every word she spoke was calculated to reveal only enough to satisfy. But then he, too, was a master at keeping his distance, giving little away. He wanted to know no one well, wanted them to know him even less. The heart was better protected that way. If no one mattered, no one could cause him to sink into despair. Protect his sanity at all costs, that was his mantra. "I assure you, you have nothing to worry over. I'd never cuckold my father. And married women have never been to my taste. I have no respect for those who engage in deceit."

He thought he caught sight of the barest of flinches. Although perhaps it was simply relief washing through her to know that once the vows were exchanged he would give her a wide berth.

With a sigh, she glanced around. "I believe I've seen enough, Lord Locksley. Your father is no doubt beginning to worry. I should return to him."

"Surely after such an intimacy, we can be a bit less formal. Please call me Locke." He offered his arm.

"I believe I can make my own way." As though to prove it, she charged forward, her heels clicking over the stones, then the wood as she crossed the threshold.

While he followed at a discrete distance, he enjoyed this view of her, the rigid set of her spine, the enticing swaying of her narrow hips. He closed the door to the terrace, followed her up the stairs, and began locking the entrance to the grand salon.

"Is that really necessary?" she asked. "With only adults living here, surely it is enough to simply tell them not to open the doors."

After securing the door, he turned to her. "Apparently my mother's ghost can't travel through locked doors, so the more of them that are locked, the more likely it is that she will remain out on the moors."

She gaped at him, her eyes rounded with surprise.

"Here now, in all the exchanged correspondence, did my father neglect to mention that the estate is haunted?"

"Surely you don't believe that."

"Of course I don't. But he does. I'm sure once he's visited your bed tonight that he'll warn you to lock your door after he departs and to never sleep with a window open. Never go out on the moors at night. She'll snatch you up."

"Cautions to make young lads behave."

"But I am no longer a young lad, yet the cautions remain."

"I suppose I should be relieved then that I don't believe in ghosts either." Pivoting on her heel, she headed down the stairs.

He liked this view very much indeed, had to enjoy it while he could. He had told her true. He would not cuckold his father. Once they were married, he was going to avoid her as though she carried the plague.

He caught up to her in the foyer, with only a few inches separating them as she strolled into the parlor. His father was slumped in the chair, eyes closed.

Her hand went to her chest. "My God." She turned to Locke, panic reflected in her eyes. "Is he dead?"

She seemed genuinely concerned, but then with his untimely death before the vows were exchanged, she would lose the dower house and anything else his sire had promised her. His father released a thundering snore. With a little screech, she hopped back.

Chuckling, Locke moved past her. "For someone who doesn't believe in ghosts, you're awfully skittish."

"I feared he was dead."

"Not yet; he's simply prone to falling asleep at odd times." He knelt beside the chair, curled his hand around his father's shoulder, and gave him a little shake. "Father, wake up."

His father's eyes fluttered open, unfocused, distant. "Is Linnie calling for me?"

His pet name for Locke's mother, Madeline, who apparently had detested being called Maddie. "No."

"Good. I have time to get ready for dinner. She despises when I'm late for dinner."

"Mrs. Gadstone is dining with you this evening."

Easier to bring him into the present than crush him by making him face the truth of his past.

"Mrs. Gadstone? I don't know a Mrs. Gadstone."

Locke looked back over his shoulder and arched a brow at Portia. *See what you're getting yourself into?*

She stepped in front of the marquess. "I'm Mrs. Gadstone, my lord. Portia Gadstone."

His father's face lit up, and he snapped his fingers. "Of course, of course. I remember now. Did you enjoy your tour of the residence, my dear?"

"It was very enlightening."

Tactfully put, Locke thought.

"Take a seat and tell me all about it, but first where's the vicar? He should be here by now."

"I'm certain he's on his way," Locke assured him. *If you did indeed inform him that he needed to be here.* He was hoping he'd only done it in his mind.

Portia returned to her chair. Locke sat on the end of the couch, nearer to her this time, although he couldn't comprehend why he wanted less distance between them. "Father, it occurred to me that it might be best to wait a few days before proceeding with the wedding, give Mrs. Gadstone an opportunity to become more accustomed to what her life here will entail."

"Neither frugal nor practical, Locke. I agreed to pay her a hundred pounds each day the wedding is delayed."

"I beg your pardon?"

"I signed a contract. If she doesn't marry today, I have to pay her a hundred pounds every day until she is wed. If I call off the wedding completely I have to pay her ten thousand quid."

Locke bolted to his feet. "Have you gone mad?" *Of course he had. He'd gone mad years ago.*

"I had to give her some sort of reassurance that she wasn't making this trip for nothing. That my intentions were honorable. That I wasn't seeking to take advantage."

But she was. Locke shifted his gaze to Portia, who was wearing a beguiling yet almost innocent smile, her eyes on him, screaming satisfaction, as though she had bested him. The little witch. She'd mentioned the contract. Had known when she walked through the door that no matter how much he might not wish it so, this marriage was going to take place, or he was going to pay her a hefty purse. She'd said as much.

He'd been so intrigued by her damned eyes that he hadn't thought to question it then. "I want to see this damned contract."

"I thought you might," she said sweetly. Reaching into her reticule she withdrew a small leatherette, untied the cord, and removed several folded sheaves of paper. He snatched them out of her hand and proceeded to scour the contents.

"Tearing them up won't help," she said blithely. "My solicitor has a copy."

"I have a copy as well."

Not helping, Father.

He read the words carefully. The Marquess of Marsden might be mad, but he wasn't an idiot. He'd have provided himself with some avenue of escape. And there it was, carefully hidden among a gibberish of words. Locke almost laughed aloud, the wily old bugger. He was clever.

Locke slid his gaze over to Portia Gadstone and, for the first time, clearly saw her for what she truly was. A mercenary, a title chaser, someone wanting to rise so badly above her station she would use any means necessary to accomplish her goal, including taking advantage of an aging gentleman. The sort of woman he could never grow to care for, could never love, could never give his heart to.

She was bloody perfect.

"I'll marry her."

Chapter 4

*I*N horror, still reeling from Locksley's proclamation, Portia watched as he turned to Marsden. "I assume you have no objections."

The marquess smiled. "None whatsoever. I was rather hoping for this outcome when all was said and done."

Locksley turned back to her. "What say you, Portia? Much better to be my wife than my mother, don't you think?"

"No." The word came out harsh, abrupt, but inside she was screaming, *No, no, no, no, no!* She could not marry the viscount. Absolutely could not. She was here to marry the marquess. An old man who thought he needed an heir when he already had one.

Not his strapping son, who caused her insides to flutter every time he looked at her, her body to warm when he touched her, her entire being to dissolve into a heated puddle when he kissed her. She could not, would not, marry *him*.

"No," she repeated with the authority of her conviction.

With a cluck of his tongue, he tossed the papers onto her lap and settled against the sofa in an insolent lounge, his arm resting along the back of it, his fingers tapping merrily. "Then the contract is null and void and we're done here."

"No." She looked imploringly at Marsden. "You and I are to marry. That's what we agreed to."

He gave her a sad smile, the wrinkles shifting over his face. "That's what we discussed in our correspondence, but the contract is worded a bit differently. It states you must provide me with an heir."

"I can't provide you with an heir if I'm not married to you."

"You provide him with an heir by providing me with one," Locksley said, his voice teeming with arrogance.

Jerking her attention to him, she wanted to snatch that smug, self-satisfied smile right off his gloriously handsome face. He thought he'd won, when he didn't even know what she was battling for, what was at stake. If she told him . . . God, if she told him he wouldn't be sympathetic, he wouldn't understand. He'd cast her out as brutally as her family had.

"The contract states that you marry and provide the Marquess of Marsden with an heir. It doesn't specify whom you marry. If you give me a son, you have in essence provided him with his heir. And actually much tidier. If you give my father a son, you've merely given him a spare. Who may or may not inherit. Give me a son, and you've provided the next heir apparent. Honestly, Portia, I don't understand why you're not throwing yourself at me. That's what you want, isn't it? A son who will inherit titles, estates, power, wealth. Is it that you object to being merely a viscountess rather than a marchioness? The marchioness title will come eventually, but perhaps not soon enough for your aspirations."

She heard the disgust, revulsion in his voice. How

could marriage to him be pleasant when he hated her before the vows were even exchanged?

But if she said no, where would she go? What would she do? How would she survive? She could not return to what her life had been. It would destroy her. *He* would destroy her.

She rose to her feet and turned to the fireplace. Cold, so cold. She wished there was a fire, but she doubted even that would warm her, as she was chilled to the very marrow of her bones. She needed to find a reason for him to cast her aside, while ensuring that Marsden would still want her. "But surely you want a noble woman, someone with a proud lineage to stand by your side."

"It wasn't one of my father's requirements. No need for it to be one of mine."

"He's a good man, my son," the marquess said. "You couldn't want for better."

"Oh, I suspect she could. Why don't you go outside and see if you can catch sight of the vicar arriving, tell him we need a little more time?"

"Jolly good idea. Give you two a moment alone to sort things out."

She heard the creak of his bones as he got up, the shuffling of his footsteps as he made his way out. She didn't want to be alone with his son. Never again did she want to be alone with him.

She was acutely aware of Locksley suddenly standing beside her, the heat and power emanating from him, even though he wasn't touching her. Why did she have to be so blasted aware of him?

"You judged me correctly, Portia, when you said I wanted to protect my father. I will do whatever necessary to shield him from anyone who would dare to take advantage of him or wish him harm."

"I've told you that I don't wish him harm. I will provide him with companionship, another child, an absence of loneliness."

"I don't trust you not to take advantage of him. As you saw, he's not always in his right mind."

She faced him. "So you will marry a woman you detest?"

"I have no interest whatsoever in love. I never have. I watched it drive my father insane. I will not follow that path. But I do require an heir. I could hardly do better than a woman who is willing to let me take her from behind, on her knees, or upside down."

She slammed her eyes closed. She'd been trying to shock him, put him in his place, get him to leave off. That approach certainly hadn't produced the results she'd wanted.

He touched his finger to her jaw. Opening her eyes, she jerked back.

He angled his head, mockingly lifted a corner of that wicked mouth. "Not exactly the response on the terrace."

"Damn you."

"You can't deny there's an attraction between us, so we'll have that at least. I can assure you that within my bed you will find pleasure."

"Not arrogant, are you."

"I've traveled the world. I've learned a good many things. You'll benefit from the knowledge."

"And outside of the bed?"

"We'll be polite to each other. Respectful. The day will be yours to do with as you please. The night will belong to me."

The way his eyes darkened with the last few words told her exactly how the night would belong to him. She didn't dread what he might do to her; she dreaded only that she might not be able to resist falling under his spell. Once before she'd tumbled head over heels for a man who exhibited confidence, boldness, assertiveness, but every aspect of him paled when compared with Locksley. He not only knew his place in the world, but he owned it, commanded it. She suspected he never had doubts, never questioned himself. She was drawn to that self-assurance like a moth to a bright flickering flame. He could destroy her so easily if she weren't careful. But without him she hadn't even a glimmer of hope for survival.

"Will I have an allowance?"

He grinned darkly. "Naturally, my little mercenary."

"How much?"

"What would please you?"

"A million quid a month."

He laughed, a deep rich sound that circled around her, through her, and took up residence in her soul. "Fifty."

"One hundred."

"Seventy-five."

She could make do with that, set aside enough to ensure she would never be penniless again, wouldn't be totally dependent on his kindness.

He cradled her face, and this time she stayed as she was, gave him leave to touch her. "You'll never suffer at my hands. I can be quite generous."

She almost scoffed. She'd heard that before, lies painted so prettily, only then she'd been young and naïve enough to believe the falsehoods, to embrace them, to pin all her hopes and dreams on them. Never again would she fall under any man's spell to such an extent that she lost sight of herself.

"Then, in case you need a reminder, there is always this."

He blanketed her mouth with his, urging her lips to

part, then his tongue was slowly stroking hers, creating sensations that she wanted to deny brought her any sort of joy. But what was to be gained?

She'd already lost her advantage. He wasn't going to step aside and allow her to marry Marsden. And she couldn't risk leaving here with nothing. He was suddenly her only hope. If she didn't anger him further, if she pleased him as a wife, perhaps he would protect her with as much vigilance and determination as he did his father.

So she rose up on her toes, wrapped her arms around his neck, and flattened her breasts to his chest. He knew her to be a widow. No sense in playing the shy miss. She knew how to pleasure a man. It would certainly be no hardship to be intimate with him.

With a growl, he crushed her to him, angled his head slightly, took the kiss deeper. Hunger thrummed through him. Need. He wanted her. She could feel just how badly he did pressed against her belly. She understood it was reckless, dangerous to accept his terms when she knew so little about him except for what she'd heard from the gossips. But he was the lesser of two unfavorable choices.

Drawing back, breathing heavily, he skimmed his thumb over her swollen, tingling lips. "Take a day to think about it. It's worth a hundred quid to me for you to be sure."

With that he released her abruptly, causing her to stagger back, and headed for the door. For some strange reason, his words erased all her doubts.

"I don't need a day."

That stopped him in his tracks. He swung back around. "You've made your decision?"

She'd made it the moment she answered the advert. She had no choice. She'd never had any choice. "I'll marry you."

LOCKE was taken aback by the sharp relief sweeping swiftly through him. He hadn't realized how desperately he wanted her to say yes. Not that he wanted a wife, but he did want her in his bed, with her luscious mouth and her tart words and her whiskey eyes. He liked the way she challenged him, suspected she'd be challenging him every night. They could have fun with each other. Not ideal for a marriage but not the worst reason either.

He held out his hand to her, watched as she inhaled deeply before crossing over to him and placing her hand in his. He squeezed her fingers before wrapping her arm around the crook of his elbow and patting her hand where it now rested on his forearm.

"It's vulgar to gloat," she said.

"You'd be doing the same if our positions were reversed." He arched a brow at her mulish expression. "You know you would."

She gave him a little half smile that made him wish the vows were already exchanged so he could close the door and take her up against the wall.

"I think we're going to get along splendidly," he said with utter belief and conviction. "We understand each other."

"Not as well as you might think."

He shrugged. "Well enough. I know all I need to know." He didn't need to know her any better, didn't want to know her any better. He wasn't going to come to care for her. She was the means to an end. A bedmate for him. An heir for Havisham. Other than that, he required nothing else from her.

As he escorted her into the foyer, the front door opened and his father stepped through, the vicar in tow, and smiled brightly. "She agreed to accept you in my stead?"

"She did indeed."

"Marvelous." He walked over, took her hand, squeezed it. "I could not be happier. You will be as well, my dear, I promise you. Allow me to introduce Reverend Browning."

Browning was only slightly older than Locke, relatively new to his post. He didn't know why it bothered him to see the man holding her hand longer than he thought necessary. He wasn't jealous. He didn't care about her enough to be jealous, but he was possessive.

"Vicar." He hadn't meant for the word to come out as a bark, but it did cause the thin man to jump back, releasing Portia, his face turning an unbecoming mottled red.

"Lord Locksley, congratulations. So shall we get to it?"

He glanced over at his bride. "Black seems a bad omen for a wedding. Is there something other than black in that trunk of yours?"

She nodded. "What woman worth her salt wouldn't have something other than black?"

He expected she was going to be worth her salt in a good many areas.

"Why don't we give my bride a chance to freshen up after her long journey?" He assumed it was long. He suddenly realized he had no idea from whence she'd traveled. It didn't matter. She could have traveled from Timbuktu for all he cared. "I need to see about my lady's trunk. Then I'll meet you gents in the library for a nip before the vows are exchanged."

Still reeling from the sudden change in plans, Portia watched her soon-to-be-husband stride out the door. Marsden patted her shoulder.

"I'm so pleased, my dear."

"I came here to marry you."

He looked at her sadly. "It's better this way."

And she wondered if her marrying his son had been

his plan all along. She'd equaled madness with stupidity. What a fool she'd been, but then she suspected most desperate souls were easily duped.

Locksley strode back into the residence, the trunk balanced on one shoulder. She'd assumed he'd fetch one of the stable lads to cart it up, had obviously misjudged his strength. He could easily kill her if he desired, might consider it if he ever learned the truth of her situation. She would have to tread very carefully where he was concerned.

"I'll show you to your room. Precede me up the stairs," he ordered.

She almost objected to his tone, but realized he'd no doubt be ordering her about quite a bit. It was the price she was paying for security. She started up the sweeping stairs. "I don't know if I've ever known a lord who can heft a trunk with such ease."

"It's often to one's advantage when traveling to see to one's own supplies and equipment."

"I would have thought you'd hire others for that."

"For some things, yes, but I like to ensure I'm never caught without." At the landing, he said, "To the left."

The hallway was wide enough that they could walk beside each other. It was dusted, tidy, but there were no flowers, no little extras to make it pleasant.

"My father's chamber is there." He turned slightly to the left. "My mother's is right beside it. It goes without saying you're never to set foot in there."

Yet he'd felt compelled to say it. She wondered if there would ever come a time when she wouldn't be irritated with him. "Where is your bedchamber?"

"End of the hallway, last door on the right."

"And mine?"

"End of the hallway, last door on the right."

She stopped walking. He turned to face her, arched a brow.

"Will I not have my own room?" she asked. Surely Marsden had prepared a room for her or had he expected her to share his? His she wouldn't have minded sharing, but Locksley's? She was fairly certain he'd dominate the space.

"I don't see the point, do you? You'll be with me all night."

"Still, it might be nice to have a place where I can be myself."

"Are you not being yourself now?"

Did he have to read something sinister into everything she said? "I simply meant that my own little sanctuary where I can relax would be very much appreciated."

"The room is large with a sitting area that should suffice. I won't bother you there during the day."

"Because you have your library. I will feel as though I'm a prisoner if I am relegated to one room."

"You can use the parlor." He spun on his heel. "What the bloody hell is in this trunk? It's heavy as the dickens."

So he was human, after all, not some god who could balance the world on his shoulders. She took grim satisfaction in the knowledge.

He reached the end of the hallway. "Can you get the door?"

She was tempted to take her sweet time doing it, but she needed to keep him in an amicable mood to ensure things between them became as pleasant as possible. After swinging open the door, she followed him in, watched as he set her trunk at the foot of a massive bed, and had no success not envisioning lying there with his large and powerful body hovering over her. Her mouth went as dry as sawdust.

Circling the room permeated with his sandalwood and orangey scent, she wasn't surprised by the absolute masculinity of it, the dark woods of the furniture, the burgundy striped paper on the walls, the burgundy cloth covering the chairs and sofa before the fireplace. There was also a starkness to the setting. Only the minimum amount of furniture, no trinkets cluttering any surfaces to provide any insight into his tastes. She supposed that was telling enough regarding his preferences. He cared only for things that were useful. She would have to ensure he considered her useful.

"There's no dressing table," she said.

"Pardon?"

Turning, she discovered him leaning negligently against one of bedposts. "Most ladies require a dressing table in order to prepare themselves properly."

"I'll see about having one ordered for you."

It was quite possible one was sitting unused in another bedchamber, but then as nothing was to be disturbed . . .

"Thank you."

"Meanwhile, I'll send Mrs. Barnaby up to assist you."

"I appreciate it. I shan't tarry."

"Take all the time you need. The vicar's not going anywhere and neither am I." He headed for the door, stopped, glanced back to her. "It's not too late to change your mind."

It had been too late before she'd ever arrived. "Your manner of courtship needs some work."

His laughter circled the room. "I think we're going to get along, Portia."

"I hope so. It will make for long years if we don't."

"We'll be waiting for you in the library. Mrs. Barnaby can show you the way."

Then he was gone, leaving her alone with her misgivings. Opening her reticule, needing something familiar to help settle her, she snatched out a peppermint and popped it into her mouth. After placing her purse on the bed, she walked to the window and gazed out on the wildness of the land surrounding the manor. If the marquess never went out, perhaps she would be allowed to tame it. And surely in this massive manor, she could claim one small room as her own.

She pressed her forehead to the glass, felt the tears threaten, and cursed her weakness to perdition. She was gaining what she wanted, just not the person with whom she'd hoped to gain it. Instead of a few years of marriage, she'd have a lifetime. It would be forever before she acquired her dower house, her independence. Whether or not she and the viscount got along, she knew the years ahead of her were going to be extremely long indeed.

STRIDING into the library, Locke was greeted with the robust laughter of his father and the vicar. He really thought a man of God should be more solemn, but Browning was obviously enjoying the spirits the marquess had offered him. Both men were sitting in front of the fireplace, each holding a glass half filled with amber liquid.

Locke went to the sideboard, poured himself two fingers of scotch, and joined them, pressing his shoulder against the mantel.

Appearing far too merry, his father lifted his glass. "Cheers to the groom."

Taking a sip, Locke considered. "There is the small matter of the license."

His father patted his chest. "Special license right here."

Locke held out his hand. "May I?"

His father reached inside the breast pocket of his jacket,

pulled out the folded paper, and handed it to Locke, who gave it a brisk snap to open it. "My name is on it."

The marquess didn't even have the decency to appear contrite. "I've been after you for two years to marry. Can you blame me for nudging things along?"

"And if I hadn't been quite so gullible?"

"I have a license in my name. I wasn't going to break my promise to the girl that she'd marry today. Don't look so disgruntled. You're drawn to her, that much was obvious in the parlor. I'd wager you kissed her when you got her alone."

He'd never doubted his father's sharpness, only his ability to remain in reality. "How much do you really know about her?"

"She's strong, healthy, and fertile. That's all that's required for her to provide you with an heir. You've imprisoned your heart, Locke. I know that, so whether you could love her was never a consideration."

Nor apparently was love a consideration for his little mercenary. "How many women responded to your advertisement?"

"She was the only one." He skewed up his face. "Seems I have a reputation for being mad. Makes me a risky prospect. Your mother wouldn't have liked it anyway, my getting married. But she will be thrilled with the news that you've taken a wife."

The vicar had begun shifting in his chair, as though just realizing that everything within this household might not be quite right. Locke couldn't recall him ever visiting. "You all right, Browning?"

"Oh, yes, just considering that all this is rather unconventional."

"Have you not heard that the St. Johns are seldom conventional?"

As though fearing he might have insulted them, he said, "The church does appreciate the new pews the marquess is providing."

So that was how he'd managed to get the vicar to agree to perform the marriage here. Should have known. Everyone had a price, including his lovely bride. He wouldn't resent it, but neither would he ever feel any warmth toward her. He would view her as little more than a high-priced—

Every thought in his head scattered as she strolled in wearing a gown of deep blue, sleeveless, revealing alabaster skin that the black had kept covered. Her neck was long, sloping down to delicate shoulders and the barest hint of swells that indicated he might have misjudged how her breasts would fill his hands. They were likely to overflow. He wanted to peel off the white gloves that rode past her elbows as slowly as she had peeled off the black. She'd tidied her hair in such a way that it demanded he mess it up.

Before he crushed his glass, he placed it on the mantel. He wanted to sweep her up into his arms, cart her to his bedchamber, and have his way with her now, this very moment. The vows could be exchanged later. The sultry look she gave him told him that she knew the exact path his thoughts traveled.

"Isn't she a vision of loveliness?" Mrs. Barnaby declared.

She was a vision of raw sensuality, and she damned well knew it. Ah, the little vixen. She fully intended to make him suffer until he could get her into bed.

Oh, yes, they were going to get along splendidly.

His long strides ate up the distance separating them. Taking her hand, he held her gaze as he pressed his lips to her gloved knuckles. "I approve."

She blinked slowly as a corner of her luscious mouth lifted. "I thought you might."

"Step aside, Locke," his father said, shoving on his shoulder. "You're not supposed to be this close to the bride until you're exchanging vows. My son is a savage. Allow me to escort you to the parlor."

He certainly felt uncivilized, barbaric as his father offered her his arm and she placed her small, delicate hand on it. He consoled himself with the knowledge that as soon as the vows were exchanged, he was taking her to bed.

Run, run, run!

Her mind played the constant refrain as the marquess escorted her to the parlor. Feeling as though she were traversing through a nightmare, Portia fought to tamp down the trembling that threatened to erupt at any moment. Never in her life had she seen such unbridled hunger in a man's eyes. When Locksley had taken her hand, pressed his lips against it, it didn't matter that she wore gloves. The heat emanating from him was such that she felt scorched.

As they entered the foyer, she knew if she were smart, she'd head straight out the door. She was no novice to men when it came to what they were capable of, but she suspected nothing in her experiences had prepared her for what Locksley would deliver. She'd thought being provocative would give her the upper hand, and all it had done was cause her to realize that she might be completely out of her element with him.

Even now, she felt his gaze boring into the nape of her neck, traveling across her bared shoulders, sliding down to her hips, back up. His hands would no doubt be taking the same journey after nightfall. Why, why, why hadn't she read the contract more carefully? Why hadn't her solicitor pointed out its flaws? Why did the viscount have to be so protective of the marquess?

As they entered the parlor, Marsden held her back while the vicar went to stand in front of the fireplace. Locksley joined him there. He dwarfed the other man. She didn't want to consider how later tonight he might dwarf her. Swallowing hard, she bucked up her resolve not to let his size or his demeanor intimidate her. Hearing the patter of feet, she turned to see three servants scurry into the room. All appeared to be only slightly younger than Marsden.

"Allow me to introduce my staff," the marquess said. "They'll serve as witnesses. Gilbert, our head butler, Mrs. Dorset, our cook, and of course, you've met Mrs. Barnaby."

They bowed, curtsied, smiled brightly, seemed completely at ease as though this were an everyday occurrence.

"A pleasure," she muttered, striving to wrap her head around the fact that this was happening, while wondering if ever there had been a stranger assortment of guests for a wedding.

"I brought you these." Mrs. Dorset extended a handful of wilted flowers, her smile bright with hope. "A bride ought to have flowers. I picked them myself from the meadow."

"Thank you. They're lovely."

The woman curtsied before stepping back into line. Marsden led Portia over to the vicar, waited while she mentally gauged her distance to the door and had a final wild thought that she should make a dash for it.

Browning cleared his throat. "Who gives this bride?"

"I do," Marsden announced, placing her hand on Locksley's arm before stepping back once and over so he was now standing by his son, apparently serving as his best man.

The vicar waxed on about the sanctity of marriage, as though neither she nor Locksley truly understood the significance of what they were doing, as though what was happening wasn't an utter and complete farce. Each word pounded into her as though delivered with a sledgehammer. If she were decent, she'd stop this outrageousness, but then if she were decent, she wouldn't be here at all. She kept her gaze focused on Locksley's neck cloth, on how perfectly it was knotted. So much easier than looking into his eyes, seeing the accusation there, the disapproval because she'd sought to marry his father for gain—only what he thought she wished to gain wasn't at all what she wanted to obtain.

After the vicar recited the vows she was to repeat, she opened her mouth, only to find Locksley's finger beneath her chin, scorching her as he lifted her head until she met his gaze. Why the devil didn't the man have the decency to wear gloves for such a solemn occasion?

"Don't make your vows to my neck cloth."

"I wasn't planning to." She took no comfort in it being one of the smallest lies she'd told this day. Why did he have to make the moment so much more difficult by insisting that they look at each other as they exchanged vows?

"Repeat the words for her, Browning," he ordered.

"I remember them," she shot back, hating the way he studied her as though he expected her to engage in some nefarious behavior. Even knowing she should walk away, she couldn't seem to make her feet move from this spot. It was more than his fingers and his eyes holding her captive. It was the absolute authority he wielded. He would never yield to another. He would defend what was his.

She knew it with absolutely certainty, and once they were married, she would be his.

She should have negotiated better terms than an allowance and the daytime belonging to her, but it was too late now. After all her careful planning and scheming, when it had mattered the most, she had given in far too easily. But she wouldn't regret it, not when she was gaining her ultimate goal.

Calmly, and with a voice far steadier than she felt, she reiterated the phrases, grateful that noticeably absent was any reference to love, that at the very least the promises they were making were honest, not hypocritical. She would cherish, honor, and obey, in sickness and in health, until death.

Still she was unprepared for the same vows being repeated in his strong, deep voice, with his eyes boring into hers as though he wanted them branded on her very soul. Finally, his finger dropped from her chin, but even with it no longer supporting her, she couldn't seem to make herself look away from him.

"Have we a ring?" the vicar finally whispered.

"Ah, yes." Marsden patted his pockets, one after another as though he'd forgotten where he'd placed it. "Here 'tis." He handed it to Locksley. "Your mother's."

With his words, Portia's gut clenched with such force and so painfully that she very nearly doubled over.

"Are you certain about this?" Locksley asked quietly.

"Quite."

Solemnly, he turned to Portia, took her hand—

She balled up her fist. "I can't." She looked at Marsden, at the hope and joy reflected in eyes as green as his son's. "You loved your wife. Your son and I don't love each other. This is simply a marriage of extreme convenience. You can't truly want me to wear her precious ring."

"Linnie wants you to wear it. I shared your letters with her. She approves of you."

Oh, God, he truly was mad. Perhaps Locksley was not only saving his father from her, but saving her from his father. Although the viscount cared not one whit about her, so why would he care if she was saddled with a madman? "Talk some sense into your father," she implored Locksley. "Tie a piece of string around my finger. That'll work just as well."

"Once he's determined his course, there is no talking any sense into him."

"But it makes a mockery of what they shared."

"No, it doesn't, my dear," Marsden said. "It's a testament to our belief that you'll be a true and good wife to our beloved son."

Only she wasn't good. If she had been, she wouldn't have been brought to this moment. If she was good, she'd walk away.

Locksley squeezed her hand. "Unfurl your fingers."

"You can't want to do this."

"Neither did I wish to get married today, yet here I am. Open your hand and let's get this done."

Reluctantly she did as he bade, watched as he slid her glove down her arm, over her hand, before passing it on to his father. Taking a deep breath, he guided the ring of tiny diamonds and emeralds onto her finger. It fit perfectly, which for some reason made it all the worse. She felt the extreme weight of it, the warmth it had absorbed from his skin as he'd held it.

"With this ring, I thee wed," he said solemnly.

She lifted her gaze to his, the magnitude of what they'd just done making it difficult to draw in breath. She was married. To Viscount Locksley. Not at all what she had schemed to occur. She had an insane urge to apologize, to tell him she was sorry. She would be as good and true a wife as she could be, but that didn't mean that he wouldn't eventually come to hate her. That she might even come to hate herself.

"I now pronounce you Lord and Lady Locksley. You may kiss the bride."

Her husband—her husband!—lowered his head, giving her what she assumed would be the very last chaste kiss he would ever bestow on her. His mouth brushed lightly over hers as though there had been no passion between them earlier. He'd barely stepped back before Marsden was bussing his lips over her cheek.

"Welcome to the family. I can't tell you how happy you've made me this day."

She wished she could claim happiness as well. Then she found herself surrounded by the servants, pumping her hand, hugging her, offering congratulations.

But as she looked over her shoulder at her husband, he was staring at her as though he'd just discovered something about her that he'd rather not know.

Chapter 5

LOCKE hadn't been able to whisk his bride up to his bedchamber following the ceremony because Mrs. Dorset had prepared a feast that would spoil if not served immediately. At the table in the small dining room, he sat across from his father, with his wife—his wife!—to Locke's left near his cold heart, and the vicar to his right.

As he sipped his wine, he considered the possibility that his mercenary wife apparently was in possession of a conscience. It had surprised him beyond all measure when she had questioned accepting the ring. He'd expected her to take one look at the sparkling jewels and salivate. But she hadn't. She wasn't comfortable with it. Even now in between courses, she fiddled with it, rotated it as though she wished she could remove it.

He didn't think it was because it symbolized she was married. It was because it symbolized love and between them there was none, not even a glimmer. Nor would there ever be. They both knew it.

"Where does your family hail from, Lady Locksley?" Browning asked, and she flinched ever so slightly, obviously not yet comfortable with the address.

Another surprise. He'd have thought she'd embrace it, insist on him addressing her as such.

"Yorkshire," she said quietly.

"The Earl of Greyling's family estate is in Yorkshire," Locke said, wondering why he hadn't thought to pose the same question to her earlier in the day. But then at the time he hadn't cared from whence she'd come. He'd cared only that she depart with all due haste. "Evermore."

For the first time since they'd taken their seats, she glanced over at him. He didn't know why he took such satisfaction in finally having her attention. "I'm not familiar with it."

"You must notify Grey and Ashe of your wedding," his father ordered. "Have them come visit. We'll celebrate."

"I look forward to meeting your friends," she said.

"They're more brothers than friends." He'd been all of six when they arrived. They'd grown up together, shared adventures, mischief, and loss, the last creating a stronger bond between them than there might have been otherwise.

"You're very fortunate to have them then."

And he suddenly wondered who was there for her. Most women filled the church with relatives and friends. "We'll have to invite your family to visit as well."

Delicately, she touched her napkin to her lips. "I have no family."

"Not a single relative who would care that you're now a viscountess?"

"Nary a one."

Then who the devil did she want to impress? Not that she wasn't gaining plenty for herself. Perhaps that was enough, that it was all about her. Her and her child. She wanted any future children to whom she gave birth to have advantages. With him as their father, they certainly would.

"Lord Marsden—" she began.

"You must call me Father," he interrupted.

"I couldn't be so presumptuous."

"We're related now. I insist."

She bowed her head slightly as though acquiescing, but he didn't believe for a single moment that she really was giving in to his father's request. She was simply striving to avoid an argument during dinner. Fast learner, his wife.

"I wondered if you might be kind enough to tell me a little bit about Locksley as a lad."

Why the devil would she ask him to do that?

Cackling, his father leaned back in his chair. "Did he not let you have your turn at an inquisition? No, I suspect he didn't."

Taking another sip of wine, Locke studied Portia, trying to gauge her angle, what she was after. It bothered him immensely that she seemed genuinely interested. She didn't care about him, so what was to be gained by learning anything at all about his past?

"He didn't like to wear shoes," his father told her. "People thought I neglected him because he was always running about barefoot, but he simply refused to keep his shoes on."

"I liked the feel of grass beneath my soles," he felt obligated to admit. "Besides, it's easier to climb in bare feet."

"Ah, yes, he was a little monkey. Climbed everything. Trees, ladders. I once found him crouched near the ceiling in my library. Nearly gave me an apoplectic fit. He had somehow wedged himself in the corner and worked his way up. He was only about three. If he'd fallen . . . I still break out in a sweat when I think about that horrendous outcome. Once I got him safely down, I thrashed him to within an inch of his life. I regretted it afterward, was afraid I'd put an end to his sense of adventure. A week later he was clambering up the shelves."

She scrutinized him with such intensity that he wanted to shift in his chair. Instead he downed more wine. He didn't want her figuring him out, deciphering him, knowing the details of his upbringing. Nothing was to be gained. As far as he was concerned they needed no words at all spoken between them.

"Weren't you frightened to be up so high?" she asked.

"I don't remember the incident at all."

"But you remember climbing?"

"Trees, outer walls. Wherever I could get a hand- or a foothold."

"Do you still climb?" She sounded truly interested, which added to his guilt, as he was interested in only one thing from her.

"On one of my journeys I scaled a small mountain. Climbing has its uses." *I'll be climbing over you before the night is done.* She suddenly blushed, and he wondered if she'd read his thoughts. "Perhaps I'll take you climbing sometime."

"I'd like that. I climbed trees when I was a girl. Enjoyed hiding out. I was a bit of a hoyden."

"From whom were you hiding?"

She laughed lightly. "Oh, you know, playing games, hide-and-seek, that sort of thing."

Based on the way she didn't hold his gaze, he wasn't certain games were at all involved. What did it matter? Why were they discussing this? He didn't want to know about her childhood, her past, or anything else. He didn't want to see her as a little girl with braids, hiking up her skirts and clambering up a tree.

What mattered now was that she was out for gain, and because of that, he'd begun his day a bachelor and ended it a husband—who had yet to fully sample the wares.

She turned her attention back to his father. "Did you climb trees, my lord?"

"Linnie was sitting in a tree when I met her. She was the climber. Coaxed me up. Dared me actually. Called me a coward. I had to show her, I tell you. So up I went. From our perch we watched as the night fell. It was so beautiful. With her I saw it as I never had before, recognized the majesty of it. But then it was time to go home. And I froze. I was all right as long as I was looking up. Looking down made my gut churn."

"How did you get down?" Portia asked.

"She took my hand. 'Keep your eyes on me,' she said. 'I won't let you fall.' I was twelve, she all of eight. Never took my eyes off her. But still I fell anyway, hard and fast."

"Were you badly hurt?"

He winked at Portia, smiled with fond remembrance. "I fell *for her*. So Locke comes by his love of climbing naturally. He got it from his mother."

He hadn't known that, had never heard the story, had known only that they'd become interested in each other at an early age. Not wanting to sadden his father, he'd avoided asking questions about his mother. Perhaps for himself as well, because he didn't want to know what he might have missed by not having both parents present in his life.

"You loved her a long time," Portia said, her voice filled with a sense of wonder.

"All my life. Well, except for the first twelve years, but they hardly count. When I met her it was as though my life began anew." He slapped the table before raising his wineglass. "And speaking of life beginning anew, we are here to celebrate a wedding. To my favorite son and my new daughter. May you never take your eyes off each other."

Portia lifted her glass, but didn't look at Locke. He suspected it was because she didn't want him to see the tears that had gathered, but her profile revealed them glistening in the corner of her eye. It was a revelation. She was sentimental, with a soft heart that she didn't want him to see.

Downing the wine that remained in his glass, he had an insane urge to tell her that he wouldn't let her fall. But he kept his thoughts to himself because he knew from experience that along that path lay madness.

𝓕OLLOWING dinner, Portia and Locke retreated to the library, where he poured them each a glass of port while his father saw the vicar to his carriage. They sat before the fireplace, in awkward silence, the only sound the crackling of the fire blazing in the hearth. Yet for all the heat it generated, she couldn't seem to get warm.

Her husband—dear God, a husband whose eyes never strayed from her as though he expected her to try to make off with the family silver. He thought her a mercenary when she knew damned good and well that money could not protect her nearly as effectively as he and his position in Society could. It occurred to her that perhaps he was mentally disrobing her, but why bother with doing that when he could escort her to his bedchamber and tear off her clothes with as much haste as he desired? Based upon his earlier fervent kisses, she suspected their coupling was going to be rough and quick. And often. She couldn't recall ever meeting a man who could appear so virile and capable when doing nothing other than sitting, sipping port, and staring at her.

"How long does it take to say goodbye to a vicar?" she finally asked, staring at the flames because it was easier than looking into his eyes and seeing the lust for her reflected there. Knowing how badly he wanted her was a sort of currency, if she could just determine how to spend it without angering him.

"I suspect my father forgot that we were waiting for him, and he has retired to his chambers."

She dared to look at him then, the way his long fingers were curled around the stem of the glass, and tried not to think about how they might close around her later. "Should you check on him?"

"He's a grown man."

Angling her head, she gave him a rueful smile. "Yet earlier today you thought him incapable of selecting a wife."

"There is a huge difference between deciding one should retire for the night and deciding one should marry."

Well, there was that, she supposed. Swallowing hard, she forced herself to hold his gaze. "I assume we're going to consummate our marriage tonight."

Never taking his eyes from her, he lowered his head slightly. "Once you've finished your port and are a bit more relaxed."

"I'm relaxed."

He simply looked at her. She wasn't, damn it. But it was imperative that they consummate the marriage, that he not be able to claim her an improper wife, that he not have any justification for an annulment. Not that she wanted him to see the desperation in her or understand the importance of his place in her life. "Perhaps I should go on up, have Mrs. Barnaby help me prepare—"

"I'll be doing all the preparing that needs to be done."

"I simply meant that she could undress me—"

"I'll undress you."

"I thought to have a few moments alone, to prepare, to slip into my nightdress—"

"You won't be needing a nightdress."

"At some point—"

"Not tonight."

"Must you constantly interrupt?"

He gave her a devilish grin that held naughty promises. "I see no point in delaying our departure upstairs with words that won't change anything. Finish your port."

She took merely a sip, because she wasn't going to be ordered about. She had expectations as well, and they didn't include bending to his every wish. He could just bloody well wait until she was ready.

Glancing around, she settled her attention on a distant corner of the room. "Is that where you wedged yourself and climbed to the ceiling?"

He didn't even bother to glance back. "As I understand it, yes."

This room had an incredibly high ceiling, a huge fireplace, massive windows, and several seating areas. "I can see why your father was terrified. If you'd fallen, you might have broken your neck."

"But I didn't fall. Would you care for something other than port?"

Shaking her head, she took another sip of the thick, sweet wine.

"You didn't drink much wine during supper," he mused.

"I've never fancied wine overly much. For me a little bit goes a long way. I suppose you drink to excess." Although she'd never heard any stories of him being three sheets to the wind.

"I prefer to keep my wits about me."

No doubt because he'd witnessed his father losing his. Although she found herself liking Marsden, thought he seemed sweet. Her own father had been a strict, controlling man. She didn't think Locksley would be living here if his father had been the same. He certainly wouldn't be intent on protecting him, to the extreme extent of marrying a woman who before this afternoon he'd never even known existed. "When you were a lad, were you afraid of your father?"

"When I was a lad, I feared nothing." He jerked his head back and to the side, indicating the far corner. "Obviously."

"Do you fear anything now?"

"Going mad. Which is surely bound to happen if I delay much longer in taking you to bed." Setting his glass aside, he rose, towering over her.

Her heart slammed against her ribs. She quickly downed what remained of her port, frantically wondering if she should ask for another. He held out his hand to her. Such a large hand. No aspect of it appeared soft. She could see calluses and evidence of nicks, tiny scars here and there. She wondered briefly what he did in order to have hands that more closely resembled those of a worker than a gentleman. No doubt they were souvenirs from his adventures.

Before she could decide if she should in fact ask him to refill her glass, he took it from her and placed it on the table beside her chair. Leaning in, he wrapped both his hands around her elbows and drew her to her feet.

"For a woman who spoke so boldly about coupling this afternoon, you seem rather nervous."

"We hardly know each other. I'm not quite certain what to expect from you."

"Expect to be grateful you're in my bed, and that our chamber is far from my father's, so he can't hear you crying out in pleasure."

"You are so blasted arro—"

His mouth slashed across hers as he hauled her up against him. Cloth provided no barrier against the heat seeping from his body into hers, as though he were already beginning to claim her, as though every aspect of him would penetrate her before the night was done.

During her short life, she'd experienced rare moments of pure terror. This was one of them. The past few months had taught her to separate her mind from the physical, had tutored her in the wisdom of not caring, of dispensing with emotion, of holding herself apart from the reality of what was actually happening. It was the reason that she had known she could lie beneath a man more than three decades her senior without nausea, without tears, without regrets.

But Locksley knocked down her barriers as though she'd built them of twigs. He wasn't content to simply take. He wanted to possess. She felt it in the thrumming of his pulse at his throat where she laid her fingers, in the vibration of his chest as he growled and took the kiss so deep that she felt as though he were mining for her soul.

She was no stranger to the ways of men, and yet he seemed to defy everything she knew and understood. She'd never known a man to emit such a powerful hunger, to give the impression that the passion rising between them would consume not only her, but him as well. That he welcomed it.

He braced his hands on either side of her head, angling her slightly to better position himself for the assault. Yet for all the voraciousness of his urgency, she never once felt as though she couldn't step away, as though she couldn't stop it. If she wanted.

But she didn't want to step away. And that alone was what terrified her. That he somehow managed to call to the wantonness inside her, that he made her long for all the dreams she'd held when she was young and innocent.

That he made her believe that perhaps they were attainable, that they did in fact exist.

Tearing his mouth from hers, breathing heavily, he stared down at her. "That's what I want. The fire and the vigor. Not the frightened mouse. I want the lioness in my bed."

A lioness? If only he knew the truth about Montie—

He swept her up into his arms as though she weighed little more than a cloud in the sky. Never before had a man carried her. She didn't want to admit how safe and secure he made her feel as he strode from the room with purpose, but then if she'd learned anything at all about him this day it was that he did everything with determination.

She knew beyond any doubt that she was on the verge of becoming his wife in truth. There would be no turning back once he claimed her.

As he took the stairs two steps at a time, guilt pricked her conscience. She should confess everything, before it was too late. Their marriage could be annulled. She could slink away in shame and mortification, find a way to survive, to protect all that needed protecting. As though a miraculous answer would suddenly reveal itself when it hadn't before.

They passed the closed door to the master's bedchamber. His strides quickly ate up the distance to the corner room at the far end of the hallway.

He wanted her. She could sense it in the tension radiating through him. She could give him anything he fancied, all he desired. He could ask anything of her and she'd not refuse his request. He could demand anything and she wouldn't fight him. She could make him grateful to have her. She could ensure he never had regrets.

As for her own regrets—she would find the strength to ignore them or to live with them. She was too close to having what she desired—what she required to survive—to let guilt win out over sensibleness. Starve or feast. Cold or warmth. Death or life.

He opened the door, walked through, and slammed it shut with a kick. She expected to find herself tossed on the bed, her skirts thrown over her head, as with a powerful thrust he took what the law now gave him the right to possess.

Instead, he lowered her feet to the floor, slowly, gently, in the center of the room. The bed loomed behind him, yet he suddenly seemed in no great hurry, as though whatever madness had urged him here with such haste had been tamed, tethered. But the fever in his eyes as he looked down on her told her that it was hovering dangerously close, that there was a primal quality to him that once unleashed could possibly destroy her.

She should have been frightened, terrified even. Yet she couldn't seem to feel anything other than wonder and an urge to take him down to the bed and order him to have his way with her. He was no longer touching her, and yet tremors cascaded through her. Her nerve endings sizzled, and her skin seemed to ache for his touch. It had been so long since she had yearned for a man's touch.

Not since she'd lost her innocence. Not since she'd known betrayal.

Leisurely, following the décolletage of her gown, he lightly skimmed the blunt tip of one long, thick finger from one shoulder down, over the swell of one breast, then the other, before traveling up to the opposite shoulder, barely touching the cloth, mostly branding her skin with heat that fairly devastated her plan to remain aloof. His eyes never left hers, and she feared he could read the confusion and weakening in her gaze.

She should have known that he wouldn't have been content with coldness in his bed.

He guided his finger back along the path until it returned to the beginning of the trail that he had mapped out like the explorer he was.

He glided his fingers down her arms, all the way to her fingertips, before going back up. "I like your arms bared," he said, his voice low, feral, deep. "Don't wear gloves in the future."

Following dinner, she hadn't put them back on. As much as she wanted to, she couldn't quite regret it at that moment. "It would be improper."

A corner of his mouth hitched up, his eyes darkened. "Before this night is done, you'll learn that I enjoy a good many improper things. Turn around."

She'd said he could take her from behind. She couldn't fault him now for wanting it. Hiking up her chin, calling forth her steely resolve, she whipped around and only then dared to squeeze her eyes shut, waiting for the assault.

"You've tensed up again," he said.

"I've told you. I don't know you well enough to know what to expect."

"And I've told you to expect pleasure."

"You're taking your sweet time at delivering it."

His heated mouth landed at the juncture where her shoulder met her neck. "We have all night, Lady Locksley." He nibbled his way to her ear. "I want you wet, hot, and begging me to take you."

A shiver of anticipation skittered along her spine. "Perhaps it will be you who begs, my lord."

His tongue outlined the shell of her ear. "I'm counting on it."

She jerked her head around, her gaze slamming into his. "You want me to make you beg?"

He grinned. "I want you to try." He pressed a kiss to her temple. "But not yet. Not until I've had the pleasure of removing your clothes."

And her hairpins apparently, because he buried his fingers in her hair, removing them one after another, tossing them onto the floor without care. Facing forward, staring at the low fire burning in the hearth, she tried to make sense of this man. He wanted her. She had no doubt there, and yet he was drawing out the torment with a sweetness to it that she'd never before experienced.

As her hair tumbled down, he growled with satisfaction and gathered some of it up in his hands. "It's been wanting to do that all day. And I've wanted to touch it. So thick and silky."

"It's unruly."

"I like unruly."

"Even in a wife?"

"That I can't say, as I've only had one for a few hours. But I like unruly in my lovers."

She hated the spark of jealousy that ripped through her, recognized the irony in her reaction. It wasn't as though she was coming to him a virgin. "How many of those have you had?"

He slowly draped her hair over one shoulder and kissed the nape of her neck. "Enough to know how to bring you pleasure."

Her eyes slid closed. It seemed his idea of pleasure involved a great deal of torment. His lips traveled across her shoulder, just before his fingers outlined her skin where it met cloth. How could so light a touch affect her so deeply, reach through her to the core of her womanhood? When she'd responded to the advert, she'd done so expecting a passionless coupling. She was hardly prepared for every sensation he was so effortlessly stirring to life.

She felt a tug on the lacings of her gown, was acutely aware of him pulling them completely free, so the material began to separate and was soon gaping. The gown was heavy enough that it began to fall from her shoulders. She jerked her hands to the bodice to hold it in place. Why didn't he douse the lights?

Aware of him brushing by her, she opened her eyes to find him standing in front of her.

"Lower your arms," he said quietly. Not an order exactly, and yet she didn't think he'd brook any disobedience. She wanted an amicable marriage, no tempers flaring, no fists flying.

Balling her hands, she lowered them to her sides. With only a single finger of each hand, he nudged the shoulders of her gown over until the silk slid down her body. His eyes drifted to the swells of her breasts, and she saw heat mirrored in the green, even though she was still covered with her corset and chemise. And once again, he traced that blasted finger along the line where cloth met skin. She wanted to push her breasts up against his palms, wanted a sure touch, a complete touch, not this irritating teasing that was setting every nerve ending on fire.

"Turn around," he ordered, and she took perverse satisfaction in the fact that he sounded as though he might be strangling. At least he wasn't completely unaffected. When it was her turn to remove his clothing, she would go just as slowly, would insist upon it. Make him suffer.

Although now that she was facing the bed, staring at it, she didn't know if she could go slowly. Her body was yearning for sure caresses, the hardness of his form pressing into the softness of hers.

A series of tugs as he loosened the lacings on her corset. Then it, too, fell away, leaving only the thin linen of her chemise. Once again he moved in front of her, his eyes darkened.

"I misjudged the size of your breasts," he said. "They're smaller than I thought."

"Disappointed?"

He slowly shook his head. "No."

He cupped her breast, and she couldn't hold back the moan as she nearly sank to the floor, nearly grabbed his free hand and pressed it to her other breast. It felt so good to have the firm touch of his large palm, his fingers gently kneading as though to test the fullness of what she had to offer. She wanted to shout for him to rip everything else away, to take her to the bed, to take her.

This time when he began to trail his finger along the décolletage, he hooked it beneath the cloth, moving it aside, approaching the mound, and she knew his finger was going to graze her nipple—

A horrendous shout, an almost feral cry, startled her, had him cursing beneath his breath before marching to the window and jerking the drapery aside.

"What was that?" she asked.

He strode to the door. "Wait here."

As though she was going to go somewhere in her half-dressed state. "What is it?"

But he was out the door, slamming it in his wake.

She scampered over to the window, pulled the heavy velvet drapery aside, and glanced out. A nearly full moon coated the land in blue, provided enough light that she could see a shadowy figure in the distance running over the moors. Then she caught sight of another figure. She recognized the shape of this one. It was her husband, racing from the house, obviously in pursuit of the person she could no longer see.

Had it been his father out there? It had to be. She

couldn't imagine Locksley rushing out after anyone else. What was the marquess doing out there, and what had he been shouting?

Although she'd heard the rumors, she hadn't believed the Marquess of Marsden—since he wasn't locked up in an asylum—was truly mad. It appeared she might have been mistaken.

Chapter 6

*L*OCKE didn't know why he bothered to run. He knew exactly where he'd find his father, where he always found him eventually. At the Marchioness of Marsden's grave.

Until tonight, he'd never understood why his father had insisted on burying his mother near a tree on their property instead of in the graveyard beside the church in the village where all his previous ancestors rested. But after hearing the tale at supper, he was left to wonder if it was that tree in which his father had first met the girl who would eventually become the love of his life.

When he saw his father nearing the grave, knew he was going straight there and wasn't planning to wander about the moors, Locke slowed his gait, settled into a walk. The moon was bright enough that he hadn't bothered with a lantern. He fought not to be irritated with the interruption. He'd certainly not wanted to abandon his bride, although he suspected curiosity had gotten the better of her and she'd glanced out the window to see father and son darting across the moors as though the hounds of hell were nipping at their heels.

No doubt by now she was beginning to realize the fate from which he'd saved her. He was still struggling to understand his rash decision to marry her. To protect his father, yes, but he could have done that by paying the exorbitant fee spelled out in the contract. Perhaps if the income from the mines were flourishing, if he didn't have better uses for the money . . .

No, even then he would have been hard-pressed to hand over a small fortune to a scheming woman who had done nothing more than answer the advert of a madman. She'd no doubt expected to be paid off, although maybe she had in fact gained exactly what she'd sought. Difficult to tell with her. What he did know was that he'd left her smoldering as though she were kindling.

He could sense the awareness sparking every time he touched his skin to hers. It didn't matter if it was nothing more than the tip of his finger. She reacted as though he'd laid his entire naked body against hers. He could hardly wait until he actually did.

He wanted to go slowly, to savor, but damnation, more than once he'd come close to ripping off her clothes, then tearing off his own. He wanted her on her back, on that bed, staring up at him as he took her. With a groan, he shoved the musings aside. Time for all that later. Right now, he had to deal with his father.

As he neared the man lying prone over the grave, he could hear the sobs, the pleas. As though a dead woman had the power to pull him from this world into the next.

He didn't think his father was in any real danger out here. There was the occasional adder and fox, but the creatures were more shy than aggressive. As a boy, Locke had once caught sight of a wolf—not that anyone believed him, as wolves weren't known for roaming these parts. For a while he'd feared that he was as mad as his father, sighting creatures that didn't exist. But surely if that was the case, he would have imagined seeing it again. The beautiful creature had mesmerized him.

So he didn't expect to find his father attacked by some wild animal. But he was frail, and a night out on the moors could serve him no good.

Locke stood, waiting until the sobs diminished, but the laments continued on.

"Why won't you come for me, Linnie? The boy is wed. He won't be alone."

So it was more than want of an heir that had prompted today's theatrics.

"I'm ready. Come and take me."

Grinding his teeth together, Locke fought not to hear the desperation in his father's voice. Finally, when he could no longer stand listening to his father's pleas, he knelt and rested his hand on the marquess's shoulder. "Father, it's time to return to the residence."

"Why doesn't she come? You're married now. My job is done."

So he'd been correct regarding today's little drama. It had all been devised as a means to secure a wife for Locke.

"I just want to be with her again," his father said.

"The fog is rolling in. The chill is going to seep into your bones. You'll catch your death. We need to leave."

"I can't." He released another sob, one that sounded as though it had been torn from his chest. "I can't leave her again. She'll come for me if I just stay here."

No, Father, she won't.

"We need to go," Locke insisted.

"Leave me here. For God's sake, this time just leave me here."

"I can't."

"I can't leave her, not again. Don't make me."

How many times had they had this conversation? How many times had Locke followed him out here? How many times had he waited until the dampness of the fog soaked through their clothes, chilled their bones? But now his father was too frail to stand up to nature's harshness. With resignation, Locke cradled his father in his arms. Ignoring his feeble protests, he stood and began trudging back toward the manor.

Normally after his father retired, Locke secured the lock on the door to the bedchamber in which his father slept. Tonight his mind had been on Portia, on escaping into the haven her body offered. He'd overlooked how quickly his father's mind could slip from reality.

His father didn't fight him. The sobs diminished, retreated completely just as they reached the manor. Locke made his way down the various hallways and up the stairs. He strode into the master bedchamber and set his father on the bed.

"Let's get you out of these damp and soiled clothes." As Locke began removing them, his father barely responded, merely stared at the window.

"I miss her, Locke. I miss her dreadfully."

"I know."

"You can't know. You've never loved a woman. You can't understand how she can become a part of your soul, a part of your whole. When she is gone, she leaves behind an emptiness, a void that no one else—nothing else—can fill."

Then he was glad not to love, not to give that much power to any one person.

When he had his father down to his drawers, Locke retrieved his nightshirt, slipped it over his head, and began working his rail-thin arms into the sleeves.

"Was I wrong to force you to marry?" the marquess asked.

"You didn't force me. We could have paid her off. Or I could have allowed you to marry her."

"You like her then?"

"I think she will prove an interesting distraction, and she is certainly comely enough."

"Perhaps you'll come to love her," his father murmured, almost distractedly.

"No," Locke assured him. "I married her because I know she is the sort I could never love."

"How did you deduce that in the small bit of time you were with her?"

"She is a title hunter."

"I think you're wrong there. No doubt she is hunting for something, but I doubt very much that it's a title."

He didn't like the uncertainty that slithered through him. He had judged her accurately. He was rather sure of it. "It doesn't matter any longer. The deed is done."

Finally, with the nightshirt in place, he lifted the covers. "Into bed with you."

"Lock the door."

"I will."

"But open the window. Perhaps your mother will come visit with me later."

No one was going to visit with him. Still Locke went to the window, turned the latch, and swung it open. It was too small for his father to crawl through—and even if he did manage it, the drop to the ground was a deterrent. While the marquess might pray for death, he wasn't one to take his own life.

Returning to the bed, Locke tucked the covers around his father before lowering the flame in the lamp. "Good night, Father."

He turned for the door and came up short at the sight of Portia standing just within the threshold. He wondered how long she'd been there, what she might have overheard. Not that it mattered. He'd been honest with her regarding why he'd married her. She'd be a fool to have illusions otherwise.

"Hello, my dear," his father said.

"I wanted to make sure you were all right." Her gaze darted between him and his father so he wasn't quite certain upon whom she was checking. She'd changed into her nightdress. With her gown and petticoats gone, he could see that she was a bit more slender than he'd realized, seemed a bit more vulnerable. He shook off that thought. There was absolutely nothing vulnerable about the woman who had challenged him that afternoon.

"Fine, my dear. Just tired." His father waved a hand. "Go on, Locke. See to your bride. I'll wait here for your mother."

Closing his eyes, he sighed as he shook his head. When he opened them, he wasn't pleased to see the pity reflected in Portia's expression.

"Sleep well, my lord," she said before stepping into the hallway.

Joining her there, Locke closed the door and twisted the key.

"Is it safe to lock him in?" she asked.

"Safer than not. Gilbert will unlock it before the sun comes up." He was taken aback by the concern in her eyes. Had he been asked, he'd have stated that she cared not one whit about anyone save herself, but she certainly seemed to have some trepidation where his father was concerned. "He'll be fine. It's better than having him out roaming over the moors. If he hadn't shouted, we might not have known until morning, and who knows what sort of state he would have been in by then?"

"So he goes out often?"

He tilted his head. "I'm usually able to catch him

before he makes it out the door. Tonight I was otherwise preoccupied."

A lamp in the hallway provided enough light that he could see her blush. She straightened her spine, angled her chin. "I suppose we should get back to it."

He wondered if it were possible for a woman to sound less delighted at the prospect of being bedded. Perhaps he'd been going a bit too slowly for her tastes. Once he had her clothes removed, she was going to be very glad to be with him. But first—

"After traipsing after my father, I'll need a bath before I rejoin you."

He thought it was relief washing over her face until she said on a breathless sigh, "Oh, a bath would be lovely."

He cursed himself for not considering that after her travels she might have preferred to do more than change her clothes. "I usually bathe in a room just off the kitchen. I could haul the tub up here—"

"No need for that. I'm perfectly happy to use whatever room is most convenient."

He'd expected her to be more demanding, more insistent that she be pampered. He didn't like these unanticipated aspects to her that he was discovering, wanted her to be precisely the sort of woman he had judged her to be: one who always put her own needs, wants, and desires first. "It'll take me a while to get the water warmed. I'll come for you when it's ready, shall I?"

"You'll do it yourself?"

"I'm not going to wake the elderly servants this time of night." Truth be told, he always prepared his own bath, took care of most of his own needs.

"I don't want you to go to that trouble for me, then."

"No trouble. I need prepare only one bath. We'll bathe together."

There was that blush again, only this time it was a ruddier hue. It wasn't very gentlemanly of him to take delight in making her blush, and yet he did. It made him want to smile and it had been a good long time since he'd honestly, completely smiled. Since there had been any true joy in his life. Not since his father's wards reached their majority and moved back to their ancestral estates.

Oh, he had a jolly good time when he saw them in London or when they traveled, but the joy here—within this manor, on this land—was practically nonexistent. He'd been content with it. It was the way of things. Yet he suddenly felt this tiny spark of something he couldn't quite identify, realized he might enjoy moments with her out of the bed as much as he was going to enjoy them in it.

Her gaze slowly roamed over him, and his body tightened in response to her perusal. When she did finally get around to touching him, he was likely to explode.

"Considering your immense size," she said, "I don't see how the two of us can fit together in the tub."

"It's a rather large tub." It was one of the few indulgences he'd allowed himself. Specially made so he could stretch out in it. Although it took heating several caldrons of water to fill it, he never minded. He enjoyed taking a leisurely bath. He was going to enjoy it all the more with her in there with him.

She nodded. "I'll need to put up my hair."

"As I said, it'll take a while to prepare it. I'll come for you."

Her lips lifted into the smallest of smiles. "I'll be waiting."

She spun on her heel, heading back toward his—their—bedchamber. Guilt pricked his conscience, made him uncomfortable. "Portia?"

She turned back to him.

Swallowing, he cleared his throat. "I don't know

how long you were standing there, what you might have heard—"

"I have no illusions regarding your opinion of me, my lord, or what it is you want from me. To be quite honest, I fully expected you to merely toss my skirt over my head and have your way with me. I'm quite relieved to discover you're willing to give me some consideration."

"You married me thinking I would force myself on you?"

"I married you knowing that women have very little say in how they are treated."

He was not going to ask about her marriage. She'd said she loved the man. Surely he had not abused her. "I told you that you would find pleasure in my bed."

"Men often lie, Lord Locksley. Or they overestimate their ability to . . . please."

With such a poor opinion of men, why the devil was she here? "Yet you sought another marriage?"

"As I mentioned, I sought security." That small smile again, as though she were amused by a private joke. "Men also tend not to listen when women speak. I'll be waiting for you."

When she walked away this time, he didn't stop her. He wasn't going to feel guilty because she was fully aware that for him, this arrangement was based on nothing more than the physical. Considering how little they cared for each other, he could probably dispense with the bath, but he wanted a long, leisurely coupling—and he wanted more than one before the night was done.

Turning on his heel, he headed down the stairs. He might have offered to bring his father a girl from the village, might have considered finding one for himself earlier in the day, but the truth was that he wasn't in the habit of taking advantage of women in the area—even the willing ones. He had an obligation to see to their welfare, not to take advantage.

He acquired his pleasures in London and he hadn't been there in a good long while. So he was quite looking forward to being intimate with his young bride, especially as she knew her way well around a man's body. His father had the right of it there. No skittish female, but one who it seemed might be able to show him a thing or two.

Although he still hadn't quite figured out how to take her upside down.

In the kitchen, he set three caldrons of water on the stove to begin heating before going into what had long ago been designated as the bathing room. He filled the copper tub halfway. Once the water on the stove began boiling he'd pour it into the tub. He liked his bath hot, steaming. He wondered if it would be agreeable to his wife.

His wife.

Barking out his laughter, he wondered how it was that term came to be associated with him. Bending over, he spread his arms wide, grabbed either side of the tub, and laughed again. Normally he was not prone to rash decisions, and he'd certainly not awoken that morning intending to be married by day's end.

Yet it had come to pass. What the hell had he been thinking? He couldn't deny that she was a fetching wench and he hadn't minded the notion of having her in his bed. But to take her as his wife when he knew absolutely nothing about her except that he could never love her?

He should have paid her off. With a bit of effort, he could have bargained her down to a reasonable amount. Only he hadn't wanted to bargain with her. Devil take him. He didn't know if he'd ever met a woman with as much backbone and daring as she. He'd wager the tin mines that she'd not truly expected to marry, that she had come here hoping to walk away with a tidy sum.

He'd wanted to best her, with her arrogance and her ability to look at him as though she knew precisely how badly he wanted to possess her. More the fool was he.

So why hadn't he simply tossed up her skirts and taken her? Because he wanted her as wet and eager for him as he was hard and desperate for her. There may be nothing between them except the physical, but by God he was going to make the most of that. He was going to torment and torture her. He was going to have her begging him to plow into her.

His laughter, harsh and deep, echoed around him. He could have had all that without marrying her. She wasn't immune to him. The few moments they were together on the terrace proved that. He could have convinced her to walk away with a paltry sum.

Only he hadn't wanted her to walk away.

That was the truth of it, and he could no more explain why than he could decipher where exactly they'd find veins of tin hidden within the earth.

Shaking his head, he pushed himself up. He was married years before he'd planned, to a woman he had no interest in knowing. Not true. He did want to know her. Her breasts, her shoulders, the haven between her thighs. He wanted to become familiar with her cries of pleasure, her hands stroking him, her tightness enveloping him.

But a bath first.

He poured only one pot of boiling water into the tub. It heated the water to a comfortable temperature. He'd save the others until he discovered how hot she liked her bathwater. Considerate of him.

As he started to leave the room to fetch her, he stopped, glanced back at the Spartan surroundings. A wooden bench he used to pull on his boots, some pegs on the walls where he hung the clothes not in use. Not the most romantic of places. They wouldn't consummate their relationship here, but they could certainly reveal themselves, taunt and tease each other—

Damnation. He was going to let her enjoy her bath alone. Wooing a woman beside a kitchen was no wooing at all. Not that she required wooing. She was his wife, but he was well aware that the first time they came together would set the tone for their marriage. He wanted pleasant, enjoyable, heated evenings with his little mercenary.

But when he arrived in his bedchamber, he discovered her curled on her side asleep on top of the covers, as though she'd merely meant to relax for a bit while waiting for him. One hand rested beneath her cheek, the other was pressed flat, almost protectively, against her stomach—the place where his child would grow within her. The babe who would make his father happy. His heir.

The weight of that landed heavily on his chest. He had planned to marry, had planned to provide an heir. Just not for a while yet, but he couldn't fault his father for pushing him. Ashe and Grey already had their heirs. It was time he did as well.

As quietly as possible, he eased closer to the bed and studied his wife. In sleep, she seemed younger, more innocent, but a woman with her tart tongue could not be wholly innocent. For the first time he wondered what her marriage had been like, how her husband may have treated her. She'd loved the man.

She'd never love Locke.

He was unprepared for the pang that thought brought with it. He didn't need love, didn't want it, and he most certainly wasn't going to give it. It angered him that he was suddenly quite curious about her. He had no interest in her except for the surcease she would provide to his body and the heir she would give him. An heir and a spare.

An image flashed of a little ginger-haired girl looking up at him with whiskey eyes. He didn't want a daughter. He didn't want to feel. He didn't want anything that challenged his sanity. It was best not to care, to become lost in work, in managing the estates, in seeing to his duty.

His duty required that he plant his seed in this woman. He would do it as unemotionally as possible. He would ensure that she never had any doubt regarding the strict businesslike tone of their relationship. He was going to use her just as she'd planned to use his father. For gain, to acquire what he needed. Other than that, she could go to the devil.

She could also bathe in the morning. It had grown late. No sense in waking her now. He didn't want a lethargic coming together.

Reaching across her, he grabbed the blankets and folded them over her. Holding his breath, he watched as she wiggled, settled beneath the covers, and he fought not to envision her wiggling and settling in beneath him.

Spinning on his heel, he headed for the bathing room, hoping to hell that the water had cooled, because now he was in desperate need of a frigid bath to douse his desires.

Chapter 7

PORTIA couldn't remember the last time she'd slept so deeply, so soundly. Feeling completely rested was almost enough to make her believe she was safe. With a low moan and a languorous stretch she slowly opened her eyes to a room awash in faint light and her husband at the washstand, slowly guiding a straight razor up his neck and over his chin.

He wore only trousers. Her mouth went dry as she took in the sight of his broad shoulders and muscled back. She'd seen and felt the evidence that he didn't spend his days lounging about, but still the perfection of his bronzed physique was a bit unsettling. Not an ounce of excess marred him. He was all corded muscle, ropy sinew, and strength. She was quite mesmerized observing the play of his muscles as he shaved.

"You're awake, I see." His deep voice sliced through the quiet.

Her gaze slammed into his, reflected in the oval mirror hanging above the washstand, and she wondered how long he might have been watching her. Her cheeks warmed.

"You didn't wake me for my bath."

"Seemed cruel." He tipped his head back, began scraping up the other side. "You seemed lost to the world. A bath is waiting for you when you're ready. It won't take Mrs. Barnaby any time at all to warm it."

Taking a deep breath, she tried to regain her equilibrium. "I suppose you're coming back to bed."

She was grateful the words came out strong and forceful, giving no hint whatsoever that she was quivering with the thought of him shucking those trousers and climbing on top of her.

A corner of his mouth hitched up, his gaze never leaving hers, even though the razor began to move along his jaw. "The sun is up. I missed my chance."

Even knowing that the room wasn't lit with candles, she sat up and stared at the window. It couldn't be much past dawn. Her gaze fell on the pillow beside hers. Indented from where his head had rested on it. He'd slept with her, but she was in a cocoon of blankets. He couldn't have touched her if he'd wanted.

She jerked her gaze back to him. "But we must consummate the marriage."

Running the towel over his face, he turned from the mirror, his grin broadening. "Anxious to have me, are you?"

"I simply want to ensure that everything is legal, that you can't annul this marriage on a whim."

She hated the way he scrutinized her, as though he had the means to explore her soul, every hidden nook and cranny of it. He angled his head to the side. "Am I going to learn something today to make me want to undo this marriage?"

"No, of course not." Hopefully he'd never learn of it. She'd do all in her power to ensure he didn't. "But as I mentioned yesterday, I sought marriage for security. I can't feel secure if you can claim that I have not seen to my wifely duties."

"Duties?" With a shake of his head, he reached for his shirt draped over a straight-backed chair. "You've convinced me that we must wait for tonight as it appears I'll need more time than I thought to ensure you don't view our coupling as a duty." He shrugged into the shirt, began buttoning it.

She scrambled out of bed. "You can take all the time you want now."

"Alas, my dear wife, I have responsibilities that require I go to the mines today. This evening will be soon enough."

It would be. She knew that. She was being silly to worry over this one aspect. What would one more day hurt? Besides, it would give her a chance to grow accustomed to the notion that she would be bedded by a young, virile, and exceedingly masculine husband rather than a bent and wrinkled one. She could shore up her defenses so she didn't give the impression that he had the ability to control her with a touch.

He snatched up his neck cloth.

"You don't have a valet," she said. A statement not a question.

"You met all the indoor servants."

She crossed over to him and lightly slapped his hands aside. "I'll do it."

"I hadn't considered this advantage to having a wife."

"You're mocking me."

"Teasing. There's a difference."

"Yesterday you didn't strike me as one who would tease."

"You didn't strike me as one who would do for others."

She lifted her gaze to his, once more unsettled by how thoroughly he seemed to be studying her. "It seems we were both wrong."

She patted the knot. "There." And snatched up his waistcoat.

He turned for the mirror, lifted his chin slightly. "You did an excellent job."

"I used to do them for Montie." Holding out the waistcoat for him, drawing it up over his arms, onto this shoulders, she grimaced at the slip of her tongue. He was far too distracting, but with any luck perhaps he hadn't paid any attention to her words.

He faced her. "Montie?"

It seemed luck wasn't going to favor her today. She began buttoning up the black silk. "My husband."

"Do you miss him?" A muscle jumped in his jaw as it tightened, making her think he wished he'd bitten back the question.

"No," she answered honestly, picking up his jacket, holding it up so he could turn and slip his arms inside. Only he didn't turn.

"I thought you loved him."

"I did. Just not so much at the end." She didn't know what had possessed her to admit that. She'd hated Montie by the end. Despised him once she discovered the hurt he was capable of inflicting, realized he wasn't deserving of her affections.

For a moment, it appeared Locksley might say something else, express his sorrow that the love had not been long lasting. Instead, he merely presented his back. She nearly laughed at her foolishness for thinking he might have cared one whit that her heart had been broken with such callous disregard.

The day before, Locksley had claimed to have no interest in love. Truthfully neither did she. It had stolen away her family and brought her to ruin, still had the ability to destroy her and wreck what she was striving to accomplish if she wasn't careful.

The jacket went into place beautifully, obviously tailored expressly for him. There was no reason to, and yet she couldn't seem to stop herself from gliding her hands across his shoulders, as though she needed to straighten the cloth.

He stepped away, brushed at one arm, although she could see no lint there. "I have to go over some papers at my desk for a bit, then I'll go into breakfast. You're welcome to join me after your bath." He looked back at her. "Although your presence isn't required. After all it is the daytime. If I don't see you there, rest assured that I shall return by nightfall, and the marriage will be consummated with all due haste."

If it was going to be done hastily, they might as well do it now. She could make that happen. "Will you help me dress?"

"Mrs. Barnaby can see to that. I have no interest whatsoever in putting clothes on you. Only in taking them off."

With that, he walked out, closing the door in his wake. She took a deep breath. For the briefest of moments there, she'd feared he might be a danger to her heart. Thank goodness she'd judged correctly yesterday. He was exactly the sort of arrogant ass she could never love.

WHEN she had awoken with that soft moan, it had taken everything within him not to pounce on the bed and take her then and there. It hadn't mattered that his face was lathered or that she'd distracted him to such an extent that he very nearly sliced open his jugular. He could think of worse ways to go than with that luscious sound ringing in his ears. How could a woman be so gloriously sensual upon awakening?

Standing at the window in the library, watching as the fog began to dissipate, he admitted that he didn't have any paperwork he needed to see to. He just wanted to give her time to bathe and perhaps join him for breakfast. He could have also delayed going to the mines, but being within reach of her without touching her would have tested his sanity. While she had offered herself during the day, they'd made a bargain he intended to keep. The day was hers; the night was his. One exception would place them on a slippery slope, and she might decide he shouldn't have all the nights, and he had no plans whatsoever to give up a single one of those.

When he finally made his way to the breakfast dining room, he was disappointed to discover it empty save for Gilbert, who immediately poured his coffee before heading out for his plate. It pricked his temper that she could disappoint him. He didn't care for her, so it made no sense whatsoever that she should elicit any emotion at all in him. It irritated him that he was still thinking about her an hour after he'd left her. Obviously she'd given him no further contemplation. She had her title, her allowance, a bath—

The last thought flew from his mind as she walked in, her cheeks flushed and pink, her dress a dark blue, buttons up to her throat, down to her wrists. At least it wasn't the ghastly black in which she'd arrived. At least she wasn't being a hypocrite and pretending to be in mourning after she'd wed another man. She was setting her grief aside, what little grief there may have been. He didn't know her husband, didn't want to know him, but still it bothered him that the man had managed to lose her love. To have had it and not appreciated it, to have not strived to hold on to it—

He shook his head, refusing to travel that path, and

came to his feet. Moving to the chair opposite his, he pulled it out.

Her flush deepened. "You don't have to wait on me."

"Just a simple courtesy for my wife."

She approached slowly, cautiously, as though she expected him to toss her on the table and have his way with her. With that particular thought crossing his mind, he realized he might have been unwise to invite her to breakfast.

As she sat, he inhaled the lingering fragrance of clean skin, her bath, and a fresh application of jasmine. His body reacted as though she'd begun undoing that enticing row of buttons. He moved quickly back to his chair before Portia could see how she affected him. Although when he was finally settled and looking at her, she gave him a secretive little uplifting of her lips that signaled she knew the impact she had on him.

He rather feared he might be blushing, damn it all to hell. Thank God Gilbert chose that moment to walk in holding a plate.

"Give it to Lady Locksley," Locke said, casually picking up the newspaper as though enough wits remained to him that he could make sense of anything he might read.

"Good morning, m'lady," Gilbert said. "Would you prefer tea or coffee?"

"Tea please."

Gilbert saw to the task while Locke read the first sentence of the main article three times. He couldn't concentrate with her at the table, in spite of his not wanting to be distracted by her. When the butler went to fetch another plate, she said, "Will your father be joining us?"

Setting down his paper, Locke realized that she looked considerably younger today, less weary, less troubled. More beautiful. Yesterday had been an apparition, an aberration. He cleared his throat. "He generally takes his meals in his room. Yesterday was an exception."

"So you dine alone?"

"I have wine to keep me company."

"At breakfast?"

He grinned. "No, then I have the paper."

"Don't let my presence stop you from reading it. You don't have to entertain me."

"I had no plans to." Could he sound any more like an ass? "Where did you travel from to get here?"

She stopped halfway to reaching for her tea, seemed to ponder her answer, or perhaps it was merely the revealing of it that gave her pause. It struck him that for all the information about him that she'd gained last night, she'd revealed very little of herself. "London."

His father no doubt knew from whence she hailed as he'd had to dispatch his correspondence to her. "You arrived in a mail coach. I would have thought my father would have sent you money so you could travel in more luxury."

"He did." She lifted the cup, took a small sip, her lips teasing the rim, the heated brew. What was wrong with him to think he'd never seen anything more provocative in his life? She licked that lower lip, then the upper. "I thought to put the funds to better use. Enhancing my wardrobe, for example."

"Surely your husband didn't leave you penniless."

"He left me nothing at all. His money was for gambling and pleasure. So I was quite destitute and desperate when I saw your father's advert." She lowered her head slightly. "Are you going to eat?"

He looked down to see a plate had been set before him. Glancing over, he saw Gilbert standing at attention in his usual spot. How the devil had he made his delivery without Locke noticing? He wasn't the most fleet of foot or the quietest. It was her. She managed to somehow garner every last bit of attention he possessed. He should stop asking her questions now. He was not going to sympathize with her scheming, no matter how bad off her husband may have left her.

"You said you were going to the mines today," she mused softly.

"Yes, immediately after breakfast."

"Will you hand over my allowance for the month before you leave?"

He almost laughed. How easy it was to forget that marriage to her had come with a price. "Of course, my little mercenary. As soon as we've finished eating."

"Then we should get to it, shouldn't we?" She turned her attention to the creamed eggs.

For the life of him, he couldn't determine why earlier he'd wanted her to join him—except for a while there, she made the room feel not quite so empty.

Chapter 8

SHE had to take such care in answering his questions that it was trying beyond measure. There had never been a husband. She wasn't a widow. But there had been a love, what she had thought was a grand love. What a fool she'd been. She wasn't going to make the mistake of falling in love again. He had no interest in it and neither did she. Which should have made them perfect for each other. Instead it served to tie her stomach into knots. She could have coerced the marquess into caring for her. She didn't stand a chance of doing that with his obstinate son.

Yet she felt this insane urge to be as honest as she could with him. If he ever discovered the full truth, he would at least see that she had limited her deception as much as she was able. Of course, if he discovered the full truth, it would all be moot, as he was likely to kill her anyway. Put those strong hands of his about her neck and choke the very life from her.

But she couldn't worry about the future. She had to concentrate on the present. And presently he was leading her down the hallway to the library. He strode into what she was certain could easily become her favorite room. While it was tidy, it still had a musty scent to it that wasn't completely a result of all the books that lined the shelves.

She wondered how long it had been since the room was aired, the carpets beaten, and the draperies washed.

He walked over to a painting of dogs on a hunt, flipped it aside as though it were a door, and revealed a safe. While she couldn't see exactly what he was doing, she heard a series of metal clicks. Then there was a clack. The clinking of coins, followed by more clanking before he swung the painting back into place.

He returned to her side, held up his hand. She extended hers, palm up. He dropped a velvet pouch into its center. She was incredibly tempted to open it and count out the money, but it had the correct heft and there should be some trust in their relationship. He gave her what she could only describe as a disappointing smile before heading for his desk.

"Go ahead and count it," he said.

"I trust you."

He glanced back over his shoulder. "No, you don't."

Had he been able to read her mind? That would be unfortunate. "If I discover it short later, I know where to find you."

He hoisted a hip onto the edge of the desk, crossed his arms over that wide chest. "Anything you require I will purchase for you, so why do you need an allowance?"

"For things that aren't required."

"Such as?"

She lifted a shoulder. "A frivolous bonnet." *A residence.* "An extra pair of slippers." *Food.* "Chocolates." *A new life. Safety. Security.*

"You are my wife, Portia. It is my duty to see after your care."

"The care of my person, yes, but the care of my heart? I daresay you no doubt draw the line there."

"I want you to find happiness here."

He almost made her feel guilty for taking advantage—almost. But too much was at stake. She held up the pouch. "I have."

He shoved himself up off the desk. "I have to get to the mines. Enjoy your day. And be prepared for tonight. You won't get another reprieve."

"I didn't ask for one," she reminded him sharply. "I was willing to have a go at it this morning, but you turned me down."

He strode up to her, stopping within a hairbreadth of her. "You can't possibly imagine what that cost me." He cradled her face with one large, powerful hand. "This will probably cost me as well in torment for the remainder of the day, but damn if you don't have the most kissable-looking lips I've ever seen."

Then his mouth was on hers, proving his point. And damn if his lips were just as kissable. They were full, his mouth broad, and his tongue so very skilled at stroking and exploring. She found herself flattened against him, not certain if she'd stepped into him or he'd drawn her near. It didn't matter. What mattered was the way his hands rubbed her back with sureness, with possession, the manner in which he angled his head to taste her more fully, providing access so she could taste him more intimately. Whatever he'd eaten for breakfast was washed away by the dark coffee he drank. She wasn't surprised he didn't begin his morning with tea. She suspected he was a man of strong desires in all matters: spirits, food, coffee, women.

He wouldn't take her lightly or gently. He might take her slowly, but when it came down to it, he would crush her, be as demanding as he was now, insist that she not hold back, that she give fully all she had.

He might be the lord of the manor, her husband, the

head of the house, but when it came to the mattress she could hold her own. She'd been tutored by the best. She wouldn't retreat, wouldn't allow him to master her between the sheets. They would be equal, true partners. A day might come when he regretted having her for a wife, but she made a vow then and there that he would never regret having her for a bed partner.

Tearing his mouth away, he stared down at her, his breaths coming swift and heavy. She slowly ran her tongue around her lips to have a final taste of him. His groan was that of a tormented creature as his eyes darkened.

"Until tonight, Lady Locksley," he ground out before spinning on his heel and charging from the room.

She could do little more than gape after him. She'd fully expected him to shove her onto the desk and take her there. Dear God, but he was a man of incredible restraint and strength of purpose. She'd not be able to bend him to her will easily.

On the other hand, it was that very aspect of him that excited her. He could stand his ground against anyone. He could safeguard her, as long as she gave him a compelling reason to want to protect her. A child would accomplish that. She needed to ensure they consummated their marriage tonight.

$\mathcal{W}$ITH her coins nestled in her skirt pocket, she spent half an hour in the library looking over the books, striving to find something to read, to occupy her time. But it wasn't the assortment of literature she wanted to explore. It was the residence itself, even if it was nothing more than a series of locked doors. Except that the locks had keys.

She made her way down to the kitchens and found Mrs. Barnaby rocking in a chair in her office, sipping a cup of tea.

"Mrs. Barnaby," she said.

The older woman's eyes widened, and she shoved herself to her feet, her bones creaking along the way. "M'lady."

"Mrs. Barnaby, I'd like to borrow your keys for a spell."

Much as she had the day before the housekeeper slapped her hand against the large ring. "They're my responsibility."

"Yes, I know. And I will return them before the day is done."

She shook her head. "I'm sorry, Lady Locksley, but I can't give them to you."

"Oh, I believe you can."

She shook her head more forcefully. "I can't."

With a deep sigh, Portia held out her hand. "You can and you will."

"You can't command me."

"I'm the lady of the manor."

"We'll see what his Lordship has to say about that."

Before Portia could respond, the woman was rushing— faster than Portia had thought her capable—out of the room. "His Lordship has gone to the mines," she called out after her.

"Not the viscount," Mrs. Barnaby shouted over her shoulder. "The marquess. He won't stand for this at all."

Portia almost called her back, almost rescinded her request, but it was a matter of pride now. She would not be cowed, nor would she bother her husband with this. She was relatively certain he would agree with her position, but it was her hope to lessen his burdens, not add to them. Whether or not the marquess was in agreement with her right to have the keys was another matter. She suspected it had to do with where his mind was this morning.

She followed Mrs. Barnaby up the stairs and waited

outside the marquess's bedchamber as the woman knocked briskly.

"Come in," he called out.

With a flourish, Mrs. Barnaby opened the door and marched in. Portia went in as well. The marquess was sitting in a thick cushioned chair near the window, looking out.

"She wants me keys," Mrs. Barnaby announced sharply.

Glancing over his shoulder, Marsden squinted. He seemed smaller today, more frail. "Who wants your keys?"

"Lady Locksley."

"Lady Locksley?"

Oh, dear Lord, had he already forgotten who she was? She stepped around Mrs. Barnaby. "My lord—"

"Ah, yes." He held up a gnarled finger. "Lady Locksley. If she wants the keys, Mrs. Barnaby, give them to her."

"But she's not the marchioness. She's not the lady of the house."

"She is my son's wife. He manages our affairs now, which makes her the lady of the house. Give her the keys."

"We don't know what she might do with them."

"I suspect, Mrs. Barnaby, that she's going to unlock a door."

"I could do that for her."

"Obviously she wants to do it for herself. It is not our place to question the viscountess, so hand over the keys."

With a mulish expression similar to the one she'd given Locksley the day before, Mrs. Barnaby unhooked the ring from her waist and held it out toward Portia, who took it, feeling as though she'd just won something significant.

"I need them back," Mrs. Barnaby said, looking as though she were on the verge of weeping.

"Yes, of course. I'll return them later this afternoon."

With a harrumph, the housekeeper marched from the room.

Portia tiptoed over to stand nearer to Marsden, although he'd given his attention back to gazing out the window.

"I'm sorry we had to disturb you with that little misunderstanding," she said softly.

"Mrs. Barnaby is a good soul but she is set in her ways. She's gone a long time without a mistress to answer to, considered herself the mistress of the household. My fault as I never corrected her. Damage was done by the time Locke finished his travels and settled in to take care of things."

"It's not a problem. She and I shall work things out and get along just fine."

"I'm sure you will, my dear." His gaze drifted back toward the window.

Portia sat in a chair opposite him. "We missed you at breakfast."

"You and my son need time alone to get to know each other better. I saw him ride out earlier, going to the mines I suspect." He winked at her. "Did he give you our heir last night?"

She supposed when one got to a certain age, he no longer felt the need to censor his tongue. "I fell asleep."

A stunned expression crossed his features. "I thought he'd have more enthusiasm, be more virile. I didn't think he'd be so sloth-like that you'd be able to go to sleep as though he wasn't even there."

She released a self-conscious laugh. "No, that's not it at all. He was preparing a bath after his journey onto the moors. I was waiting for him and drifted off."

"Ah, and he was too polite to wake you." He shook

his head. "A man shouldn't be that polite on his wedding night. Prepare yourself. He'll be twice as randy tonight."

Her cheeks grew so warm she was surprised they didn't ignite. She had a need to turn the conversation away from being bedded by his son. "Are you searching for your wife?"

He shook his head. "She doesn't come out during the day. Sun doesn't agree with her. So I just wait, watch the shadows move with the daylight, lengthen as it weakens, until the darkness brings her back to me."

"You loved her very much."

"She was everything. Still is." He wrinkled his nose. "She gets angry at me. Says I wasted my life. But Ashe, Albert, and Edward all married for love. Even if Albert and Edward married the same woman."

She knew that Albert had died and Edward had married his brother's widow in Switzerland, which had created quite the scandal among the peerage.

"And now Locke is married. I didn't do bad by them, so how could I have wasted my life?"

"I don't think you did," she said with conviction.

"You're a sweet thing. Locke will come around to loving you."

Her chest tightened. "I don't require his love, my lord."

"We all require love, my dear. The more we think we don't need it, the more we do."

Again, another topic she wanted to leave behind. "Would you like for me to read to you?"

He shook his head. "Go do whatever it was you wanted to do with the keys."

"I wish to explore the residence a bit, but I won't disturb anything."

He nodded, a faraway look coming into his eyes, and she suspected that she'd lost him, that he was out on the moors with his love. Standing, she leaned over and pressed a kiss to the top of his head. He barely acknowledged her.

Clutching the keys, she walked from the room, wondering where to start. With the bedchambers. She could find one to secretly make into her own, except that Locksley was correct. When would she use it? Every hour of the night would be spent in his bed.

Surely there was another room that would serve better. A small library, a sitting room, a parlor, a little haven hidden away where she could escape to find peace. She wouldn't have to tell anyone about it. It would be her private sanctuary. And as the marquess appeared to not wander about, her actions weren't likely to upset him, as he probably wouldn't stumble across whatever room she decided to clean.

And cleaning it would be the first order of business. She'd seen evidence of the neglect when Locksley had shown her the ballroom, and it was repeated in every room into which she stepped. Cobwebs, dust, decayed flowers. The suffocating odor of disuse. She needed a room with an abundance of windows so she could air it out quickly.

But as she wandered from various parlors and sitting rooms to drawing rooms and conservatories, melancholy began to take hold, to blot out any optimism. She could envision a time when all these rooms were well maintained, warm, and welcoming. They would have brought pride to the marquess and marchioness.

An even greater sadness washed through her as she realized that Locksley would have known none of what had once been. He grew up with the abandonment and dilapidation. Locks on doors couldn't contain it. Knowing what rested on the other side of the doors, she could now feel it seeping into the hallways. It might have been better for all had the structure burned to the ground after the marchioness's passing.

Then she opened a door that made her grateful the residence still stood. Light filtered in through a narrow parting between the draperies, but it was enough for her to see that she had stepped into a magnificent music room. Windows lined one wall. Near them rested the largest pianoforte she'd ever seen. So grand. Or it would be if the dark wood was polished to a sheen.

She approached with the reverence it deserved.

It had been years since she'd set fingers to keyboard, not since she'd left home. She'd offered to play for Montie, but he'd explained that when it came to her he was only interested in the music of passion that was created between the sheets. She'd been flattered, swept away by the notion that he wanted her so badly. It was a while before she understood that being wanted for only one purpose created a very lonely existence.

The type she would have with Locksley. At least he was honest with her, being forthright that he wanted from her only what Montie had wanted, but Montie had wooed her with pretty words and promises of love. Even if Locksley offered them, she was too wise now to believe them. She would not open her heart to him, merely her thighs.

As she neared the piano, she wanted to weep because it had gone years without being played, without anyone listening to the glorious music with which it would fill the air. Unappreciated, unloved, its potential unrealized. Tapping a key, cringing as a tinny sound reverberated, she wasn't surprised it was in need of tuning, but that could be handled easily enough.

Slowly she began to turn in a circle, stopping when she noticed the life-size portrait of a woman hanging over the massive stone fireplace. She wasn't particularly fetching, but there was warmth in her eyes, her smile. Portia had never known anyone to grin during a sitting, yet she couldn't imagine this woman without a happy expression. Finding herself drawn to the painting, she took a couple of steps nearer. Based on the style of her royal blue gown, she had to be a recent marchioness, no doubt Marsden's dead wife. She was covered in dust and cobwebs, and yet there was an ethereal quality to her that seemed to glow when her surroundings should have dulled the painting.

"How fortunate you were to be so loved," she whispered.

Holding out her arms, Portia completed her circle, her joy burgeoning as she took in the various sitting areas, the shelves displaying books, statuettes, and vases, and the various decorations arranged throughout waiting to be released from their shroud of dust.

Clapping her hands together, she released the smallest of squeals. She had found her room.

$\mathcal{I}$T was late afternoon by the time Locke, covered in sweat and grime, strode into the kitchen. He didn't know why he believed that if he worked in the mines alongside the miners that fortune was more likely to smile on them and they'd discover a tin-rich vein after two years of nothing. It had made the men uncomfortable when he'd begun digging beside them. He was a lord. It had taken them a while to accept his help, his determination. But he enjoyed stretching his muscles, pushing himself to the limit of near physical exhaustion. It kept his mind from traveling the path of despair. Today it had kept him from breaking his promise to his wife that the day belonged to her.

He shouldn't have kissed her before he walked out, because her taste had stayed with him far too long, had kept his body tense and in need until he'd gone down into the pits where there was always a danger that he wouldn't come out.

So perhaps his father had the right of it. He really did need to get the next heir lined up. Robbie would no doubt let the mines go, sell the land, since it wasn't part of the entailment. He wouldn't appreciate his heritage or what the marquesses who had come before him had built.

"You're a bit early," Mrs. Dorset told him, a knowing smile on her face. "Although to be honest, I was expecting you sooner, what with a new bride and all. Been warming your bathwater for some time now."

He was in the habit of bathing after a day in the mines, which was the reason he'd established a room for bathing near the kitchen. For the convenience of procuring hot water and not tracking dirt through the residence. While he wasn't particularly pleased with how anxious he was to be with his wife, he had no wish for her to see him in this state, to know he engaged in backbreaking work to secure their future—or how much that seventy-five quid a month was really costing him. They were not truly a couple who shared joys and burdens. They were merely bedmates. Or they would be by night's end.

Still, when he was finished with his bath and shave, he did find himself missing her fingers knotting his neck cloth as he put on the clothes he'd changed out of that morning before leaving. For the mines he needed sturdier material.

When he stepped out of the bathing room, he nearly tripped over Mrs. Barnaby, who it seemed had been awaiting his appearance.

"She took me keys," she announced, her hands clutched at her waist, her brow deeply furrowed.

"She?"

"Your wife."

"For what purpose?"

She gave her eyes an exaggerated roll. "To open doors."

He'd assumed as much. In hindsight his question was rather pointless. He hadn't even bothered to consider how Portia would fill her day. Obviously by wandering the hallways and sticking her nose where it didn't belong.

"She's yet to return them, and it's nearly dark. They're my responsibility. I warned his Lordship—"

"You spoke to my father about them?"

She nodded. "I wanted his approval before handing them over to her. She's not the marchioness."

"She is, however, the lady of the manor."

Her eyes widened at his forceful tone, which he had not meant to come out so sharp, but regardless of how little he might personally care for Portia and her greedy little fingers, she was his wife and as such would be accorded the respect she deserved.

Mrs. Barnaby's mouth turned down. "Your father said the same thing."

Of course he had.

"Where will I find Lady Locksley?" he asked.

"I don't know. I'm not her keeper. Wandering about somewhere I suppose."

He wasn't particularly pleased with her answer. He and his father before him had been rather lax with the servants. Perhaps it was time he prodded Mrs. Barnaby toward retirement. He'd consider it. Meanwhile he had a wife to locate.

She could be anywhere in this massive mausoleum. As he began trudging through it, he considered that she had probably gone in search of a bedchamber that she could claim without his knowing. Upstairs then. He should have asked how long she'd been in possession of the keys.

There were maybe fifty bedchambers. How long would it take her to go through them, to find one that suited her?

Having her own bedchamber would be a waste. She had to understand that. Every moment of every night was going to be spent with him. He'd made that clear.

He was halfway up the stairs when he stopped, considered. Perhaps she'd merely wanted to explore. He and his father's wards had certainly done their share of nicking the housekeeper's keys and sneaking into rooms at midnight. Perhaps he'd plan a little adventure for his wife, take her on a tour in the wee hours when everything creaked and moaned. He thought of her clinging to him—

No, she wasn't one to cling. He knew that instinctively. She'd probably be leading the way.

Night was falling. Soon she would be looking for him. He should simply settle in his library and wait. Only as he headed back down the stairs, he wasn't in the mood to wait for her. He wanted to find her, discover exactly what she was up to. It was possible that she was planning to collect small items that would fetch a pretty penny, things that she believed wouldn't be noticed missing. Although the truth was that he couldn't see her as a thief, no matter how much money seemed to matter to her. It had irritated him when she'd asked for her seventy-five pounds that morning, had irritated him more when he could tell that she wanted to count it. Theirs was a business arrangement. Security for an heir. It was silly of him to fault her now when he'd known all along that she cared about only titles and coin.

She wasn't going to steal anything, but he suspected she was taking inventory, striving to determine how much they were worth. She would no doubt be methodical about it. If she was unlocking every door, examining the contents of every room, he doubted that she'd have made it upstairs yet. No doubt, she was still on the main level somewhere.

He strode briskly down hallways, trying doors. Locked, locked, locked.

But as he came to the end of one monstrously long and wide hallway, he could see a faint swath of light that could only come from an open doorway. Quieting his tread, he cautiously approached and peered inside, completely unprepared for the sight that greeted him.

With a scarf covering her hair and her sleeves rolled up past her elbows, she was on her knees near a bookshelf, pulling items off the bottom shelf, wiping them, setting them aside. Suddenly with a screech, she jumped up and back. He saw the huge spider scurrying out, racing past—

She lifted her skirt slightly and stopped the creature's progress forever with a hard stomp.

He stared at the foot, which had come down with unerring determination. "Are you wearing one of my Hessians?" he asked incredulously.

With a start, she faced him squarely, her eyes wide, that luscious lovely mouth of hers slightly open. "You're home."

He didn't like the way that her words seemed to pierce his armor, made him glad that he was in the residence. He was accustomed to having his bath, a drink, a quiet dinner, an evening reading. Alone. Always alone until he looked in on his father before retiring. Solitude had been the order of the night. She was going to change all that, whether he wanted her to or not. "Indeed I am. The boot?"

Raising her skirt, she extended the foot, turning it one way then the other as though surprised to find the polished black leather encasing a good part of her leg. "Your feet are much larger than mine, which makes it easier to kill the spiders and provides a little distance from them as I do so." She glanced up at him. "There are an inordinate number in here. And they are remarkably large. And beastly ugly."

"Cardinal spiders, no doubt. They say Wolsey had an aversion to them."

"Smart man."

Approaching her, he wondered why it was that he found himself drawn to her more than ever. She more closely resembled a street sweeper than the wife of a lord. Yet drawn to her he was. "You have a spider web in your hair—"

"What? No!" She began slapping at her head.

He grabbed her wrists. "Hold still."

Although she looked fairly petrified, she moved not at all. He wasn't even certain she was breathing. Those whiskey eyes held a measure of trust that he didn't want to disappoint. Somehow she seemed more vulnerable with the trail of dust along her cheek. He didn't like her appearing in such a state. He preferred her strong and tough. He brushed the back of his hand across the silken strands that rested against her hair and scarf, drawing them away. "There. All gone."

"I hate spiders."

"Then you'd despise going into the mines."

Her brow furrowed. "Do you go into them?"

He hadn't meant to disclose how he spent his day. "Occasionally. After all, we own them; therefore, it behooves me to give them a look." A change in topic was in order. "What are you doing in here?"

"I would think that answer is obvious."

With the danger of the spiders gone, she was back to her tart self. Much easier to deal with. "Then I suppose the better question is why are you doing it when I've already stated that change upsets my father?"

"Surely this room is far enough away from him that he'll never know what I've done." She stepped away, swept her arms wide as though to encompass everything surrounding them. "It's such a glorious room. How could I leave it in disarray?"

She rushed over to the piano. The fading light cast her in silhouette, and yet still he could see her brilliant smile. "Isn't this gorgeous? Or it will be once I've polished it. I could play for you in the evenings."

"I had a different sort of *play* in mind."

Her shoulders slumped, and all the exuberance seemed to leak out of her as air did from a balloon. "Yes, of course. Silly of me to think we might have more." She trailed a finger along a curved edge, inhaled deeply. Disappointment radiated from her.

He hated that he'd killed her smile. "Do you play?"

She glanced over at him. "I do. Not since I left home, so I'm terribly out of practice, and the pianoforte needs tuning, so it would no doubt not be a pleasurable experience for you. But this room . . . it must have been so magnificent once."

He fought to convince himself that she wanted that magnificence for herself. That she wanted the grandness of this room to enhance her own majesty, and yet he couldn't quite persuade himself of the truth of that. There was an honesty in her voice when she spoke of the room that made him think she was being more candid with him at that moment than she'd been since he opened the door to her yesterday afternoon. It had nothing to do with baubles, coin, title, or gain. She saw this room as it might have once been. All his life he'd strived not to see any of the chambers as they'd appeared in the past, hadn't wanted to see the potential in them, had never wanted to envision laughter echoing between the walls, joy spreading to the ceilings, gladness sweeping along the floor. These rooms merely served as evidence that no good could come from love, that it was best to avoid—

"Is that your mother?" she asked tenderly, cutting into his thoughts.

He didn't want her to be tender or soft. He wanted her to be as cold as the coins she craved. Still he followed her gaze toward the portrait hanging over the fireplace. His father possessed a miniature of the same woman that he always carried with him and sometimes showed to Locke. Her eyes, her smile always drew him in. As a lad, he'd resented her for dying, for leaving him. It was many years before he understood she'd had no choice.

Staring at her behind a film of grime, he could understand why his father had loved her. Even though she existed now only in oils, her image seemed vibrant. She possessed the ability to warm his heart, to make him feel guilty that he hadn't accepted Portia's offer to play the pianoforte for him. "Yes."

"I didn't think so at first, but the more I've gazed at her from different angles, I've decided she was very beautiful."

"Beautiful enough to drive a man insane."

"Losing her drove him insane, not her. There is a difference."

He looked over at her. A corner of her mouth and one brow tilted up ever so slightly.

"You would go mad if I were to die," she said teasingly.

Slowly he shook his head, unwilling to take this matter lightly. "I'll not give you my heart, Portia. I was clear on that aspect of our relationship. We can have the marriage annulled tomorrow if you went into this arrangement believing you could somehow acquire it."

She paled, no doubt at the mention of an annulled marriage that would deny her all she sought to gain. "I have no illusions regarding what you want of me, my lord. I suppose we should make haste toward the consummation of this marriage."

Why was it that her haughty tone could make him feel like such an ass, when it should merely confirm why she'd sought the marriage with his father to begin with? He touched the dirt on her cheek, and she went still, so very still. With his gaze following, he trailed his finger along the smudge that journeyed past her mouth to her chin. "You're in need of a bath. I'll cart the tub up to the bedchamber."

"You don't have to go to that bother."

He didn't want her to be considerate, damn it. He needed her to demand spoiling. "As you no doubt discovered this morning, the bathing room stays chilly." Pressing his thumb to her chin, he rubbed at the dirt, wondering why it fascinated him, why he liked seeing her in such a disheveled state. "Mrs. Barnaby wants her keys returned."

"Of course. I'll see to that immediately."

He moved his thumb up to her lower lip, stroked it, considered nipping at it, but if his mouth got anywhere near hers, he was likely to toss her on top of that piano she seemed rather fond of and possess her then and there. That would certainly give it a polishing. But she needed a bath. He needed food and drink. And he didn't want to take her quickly or roughly. Not the first time anyway.

Every other aspect of their relationship might be stiff and awkward, but he wasn't going to tolerate it in the bedchamber. That required patience on his part. He would live with the torment of not possessing her for now. But before the night was done, he would claim her body as his own.

As he escorted her from the room, Portia was a bit surprised—based upon the way his eyes had darkened as he'd rubbed her chin—that he hadn't tossed her on a nearby sofa and hefted up her skirts.

Once outside, she locked the door, already dreading the encounter she would have with Mrs. Barnaby regarding the keys in the morning. She was going to reclaim the room whether Locksley liked it or not. When he wasn't around, she would entertain herself by playing the piano. She understood it was his house and his rules, but some were in need of breaking.

Carrying on down the hallway, she became very aware of her uneven gait, her slipper whispering along the floor, his boot clomping.

"How are you managing to keep my boot on?" he asked.

"I stuffed newspaper into the toe and around the sides filling up the space around my foot. A trick I learned from my mother, who always bought our shoes a bit large so we could grow into them and they'd last longer."

"*Our* shoes? You had siblings?"

She grimaced. The less he knew about her, the better things would be for her. While she'd been ghastly disappointed that he had no interest in her playing the pianoforte for him, she found some solace in his merely wanting her body. He wasn't likely to ask questions or delve into her past. But she wanted to limit her lies, because the truth was always easier to remember. "Two sisters and a brother."

"Last night, you said you had no family."

Because I don't.

"Are they dead?"

It would be so much simpler to say yes. "No. But they did not approve of Montie. So I had to choose him or them."

"You chose him."

She nodded.

"But surely after he died . . ."

"They want nothing to do with me."

"Even though you are now married to a peer?"

"I could marry a prince of England and they wouldn't forgive me." She could feel him studying her. She'd said too much. He was going to continue to question, and when he learned the truth the annulment he'd suggested earlier would become a reality. What was she thinking to be so careless with what she revealed?

"This way," he said, turning down a hallway.

Confused by the direction, she stopped, pointed toward another corridor. "That way leads to the kitchens. I'm fairly certain of it."

"We're taking a detour."

"For what purpose?"

"It's not a woman's place to question her husband."

Or any man for that matter, she was well aware. If she'd questioned Montie she might not have found herself in this unconscionable position. But she wasn't going to make the mistake of trusting blindly again. "You did not strike me as the sort who would want a sheep for a wife."

"As you're well aware I didn't want a wife at all."

There was that, she supposed. So when he started off again, she followed. She'd opened the doors in this hallway earlier in the day. She knew they contained nothing nefarious, nothing that should give her cause for worry. "But you require an heir, so eventually you would have wanted a wife."

"Not wanted, never wanted, but eventually I would have taken one."

"So my arrival simply moved up your timetable."

Stopping in front of a door, he faced her. "Don't say it as though it was a small matter and you did me a great favor." Before she could come up with some quip, he held out his hand. "The keys."

"There's only a study beyond the door."

"I know." He snapped his fingers. "Keys."

She dropped the ring into his broad palm, and he began sorting through the iron. "You didn't take a very close or detailed inventory of the rooms," he muttered.

"I didn't inventory them at all." For some reason, she was insulted by his belief that she would. "Did you think I was searching for silver? I was merely hoping to find a room that would serve as a sanctuary."

He held a key between his thumb and forefinger. "So you merely peered inside and carried on?"

"For the most part, yes. Until I discovered the music room. It was as though it spoke to me."

He arched a thick dark eyebrow over those penetrating green eyes. "You do realize that makes you sound mad."

She scoffed. "The walls didn't literally speak to me, you ninny. I simply meant that I found the room to be welcoming."

"Even with the spiders?"

She twisted her lips. "Not so much once I discovered them." She tapped his boot on the floor. "But I was able to make short work of them."

"So you did."

Before he turned, she almost thought she caught sight of admiration twinkling in his eyes. He unlocked the door, swung it open, and stepped inside. She followed.

"This was the marchioness's study," he announced as he crossed over to a small secretary desk.

She could see it now. With the daintier furniture, the lighter colors. It might have been a cheerful room had it more than one narrow window.

On the desk, he lowered a door to reveal an assortment of nooks and crannies. Pulling open a drawer, he reached inside and withdrew a ring of keys, the metal circle much smaller than the one the housekeeper used. He held it out to her. "So you don't have to bother Mrs. Barnaby for the keys in the future."

She stared at the offering, wondering why her eyes were stinging. He was doing more than handing her bits of iron. He was demonstrating that he trusted her, that she had a true place within the household, in his life. He was handing her freedom, more than she'd had in a good long while. Slowly, reverently, she took them from him. "I don't know what to say."

"There's nothing to say. You're the lady of the manor. You're entitled to a set of the keys."

Of course he would ruin the gesture with a curt tone, but she wasn't going to let him dampen her spirits entirely. "How did you know they were here?"

"I'll tell you during dinner. Meanwhile, I'm quite famished and you still need your bath."

"I'm looking rather forward to the telling." She turned to go.

"Remember," he called after her. "Don't wear gloves."

She glanced over her shoulder, giving him her most wicked smile. "I haven't forgotten. As a matter of fact, I intend to wear very little except for my gown. Less for you to bother with later. Ponder on that during dinner."

With her mismatched footwear, her exit wasn't nearly

as poised as she would have liked, but his low groan, bowed head, and fingers digging into the desk behind him managed to give her a great deal of satisfaction. The night might belong to him, but it was going to belong to him only on her terms.

Chapter 9

*S*HE was going to drive him mad. He was fairly certain of it as he sipped his scotch, stared out the window of the library into the darkness, and waited for her arrival.

After hauling up the tub and water, he'd been incredibly tempted to lounge against the wall and watch as she removed her clothes, as she stepped into the bath, as she dribbled water over her skin. But if he'd stayed, he doubted that she'd get so much as her tiniest toe wet before he had her on her back. He yearned for her with a fierceness he didn't want to acknowledge. Never before had any woman affected him as she did.

So he'd walked out simply to prove—more to himself than to her—that he could.

He never would have expected to find Portia on her hands and knees cleaning. Granted, Mrs. Barnaby was no spring chicken and her efforts yesterday with the parlor had been sadly lacking, but she'd made the room habitable. And she was the housekeeper. It was her job to keep house.

But Portia had begun seeing to things herself, had been uncomfortable with him preparing her bath. She didn't want to be pampered. He hadn't expected that, didn't know quite what to make of her. Every woman he'd ever been with had wanted to be spoiled, had insisted upon it. In fact, they'd wanted constant compliments, numerous baubles, and his undivided attention.

Based upon Portia's reasons for being here, what she hoped to gain, what she sought, she should seek to be spoiled more than any woman he'd ever known. But she'd been covered in dust and cobwebs, with grime on her face and hands. Something was wrong with him for finding that so incredibly sensual. Wives of lords did not crawl about in the muck. Yet she'd seemed comfortable with it.

Who *was* Portia Gadstone St. John?

A bit late to be wondering that, old chap.

He didn't want to be intrigued or fascinated by her. He didn't want to know her. He merely wanted to bed her, slake his lust, ensure she earned the title that marriage to him had gained her.

Hearing light footsteps, he glanced over his shoulder. Christ, she was gorgeous. If she entered a ballroom wearing that deep purple gown that revealed her shoulders so enticingly and suggestively, she would have had a hundred suitors. Why answer an old man's advert? What did it matter now? She was his wife.

"You did away with the Hessian, I see," he said as she approached, her satin slippers occasionally peering out from beneath the hem of her skirt.

"You're here now. I'm sure you'll save me from any hideous eight-legged creatures."

He had the passing thought that he would save her from anything.

"Based on the flow of your skirts, it appears you're not wearing petticoats." He hadn't truly expected her to honor her words about not wearing any undergarments. She'd merely been attempting to taunt him.

She angled her head, a wickedness in her smile. "No

petticoats. Only a corset, otherwise my bodice would droop unbecomingly."

His mouth went dry. "Only a corset?"

"Only a corset. Well, and stockings. They were needed for the shoes. But you don't have to remove the silk to have your way with me. Or the shoes for that matter."

He imagined her naked, except for the stockings and shoes, her legs in the air—

"Drawers?"

She shook her head, her teeth pressing into her lower lip.

"Chemise?"

Another teasing smile. "Corset only."

"Jesus." As he downed what remained of his scotch, he didn't miss her look of satisfaction. His father was correct. There were definite advantages to taking to wife a woman with experience. He was beginning to wonder why men so highly coveted virginity in their brides. "A drink before dinner?"

"No, thank you."

Well, he needed another. On his way to the sideboard, he passed the desk. It occurred to him that he could just take her there. Unencumbered by petticoats, ease those skirts up to her waist, unfasten his trousers, sink into her before they dined. But he had the impression that she would view it as a victory. He would resist for a while longer.

"Dinner is served, my lord," Gilbert announced.

A pity. The drink would wait.

Walking over to Portia, he extended his arm. She placed her hand on it, squeezed.

"I wouldn't have objected to the desk," she said sweetly, before releasing her hold and walking from the room, her hips swaying provocatively.

Through gritted teeth, he released a feral curse. He'd

been so focused on saving his father from Portia that he hadn't considered the need to save himself.

MONTIE had been attracted to her, had wanted her. He'd made that clear the evening he introduced himself. But he'd never looked at her with the smoldering intensity that Locksley did. While he sat across from her, several feet away, she was acutely aware of the desire thrumming off him as the wine was poured. Although *desire* seemed too tame a word.

He'd wanted to spread her out on the desk and have his way with her. She'd seen it in his eyes. She didn't know whether to be flattered or insulted that he managed to keep his urges under control.

She would be wise not to taunt him so brazenly, not to give the impression that she was somewhat of a wanton, but she needed the marriage consummated before the sun next rose. It was the only way to ensure this arrangement couldn't be easily undone, was the only way to guarantee a measure of protection should Montie discover where she was hiding.

She'd been careful, never using her name during her travels, never using a main system of transportation. Hence the journey on the mail coach where no questions had been asked, other than her destination. She felt relatively safe, and there was always a chance that Montie would welcome her absence when he discovered it.

Still, a consummated marriage was essential to her strategy. She refused to feel guilty because her plan had gone awry and she was now the wife of the viscount rather than the marquess. She wasn't going to reconsider her plan simply because Locksley had shown a momentary kindness and given her a set of keys. Or because he truly seemed to care for his father. Or because he seemed capable of destroying her with little more than a touch.

And while she might tell herself that she wanted this marriage consummated for her own personal gain, she couldn't deny that the glimpse he'd given her of the passion that awaited her in his bed now had her own body thrumming with needs that made her wish he had indeed taken her on the blasted desk. Be done with it. Stop torturing her by being so strong-willed.

Gilbert interrupted her thoughts as he set a bowl of turtle soup before her. Then he placed one before the viscount.

Locksley's brow furrowed. "You can bring out all the food, Gilbert. We've no guests tonight."

So he took his dinner the same way as he did his breakfast—with ease for the servants and no fanfare. She couldn't imagine Montie being so considerate, knew beyond a doubt he wouldn't be. Servants served and he lived to be served. He'd never been abusive but he was extremely skilled at ensuring those around him understood their place. Her heart had shattered when she'd finally come to understand hers.

"Mrs. Dorset says we can't be serving everything on one plate anymore, not now that there's a lady in the house," Gilbert explained, looking somewhat guilty.

"So you're going to traipse back and forth all during dinner?"

"Apparently so, m'lord."

Locksley sighed. "Then for God's sake, at least put the wine on the table so I can serve myself."

"Mrs. Dorset—"

"Will never know."

"Very good, sir." After seeing to the wine, he retreated to stand by the wall.

Her husband appeared disgruntled, a man who didn't relish being waited on. She refused to let that discovery make her like him. He'd ruined her carefully laid-out plans—even if his reasons were to be commended. She tasted the soup. Delicious. Little wonder no one argued with Mrs. Dorset regarding how the meal was to be served.

"You were going to tell me how you knew about the keys," she said quietly.

Amusement dancing in his eyes, he leaned back and lifted his wineglass. "So I was. My father's wards and I fancied ourselves intrepid adventurers. We'd nick the keys from Mrs. Barnaby after she fell asleep and explore the various rooms during the late hours of the night."

"With the size of this place, that could have taken years."

He nodded, sipped his wine. "Nearly three, as I recall. We were like archeologists sorting through the rubble of an archaic civilization, cataloguing our finds, but ensuring that nothing appeared disturbed."

While he said it with ease, she didn't miss the sadness—and guilt—that briefly touched the green of his eyes. The archaic civilization had been his parents' life. She wondered what it had been like to grow up with so little known of the past. "And when you grew up, you continued to explore, but moved on to the world."

"For a while."

"Do you miss it?"

Gilbert took their bowls, disappeared through a doorway. Locksley tapped his wineglass. "I do hope she didn't prepare an abundance of food. I don't like waste."

"I'll speak with her tomorrow, shall I? Approve the menu. Ensure it's not too much."

He nodded. "You'll no doubt find her easier to deal with than you did Mrs. Barnaby."

A woman who ruled a kitchen? She very much doubted it, but she'd been raised to manage a household. She could take on this task easily enough. "You didn't answer my question. Do you miss traveling?"

"Sometimes." He gave her a tantalizingly wicked grin. "But then exploring is going to be in my very near future, isn't it, Lady Locksley?"

Heat flushed her skin. "Must you always turn the discussion in that direction?"

"You're the one sitting there without your drawers."

"It's quite lovely actually. The silk of my gown against my nether regions."

He laughed darkly. "God, you are a tease. Most women are bashful about bedding."

"You like that I am not."

He lifted his glass in a salute. "Damned if I don't."

She didn't quite trust the smile he gave her. He let her win too easily. She had a feeling he was going to make her pay for it later—in screams of pleasure that might shatter the windows. She suspected what she knew of pleasure was going to pale beside whatever he delivered. She anticipated and dreaded it.

Gilbert strode in and set a plate of broiled lamb and potatoes before her. She lifted her gaze to find Locksley studying her. She was beginning to wish she'd at least put on her drawers. "How was everything at the mines?"

He narrowed his eyes, his face shifting into a cold resolve. "Don't worry, my little mercenary, your pin money is safe."

"I wasn't—" She stopped, unable to blame him for his low regard for her. She'd certainly given the impression that she was merely here for gain. His dislike and distrust of her provided her with a shield. But it was becoming quite heavy to keep in place. "I was merely asking after your day. If you found it satisfactory. That is what good wives do."

A corner of his mouth tilted up. "Are you planning to be a good wife?"

"Within reason."

He laughed deeply. "At least you're honest."

Only she wasn't. She wished she could be, but his opinion of her was low enough as it was. Instead of taking her to bed, he'd rid himself of her. With all due haste. "I want things to be pleasant between us."

"Once we're finished with dinner, they're going to be very pleasant between us."

She released a very unladylike snort. "Again, must your mind always go there?" She wanted a man to desire her for more than her body. Marsden would have wanted companionship. She should have insisted that she marry the marquess. Not that this stubborn, obstinate man would have allowed it, no matter what reasons she gave.

"I thought of you for a good part of the day," he said quietly.

She rolled her eyes. "Bedding me, I'm sure."

"Sometimes." He shifted his gaze to his wineglass, trailed his finger slowly up and down the stem just as he would no doubt be trailing it over her before long. Seemed he wasn't the only one whose mind continued to journey to bedchambers. "Sometimes I find myself wondering what truly brought you here."

His gaze, compelling and demanding, slammed into hers. If she thought for a moment that he truly cared, that he would be decent about it, she might confess all. "Your father's advert." She hated that the words came out on a croak.

"Did you know they call him the mad Marquess of Marsden?"

She gave a slight nod. "Is that the reason you spend so little time in London?"

"How do you know how much time I spend in London?"

"I believe I mentioned the gossip sheets. Truth be told, I'm rather addicted to reading them. You and the other Hellions are frequently reported on." She creased her brow. "How did the moniker come about, by the way?"

"We tended to break the rules in our youth. But we're always forgiven. Our pasts made us such tragic figures we could get away with a good deal of bad behavior."

"You were also known for being reckless."

"We were indeed. Ashe almost became a lion's dinner once. And of course Albert died on safari, leaving Edward to inherit the title, after pretending for months to be Albert. It was madness."

"I remember it in the papers. It created quite the scandal when his duplicity was discovered."

"It did. Then he did something even more audacious by taking his brother's widow to Switzerland and marrying her. They're not quite accepted yet, but people are beginning to come around. When they visit here, I shall expect you to welcome them."

"Of course. I am not one to cast stones."

He held her gaze. "And why is that, Lady Locksley?"

She stilled, her breath timid about leaving her lungs. *I know what it is to be disgraced, ostracized, cast out.*

"Had a few stones cast your way?" he asked.

More than a few. "As I mentioned, my family did not approve of Montie. His did not approve of me. But our love was grand enough that it didn't matter." The last had turned out to be a lie, but her younger self had believed it with all her heart.

"But you're not seeking love now."

"No, my lord. I've closed my heart to it. It's easier that

way." Another lie, this one perpetuated by her cynical self because she knew he would never love her and it was pointless to wish otherwise. On the other hand, neither would she ever love him.

But life with Montie had taught her to hide her feelings, and she'd become very good at it. She hoped only that she hadn't learned to hide them from herself.

SHE licked the pudding from her spoon, slowly, provocatively, all the while making little moaning sounds that caused him to harden, his skin to tighten, his breath to hitch. He had no doubt that she knew precisely how much she was tormenting him and was taking delight in doing so.

He wanted to throttle her. He wanted to kiss every inch of her. He wanted to laugh, a large boisterous guffaw that would echo through every corner of the manor. He couldn't remember a time when he'd enjoyed a woman so much—and he had yet to enjoy her fully.

His own pudding remained untouched. "Perhaps you'd care to partake of my dessert," he offered when she finally set her spoon aside.

"Don't you like pudding?" she asked.

"I haven't much fondness for sweets, which must be why I like you. You're so tart."

Surprise washed over her features. "You like me?"

Had he said that? Damn it all to hell, he had. Without thinking of the repercussions or how she might interpret the words. That she might find hope in them for something more between them. "You challenge me, Portia. I can't deny that I enjoy that aspect of our relationship. I've never much cared for mewling misses."

She gave him a lascivious look. "How about purring ones?"

Oh, yes, he definitely wanted her purring. "Is there anything else to be brought out, Gilbert?"

"No, my lord. The pudding was the last bit."

Thank God. He shoved back his chair, stood. He considered for half a heartbeat inviting her to the library for an after-dinner cognac. But he was weary of delaying the inevitable, of pretending to be a gentleman when she managed so easily to turn him into a barbarian who wanted only to ravish her from head to toe.

He felt rather predatory walking to her end of the table, and some of his thoughts must have shown because quite suddenly she appeared a trifle wary of him. Good. She might have the upper hand out of the bed, keeping him hard and ready for her, but by God, he would have the advantage once they landed on the mattress. He pulled out her chair, waited as she rose with such elegance, stepped away from the table—

He swept her up into his arms, taking satisfaction in her small squeak.

Her face level with his, she stared at him. "Surely you plan to enjoy a drink after dinner."

All he wanted was to drink in the whiskey of her eyes. Not that he was fool enough to state such drivel. "I think we've delayed matters long enough."

He watched the delicate movements of her throat as she swallowed. He was going to nibble on those fragile tendons quite soon. Then he became incredibly aware of the outline of her legs, their warmth seeping into his arms. No damn petticoats. He rather liked it.

He thought he detected a tremor traveling through her before that rounded little chin of hers jutted out a fraction and she gave a barely imperceptible nod. As she licked her lips, she placed her hand just below his jaw, her fingers coming to rest against his neck where his pulse was pounding in an erratic rhythm. She lowered her eyelashes slightly, invitingly. "I'm anxious to discover if you're as good as you claim."

If he'd known wives taunted and teased more provocatively than the highest-paid light skirt he'd ever experienced, he might have taken one sooner. He may have growled or perhaps he sounded as though he was strangling, because as he began striding from the room with urgency, she laughed lightly, running a hand over a portion of his chest and shoulder, whatever she could reach. Leaning in, she nipped at his ear.

"Keep that up, you little minx, and I won't be able to walk up the stairs."

"I like that you want me."

Want was too tame a word, but he had no wish to frighten her by revealing the full extent of how desperately he desired her. Nor did he wish to give her quite that much power over him. She was going to be the one unable to walk before the night was done. He already knew once wouldn't be enough for him. Hell, a dozen times might not be enough.

As he reached the stairs, she settled her head on his shoulder, and a fierce protectiveness swept through him that nearly caused him to stumble back. Something about the trusting gesture made him regret that he wanted her for only one purpose: to warm his bed. From the moment he'd opened the door to her, he'd had an insane desire to possess her, to claim her . . . to win.

He didn't trust her or her motives for agreeing to marry his father. That hadn't changed. He'd been determined to best her at her own game—in hindsight, it occurred to him that he might have walked right into her trap, yet he couldn't seem to regret it. Not when it guaranteed she would be writhing beneath him. And writhe she would.

She might tempt him and play the naughty flirt, but he was the master of the night.

At the top of the stairs, he turned down the hallway toward his bedchamber, was acutely aware of her breaths shortening, of the anticipation thrumming through her. She incited his own desires with so little effort. He was mad to want her this desperately.

He strode past his father's room, stopped, cursed. He wanted no disturbances this night, no interruptions. Once he had her in his bedchamber with the door closed, he didn't want it opened until dawn.

"We should check in on your father," she said softly.

He didn't like the tightness in his chest because she sounded as though she truly cared about his sire. It didn't matter how she felt about the marquess. Locke wasn't going to care about her, refused to allow himself to soften toward her, to be wrapped around her finger. Theirs was a relationship defined by emotional distance. It suited them both. Still, he lowered her feet to the floor. "I won't be but a moment. Wait here."

He was leaning in to give her a quick peck on the lips when the anger rushed over her features and stilled him.

"I'm not a dog to be commanded about," she said. "I wish to say good night to the marquess, and so I shall, with or without your approval."

He considered reminding her of a woman's place—to obey her husband in all matters—but that would no doubt result in a quarrel, as she wasn't the sort to obey anyone. It was one of the aspects to her that drew him in. Besides, he liked that she wasn't a withering violet, that she stood toe to toe against him, would even stomp on his toe if need be. But he required some sort of victory, so he darted in for a quick kiss before turning to the door and giving it a sharp rap.

"Come in," his father announced.

Opening the door, he indicated for her to precede him. She waltzed in with a victorious flourish. She was in need of taming, but he didn't have it within him to kill her spirit. Standing behind her, he fought not to estimate how many seconds it would take him to undo the lacings of her gown.

"Twelve," his father announced.

Locke looked over her shoulder to where his father sat by the window. "Pardon?"

"It'll take you twelve seconds to get those lacings undone."

His jaw tautened. He didn't like being so easy to read. "Eight."

"We're not here to discuss my lacings," she chastised, and he liked that she didn't wither or stammer with the knowledge that they were discussing what was to come. "We're here to see if you require anything before we retire."

"An heir. But I'll get that after you retire."

"Honestly, my lord, you need to expand your interests. Perhaps you'd like for me to read to you for a bit."

"No," Locke growled.

She glanced back innocently, and he knew there was no innocence in her. Wicked woman was only seeking to torment him further. "We are not reading to him tonight," he ground out.

"As you wish." She turned back to his father. "We missed you during dinner."

"I prefer to dine here."

"Solitude does not become you, my lord."

"I'm never alone, my dear, and you must call me Father."

She did blush then. She really wasn't comfortable with

it, and he briefly wondered why. "Well, if there's nothing you need, we'll be off to bed," he said.

"Bit early for bed."

Locke fought not to stare. Had they not just been discussing her lacings and an heir? "I've had a long day."

The wrinkles on his father's face shifted downward. "I saw you riding out, to the mines I assume. You've been going there a lot lately. Is something amiss?"

He didn't plan to discuss the troubles with him ever, but especially not tonight. "Everything is fine."

Portia gave him a speculative look that he didn't want to interpret.

"I'll be locking the door now," he told the marquess gently. "I just wanted you to know."

His father waved a hand as though bothered by a fly. "Go ahead. Your mother will be here soon."

Locke didn't want to feel guilty about this. It was for his father's protection as much as anything. "Are you certain you have everything you need?"

"I haven't had everything I need since your mother died. But no matter. You don't need to listen to an old man's grumblings. Go bed your wife. Give me my heir."

With those words, his guilt eased, and he noticed that the top of Portia's ears turned red. Maybe she blushed more than he thought. Just not always on her face. Interesting. He'd have to explore the possibility further. He liked the idea of her blushing in other areas.

Walking forward, she kissed his father on the cheek. "Sweet dreams, my lord."

"Father," the marquess insisted.

She smiled, nodded, tried to look contrite, but she didn't repeat the word. Locke had a feeling she never would. She walked past him, out the door.

"She's a beauty, isn't she?" his father asked, regaining

Locke's attention. "Prettier than your mother, but don't tell your mother that." He patted his chest. "Your mother's beauty was all inside. Portia has a good bit in there as well. Don't forget to look there."

The woman was a conniving vixen. That his father failed to see it only reaffirmed that Locke had made the correct decision in marrying her. She would have had his father wrapped around her finger five seconds after the marriage papers were signed.

"I require only that she warms my bed. I don't have to like her for that."

"Don't be a fool, Locke. Open that damned heart of yours."

So I can live my life in misery should she die? Not likely. "Sleep well, Father."

As for himself, he didn't plan to sleep a single wink.

Chapter 10

STANDING in the hallway, she fought to ignore his telling his father that he didn't like her. She took some consolation in the fact that he didn't seem to despise her. And he'd given her the keys. There might be no affection lost between them, but theirs would be a civil relationship. At least outside the bed. She suspected it was going to be quite untamed within it.

Stepping out, he closed the door, turned the key, waited a heartbeat as though needing a moment to shirk off the pall that came over him after spending time with his father. Then he faced her, giving away nothing, none of his doubts, his concerns, his troubles.

"What's wrong at the mines?" she asked.

His jaw tautened, his eyes narrowed. "Nothing is wrong at the mines."

"You answered so quickly"—so tersely—"that I was rather sure you didn't want to discuss the matter with him."

"I didn't." He took a step nearer to her. "My father loves his mines. Get him started on them, and he can go on for hours. I have little patience for it tonight."

He lifted her up into his arms and began striding toward his bedchamber.

"Seems you haven't any patience at all," she said.

"Be grateful for it."

So brusque, and yet he wasn't a hard man, a man she should fear. A hard man would have seen his father placed in a mental asylum. A hard man wouldn't make allowances for idiosyncratic servants. A hard man would have taken her already.

He crossed the threshold, kicking the door closed in his wake. This time he set her down nearer to the bed, within tossing distance of the mattress. "Turn around," he ordered.

Shoving back any trepidation, any desire to know him better before he had his way with her, she spun around, her gaze falling on the thick comforter, wondering if she should move it aside, but she suspected nothing about what was to follow would be very tidy.

Seven seconds was all it took for him to have the lacings of her gown undone. His callused finger skimmed the lower edge of her corset, just below the small of her back, over the curve of her buttocks. Then his mouth, hot and damp, was following the same path, causing heated dew to gather between her legs. The sweet torture was almost more than she could stand. Finally, he straightened and began working on the laces of her corset. Thank God, because she could barely breathe as anticipation coursed through her.

She'd wanted to tease him with what she wasn't wearing, but the thought had flittered at the edge of her mind that he would be able to claim her so easily. So little separated her skin, her womanhood from him.

Six seconds on the corset. She pressed her hand against her stomach to keep her clothes from falling. He was definitely moving faster tonight. In less than a minute she was going to be on her back. He trailed his finger along her spine, down, up. He flattened his palms against her shoulder blades and slowly moved his hands around her shoulders, easing her gown aside until it fell to the floor. The corset followed it down.

"Who would have thought that someone with such a delicate back would have such backbone?" he asked, and she could have sworn she heard admiration in his voice. "Step out of the clothes."

She did as he bade, then swung around. "Are you just—" *Going to command me all night?* died on her lips. She didn't know if anyone had ever looked at her with such hunger, a starving beast willing to do anything to satiate his desires.

"Christ, you're beautiful." He cupped his hands beneath her breasts, his thumb and forefinger pinching her nipples, not too hard, not too softly, as though he knew exactly what she required.

Swallowing hard, she resisted the urge to snatch up her gown and cover herself. His perusal, so heated, so intense, made her feel exposed. Hell, she was exposed, at a disadvantage. "Remove your jacket."

He grinned darkly. "Only my jacket?"

She angled her chin, striving to appear bolder than she felt. "Everything."

That smile grew, so wicked, so taunting, so full of promise. "As my lady commands."

She hadn't really expected him to obey, had never truly felt an equal in her relationship with Montie, but Locksley didn't lord himself over her. He tossed his jacket to the floor. His fingers went to the buttons of his waistcoat. Without thinking, she stepped forward and covered his hands with hers. She could feel the tension radiating through him. What was he trying to prove by not yet taking her? That he could resist her charms? She could sense how difficult the battle was. She should take pity on him. Too bad that she wanted his surrender. "I'll do it."

Never taking his eyes from hers, he lowered his head in acquiescence, spread his arms wide. She didn't mistake the gesture for submission, knew it was merely a pause in the war. "We don't have to be at odds," she said quietly as she worked on the buttons.

"We're not. I daresay, we have the same goal: getting you bedded." He shirked out of his waistcoat, sent it flying to where the jacket had landed.

She unknotted his neck cloth. "Yet I feel we're going about it as though it were a competition."

His hand came to rest just beneath her jaw and—with the slightest of prompting—he tilted back her head. "You want to best me."

She did, damn it. She wanted him to yearn for her, to beg, to be at her mercy. She wanted to be in control because she hadn't been before. After pulling his neck cloth free, she tossed it aside. "You don't love me." She unbuttoned his shirt. "You will never love me." She removed the black-onyx-studded cufflinks, cradling them in her palm, not certain what to do with something so obviously expensive and well crafted.

He scooped them up, carried them to the bedside table, set them down. He dragged his shirt over his head, tossed it to the floor before facing her. She'd seen his magnificent form when she'd awoken that morning, and yet still it took her breath. The sinew and muscle, the way his skin was stretched taut over a form molded to perfection.

His eyes never leaving her, he dropped into a nearby chair and began removing his boots.

"You don't like me," she continued, hating that she sounded so breathless, that her voice had gone so raspy and deep at the mere thought of flicking her tongue over his nipple, along his ribs, going lower until she tasted his very essence.

"I mentioned liking you earlier."

"Comparing me to pudding, which is so very flattering. Then you told your father that you don't have to like me to bed me."

He narrowed his eyes. "You weren't supposed to hear that."

"Yet I did. But I'm not bothered by it." Much. "I don't fancy you either." A small lie. It was difficult not to fancy a man who exuded such sensual awareness, who moved about like some predatory animal. "However, I at least want to ensure you desire me."

His task completed, he stood and ambled over to her, his gaze roaming over every inch visible to him, and she wished she'd thought to take off her stockings and slippers while he removed his boots. She felt rather silly with them still in place.

Stopping, he cradled one of her breasts, flicked his thumb over her pearled nipple. "I've never desired anyone more."

His mouth came down on hers, hard, demanding. His arms closed around her, flattening her breasts to his chest, as his hands bracketed either side of her spine and journeyed up. Torrid heat swamped her, her legs went weak, and she scraped her fingers over his broad back so she had something solid to hold on to.

He dragged his lips down her throat, along her collarbone, nipping and licking as he went, leaving behind the promise of devouring her when all was said and done. She had little doubt that she would awaken in the morning to discover herself covered in tiny love bruises. Love. She very nearly scoffed. There would never be any love between them. Even what was passing between them now resembled love not in the least. It was all about possession, claiming what he had gained through marriage, taking ownership of what was now rightfully his.

She should have resented it, how easily he made her want to surrender, how simply he flamed the fires of her own desires. She'd never clamored for a man to take full possession of her the way she did for him to join his body with hers. Not even Montie. Regardless of her love for him, she'd never felt this intense need, this fear that if he suddenly released her and walked away, she might very well die.

He moved his mouth lower, and she arched back, her breasts an offering as though to a god. His mouth latched onto her nipple, and he suckled with purpose. Crying out with unguarded pleasure ripping through her, she lifted her leg to his hip, pressing her feminine core against the firm rigid length of him. Even through the cloth she could feel the scalding heat.

Groaning low, one hand—fingers splayed—supporting her back, he moved to her other breast and took while his free hand cupped the round backside of her raised leg and journeyed along it to her knee, back down, back up, as he undulated against her, causing her to grow wet, to crave a deeper intimacy. Where had her breath gone? Why could her heart not slow?

Quite suddenly, she found herself in his arms once again and before she could fully appreciate her position, he tossed her onto the bed, followed her down with a feral growl, once more taking her mouth, his tongue delving deeply as though he feared leaving bits of it unexplored, and yet how could he when he gave it such a thorough mapping? She'd never been so affected by a kiss, but then he'd stirred sparks within her to life the first time that he'd plastered his mouth to hers. She hated admitting that she could spend a lifetime kissing him and never have enough.

*H*E was reluctant to admit that he might never have enough of simply kissing her. The way her luscious mouth moved beneath his, welcomed him, had him anticipating her notch welcoming and closing around his cock. Because he wanted her so desperately, he fought to curb his body's aching needs, refusing to give in too quickly to the temptation of her. But before the night was done, he planned to know her in every way possible.

She was remarkably beautiful, every inch of her flawless. She could bring any man she wanted to his knees. He vowed then and there to never go to his knees for her.

Breathing harshly, he tore his mouth from hers, plowed his fingers into the thick silken strands of her hair, and began removing pins.

Gasping for breath, she said, "It would have been easier if you'd done that whilst standing."

"I didn't want anything to obstruct my view." He combed her hair out over the pillows, the glorious red in stark contrast to the pristine white. All the while her hands glided over his chest, his shoulders, his back as though she couldn't get enough of touching him. The satisfaction in knowing that she wanted him as much as he did her was unlike anything he'd ever known.

Leaning up, she stroked her tongue around his nipple. Placing his hand beneath the back of her head, he braced her and relished the torment of her scraping her teeth over the sensitive skin before taking a quick bite that caused his bollocks to tighten. He'd never been with a woman he considered his equal when it came to pleasuring. Her boldness inflamed him. If he hadn't kept his trousers on, he'd already be buried deeply inside her—which was the very reason he had yet to remove them. He didn't know why but when it came to her he wanted more than slaking his lust. If this was all they'd ever have, he wanted it worth the price of his freedom that he'd paid for it.

He might not love her, might not be particularly fond of her, might not trust her completely, but he would honor the vows he'd given her. He would remain faithful, he would respect her, he would honor her as a wife was to be honored. But behind a closed door, he wanted her untamed and wild, brazen and bold, a vixen of the first order.

She nipped at him, dug her fingernails into his buttocks. Pulling back on her hair—gentle but forceful—he scraped his teeth along the lengthy column of her throat. Her eyes shuttered closed, her lips parted slightly. At least she didn't try to feign an immunity to his charms. He'd worried that she'd take the tack of being cold and brittle, of striving to hold back what he wanted most from her.

But here at least there were no games between them. There was only raw need that threatened to destroy his sanity.

ABRUPTLY he released her, his mouth left her, and Portia flopped back on the mound of soft pillows. She was accustomed to being taken swiftly, to having very little play beforehand. She thought she might die if he didn't unfasten his trousers and get down to business. He was between her thighs, sitting back on his heels. It would be easy enough for him to loosen the buttons and set himself free to plunder. She was wet enough. He'd slide right in.

His gaze grazed over her and she felt it almost as clearly as she'd felt his teeth a moment earlier. He began slowly trailing his fingers along the inside of her thighs, from the top of her stockings to her auburn curls. Up. Down. Up.

She grabbed his wrists. "Stop torturing me."

His eyes darkened, his grin was sensual. "I've only just begun."

He moved nearer to her feet.

"I thought you wanted me." She hated the petulant tone, and yet she seemed unable to keep herself from revealing her disappointment that he wasn't already going at her like a man possessed.

"Oh, I do. I'm just not convinced you want me."

How could she not want him? He was all firm muscle and corded sinew. Broad chest and flat stomach. She watched those muscles bunch and stretch as he peeled off her slipper, tossed it aside, then did the same with the other. He folded his large, powerful hands around her left foot. He began kneading the ball of her foot, her arch, her heel, all the while studying her foot as though it were the most interesting aspect to her.

She'd never had her feet treated to such wondrous care. It felt so lovely that she wanted to close her eyes and sink into the sensations, but she couldn't seem to take her gaze off him, didn't want to miss out on seeing his movements, of the way his lips parted as he lifted her foot to his mouth and pressed a kiss to her toes, her instep, her ankle, before shifting his gaze to her, a dare in the green depths as he placed her stocking-covered foot against the fall of his trousers, against the hard ridge.

Accepting the challenge, she began rubbing her foot along the marvelous, somewhat startling, length of him. She wanted to see him, all of him, as bared as she was.

Leaning forward slightly, he began untying the ribbon that held her stocking in place above her knee. When it was loose, he gathered the stocking up, revealing an inch of skin, before rolling it back up to cover half an inch. Down an inch, up a half, the tips of his fingers playing along her skin, creating delicious little tremors that bubbled through her. She very nearly went insane before the stocking was completely removed, leaving her bare foot against his trousers. She pressed harder, taking great satisfaction in the tautening of his jaw.

Without waiting for him to give attention to her other foot, she placed it on his chest, gave her toes freedom to circle his nipple. This stocking came off with such speed that she wouldn't be surprised to discover it torn when she gathered it from the floor later.

With a feral growl, he spread her legs wide, settled onto his stomach, and blew a cool breath, stirring the curls between her thighs. Then his mouth was on her, his fingers parting the folds, his tongue slowly stroking. She cried out at the unexpectedness of the pleasure that rippled through her.

She squeezed her eyes shut, not wanting to see him gloating at her reaction, but how could he gloat when his mouth continued to work its magic, suckling and nipping, stroking and flicking the swollen bud? When she finally opened her eyes, she saw no reveling, simply a man intent on creating wave upon wave of sensation.

Sliding his arms beneath her thighs, lifting them slightly, he cupped her breasts, his fingers toying with her nipples. Her hips rocked up, giving him easier access and he took. The build was slow, yet intense. She plowed her fingers through his hair, scraped her fingers over his sturdy shoulders. He'd promised her pleasure. She'd certainly not expected him to deliver it like this. She hadn't even known this was possible.

She felt more treasured at that moment than she'd ever felt with a man she loved. Tears pricked her eyes. Tears because she'd been a fool. Tears because she was probably a fool now to give her body free rein to experience all the sensations that Locksley was bringing to life within her.

With his tongue, his lips, his fingers, his murmurs he urged her to let go, to fly. Long, slow strokes of his tongue, rough velvet to silk, two of his fingers slipping inside of her, spreading her before his tongue licked at her quim. He explored so thoroughly, so intensely. She wanted to resist the lure of complete and total release—and at the same time she wanted to accept this absolute, unselfish gift.

Her body stretched, reached . . . surrendered.

Pleasure ripped through her, through every nerve ending, every muscle, every inch of skin, from the tips of her toes through her scalp, tingling, expanding, contracting.

Squeezing her eyes shut tightly, she cried out—a benediction, a curse—as her body convulsed and her limbs thrashed about. His hands cradling her ribs were the only things keeping her anchored to the bed. She fought for breath, for equilibrium, even as her lips spread into a smile of satisfaction. He released his hold on her, moved away.

The bed shifted with his movements, but she was too lethargic to care. When she could finally gather up the strength to open her eyes, he was raised above her, his trousers gone, his thick cock jutting out proudly, the sight of it taking what little breath remained to her. He was magnificent, powerful.

"You seemed to enjoy that," he said.

"Don't be so smug," she ordered.

He laughed darkly as he bent his elbows, leaned down, and nibbled on her lips. "I knew things between us would be good in bed."

Only they hadn't been good for him, not yet. And she

needed that, needed him to spill his seed inside her. Pushing herself up, she pressed her mouth to his throat, lifting
her hips, aware of him hovering so near. "Take me. Make
me yours."

With a growl, he thrust his hips forward, his shaft sliding sure and deep, stretching her, filling the valley between her thighs.

"Oh, Christ," she murmured. She thought it should
have hurt, because he was much larger than what she was
accustomed to, and yet he'd ensured that she was glistening with dew, more than ready to receive him. She didn't
want him being that considerate. Didn't want to like him.
It would all be so much easier if she felt nothing at all
for him.

But as he rocked against her, she feared she might
have misjudged the power of the intimacy they would
share. Even now he wasn't mindlessly rutting, striving
to acquire his own release. He fondled her breast, closed
his mouth around the tip, suckled. He skimmed his hand
along her back, over her hip, adjusted the position so he
could delve more deeply. It was marvelous, each thrust
delivered with purpose, with a goal. She could feel him
tensing beneath her fingertips, knew he was hovering
at the cusp, that the next thrust might be his last, might
fill her with his seed. The thought of him climaxing inflamed her. She couldn't take her eyes off him. Even his
black hair was involved, flapping against his brow with
his efforts. Her own pleasure began mounting again, the
pressure building.

She didn't want these sensations, didn't want the way
they made her body curl around him, cling to him as
though he were her only hope for salvation. Yet he refused
to be denied. He continued to torment her with his mouth,

hands, and cock—all working in tandem to ensure she became lost in the whirlwind of pleasure.

Bucking beneath him, she was once again crying out as an orgasm tore through her and stars exploded within her. He gave one last mighty thrust that nearly lifted her off the bed, his own throaty groan echoing around her as his muscles spasmed beneath her fingers. He buried his face in the curve of her shoulder, his mouth coating her neck in dew as he fought to regain his breath. He kept his weight off her, but as reason began to return to her, she realized his arms were trembling with the strain. She folded her hands around them.

"Relax," she urged.

"I'll crush you."

"I'm stronger than I look."

He laughed, and for the first time, she thought the sound might have been laced with a bit of joy. He rose up on his elbows, placed his hands on either side of her face, and skimmed his knuckles along her cheeks. "I'm thinking now that perhaps you could move that chair across the parlor."

"Not now; I can barely lift a finger at the moment. In the morning perhaps."

He grinned as though they were sharing a private joke, and she realized that grin could be devastating to her heart. She liked it far too much, liked how approachable it made him.

He rolled off her, rolled off the bed, and began striding away from her.

Sitting up, she swung her legs over the side.

"Wait there," he said as he reached the washstand and dipped a cloth into the water. "I'll clean you."

She stilled, not because of his words, but because

Montie had never extended such a courtesy to her. She was the one who saw to matters when they were finished. "You don't have to."

He glanced over his shoulder. "I want to." With a wicked gleam in his eye, he started back. "If I'm lucky and do it properly, it'll lead to another round."

Chapter 11

$\mathcal{H}$E did it properly. It led to another round. One that went a little quicker than the first, but was no less intense. She was so blasted tight that at first he'd thought she was a virgin. But there had been no blood to clean up. And she was far too comfortable with a man's body not to have been around one before. Still if he didn't know better, he'd think the pleasure she'd experienced had taken her by surprise.

They'd finally gotten around to moving the bedding aside. She was lying on her back, one arm raised, her hand toying with strands of his hair, while he rested up on an elbow and trailed his fingers over her sternum, along her ribs. He'd tried going down her side to her hips only to discover she was a bit ticklish. Who'd have thought?

"I've never done this," she said quietly.

He stilled, his hand a quarter of an inch away from cupping her breast. "You were a virgin? But you were married. There was no blood."

She laughed lightly, running her fingers up over his scalp. "No, just lay here afterward, just . . . I don't know. It's as though the pleasure hasn't quite dissipated completely, and we're keeping it alive by still touching."

"Your husband didn't touch you afterward?" He

wanted to bite his tongue for asking the question, hated even more the spark of jealousy that ignited within him because another man had known her as he had.

She shook her head. "He always fell asleep right after."

He cupped her breast. "And you?"

She lifted a shoulder. "Would watch him. Feel lonely." She emitted a sound that was part scoff, part laugh. "I'm being silly. I don't want to talk about before."

He didn't want to know that she'd found her love less than satisfactory, that she might have learned it wasn't worth the pain it could bring. He bracketed her ribs, felt her stiffen—no doubt in anticipation of his going along her side to torment her with tickles. Another night he might. Not tonight. Tonight was about building trust so every night would be as good as or better than this one.

"Afterglow," he said.

"Pardon?"

"A woman I once . . . spent time with described the way she felt after sex as a glowing, told me I couldn't leave her or fall asleep until the glow went away. She would refer to it as the afterglow."

"It does rather feel that way. Was she pretty?" She shook her head. "I'm sorry. You don't have to answer that."

He liked that she sounded almost jealous. "Can you imagine me with an ugly woman?"

She studied him until he became uncomfortable with her perusal and was considering that it was time to plow into her again, before this conversation went someplace he didn't want it to go.

"Yes," she finally said. "But you would be with her out of kindness."

"I'm not a saint. I like beauty in my women." Leaning down, he laved his tongue over her nipple, took satisfaction in her soft sigh, before lifting his head to look at her again. "But there is all kinds of beauty in the world, some of it not always clearly visible. Even those spiders you hate have it within them to create the most intricate and beautiful webs."

"You look below the surface of things."

"I recognize that not all things should be judged by their appearance."

"Would you have married me if I were a toad?"

If those whiskey eyes of hers had still held the challenge that they did— "Probably. Although I am quite grateful that you're not a toad."

Her lips quirked up slightly as she moved her hand around to the nape of his neck and began kneading. "Well, you have the toad's voice anyway."

"Pardon?"

Her cheeks flushed a pale pink. "My voice. It's deep. Like a toad's."

"It's one of the most sensual things about you."

She seemed genuinely surprised.

"Did you not know that?" he asked.

Slowly, she shook her head. "I've been told it's rather unbecoming."

"By your husband?"

Her response was nothing more than her blush deepening. He couldn't help himself. "Forgive me for asking, but why the devil did you marry him? He sounds like a complete ass."

Laughing, she rolled onto her side and buried her face against his chest. He didn't want to admit how much he enjoyed having her there, her breaths skimming along his skin, the feel of her smile broadening. "He was. I simply didn't realize it until it was too late."

Her slender, delicate shoulders were shaking with her

laughter as he closed his arms around her and held her close. Dear God, but love never did anyone any favors. It had caused his father to go mad, had caused Portia to marry a man undeserving of her. He should leave it there. He knew all he needed to know, and yet his competitive nature refused to remain silent. "Did you find satisfaction in his bed?"

Her laughter abruptly stopped. She tilted her head back, while he tipped his down. He didn't know why it was imperative that he look into her eyes when she answered. Even if her answer was *none of your business; go to the devil*.

"Sometimes," she whispered. "But not like I did in yours tonight."

His mouth came down on hers, hard and demanding. She was going to find satisfaction in his bed at least once more before she went to sleep.

LOCKE woke her up before dawn so he could have her before sunlight stole into the room. Then—even though she invited him to stay—to prove to himself he still possessed enough willpower to resist her charms, he dressed and went to the library to study his ledgers. Instead, he kept seeing her sitting in the chair before the fireplace that first night. They would probably spend many a night there. Either there or in his bedchamber or wandering the hallways. It wasn't as though he was providing her with an abundance of options.

Not that she needed any options. She was there to warm his bed, provide him with an heir. She wasn't supposed to make him want to laugh. She wasn't supposed to make him want to give her more.

Nor was she supposed to make him glad for her presence when he walked into the breakfast dining room after growing tired of staring at her empty chair in the library. She was dressed in the dark blue she'd worn the day before, which he supposed signaled that she was going to tidy up the music room a bit more. He refrained from lifting her skirts to see if she was again sporting one of his Hessians.

"Good morning," he said as he took his seat. "Again."

She blushed. "Good morning, my lord. I didn't have the opportunity to voice the words earlier."

"You communicated quite well without them and provided me with a good morning indeed." He nearly laughed watching Gilbert turn red as a beet while he poured Locke's coffee.

"I'll get your plate, m'lord," he said gruffly before quickly vacating the room.

"I think you embarrassed him," Portia said, lifting her teacup.

"I'm not certain he's ever had a woman."

Her eyes widened. "Truly?"

"It's not as though Havisham is teeming with opportunities for dalliances. Why do you think I traveled the world?"

"For the adventures."

"Most women are an adventure."

She began slicing her bacon. "In comparison, I'm certain I pale."

"Looking for a compliment?"

Lifting her head, she held his gaze, shook her head. "No."

He might have let it go if he hadn't known about the ass she'd married. "I've never been more intrigued by a woman."

"But you must have known some exotic women."

"A few, and if we keep talking about them, perhaps I'll remember them well enough to change my answer."

"None were memorable?"

Not since she walked through the door.

Gilbert reentered and set the plate before Locke, then took up his position by the wall. Locke had no desire to discuss his conquests in front of the butler or to give the impression there was a need to reassure his wife. Servants weren't supposed to have opinions but still he didn't want the old gent's censure. He scooped up some egg. "I've a need to go to the village. I realize the day is yours and I don't mean to interfere with that, but I thought you might want to come with."

He tried to sneak a glance at her face, to judge her reaction, then gave up the pretense of caring about the food on his plate and looked at her directly. He didn't care for finding her surprise so rewarding.

"I'd like that very much," she said.

He cared even less for the relief that went through him with her answer. "Good. I thought to place an advert in the *Village Cryer*, the local newspaper, letting it be known that we're seeking a couple of maids of all work and some lads to haul things around until you can get in touch with the servant registry office in London in order to hire some proper footmen."

"You're hiring servants?"

"I can't have my wife messing around in the muck. If you're intent on cleaning the music room, you need someone on hand to do it. And you'll want to hire a lady's maid. Mrs. Barnaby shouldn't be traipsing up and down the stairs with her creaking knees."

The smile she bestowed upon him made his chest tighten uncomfortably. It was as though she thought he'd bestowed upon her the grandest gift in the world.

"I don't need to send to London for proper footmen or any servants. I like the notion of hiring locally. I can teach the girls what they need to know—with Mrs. Barn-aby's help, of course."

Smart girl, to make certain the housekeeper felt useful.

"And Gilbert could teach the lads how a footman be-haves. Couldn't you, Gilbert?" she asked.

In his entire life, Locke had never seen the butler stand so straight. He nodded. "Starting out as a footman here, myself, I welcome the opportunity to keep a couple of lads out of the mines. Lost two brothers to them. They were just boys at the time."

Sadness touched her eyes. "I'm so sorry for your loss."

"I appreciate it, m'lady, but it was nearly forty years ago now."

"Mining is safer these days," Locke said.

"It's never safe when you're going beneath the ground," Gilbert grumbled.

"Not contradicting the man who pays your salary, are you, Gilbert?" Locke asked.

"No, m'lord." He stared straight ahead.

"Are the mines safer?" Portia asked Locke.

"They are, and I don't allow children to work in them."

She leaned back as though she'd discovered something important about him. "You care for children."

"I care that work is done properly, and children are sometimes careless." He didn't know why he didn't tell her that he'd once seen a lifeless child carried from the mines, and didn't want to be responsible for the death of another body that small. "They are better suited to play than work."

"You can sound as gruff as you like. I think you care about them."

"Think what you want. It was a business decision."

"I always think what I want. Therefore, I am more convinced than ever that sending to London for servants is not the way to go. We can educate staff here, provide other opportunities for employment."

"We're not opening a school for servants. Two maids-of-all-work and two footmen."

"And a lady's maid," she reminded him.

He nodded.

"And a valet," she said.

"I don't need a valet."

"You're a lord."

"I don't need a valet."

She twisted her lips into a show of disapproval—no doubt at his stubbornness rather than his lack of a man to dress him. "Perhaps your father should have one."

"He seldom leaves his room. What would the chap do?"

"I suppose you have a point."

Of course he did. He wasn't one to argue simply for the sake of arguing, although he had to admit that he'd never enjoyed pitting himself against anyone as much as he did against her. He liked that she challenged him, wasn't afraid to let her position be known. He returned his attention to his eggs. "Do you have a riding habit?"

"I don't like horses. They're so large with such enormous teeth. I'd rather go in a carriage."

Her words surprised him as he'd pictured her as someone who would relish galloping over the moors, with her hair coming loose and blowing wildly behind her. "I thought you fearless."

"Not when it comes to horses. An incident as a child forever scarred me."

"I didn't notice any scars on you, and I gave you quite a thorough examination."

She gave him a pointed glare and patted her chest. "In here."

It had to have been quite horrific to leave her with a

fear of riding. He almost asked her for the details, but he didn't want to know of anything unhappy that might have happened during her childhood, didn't want to feel any sympathy for her. "A carriage it is then. For today. Although we may have to work on your aversion to horses. I enjoy riding. I suspect you would as well."

"At night? Over the moors? That's the only time left to us as I promise you that I would never ride a horse during an hour that belongs to me."

"I often ride over the moors at night. It can be quite invigorating."

"I thought you were warned not to go out at night—unless you absolutely had to."

"Do I strike you as one who heeds warnings?"

"No." She gave him a wicked little smile. "When did you first break that rule?"

"When I was fifteen. There was the largest moon in the sky, a blood moon. I wanted to be beneath its light so I snuck out, saddled up a horse, and rode until dawn."

"During all that time, you never saw your mother's ghost?"

"Not once."

"Maybe when you snuck out, she snuck in."

"I doubt it."

A sadness coming into her eyes, she gazed toward the windows. "There's a part of me that wishes your father did indeed see her."

"Perhaps it's enough that he believes he does."

She gave her attention back to him, a slight crease between her brows. "I can't imagine a love that grand."

"Wasn't yours?"

Slowly she shook her head, melancholy washing off her in waves. "No, not even in the beginning, when our love was new and untried."

"What of your parents? Did they not love each other?"

"In their own way I suppose they did." She stood, signaling the end to that topic. He wasn't even certain why he'd asked. "I should get ready for our outing."

She walked from the room, and he had the oddest realization: he rather wished the love that had cost her so much had been a grand one.

Chapter 12

THE open buggy contained a single bench, so Portia sat beside Locksley while he expertly handled the two horses. She wasn't surprised by his skill or the fact that he hadn't chosen a vehicle that required a driver. He was accustomed to doing for himself. He didn't seem to mind it or consider being pampered as his due. She knew she needed to stop comparing him to other men she'd known, and yet she couldn't quite seem to help herself. He possessed not only a physical strength but an inner one as well. She couldn't imagine him succumbing to madness, doubting himself, questioning his abilities—couldn't imagine him ever being anything except confident in his beliefs and actions.

She was rather glad he'd asked her to join him. While she welcomed time to herself, she wanted to be more than simply his bedmate. She wanted to mean something to him, which was a silly thing to wish and yet she did.

Although they didn't speak, there was a comfortableness to the quiet. She found it pleasant being with him in the silence, because he wasn't striving to figure her out. Sometimes when he asked his questions, her guard would shoot up, and she'd worry that he might uncover something she didn't wish him to know. He was too smart, too discerning by half. If he weren't, she'd now be married to his father. She wouldn't be taking a ride with her husband.

The village came into view, sooner than she'd expected. "We could have walked," she murmured.

"I haven't the time. I need to get to the mines."

"Do you not have a foreman to oversee matters?" she asked.

"I like to keep my eye on things."

"Including me, I suppose."

"Especially you."

She was taken aback by the pang his words brought. "I'm not going to run off with the silver."

"I didn't think you would. You're smart enough to know that I would find you—and make you pay."

She suspected he'd make her pay in the most pleasant of ways. He didn't strike her as a man who would ever harm a woman.

Slowing the carriage, he brought the horses to a halt in front of a shop with a sign that read "Village Cryer." In the window was what looked to be the front page of a recent edition. It proclaimed, "Lord Locksley Takes Wife!"

"It seems the vicar's been a busy fellow spreading the word of our marriage," Locksley groused.

She didn't know whether to be flattered or alarmed. "How far a reach does this newspaper have?"

"The window there is it, but I'm sure we could have another printed if you wish to put it in the post to your family."

She looked over, not surprised to find him studying her, gauging her reaction. "They wouldn't care."

"It wouldn't give you a sense of satisfaction to let them know you haven't done too badly for yourself?"

"I am not so petty as to take delight in boasting my

good fortune. Do you think the vicar reported our marriage to the *Times*?"

"I doubt that it occurred to him that London would care."

"It would occur to your father."

"Unlikely. His life centers around Havisham. He doesn't care who knows I'm married. He only cared that I married."

Locksley climbed out, secured the horses, and walked around to offer her his hand. "Are you disappointed not to have your newly acquired position heralded?"

She didn't blame him for thinking so poorly of her, but she was growing weary of it, especially after last night, especially when he had seemed to be glad they were together. Placing her hand in his, she tilted up her chin. "But it is heralded. The entire village must know."

Although no one wandering the streets was rushing over to congratulate them, which bothered her not in the least. She'd merely wanted to be reassured that news of her nuptials had not yet reached the *Times*. The possibility that it might never appear in the London paper brought her more relief than he could ever know. She was safe, secure, protected, hidden away exactly as she wanted.

She stepped down, went to remove her hand, only his fingers closed more securely around it.

"Why am I always left with the impression that you're not quite honest with me?" he asked.

"Why am I always left with the impression that you're an incredibly suspicious sort?" she offered in rebuttal. She wanted to respond that she'd never lied to him, but there had been a thing or two that she'd told him that wasn't completely true or exactly as she'd revealed it.

"If I weren't, you'd be married to my father. Can you deny, after last night, that you're glad you're not?"

"I suspect I'd get more sleep if I were married to him."

He grinned, and she refrained from reaching up to touch the corner of that luscious mouth that had done such wicked things to her after the sun had set. "I suggest you nap when we return to Havisham, if sleep is what you covet, as you'll have even less of it tonight."

"And when will you sleep, my lord?"

"When I've had my fill of you."

"Are you challenging me to ensure you never do?"

"Would you accept if I were?"

She began to curl her lips into her sauciest smile, then stopped. She had no desire to play games with him, to be to him what she'd been to Montie. "I'd give it my best if that's what you wanted."

His eyebrows knitted together. "What were you thinking just then?"

She shook her head. "Something silly. Impossible. We should get to our errands, shouldn't we? Before people begin speculating as to why we're merely standing here as though we're a couple of fools."

"You may be many things, Portia, but foolish is not one of them. I'd bet my life on that."

"And here I was just getting accustomed to having you around."

"Are you admitting I'd lose that bet?"

"We are all foolish at one time or another, my lord. It is the only way in which we can become wise."

"Perhaps someday you'll tell me about those foolish lessons."

"Don't hold your breath."

"Wouldn't dream of it. Let's get you some servants, shall we?"

His fingers loosened their hold, and he took her hand, placing it on his forearm, before leading her into the newspaper office. The smell of ink was sharp, the printing press taking up a good portion of the small space.

"Lord Locksley!" a man with salt-and-pepper hair sitting behind a desk exclaimed as he jumped to his feet. "Congratulations are in order, I hear."

"I daresay, Mr. Moore, that you wrote as much."

The man's face turned a mottled red, the blush creeping up until it disappeared in his receding hairline. "The vicar said nuptials had taken place, and as it is my job to report the news, I did so immediately. Did I offend?"

"Not at all. Lady Locksley, allow me to introduce Mr. Moore, our intrepid newspaper owner and reporter."

His fingers were ink-stained, the lenses of his spectacles thick, and she imagined him working late into the night striving to determine the best words to herald whatever news he needed to announce. "It's a pleasure, Mr. Moore," she said.

He bestowed upon her a sweeping bow. "The pleasure is mine, m'lady. Reverend Browning claimed you were a beaut. Good to know a man of the cloth doesn't lie."

She was aware of the heat fanning her cheeks, and Locksley giving his throat a harsh clearing as though warning the man he'd been entirely inappropriate with his praise. Moore jumped, stepped back, and darted his gaze between her and the viscount.

"How may I be of service?" he asked.

"The *viscountess* is in need of some servants," Locksley said, emphasizing her title. "We wish to place an advertisement in the *Cryer*."

Moore perked up even more, and she wondered if it was the idea of a lord making use of his beloved newspaper or the notion of coins in his pockets. "Very good, m'lord."

"We are also in need of someone to tune a piano." Her

husband's words startled her, as she'd thought the notion of tuning the piano forbidden and the discussion closed. "Is there anyone local or must we send to London?"

"Mr. Holt would be your man, there. He keeps the organ going at the church."

"Send word to him, then, that he's needed at Havisham."

"Yes, m'lord. How would you like your advert to read?"

"I shall leave that to Lady Locksley." He walked over to the window and gazed out, while she followed Moore back to his cluttered desk. She thought perhaps her husband was disgusted with himself for inquiring about the tuner, for indicating that she had his permission to play the piano. Or perhaps it was simply that he wasn't comfortable with the changes she wanted to make.

And yet the joy spiraling through her was sharp and unmistakable. He might grumble, but he wasn't going to deny her what she wanted. She didn't want him to be extraordinarily kind, didn't want to like him, because it only added weight to her guilt. She would do all she could to make his home a pleasant place in which to dwell.

How odd that when she'd run away from home, she'd believed she was gaining freedom, and now in marriage, she was finding more than she'd ever known.

When the advert was written to her satisfaction, she strolled over to join her husband at the window. "We're finished."

"Very good." He offered his arm and she took it. "Thank you, Mr. Moore," he said before escorting her out.

Once they were on the boardwalk, she said, "The advert will be in tomorrow's paper, so I suppose I shall begin interviewing then."

"I suspect you'll begin interviewing today. The newsprint is merely a formality. Moore is the biggest gossip in the village."

She laughed lightly. "Truly?"

He gave her a laconic smile. "He is rather good at not spreading false tales but he is more the 'crier' than his paper."

"You didn't like that he finds me beautiful."

"I didn't like that his words were inappropriate. You're a lady, not a doxy, but as it's been a little over thirty years since there was a lady about, I suppose the villagers may have become lax in their manners. It's the only reason I didn't plow my fist into his nose."

She blinked, stared, taken aback by his words. "You would have struck him?"

"You are my wife, Portia. You will be given the respect you deserve as such or I shall know the reason why."

And if she didn't deserve the respect? She wouldn't think about that, would put the past behind her, would become a woman who did deserve his respect, who was worthy of being his wife. "Do *you* respect me?" she asked.

"How I perceive you is not the point. Now I have another matter to see to. Shall we walk?"

"I would enjoy getting a sense of the village. I suppose I shall spend some time here."

"Divesting yourself of your monthly allowance?" he asked as they began strolling north.

She wasn't going to spend a penny. She was going to hoard it all away in case a time came when she found herself again on her own. "I thought you were going to purchase everything I require."

"Nothing frivolous."

Like the tuning of a piano? She truly didn't know what to make of this man. "Who will decide if it's frivolous?"

"I shall, of course."

"I can't quite figure you out, Locksley. On the one hand, you appear to be incredibly domineering, and yet on the other hand, you're incredibly kind."

He scowled, the furrows in his brow deep, his eyes as hard as the gems their shade mirrored. "I am not kind."

"You gave me the keys."

"Because I did not want to have to deal with an upset Mrs. Barnaby every day. Never confuse practicality with kindness."

"I shall keep that in mind." She wondered why he was so intent on not gaining her affection. She supposed it had to do with his aversion to love. Perhaps he feared that if she came to care for him, he might reciprocate.

It was obvious, as they wandered the streets, that many of the villagers knew Locksley, but there was a deference to their greetings: a doff of the hat, a quick curtsy, a quietly spoken "M'lord, m'lady." A very different approach from their encounter with Mr. Moore. She'd no doubt provide some sort of gift to the villagers at Christmas. The village in which she'd been raised had been near an earl's estate, and the countess had always delivered a basket of food to Portia's family on Christmas. Portia had considered the woman so elegant, so refined, so well dressed, but it had been equally obvious that duty alone had brought her to their home. Portia did not intend to give the impression that she considered herself above these people, that she considered the task her duty. For her, it would be a pleasure to be able to do something for those less fortunate, no matter how small or trivial the contribution might be.

As they walked, she counted five taverns. She suspected her husband had frequented them all.

Locksley turned them onto another street. They passed

a hostelry and a blacksmith. At the end of the road stood a large building with huge doors that hung open. The sign above them read "Cabinetry and Such."

Locksley began guiding her toward it. She was rather certain why they were here, and quite suddenly she didn't want him to give her another gift. Digging in her heels, she resisted until he stopped and looked at her. She shook her head. "I don't need a dressing table."

"You told me that ladies require them."

"I was being difficult."

He arched a brow. "As opposed to now when you are being so accommodating?"

"You're allowing me to have servants. You're arranging for the piano to be tuned. I can go without a dressing table. Or I can find one in an abandoned bedchamber."

"I've already stated that's not an option."

She couldn't explain why she wasn't comfortable with it. She just wasn't. "I didn't expect you to be so generous."

"I told you that I would be. Did you think me a liar?"

"No, I just . . . it's all too much, too soon." Although it was reassuring to know that he wasn't striving to be kind but was merely honoring his word.

"I don't have time to argue, Portia. I need to get to the mines. We're here, and if we don't see to it now, I'll have to come to the village another day. So let's get to it, shall we?"

He didn't wait for her to answer, but simply placed her hand back on his arm and led her into the massive building. Wood shavings littered the floor; the tart fragrance of cedar filled the air. Three men were working. Two of them appeared to be a bit older than Locksley, the last considerably younger. One of the older men stopped planing a plank and walked toward them. A fine layer of sawdust covered his face and clothes.

"M'lord," he said when he reached them. He bowed his

head toward her. "M'lady. Congratulations to you both on the recent nuptials."

She supposed her clothing gave away that she was the new viscountess. The last thing she'd ever expected was to be considered nobility, regardless of her marriage.

"Thank you, Mr. Wortham," Locksley said. "We're here as Lady Locksley is in need of a dressing table. I thought you might be up to the task."

"Indeed, m'lord, I'd be honored. I'd wager it's been nearly thirty years since we fashioned anything for Havisham Hall. That privilege went to my father."

"Then it seems we're long overdue," Locksley said.

"Perhaps, m'lord." Wortham's gaze darted between her and Locksley. "However, the last piece we made for Havisham was never delivered. And it just happens to be a dressing table. The marquess was having it made for his wife"—he shifted his weight from one foot to the other—"as a surprise for after . . ." He cleared his throat. ". . . she gave birth. Then he didn't want it. But we've kept it. Would you like to see it?"

"Yes," Locksley said succinctly.

Wortham turned; Locksley took a step to follow him; Portia grabbed his arm. He stopped, stared at her.

"You can't be thinking of taking it," she told him.

Locksley held her gaze. "Why not?"

"It was to be a gift from your father to your mother."

"Which he never collected, so it's merely been sitting here for thirty years."

She wanted to grab onto his shoulders and shake some sense into him. "Haven't you a sentimental bone in your body?"

He sighed deeply as though reaching the end of the tether of his patience with her. "Mr. Wortham, has it been paid for?" he called out.

"Yes, m'lord."

Locksley gave her a pointed look. "It's impractical to have another one made when we have a perfectly good one sitting here unused."

"And if your father should happen to see it—"

"That's not going to happen. There is no reason for him to come into our bedchamber."

"But should he see it being carted down the hallway to said bedchamber?"

"I doubt he remembers it, Portia. He seldom remembers what day of the week it is."

"But it was his gift for her."

Breath rushed out of him on a quick huff. "At least look at it. If it's hideous we'll have another crafted."

Only it wasn't hideous. It was quite simply the most beautiful piece of furniture she'd ever seen. It had six side drawers, three on each side of the large oval mirror. The mirror's frame was a circlet of carved roses. The table's legs were thick and curved, with whittled ribbons of flowers winding around them. "It's gorgeous."

"The rosewood gives it an elegant look," Wortham said.

It was more than the wood. It was all the intricate detailing. "Do you think Lady Marsden knew that something so fine was being made for her?"

"I don't think so, m'lady."

"How very sad."

"We didn't know what to do with it since his Lordship paid for it. We've been keeping it polished and well cared for all these years. A shame for it not to be used."

She glanced over at Locksley. He was studying the dressing table as though it were merely a block of wood, not something that had been created with a great deal of care. "Your father was very skilled, Mr. Wortham."

"Aye, m'lady, he was. He would be right pleased to know that it was being appreciated and put to use."

"I suspect my mother would as well," Locksley said quietly.

Portia jerked her gaze to him. He merely shrugged. "From what I understand she was a very generous woman. She would hate seeing this piece wasted."

Portia nodded. "I suppose it makes sense to take it."

"When can you deliver it, Mr. Wortham?" Locksley asked.

"Tomorrow, m'lord."

"Very good. I shall be sending you a payment double your usual rate for delivery and I'll be providing a bonus for the care you've given this piece over the years."

"No need for that, m'lord."

"There might not be a need for it, but it's definitely warranted."

"It's best not to argue with him," Portia told Mr. Wortham. "Once he's set his mind to something he can be quite stubborn."

She caught the sight of Locksley's mouth curling up as he turned away from her. She didn't know why it always pleased her to make him smile, or why her comment to Wortham made her feel so wifely. Coming to know her husband filled her with a sense of satisfaction as well as a measure of dread, because she feared he had the power to shatter what remained of her fragile heart.

So she thought she knew him, did she? Well enough to speak of him to a laborer as though they were friends. He didn't like that she might actually be figuring him out, liked even less the things that he was coming to anticipate about her. He'd known her eyes would widen in surprise and pleasure when he asked about the blasted tuner for the piano. He'd known she wouldn't be entirely comfortable taking the dressing table. But it was ridiculous to spend coin to have another made when his father had already purchased one that had gone unused for more than a quarter of a century.

He didn't take any satisfaction in his ability to predict her reactions. Took far less in her ability to predict his. Therefore, he had decided to do something entirely unpredictable and bring her to Lydia's Teas and Cakes before they returned to Havisham. As they'd entered, those whiskey-shaded eyes of hers had glowed with absolute delight. And he'd cursed his stupidity. He was being far too accommodating. It didn't help matters that it always caused this odd sense of swelling in his chest that made it difficult to breathe for a few seconds whenever she flashed him a quick smile.

He did not want her smiles. He did not want her eyes sparkling. He did not want her to express gratitude to him.

As they sat at a table by the window, she began slowly peeling off her gloves. He'd not objected when she'd worn them for the journey. It was proper after all, and he needed his wife to be proper. But did she have to remove them in such a salacious manner that made him want to carry her to an upper room in the tavern across the street and strip away every piece of clothing she wore?

Clearing his throat, he turned his attention to the activity beyond the window, to the people wandering by, carrying on with their business. He spent very little time in the village, something that should no doubt be remedied now that he had a wife. They should have more presence in the future, ensure they were respected rather than feared for being mad.

"It was very kind of you to double the amount you'll be paying for the delivery," she said.

"Practical, Portia. It'll make it easier for Wortham to find someone willing to cart the dressing table out there and haul it inside." He could feel her gaze boring into him. He shifted his attention back to her. "Just as we'll be paying your servants double the going rate. No one likes to spend time at haunted Havisham Hall."

"With whom did you play?" she asked. "Before your father's wards arrived?"

"No one."

Her expression reflected sorrow. "Don't look so sad, Portia. I knew no different so it wasn't as though I were lonely."

Her brow knitted, and he refrained from reaching across to smooth out the delicate folds with his thumb. "You can't recall climbing to the ceiling in your father's library but you recall that you weren't lonely?"

"I should think had I been lonely that it would have made an impression and I would remember it. I don't. Just as I wasn't lonely before your arrival. I'm content with my own company." Not entirely true. He'd begun to have a sense of something missing, of a need for something more, but he wasn't going to share that with her and give her any sort of power. She was a pleasant-enough distraction, but he didn't *need* her in his life.

A young woman brought over a teapot and a plate of cakes. After she left, Portia poured tea into Locke's cup and then her own. "Your father doesn't enjoy tea, does he?"

"He detests it. What gave him away?"

Her lips curled up into the barest hint of a smile. "The abundance of sugar he requested, followed by the fact that he failed to take so much as a sip."

"You're keenly observant."

"I try to be. Leads to less heartache."

Watching as she nibbled delicately on a cake, he told

himself that her heartache was none of his concern. He
certainly wouldn't be causing her any, as that would require she care for him, and he wasn't going to give her
cause to follow that route. Still, it nagged at him. "Did
you learn that the hard way?"

She took a sip of her tea, seemed to be contemplating
her answer. "In my youth I tended to view things as I
wanted them to be, rather than as they were. I was apt to
misjudge people and their intentions."

He leaned forward. "What did he do to lose your love,
Portia? Your husband? Have an affair?"

She looked down at her cup, circled her finger along
the rim. "He did have a penchant for unmarried ladies,"
she said so softly that he almost didn't hear her.

"You need never worry that I shall be unfaithful. I take
the vows we made quite seriously."

She peered up at him through lowered lashes. "And if
you fall in love with someone else?"

"I've told you. Love is not for me, so that shan't happen."

"I have found that love is not quite so easily controlled."

"In my thirty years upon this earth, I've not even felt
the spark of it."

"Not true. You love your father. Otherwise, you
wouldn't be as protective of him as you are."

"I'm merely exhibiting a son's duty."

Biting her lower lip, she shook her head, rolled her
eyes. "You're delusional if you believe that."

He did love his father. Loved Ashe and Edward . . . and
had loved Albert. Missed him still. But a woman? He'd
never loved a woman. He'd long ago closed his heart to
the possibility of harboring deep feelings for any lady.

"M'lord, m'lady?" a feminine voice asked hesitantly.

Welcoming the interruption to his thoughts, to this
discussion, he turned to the young woman clasping her

hands in front of her. Her dress was modest, a bit frayed at the cuffs and collar, but she was tidy. Not a single strand of her blond hair was out of place. He shoved back his chair, stood. "Yes?"

"I'm Cullie Smythe. I don't mean to interrupt, but I heard you were seeking a maid-of-all-work. I'd like to apply for the position, and I was wondering if it would be all right if I come out to the manor this afternoon to see about it."

"No need to wait," Locke said, drawing the chair back farther. "Take a seat, Miss Smythe. Lady Locksley can interview you now."

"Now?" his wife asked, her eyes huge and round.

"Why not? We're here. She's here." And her arrival had effectively ended an unwanted conversation. Besides, he was anxious to see how Portia conducted herself, since it was unlikely he'd be present for the other interviews.

"Yes, please sit, Miss Smythe," Portia said.

After assisting the woman, Locke turned his attention to the outdoors, trying to give the impression that he wasn't the least bit interested in what was going on, when in truth he had enough curiosity to kill a dozen cats. He didn't know why every single aspect of Portia fascinated him. He wanted to watch her interacting with other people. He wanted to observe her from afar but near enough to listen.

"Have you any experience?" he heard her ask Miss Smythe.

"I've kept me da's house for two years now, ever since me mum passed."

Out of the corner of his eye, he saw Portia reach across the table and place her hand over Miss Smythe's in a comforting gesture that for some unaccountable reason made his chest tighten. "I'm sorry for your loss," she said softly with genuine sorrow reflected in her voice. "I know it's very hard to lose your mother. How old are you?"

"Seventeen."

"If you come to work at Havisham, you will reside there. Do you fear ghosts, Miss Smythe?"

"Not as much as I fear going hungry."

"Is that a possibility?" True concern in Portia's voice indicated she would be a fair mistress. Locke didn't want her abusing the servants, but neither did he want her to care so deeply. Everything he learned about her contradicted what he'd originally assumed, and that unsettled him.

"Aye," Miss Smythe said. "I've been thinking of going to London in hopes of securing a position, but working at Havisham would allow me to stay closer to home, which would be a godsend, as I've no desire to leave, not really."

"Who would care for your father's house?"

Again, her concern for something that shouldn't weigh into her decision at all. It was not their place to worry over why people did what they did.

"My sister," Miss Smythe answered. "She's old enough now to manage things."

"Did she style your hair? I like it very much."

"No, m'lady. I fixed it meself."

"Would you consider serving as my lady's maid rather than a maid-of-all-work?"

Locke shifted his attention back to the table. He could see only Portia, but her expression was soft, hopeful, filled with kindness—nowhere near the cold expression she'd exhibited when he'd questioned her that first afternoon. If she had looked at him like she now looked at Miss Smythe—he could have resisted her, seen her as a danger to his heart, and easily sent her on her way with a heavier purse.

"Oh, m'lady. I'd be putting on airs to go for a position such as that."

Portia smiled. "Exactly why I want you in the position, Miss Smythe. I appreciate modesty."

Locke almost scoffed. Portia didn't have a modest bone in her body, but then he was hit with the startling realization that perhaps she once had, that maybe she had been as eager and innocent as Miss Smythe—before her husband had betrayed her love and trust in him. He had an unsettling image of her young and naïve, giving her heart to a scoundrel who didn't deserve it. For an insane moment, he wished he'd known her then, only long enough for a passing glance. He would have kept his distance, wouldn't have wanted to be ensnared by her guileless charms. Not that he would have been. Such had never appealed to him, and he almost regretted that.

"I don't know what to say, m'lady."

"Say yes."

"But I don't know how to be a lady's maid."

"I'll teach you."

"Caw. Well, I'd be a fool to say no then, I suppose, wouldn't I?"

"You don't strike me as a fool, Miss Smythe."

"Then I'd be pleased to take the position. And I'll give it my best."

"I would expect no less. Could you move in tomorrow?"

"I can move in this afternoon."

Portia smiled sublimely. "I shall look forward to welcoming you to Havisham Hall."

Her words were like a kick to Locke's gut. When was the last time that anyone had been welcomed to Havisham Hall? He'd be hard-pressed to say his father's wards had been welcomed, at least at first. Other than Ashe and

Edward, with their families, no one ever visited Havisham. No one was ever welcomed there.

His mind reeling with his awareness of the change to routine that Portia was bringing to Havisham, he barely acknowledged Miss Smythe's leaving.

"Are you all right?" Portia asked.

Again, her concern—except it was directed at him, and he didn't want it. He nodded brusquely. "Yes, but we've delayed our return to the manor long enough. You should finish your tea."

"I'm finished."

She began to scrape back her chair. He darted over to assist her. When she was standing, he said, "It was very kind of you to give her such an elevated position in the household."

"She was desperate—approaching us here, not willing to wait until an appropriate time, not willing to risk losing her chance to gain a position. She'll work hard to further herself."

"Perhaps she was merely ambitious."

She shook her head. "No. I know the look of desperation and the lengths to which one will go when backed into a corner. Besides, I like her. I think we'll get along famously."

Skirting past him, she headed for the door. Following after her, he hoped she hadn't come to know the look of desperation while gazing at her reflection in a mirror.

Chapter 13

*H*E thought about Portia while he was at the mines. He thought about her while he galloped his horse over the moors toward the manor. He thought about her as he bathed, while he strode through the hallways in search of her, fairly certain where he'd find her.

In the music room. He wasn't disappointed.

Crossing his arms over his chest, he leaned against the doorjamb and simply watched. Standing on a ladder, dusting his mother's portrait, she was dressed much as she'd been the day before, sans his Hessian, as she now had two strapping lads, one about six inches taller than the other, to deal with the pesky spiders. The new footmen were moving furniture so two young women—one of them Cullie—could roll up the various carpets. He suspected they'd be getting a beating in the morning, along with the draperies that had already been removed. Another young woman was using a long-handled broom to sweep away the dust and cobwebs from the walls. White sheeting had been placed over the piano to protect it from any dust swirling about.

So much activity in this room, yet everyone seemed to know what they were to do. What he didn't understand was why Portia—a title hunter, a woman seeking prestige and position—was in the thick of things rather than standing off to the side merely ordering her new servants about. If a stranger strode in, he was going to mistake her for a maid. Why wasn't she lording her position over these people?

Although he couldn't deny that he enjoyed watching her movements: her hips swaying as she dusted, the way the cloth of her bodice tautened along the side as she reached for the intricately carved corner of the gilded frame.

Hearing a short high-pitched squeal, he was about to turn in the direction of the sound—no doubt the maid at the window—when he saw Portia doing the same, only her perch was precarious. She moved too quickly, too sharply. Suddenly she gasped, her arms flailing—

He'd managed only half a dozen frenzied leaps in her direction before she landed in the arms of the taller footman, who grinned stupidly down on her as though he'd acquired the prize at some county fair game. Locke was completely unprepared for the rage rampaging through him because the man was holding his wife. It didn't matter that he'd saved her from harm. It only mattered that he grinned like a buffoon.

Portia smiled at him, patted his shoulder. "You can release me now, George."

He did so, slowly lowering her feet to the floor. Stepping away, she brushed at her skirts before looking up and spying Locke. The only thing that prevented him from permanently removing the grin from the lad's face was the fact that the smile she gave Locke was brighter and more welcoming than the one she'd given the footman.

"You've returned," she said.

What the devil was the matter with him? What did he care if she was glad to see him? Why should he be angry that a muscled laborer saved his wife from a crack on the head? He should be grateful for it. Instead he was ready to sack the man.

"Why are you working when we have hired servants to see to things?" he demanded to know. He jerked his head toward the ladder. "You could have broken your neck."

"Unlikely. It wasn't that far a drop. At the most I'd have bruised my backside. Although I am grateful to George for rescuing me." She patted George's arm before glancing toward the windows. "Sylvie, why did you squeak? Is everything all right?"

Sylvie, of the black hair and blue eyes that were far too round, curtsied. "I saw his Lordship standing there in the doorway. His presence took me by surprise."

"I've told you that you don't have to curtsy every time you're addressed."

The girl curtsied. "Yes, m'lady."

With a patient shake of her head, Portia turned back to Locke. "How long were you standing there?"

"Not long, but again, Portia, why are you climbing ladders and dusting?"

"There's so much to be done. I didn't see the harm in helping."

"I don't want you scaling ladders"—and falling into the arms of well-built young men—"and putting my heir at risk should you already be with child."

She paled to such an extent that he was surprised she didn't swoon. "Yes, of course. I wasn't thinking." She shook her head. "You're quite right. I shan't ascend ladders anymore. I'll find another way to help."

He didn't know why he didn't feel victorious with her acquiescence. Why did the woman have to constantly confound him? He'd determined her character before he married her. She had no right not to be as he knew her to be. "I'll have your bath prepared," he said, far more curtly than he'd intended.

"No need. George and Thomas can see to hauling the tub and water up. Since you want them doing their job."

As long as they weren't imagining her in that water. What the devil was the matter with him? He'd had women in his life and never experienced jealousy—even when he was fully aware that he wasn't their only lover. But this was different. She was his wife. They'd exchanged vows. So it wasn't jealousy he was experiencing, merely conscientiousness of a certain expectation from her and those around her. The male servants shouldn't be lusting after her, grinning at her, or cradling her in their arms. Training was definitely in order. He'd speak to Gilbert about it.

"You're quite right," he said now. "We'll have the footmen see to it."

"Very good. Allow me to introduce you." She turned to the others in the room and clapped her hands. "Please come forward." They did as she bid, albeit a bit hesitantly. "Queue up," she ordered. "Straight line, stand tall."

Once they were positioned to her satisfaction, she moved to one end. "Cullie you've met, of course."

He nodded toward the girl. "Cullie."

"M'lord." A quick bob of a curtsy.

"Sylvie."

Who gave him three curtsies. He assumed she would have curtsied until her knees gave out if Portia hadn't placed her hand on her arm and said, "That's sufficient."

Marta was the final housemaid. One very nice curtsy from her. The lads, George and Thomas, followed with bows.

"It's a pleasure to have you all at Havisham Hall," Locke said.

"Is it really haunted?" Marta asked.

Sylvie jabbed her elbow into Marta's side. "You're not supposed to ask questions of his Lordship."

"It's quite all right," Locke said. "But, no, it is not haunted."

"I've seen her ghost on the moors," George said.

"Merely swirling mist, I assure you," Locke told him.

"But—"

"You don't contradict his Lordship," Portia said sternly.

" 'Cuz the nobility is never wrong." There was a snide quality to his tone.

Before Locke could bring him to task, Portia was standing before him. "George, have I misjudged your readiness for this position?"

The lad clenched his jaw, shook his head. "No, m'lady."

"I shall hope not, but bear in mind that I shan't tolerate any behavior that is not to my liking, nor shall I keep in our employ anyone who vexes me or his Lordship."

"Yes, m'lady, but I *did* see her."

"It might be best to keep that to yourself."

"Yes, m'lady."

She faced Locke. "Did you wish to add anything?"

He slowly shook his head. The woman was mercurial. One moment she was acting as though she were the servants' equal and the next she reasserted herself as mistress of the household. A chameleon of sorts. During his travels, he'd seen enough creatures with the ability to blend into their surroundings that he knew they could be quite dangerous, had the sense that the same could be said of her. "No, I believe you handled it well enough."

"Right." She clapped her hands again to gain everyone's attention. "As it's nearly nightfall, I shall begin my preparation for dinner. Cullie, come with me. Sylvie and Marta, assist Mrs. Dorset in the kitchen. Thomas and George, report to Mr. Gilbert once you've seen to my bath. Will you be waiting for me in the library, my lord?"

As though there was anyplace else for him to wait. "Yes, I will."

It would take her a while, though, so he decided to visit with his father. He went to the library first to secure them each a glass of scotch before making his way to the master bedchamber. He knocked on the door, waited for his father to invite him in. Once inside, he handed his father a glass, leaned a shoulder against the window near where his father sat, and watched the sky turning a darker gray and shadows spreading over the land.

"I wanted you to know that we've hired a few servants," he told his father.

"I'm aware. Portia introduced them to me earlier. That George is going to be a handful, I think. Bears watching."

"She can keep him in his place."

"Is that respect I hear in your voice?" his father asked.

He sipped his scotch, kept his gaze on the land. "Merely an observation."

"Careful, Locke, you're going to start liking the girl."

"I don't dislike her." He placed his back against the wall, studied the amber liquid in his glass. The rich hue reminded him of her eyes. "She's comfortable ordering people about. She's equally comfortable doing the work. One moment she gives the impression she's a country lass, the next she takes on the airs of the nobility. What is her background exactly?"

His father remained silent. Locke glowered at him. "No harm in telling me."

"Commoner, as she said."

"What of her husband?"

"Well off enough that she managed a household. At least she claimed to manage one."

"Yet he left her with nothing."

"Men are not always the best that they can be. Nor, unfortunately, do they always appreciate the women in their lives. Or he was young enough to think there was plenty of time to make arrangements for her in the event of his death. That's probably it. You never expect to go young. Always time to see to business later."

Locke glanced back to the moors. Almost dark now. "I should like to read the letters that she wrote to you."

His father chuckled low. "That would be too easy. If you want to know something more about her, ask her. Talk with her, have a discourse. Flirt."

He glared at his sire. "A man doesn't flirt with his wife."

His father looked at him as though he'd caught him doing something he shouldn't. "Don't be a fool, boy. Of course he does."

"He's obtained her. What's the point?"

"The point is to make her eyes sparkle like the rarest of jewels, to bring color to her cheeks, to cause the corners of her mouth to turn up ever so slightly. To let her know she is appreciated, still regarded as special, worth the effort. To give her cause to fall a little bit more in love. I flirted with your mother until the day she died." He lifted a slender shoulder, rounded with age. "Still do from time to time."

It took everything within Locke not to roll his eyes. "Trust me, she felt bloody well special last night in my bed."

His father *didn't* refrain from rolling *his* eyes, did so with a great deal of exaggeration and obvious disappointment. "Courtship is just as important outside of the bed as in it—in some ways more so. I have failed miserably in educating you when it comes to women."

"I am well educated in regard to women."

"When it comes to their physical pleasure, I've no doubt. But a relationship requires more than that to flourish."

Locke downed the remainder of his drink. He needed nothing to flourish. "You should join us for dinner."

"You need time alone with your wife."

"I have all night to enjoy her without company."

"And you do enjoy her."

No point in not admitting it. "More than I expected."

"Then I shan't interfere."

"You wouldn't be interfering. I suspect she'd welcome your presence."

His father scratched his chin, the scrape of his fingers over bristle creating a soft grating sound. "Not tonight."

"Perhaps we should hire a valet for you."

His father shook his head. "Gilbert serves well enough. Shouldn't you be with your wife now?"

"She's preparing for the evening. But yes, I should be off." He pushed himself away from the wall, headed for the door.

"Locke?"

He turned back.

"If you want to know more about her past, ask her. I suspect she'd welcome your interest."

"I know all I need to know, Father. I was merely making conversation."

"It's an unwise man who lies to himself."

Then he supposed he was going to go to his grave as an incredibly unwise man.

Chapter 14

THREE evenings later, after returning from a day at the mines, Locke was disappointed to find the door to the music room locked. He'd grown accustomed to finding his wife there, to having a few minutes to observe her before someone spotted him lurking in the doorway and gasped or shrieked in surprise. In spite of his assurances that no ghost was hovering about, it seemed some were still expecting the sudden appearance of a wraith.

He didn't much like that he anticipated seeing Portia at the end of the day, that she had so quickly become an intricate part of his life. He awoke with her in his arms, and if he were fortunate enough to find the sun had yet to appear, then he began his morning with a rousing sexual encounter. She was the most enthusiastic partner he'd ever known—or perhaps it was simply that he took such satisfaction in pleasuring her. Her moans and cries inflamed his desires.

Even now, standing before the blasted locked door, he wanted her. But he wouldn't take her, not until they dined. He was determined to maintain some control, to not let her see how desperately he wanted her naked and beneath him.

He pressed his ear to the door, listening intently to ensure she and the servants weren't inside, hadn't locked him out unintentionally—or intentionally, for that matter. He considered fetching the keys from Mrs. Barnaby in order to make certain that no one was within the room, but it was so quiet on the other side that it seemed highly unlikely that anyone was hidden away in there. So where was she? And why did it irritate the devil out of him that it had been half an hour since his bath and he had yet to see her?

He nearly pounded a fist on the damned door, was glad he hadn't when he spun around to find her standing in the hallway, her head half-cocked as though she'd been studying him for a while.

She was already dressed for the evening in her blue gown with her hair piled up in that intriguing style that called for his fingers to muss it up. Now that she had her servants, she was no longer dependent upon him for her bath. He was not going to be jealous of a couple of footmen because they could see to her needs. They were lugging water, for God's sake, not bringing her pleasure.

"Were you looking for me?" she asked, her smile one of immense satisfaction, as though she already knew the answer, which of course she did.

"It is almost night."

"So it is." She offered him a sultry look, half lowering her lashes. Damn it. He began silently uttering the refrain *Dinner first. Dinner first. Dinner first.*

"I wasn't expecting to find the door locked," he said, wondering why he sounded so disgruntled. Because he wanted her—now. And he was denying himself.

"We finished tidying the room this afternoon. I thought I would give it an official unveiling after dinner. Perhaps even play for you."

He began stalking toward her. "What sort of games did you have in mind?"

Pressing her lips together, she rolled her eyes. "I meant the pianoforte. It's been tuned, sounds quite marvelous now."

He didn't stop until his legs were brushing her skirts and his hand was cradling her jaw. "Perhaps one song."

Then his resistance broke and he claimed her mouth as his own. He didn't understand this need to possess her that continually rifled through him. Perhaps it was the eagerness with which she welcomed him, the speed with which she wrapped her arms around his neck or pressed her body to his. Perhaps it was the fervor with which her tongue explored and demanded that he not hold back. Her zeal when it came to passion was equal to his. He didn't set the tempo or nurture a spark into a flame. She matched him step for step. She created a conflagration with her first touch.

She was bold and daring and intrepid within the bed and out of it. He thought of his father's advert. He'd sought the wrong things in a wife, and yet somehow Locke had ended up with one that exceeded expectations.

He tore his mouth from hers, stared down into those smoldering whiskey eyes. Her lips were wet and swollen. He was going to make other parts of her wet and swollen after dinner.

He cringed. No, after a tune in the music room. One tune. To humor her. To give the impression of being a good husband instead of the randy one he was. Christ, by now he should have lost some interest in her, the novelty should have worn off. Instead it all seemed to have increased tenfold. If he believed in witches, he might have thought her one.

"I need a drink before dinner," he stated, striving for a neutral tone that wouldn't give away the war raging

within him to go ahead and have her now, here in this
hallway, up against a wall.

"I'll join you."

As though she had a choice. He could see through
the windows at the end of the corridor that darkness had
fallen. She was his now. Absolutely and completely—
until the sun once again emerged.

ANTICIPATION was an aphrodisiac. Portia could not
help but believe that as she enjoyed her dessert. She had
been tempted earlier to unlock the door, to share with
Locksley then and there the results of her—and her
servants'—efforts. But all through dinner she tingled
with the awareness of what was to come. While she knew
it was quite likely he would not be as taken with the room
as she was now that it was put back together, her enthusiasm for sharing it was not dimmed. It was her sanctuary.
She had made it so with each spider killed, each cobweb
swept away, each fleck of dust removed, every inch of
wood polished, every bit of cloth and carpet beaten until
the years of neglect faded away.

With that one room tidied and vibrant again, she could
envision the magnificence that had once encompassed the
entire residence. It was a shame, a crime even, that this
house had been left to ruin. She wanted to give back to
Locksley what it had once been.

That he had grown up with such decay and neglect
saddened her beyond all reason. She knew he fancied her
for only the physical comforts she could provide but she
viewed him as more, wanted more between them. She
had no doubt that it would be slow in coming, but perhaps
in a few years once she had filled his life with the laughter
of children . . .

If for no other reason, this residence needed to be set to rights so their children would know joy and comfort and gladness. This wallowing about, allowing the residence to continue its slow decline, could not stand. She wouldn't allow it, even though she knew she had to move unhurriedly and with caution to bring him over to her side of things. She might have entered into this marriage as a last resort, but she was determined that neither of them would ever regret it.

As she took her final bite of pudding and set aside her spoon, Thomas moved in to take the dish away. She wasn't certain where Gilbert had found the livery for the footmen or Mrs. Barnaby had secured the clothing for the maids. As the servants now reeked heavily of cedar, she assumed the items had been packed away in cedar chests somewhere, simply waiting for the day when the residence would be brought back to life.

She looked to the end of the table. Her husband had finished off his wine and was lounging back, his elbow resting on the arm of the chair, his chin supported by his hand, his finger stroking just below his lower lip. That finger would be stroking her later.

"What are you thinking?" she asked.

"I'm not certain I've ever witnessed anyone exhibiting such pleasure while eating dessert. In the beginning, I thought it was because you'd gone a while without sweets, but if that were the case you should be accustomed to it by now. But I can actually see your excitement building as we near the end of the meal."

"We had dessert only on rare occasions when I was growing up. My father was a strict man who didn't believe in indulging in practices that brought pleasure."

"You don't have seemed to have adopted his beliefs."

She shook her head. "I believe we must secure happiness where we can. I'm happy when I eat pudding, and where is the harm? I'm also happy when I'm playing the piano. Shall we adjourn to the music room?"

He shoved back his chair, stood, and began walking toward her. "I'll want to drop by the library first for a bit of port."

He stopped by her chair, pulled it out, and extended his hand. Not until she was standing did she say, "I added decanters of liquor to the music room."

A corner of his mouth quirked up. "You're very good at determining my needs."

She smiled. "I try."

The way his eyes darkened, she doubted she'd make it through the first song before he was whisking her up to his bedchamber. She supposed there were worst things than being madly desired by one's husband.

She placed her hand on his proffered arm and fought back the nerves that suddenly made an appearance, causing her to doubt that he would take any pleasure at all in her efforts, that he would care about the room, that he would ever care about her.

She did not need love, but quite suddenly she found herself wanting it. Which made her a very silly girl indeed, as he was not a man to love, but perhaps with time he would feel some affection toward her. For tonight, she merely wanted him to favor the room half as much as she did.

When they reached their destination, she removed the key from a small hidden pocket in her gown and extended it to him. "You may do the honors."

With a tilt of his head in acknowledgment, he took the offering, unlocked the door, and swung it open. She glided over the threshold, then turned quickly to gauge his reaction as he followed her inside.

Locke was familiar with the surroundings, of course. He'd explored them as a boy, and he'd watched her and the servants working to tidy things up. Yet he was unprepared for the magnificence that greeted him. Every wooden, glass, and marble surface gleamed. Fresh flowers in vases scented the air. The draperies over the windows were drawn back to reveal the night. "You changed the furniture."

It seemed an insignificant thing to say but he was having difficulty reconciling this room with what he'd always known.

"Moths did quite a bit of feasting in here. I kept what was salvageable. Mr. Wortham reupholstered several pieces. A few are still with him, but I was too impatient to share the room. I'm very pleased with how it all came together."

And she was nervous as well. He could hear it in the tinny pitch of her voice. Usually so raspy and sultry. His opinion mattered to her. He didn't want to matter to her; didn't want her to matter to him. But he couldn't deny her the truth. "You've done a remarkable job."

He glanced over at the portrait over the fireplace. He'd never known the colors to look so rich, for the painting to seem so lifelike that for a moment it appeared his mother might actually step off the canvas and into the room. He took several strides toward it.

"I was very glad to discover it was merely dust dulling the portrait," Portia said.

Other portraits were scattered on the walls throughout the room, but his mother's dominated.

"I wish I'd known her," Portia mused softly.

"My father seldom spoke of her."

"Perhaps you should ask him about her."

"It will only make him more sad." He spun toward the corner where he had earlier spied the decanters. "Would you care for something to drink?"

"No, thank you."

He poured himself a finger of scotch, downed it, poured two more fingers' worth before facing her.

"Does the room upset you?" she asked.

It didn't upset him, but it did unsettle him. He was accustomed to the decay. This was change. Perhaps he wasn't that different from his father. He didn't like alterations. "It will take some getting used to, I suppose."

"Would you prefer to return to the library to finish your drink?"

He wanted to go to their bedchamber, but to do so would make him feel as though this room had somehow beaten him. It unsettled him further because she was able to tell that he wasn't completely comfortable here. He didn't want her to know him that well. So while he might want to leave, he would stay. "I would like to hear you play the piano."

The smile she gave him took his breath, and he could not comprehend why her husband would have wandered. He, himself, had an irrational urge to do whatever necessary to keep her smiling.

"Make yourself comfortable," she said before spinning on her heel and strolling to the shining instrument. He suspected she had polished it herself, with care, using strokes very similar to the caresses one gave a lover.

As he settled into a nearby chair, not a single speck of dust rose up. Before his mother's death, he suspected all the rooms had been kept as pristine. He had a momentary flash of thought that his father had done his mother a disservice to allow the residence to fall into neglect. It had never mattered before Portia arrived. There was no one to see it except for those who resided within these walls. And what did they care?

It bothered him to realize that perhaps they should have cared a great deal.

He refocused his thoughts on more pleasant matters, on Portia, as she lowered herself to the bench. "I'm a bit out of practice," she said, "so don't judge too harshly."

He almost responded that he wasn't one to judge but they would both know that for the lie it was. He'd judged her before she'd even arrived at Havisham Hall, before he knew the color of her eyes or the shade of her hair, before he knew her tart tongue could slay him with words and kisses. "I have made it a habit to avoid musical entertainments as much as possible, so I have little against which to compare you. So please proceed in the knowledge that I am not likely to be disappointed."

She placed her fingers on the keys. He sipped his scotch and waited. Her eyes closed.

The first chord struck deep, reverberating throughout the room, and what followed was a haunting melody that wove through him and threatened to draw him in. He watched the way Portia swayed with the movements of her fingers. Her head tipped back slightly and she seemed to be lost in ecstasy—without him. He refused to be jealous of a damned musical instrument.

But dear God, to observe her was in itself a sexual experience. He was beginning to understand what she might have felt when she strode into this room and first saw the abandoned piano, why she had needed to set this chamber to rights. It had called to her soul and now she was setting that soul free, absorbed by the music that she so skillfully created.

He shouldn't have been surprised. From the moment

she had walked through the front door, she had thrown herself into everything with complete abandon, whether it was besting him during an inquisition, kissing him, tidying a room, eating dessert. She possessed a passionate nature that he had barely tapped into. At this moment, she mesmerized him, drew him in as though she'd woven a web around him and was gently tugging him forward.

He didn't want to be on the edge observing. He wanted to be in the midst of her passion, wanted to experience it, enhance it. Setting aside his glass, he stood. As quietly as possible, so as not to disturb her, he crept toward her. When he was near enough, he knelt and wrapped his hand around the hem of her skirt. Her eyes flew open and she stared down at him.

"Keep playing," he ordered, lifting her skirts and positioning himself between her legs.

KEEP playing? Was he mad? If not for the wicked challenge in his eyes before he disappeared beneath her skirts, she might have kicked him out of the way. Instead she returned her fingers to the keys while he bracketed her hips and slid her to the very edge of the bench. She struck a wrong chord, cringed. She was not going to allow the kisses he was trailing along the inside of her thigh to distract her. It mattered not that she could scarcely breathe or that she was suddenly so warm she could have sworn the room had caught afire.

Then his mouth landed on the bud of her desire and she nearly came up off the bench. Instead she pounded the keys as his tongue circled, as the pleasure mounted. She dropped her head back, unable to concentrate on the tune, simply striking random chords. What did it matter when he was doing such wicked, wicked things, when he was distracting her, causing her to be perched on the threshold of so many incredible sensations swirling through her, urging her to cry out—

"Locke, what the devil—"

With a screech at the sound of Marsden's voice, Portia leaped to her feet, heard a mash of chords striking as Locksley's head hit the underside of the piano. With a harsh curse, he crawled out from beneath her skirts, out from beneath the piano, until he was standing beside her, none too pleased by the interruption based upon the hard expression marring his face.

"What were you doing down there?" the marquess asked.

Her husband's cheeks burned a bright red that at any other time she would have taken satisfaction from and teased him about. "Listening for any chords that needed to be tuned."

"It seems as though you could have done that just as well—if not better—from over here."

The absurdity of it all. She couldn't help it. She began laughing so hard that tears formed and her legs weakened. Covering her mouth with her hand, she dropped back down onto the bench.

"It's not funny, Portia," Locksley stated succinctly, clearly as irritated with her now as he was with his father.

"I'm sorry." But she couldn't seem to stop the peals of laughter from rolling out. She was mortified to have been caught with her husband's head nestled between her thighs. It was either cry or laugh, and she'd learned long ago that it was always better to laugh. Taking a deep breath, working to stifle the chuckles, she pressed her palms against her burning cheeks. They were no doubt as red as Locksley's.

"What the deuce are you doing here?" he asked his father.

"I heard the piano." He took a step forward. He'd obviously donned his jacket quickly as one side of the collar was tucked under, caught beneath the cloth at his shoulder. "I thought it was Linnie playing. She loved to play the pianoforte. She was so good at it."

"I'm not very good," Portia felt compelled to say.

"You were wonderful. Will you play for me?" Before she could answer, he added, "Locke, fetch me some scotch." Then he dropped down into the chair that Locksley had vacated.

With a sigh, Locksley strode toward the corner, stopping to pick up his glass along the way. She watched as he added scotch to his glass before pouring some for his father. She turned toward Marsden. "I feared you might be upset that I had tidied this room."

He glanced around as though only just noticing. "I haven't been in here since I lost her. It was her favorite place to be. Other than in my bed, of course."

The heat that had been fading from Portia's cheeks returned. She was grateful that he hadn't seen what had become of this room, was even gladder that she had set it to rights.

"Your inappropriate mention of your bed is making my wife blush," Locksley said as he handed his father a glass.

"Why is it that lovemaking, which can be so glorious, is only whispered about as though it's something tawdry?" the marquess asked. "Or done beneath a piano."

She could have sworn that she heard Locksley growl. "I told you. I was striving to hear the chords more clearly."

"Going deaf, are you?"

Locksley sat in a chair near his father. "I would be grateful not to hear you talking."

"You never were one for being teased. Besides, I fully

understand how this room and the music can seduce. I think you were conceived on top of that piano."

"Oh, dear God," Locksley muttered. "There are some things I'd rather not know."

"And too many things that you should but I have failed to tell you. She's watching us now, you know. Your mother. I think it pleases her to peek through the parted draperies and see us sitting here."

She watched as sadness drifted slowly over her husband's face, and knew that he was bothered by his father's fantasy that the Marchioness of Marsden was still able to look in on them. "Shall I play now?" she asked, hoping to brighten Locksley's mood.

Marsden lifted his glass. "Please."

Rather than play from memory as she'd done before, she used the sheet music that had been in a position on the piano to indicate that it was probably the last song to have been played, or perhaps it had merely been queued up to be played in the future. It didn't matter. She was rather certain that at some point, the Marchioness of Marsden had performed the tune for her husband.

As her fingers flew over the keyboard, she dared a quick glance at the marquess. He looked at peace, his eyes closed, his mouth turned up ever so slightly at the corners. She did hope he was recalling pleasant memories.

And she wondered if a time would ever come when her own husband would recall pleasant memories about her.

Chapter 15

A WEEK later, Portia unlocked a door and led her newest staff members into a room that she was fairly certain had been at least one marchioness's morning room. At the far end, the windows jutted out to create a little alcove, with bookshelves along the wall on either side. She could imagine herself curling up—book in hand—in one of the two large plush chairs near the windows and reading to a little girl nestled in the other.

"Let's get started, shall we?" she ordered as she whipped the draperies open, coughing as the dust floated around her.

Since the marquess hadn't seemed disturbed by the tidying of the music room—in fact he seemed to relish it, since he joined them there each evening shortly after she began to play—she had attacked the marchioness's study with gusto. Now she had a place where she could write letters—if she'd had anyone who would welcome receiving a letter from her. The cook met her there each morning to go over the menu for the evening meal. She kept the midday fare simple—bread, cheese, sometimes soup. She would have a tray carried up to Marsden's bedchamber and she would take her meal there. Without much prompting, she could entice him into speaking about his love. She thought it the most wonderful thing in the world that after so many years, he could still love his Linnie so deeply. She wished she'd an opportunity to know the woman, although through her afternoon visits with the marquess, Portia was beginning to have a sense of his wife's personality and temperament. Of course, over the years, he'd no doubt idealized her, for surely no woman could be that perfect.

But she had obviously been perfect for the marquess. Unlike Portia, who was the absolute worst choice for a wife that the viscount could have made. Although of late, she was finding it a bit difficult to keep up with him in the evenings. She'd begun taking a short nap following her time with the marquess so she wouldn't be completely exhausted when her husband wasn't content with one session of lovemaking but was in the mood for two or three, usually keeping them going until long past midnight. Not that she minded. He was incredibly thorough and was never satisfied unless her pleasure equaled or exceeded his. She wasn't accustomed to such considerations. Sometimes guilt nagged at her because he was a far better husband than she was a wife.

As she began examining each piece of furniture to determine which might need to be taken to Mr. Wortham for a bit of repair, she supposed she'd have more energy for the evenings if she stopped helping the staff as they worked to make each room habitable. But being involved made the days pass more quickly. She'd had two years of being little more than an ornament, waiting to be taken off the shelf. She delighted in all the activity during the day, although she had begun finishing up an hour earlier so she could be bathed and dressed by the time Locksley returned from the mines. He was rather punctual, always arriving home just before the sun set.

Once the furniture was sorted, moved about, rugs rolled up and draperies pulled down so they could all receive a good beating, Portia began on a set of shelves, removing the books one by one and carefully wiping the years of collected dust from them. She didn't know why Locksley insisted on going to the mines every day. She thought he would be better served to hire a capable foreman to see to matters. After all, Locksley was born to be a lord, not a laborer.

But whenever she tried to speak to him of the mines, of why he needed to keep such a close watch on things, he'd merely say, "Not to worry, Portia. I have the means to provide you with your allowance."

His tone was always so blasted snide that she sometimes wanted to reach across the table and tweak his nose. It was the one aspect of their arrangement that disappointed her—that he found fault with her for wanting financial security. If she had insisted Montie provide her with an allowance—and if she'd had the foresight to save it—she would have had options, she wouldn't have been forced to choose a route that left her sick to her stomach. But she had loved him and trusted him and believed him when he'd promised to always take care of her. Was there a greater fool in all of England than she? She would not be so foolish this time around.

"There's his Lordship, returning from the mines," Cullie announced.

Blinking, Portia looked up from the stack of books she'd been sorting—she wanted them returned to the shelves according to author—and gazed out the windows. The afternoon had gotten away from her. She'd learned to judge the hour by the shadows as she couldn't quite bring herself to start the clocks keeping time again. *That*, she had decided, might indeed upset the marquess.

She shoved herself to her feet and walked into the alcove to get a better view of the rider. He seemed to be the same size as Locksley but his clothing was wrong. Instead of the well-tailored clothes the viscount wore, the man's attire was coarse and didn't mold itself to the shape of his body.

"When this room is ready," Cullie said, "you can sit here in the afternoons and await his Lordship's return."

"Only that's not his Lord—" The man was nearer now. His worn hat was pulled low over his brow, shadowing much of his face, but she could see the strong square cut of his jaw. She shook her head. "Why is he wearing such drab clothing?"

"Well, he don't want to wear his finery down into the mines. They'd get ruined right quick while he was working," Cullie said.

Portia's brow was furrowing so deeply that she thought she might give herself a megrim. "He doesn't actually labor in the mines."

When Cullie remained silent, Portia turned to her. The girl looked as though she feared getting sacked. "Cullie? He doesn't labor in the mines."

Cullie's gaze darted around the room, landing on each servant in turn as though she expected one of them to speak. Finally, she settled her eyes back on Portia, licked her lips, took a deep breath. "Yes, m'lady, he does."

"No, he goes in occasionally to check on things." He'd told her as much. "That's the extent of his involvement."

Cullie shook her head. "No, m'lady. He works in the mines."

"You mean digging for ore?"

"Yes, m'lady, and it took some time for the miners to get used to him being beside them, but since the tin played out, he's been trying to help them find more."

Played out? She swung back around, but she could no longer see Locksley. He always came to her smelling of a recent bath. Part of the reason that she'd begun readying herself earlier was so the tub would be back in the bathing room when he returned home. She'd thought he was simply meticulous about being clean. Instead, he'd been working to rid himself of any evidence of his efforts.

"We're finished in here for the day," she called out as she began marching from the room.

"Will you be wanting a bath before dinner?" Cullie asked.

"Later."

First she needed a word with her husband.

LOCKE poured the steaming water into the tub in the bathing room. Mrs. Dorset didn't understand why he didn't have one of the footmen prepare his bath, but the servants were Portia's, not his. He didn't need to take them away from whatever chores his wife had them doing. Besides, the fewer people who saw him in this ragtag state, the better.

After setting down the pail, he arched his back and looked up at the ceiling. Christ, he was tired. But he knew once he saw Portia, the weariness would fade away. Her smile of greeting always seemed to revitalize him. He'd even begun to enjoy her evening recitals, no longer viewing them as an irritating delay to his possessing her, but rather embracing them as a slow, sensual building of awareness. She found a bit of ecstasy in gliding her fingers over the ivory, and he became enthralled watching her.

She was a siren, luring his father out of his reclusiveness. Each evening, he made his way down to the music room. Locke had begun pouring a scotch and setting it on the table beside his father's favorite chair in anticipation

of the marquess's arrival. Sometimes his father spoke of
the love of his life. In the past several nights Locke had
learned more about his mother than he'd learned in all the
years prior.

Apparently, she'd been a bit of a hellion herself: brave,
strong, and bold. He'd only ever known his father as a
broken man, but perhaps he wasn't quite as damaged as
Locke had always thought.

Groaning, he stretched his arms overhead, then lowered his fingers to the water. Too tepid. Another bucket
of boiling water should do the trick. Swinging around, he
came up short at the sight of Portia standing just inside
the doorway. He'd already set aside his dirt-covered
jacket and removed his gloves, but grime had settled into
the creases of his face and neck. He was well aware of his
disheveled—and horribly smelly—state.

Her gaze roamed slowly over him as though she'd
never seen him before. "You work the mines," she stated
quietly but with confidence.

He'd known sooner or later she might learn the truth
of it. He'd have preferred later, but considering that she
now had a few additional servants, and each of them were
no doubt related to someone who labored in the mines,
he saw no point in denying the truth, although he wasn't
going to confess it either. Apparently she had the wisdom
to accurately interpret his silence.

"Does your father know?" she asked into the silence
that followed her earlier words.

"No, and I prefer that he not. I also prefer that you
leave so I may see to my bath."

"How long has it been since there was any tin?"

"I'm not discussing the mines with you but rest assured, you will receive your allowance—"

"Damn you, Locksley!" she cut in with such vehemence that he snapped his head back as though she'd slapped him. Although God help him, the fire burning in her eyes was an aphrodisiac that might have drawn him in if he wasn't embarrassed that she'd learned the truth of his days. "Do you honestly believe that's the reason I'm asking? You're a lord. You're not supposed to be digging in the mines."

"I'm another set of hands, hands for which I don't have to provide a salary."

"So it's been a while." Her tone reflected a fact in the same way a solicitor might make his case before the bench. Why did he feel as though he were the one in the prisoner box?

She took a step toward him. He backed up, slammed into the tub, cursed, pushed out the flat of his palm to still her. "Don't come near me. I reek to high heavens and am likely to cause you to swoon."

A corner of her mouth tilted up. "I'm not as delicate as all that. Why didn't you tell me?"

"Because it's not your business."

Now she was the one to jerk back as though she'd been slapped. "I'm your wife."

"Your job is to warm my bed and provide my heir. That is the extent of your wifely duties. The estate, the management of it, the income are my duties. Nothing is to be gained by discussing them."

"A lessening of your burdens, perhaps?"

"More likely an adding to them, as you'll no doubt begin pestering me for details or resenting if I suggest you not spend so frivolously. You'll not do without, Portia, so I don't see that you need to concern yourself with my troubles."

She gave a brusque nod. "Sometimes, Locksley, you are an utter ass."

With that, she spun on her heel and quit the room.

For reasons he couldn't fathom, he laughed. Long, loud, and hard. Then he did something even more confounding. He moved to the side of the tub, grabbed the edge, and heaved with all his might until he upended it and sent water cascading over the floor.

Bowing his head, he clenched his fists. *Damn. Damn. Damn.* He had never wanted her to learn the truth of how he spent his days, frantically tunneling at the earth, desperate to find even the tiniest vein of ore, to uncover some evidence that more tin existed, that their financial future wasn't completely and utterly hopeless.

𝒩EARLY an hour and a half later, he stood at the window in the library, downing scotch. He'd come straight here from the bathing room, now wearing the clothes he'd donned that morning before changing into the sturdier and rougher attire that he sported when going to the mines.

Portia was correct. He'd been an ass. Was still in danger of behaving as one because he couldn't shake off the anger that riveted through him now that she knew the truth of his situation. He was embarrassed that he got his hands dirty, that he engaged in backbreaking labor that no gentleman should. That he hadn't paid more attention to the mines when he reached his majority, that he hadn't noticed sooner that his father was not the best steward for the estate.

That he returned to the manor each evening covered in sweat and grime. It was bad enough the local villagers knew. But he could envision Portia in London attending a tea, tittering with a group of ladies, laughing at the notion of him working for his supper as though he hadn't been born into an elevated position in Society.

Hearing the footsteps, he turned slightly and watched as she charged into the room, wearing the deep blue gown that always made her appear so incredibly striking, that always made him want to remove the silk in all due haste. It taunted him now because he suspected she was going to object when next he went to touch her with hands that toiled. She had married him assuming him to be a gentleman, but a gentleman did not spend his day in the dank and chilled air beneath ground. A gentleman didn't stink of labor rather than play.

He hadn't been certain she'd join him for dinner now that she knew the truth. He hated the relief that swamped him because she was here, that she wasn't leaving him to stew in solitude.

She came to an abrupt halt before him, her whiskey eyes searching his features, and he wondered what she saw now when she looked at him. A man who feared he might be a worse steward than his father, a man who shouldn't have taken her to wife, who shouldn't be striving to get her with child when he wasn't certain if the lands would ever again be profitable. He shouldn't yet be bringing an heir into this world, and yet he seemed incapable of not plowing into her each night. For a while, when he was lost in the heat of her, his troubles faded away. Yet they always returned with the sun, always—

His thoughts slammed to a halt as he realized she was holding something toward him. Glancing down, he saw resting in her palm the velvet pouch that he'd handed her the morning after they'd married.

"I'm returning the coins to you. I'll keep a tally of what I'm owed, and you can pay me the amount when the mines are again profitable."

"I don't need the coins returned."

"Still, I'm returning them."

"I don't want them."

She spun on her heel, marched to the desk, and tossed them onto the center of it. "I'm giving them back. You don't have a choice."

THE growl that echoed through the room was that of a wounded animal. Portia spun around to see Locksley charging toward her. She almost hiked up her skirts and ran. But she'd fled twice before in her life, and nothing good had come from it.

This time she stood her ground. He tossed his glass aside. It landed on the rug without shattering. Then his hands were on her waist, and he was lifting her onto the desk, coming to stand between her legs.

His green eyes were feral, filled with rage. She thought she should have been frightened, but she trusted that no matter how mad he might get he wouldn't hurt her. His pride was bruised, scored, battered. She could see that now, wished she'd understood earlier what it was costing him to toil in the mines. Why could he not see how remarkable it made him that he didn't simply sit back and hope for the best? That like her, he would do what he must to right a horrendous situation?

"I don't want the bloody money," he ground out. "I don't want you to be kind or generous or understanding."

She tossed her chin. "Never mistake practicality for kindness. You need the funds now to ensure we have more in the future."

His dark laughter echoing around them, he shook his head. "I don't want you to be practical. I don't want you bringing music and sunshine and smiles into this house. I want you for one thing and one thing only." With those large strong hands that had brought her so much pleasure, he grabbed her bodice, corset, chemise, and ripped them all asunder with one mighty tug that caused her breasts to spill out. "This is all I want of you," he growled before taking one nipple in his mouth and sucking hard.

She dropped her head back as pleasure tore through her. "I know."

"I don't want you making me anticipate the end of the day."

He moved to the other breast, closing his mouth around the turgid pearl and tugging. "I know," she barely managed as sensations coursed through her.

"I'm not going to like you. I'm not going to care for you. I'm not going to love you." He bracketed her face, his gaze boring into hers. "I'm not going to give you my heart. Ever."

She nodded jerkily. "I know."

"I don't want you in my life. I want you only in my bed."

"I know," she repeated, for what else could she say? She did know.

He buried his face against her breasts, closed his arms tightly around her. "I will not love you," he emphasized slowly, ardently, and she couldn't help but wonder if he was striving to convince himself more than her that the words he spoke were true.

She also wondered if it would be enough for them if she loved him. Combing her fingers gently through his hair, she repeated softly, "I know."

He pressed his lips to the inside of one breast, needing only to turn his head slightly to kiss the other. "I don't want you to taste so damn good, to feel so damned good."

Raising her legs, she wrapped them around him as securely as she could, considering all the inconvenient petticoats she wore. Perhaps she should apply his rule regarding gloves to her undergarments—never to be worn in the residence. She scraped her fingers through his hair, brought her hands around until she was cupping his face between her palms, tilting his head up so she could hold his gaze. "I know precisely what you don't want. What *do* you want, my lord?"

His harsh curse just before he swooped in to claim her mouth should not have delighted her, but the raw intensity of it had pleasure and satisfaction spiraling through her. She thought he might very well devour her with the feverishness with which he took possession of her lips, her tongue. Always there was a wildness between them, but at that moment it was more untamed, more uncivilized than it had ever been.

She knew he had been battered and bruised by her discovery, but the truth of it was that it only made her want him more. They were more alike than he'd ever realize, willing to do whatever was necessary to protect those who needed protecting, to ensure a safe future for those they loved. Although he would claim to love no one, she was well aware that he cared deeply for his father, for the estates, for the land. She was reckless to hope that some of his caring would be directed her way.

Yet when his heated mouth branded her throat with a series of kisses and bites, she couldn't help but feel that within the realm of pleasure, she belonged to him as he did to her. Here they communicated more honestly than they did at any other time. Here there were no barriers, no lies, no deceptions. Here at least there was raw need, primitive desires, and bared wants.

With an arm around her hips, he dragged her to the very edge of the desk, shoved up her skirts, unfastened his trousers, and plunged deep and sure. Her cry of pleasure mingled with his groan of satisfaction.

"You feel so damned good," he growled, before again

capturing her mouth, his tongue thrusting in a rhythm that matched the movements of his hips, his arm at her back supporting her.

Clinging to him, she tightened her arms around his shoulders. She was a wanton to enjoy this inappropriate coupling so much, with the cool air wafting over her breasts, her straining nipples tingling as his jacket rubbed over them. Here in the library, on the desk, he pumped into her hard and fast. His mouth left hers to taste her elsewhere: her chin, her throat, the sensitive skin just below her ear where her pulse thrummed wildly.

Trying to hold back her cries, she bit her lower lip, but the action did nothing to muffle her scream when she finally came apart in his arms, trembling with the force of her release. His groan was that of a conqueror as he tensed, pouring his seed into her. With her legs, she squeezed his hips, tightened her muscles around him. He jerked, grunted before dropping his head to her shoulder.

"You have ruined this desk for me," he said, his breaths coming in hard, short bursts. "How can I work here now without seeing you sprawled over it?"

"I'm not sprawled."

Lifting his head, he held her gaze briefly before lowering his eyes to her breasts. "You can't go into dinner like that."

She laughed lightly. "No, I suppose I can't."

Stepping back, he lowered her skirts, then began to fasten his trousers. She didn't want to acknowledge how bereft she felt with his leaving. He whipped off his jacket and draped it over her shoulders. She'd barely clutched the opening closed when she suddenly found herself in his arms, being carried from the room.

"I can walk," she said.

"After the way you cried out, I assume you're far too weak. Your legs are still trembling."

She felt the heat suffuse her face. "You weren't so quiet yourself, you know."

"And whose fault is that?"

She didn't bother to hide her smile as she laid her head against his shoulder.

Gilbert stepped into the hallway. "My lord, dinner—is Lady Locksley all right, my lord?"

"She has come apart at the seams, Gilbert."

Portia slapped her hand over her mouth to stop her laughter from erupting.

"My lord?"

"My London seamstress is not as accomplished with a needle as I was led to believe," Portia said, surprised she was able to keep her voice so steady. "Her stitching didn't hold as it should."

"As you can well imagine, Gilbert, Lady Locksley has had quite a shock. We'll be dining in our bedchamber. Have Cullie bring up a tray in an hour."

"In an hour, sir?" Gilbert asked as he managed in spite of his arthritic knees to hop out of the way as Locksley barged past him and into the foyer.

"An hour, Gilbert. I need to settle my wife's nerves first."

Once they were headed up the stairs, she took his earlobe between her teeth and nipped gently, relishing his groan but wanting it to sound more tortured. "When we get to our bedchamber, you might as well rip everything off. It's beyond saving."

His responding growl served to make her wish he'd walk faster.

ℋE'D never known a woman like her—ever. Following along with his tale about the seams, she matched Lady

Godiva for boldness, and he could well imagine her riding naked through the streets without a single blush forming anywhere on her person. And damned if he didn't want her again with a fierceness that made him feel barbaric.

After he kicked the door to his bedchamber closed behind them, he did precisely as she suggested and ripped what remained of her clothing from her body. There was something immensely satisfying and feral in the rasp of rending satin and silk, in the way that Portia simply stood there and let him have his way with her, her eyes smoldering with needs that matched his own. When she was completely bared, he lifted her back into his arms, carried her to the foot of the bed, and tossed her onto her stomach, leaving her legs to dangle over the mattress.

Breathing heavily, she rose up onto her elbows and gazed back over her shoulder at him as he tore off his own clothes, buttons popping off and pinging onto the floor with his haste. So desperate to possess her, he'd considered merely unfastening his trousers again but he enjoyed too much the feel of her silken skin against his. He was going to take her fast and hard, but by God, he wanted no cloth between them this time.

When he'd shed the last of his clothing, he stepped between her thighs, parted them with a spreading of his own legs. Leaning over her, he layered a series of kisses along her shoulder, following the curve of her neck. "You said I could take you from behind," he rasped.

Her eyes heated. "So I did."

He bracketed her hips, lifted them slightly, and plunged into the molten depths, her cry of satisfaction echoing between them. He slid one hand around until he brushed the tight curls at her apex, then parted the folds and pressed a finger to the swollen nubbin. He applied more pressure, caressing her outwardly while slowly stroking her inwardly. She whimpered and wiggled. He rained kisses between her shoulder blades, could feel her tightening around him as her whimpers turned to throaty moans and her breaths became uneven.

"Fly, Portia," he rasped near her ear before swirling his tongue along the delicate shell. "Fly."

Her cry came as she bucked against him, and her muscles closed tightly around him. He grabbed her hips and pounded into her a mere handful of times before his own release tore through him, darkening the edges of his vision until all he could see was her profile, with lashes half lowered, lips parted in wonder.

Sinking down, he pressed his cheek to hers, placing his arms so he bore his weight, and his chest barely skimmed her back. But it was enough to tame the beast that raged within him, the one that wanted her to be different than she was, to be the fortune-hunting title chaser that he'd thought he married.

She shifted her arm slightly, and her hand was suddenly in his hair, holding him near. And he realized with unerring accuracy that he had made many mistakes in his life, but when it came to her, he may have made the greatest one of all, because it was quite possible that he could come to care for her a great deal.

And that was the very last thing he wanted. Unfortunately he feared it might be too late to worry over what he wanted.

Chapter 16

$\mathcal{P}$ORTIA leaned forward from her comfy pillows, snagged a grape from the tray that rested near her knees, and popped the dark red fruit into her mouth.

Lounging at the foot of the bed where a short time ago he'd taken her with such unbridled enthusiasm, her husband sipped his burgundy wine. His gaze drifted to her chest. Perhaps because she hadn't pulled her dressing gown as tightly around her as she might have and she'd left a good bit of flesh visible. She didn't know why she took such delight in teasing him with flashes of skin.

"Be sure to send word to your London seamstress that you're in need of another blue gown," he said.

She shook her head. "I have enough gowns."

His jaw tautened for a heartbeat before relaxing, and she knew he was taking exception to her frugality, that he was insulted by the notion that he couldn't properly provide for her. "Not in that shade of blue. It's my favorite as it brings out the red in your hair."

She laughed lightly. "As though I need anything to bring out the red in my hair. The devil's doing, my father often said." When his eyes narrowed, she wished she'd bit back the words—better yet bitten off her tongue.

"Why would he say that?" Locksley asked.

Sighing, she popped another grape into her mouth, chewed slowly. She didn't think the tray of fruit, cheeses, and sliced meats had originally been prepared for supper but she suspected Mrs. Dorset had decided simpler fare was required for dinner in a bedchamber. Portia swallowed. "Because neither my father nor my mother has red hair. Hers is a dark brown, his blond. Although I always thought his mustache hinted at red when the sun hit it just right, but he never acknowledged that."

"Did he accuse your mother of being unfaithful?"

"No, he merely thought I had more of the devil in me than I should." And on occasion believed he could beat it out of her. But she didn't want to travel down that path, and as Locksley had asked a personal question—

"How long has it been since the mines produced tin?"

He reached for the bottle of wine on the tray and poured more into his glass. "Close to two years."

"That's the reason you stopped traveling."

He took a sip, nodded. "It seemed prudent. The mines were still producing but their output was dwindling. In all his years of hiding away here, my father never neglected the estates, but the steward expressed concerns that the marquess wasn't taking the diminishing income seriously." He lifted a shoulder, dropped it back down. "I realized it was time I stepped up to the task. I discovered I liked the challenge of it, especially as everything wasn't moving along swimmingly well. I think I might find it boring if there was nothing to worry over."

She suspected he would. A man who scaled mountains certainly wouldn't be content to merely stroll over even ground.

"Then about six months after I took over, the mines stopped producing altogether," he added.

"And you began to work in them," she stated.

"I thought I might have more luck finding what the miners had missed. Not to mention that it drove me to distraction to be sitting about waiting for word that a new source of ore had been struck."

"The lords I've known wouldn't have cared. They'd have continued to play and let their fathers worry over it."

"Then I suspect they'll find their estates in ruination when they inherit. Things are changing for the aristocracy. I don't think we can blithely go on without recognizing that we are on the cusp of becoming obsolete."

"There will always be an aristocracy."

"But our role is diminishing. Or at the very least our carefree lifestyle must change. We can't continue to be pampered without realizing it comes at a cost."

He placed a slice of ham and some cheese on a cracker and ate it as though to signal the end to the conversation. But she wasn't yet ready to let it go. "I can't imagine you were ever pampered."

"Not here, not really. We had so few servants. I like doing for myself. One of my first evenings at a gentleman's club—I was in the drawing room, sitting near the fire, enjoying a bit of brandy. An older gentleman, an earl, was sitting nearby. He called a footman over because the fire needed stirring and a log added. And I thought, 'If you're chilled then get up off your bloody ass and stir the fire yourself.' Here we never called a servant into a room to take care of something we could take care of ourselves. It was both enlightening and disturbing once we began moving about in London."

Adjusting a pillow behind her back, she settled against it. "You must have ground your back teeth that first afternoon when I said I would call in a footman to move the chair for me."

He studied her intently, so thoroughly that she felt a

need to squirm, and it was all she could do to hold still. "You lied that afternoon, Portia. You wouldn't call in a footman. You'd move it yourself. Why did you wish us to think otherwise, to see you as a snobbish haughty woman?"

"Like your earl who wouldn't stir his own embers, every aristocratic woman I've met comes across as quite helpless. I thought the same behavior would be expected of me."

"What else did you lie about?"

So much. With a low fire crackling on the hearth, her body sated by pleasure and food, her husband speaking with her as though she were his equal, she almost told him everything—but what good would come of it now? The pleasantness between them would shatter, utterly and completely, never to return. Of that she was certain.

"You should tell your father about the mines," she said instead, shoving any possible confession into the furthest corners of her mind.

He flashed a quick grin that reflected both his expectation that she'd avoid his question and turn the tables back on him, and his disappointment that she had. He was beginning to know her far too well, but all the deciphering of her actions wouldn't uncover her secrets. "He doesn't need to be worrying over them."

"But if, as you claim, he managed them quite well until recently he might have some insights to offer."

"He's not going to know precisely where we'll find more ore. It's not as though he has the ability to see through the ground and into the earth."

"So you'll just keep digging and being frustrated when your efforts reap no rewards?"

"For now. I'm not ready to give up on it. Somewhere there must be more."

And until then he'd simply continue to tear into the earth alongside the miners, to put himself at risk. She'd heard of cave-ins. "Is it safe?"

"We reinforce the walls as we go. There hasn't been an accident in years."

She nodded but took very little solace from his words. While she admired his determination to go into the mines and work beside those who toiled and provided an income for the estate, she also detested that he placed himself in danger. For what? A few bob? She wanted to lessen his burdens, but suspected she'd only added to them. "I could let a footman and maid go. I can let them all go."

"We're not quite destitute yet, Portia. Speaking of the servants, are you finished here?" He waved his hand over the tray.

"Yes. Shall I ring for someone to take it away?"

"I'll see to it." He rolled off the bed, picked up the tray, and carried it over to the low table by the fire. When he returned he stretched out beside her, resting on an elbow, and trailed the fingers of his free hand along her collar-bone. "What I said earlier, when we were in the library, is inexcusable."

"You were upset that I uncovered your secret." Perhaps even a bit embarrassed to be caught working when nobility did not labor. Although she wasn't going to point that out to him. "Besides, Locksley, I have no illusions regarding your feelings toward me."

He slid his hand up her neck, stopping just short of her jaw, his thumb stroking the delicate skin where her pulse thrummed. "I like you, Portia. A great deal more than is wise."

"I've never much cared for wise men."

He flashed her a grin. "I do so love your rejoinders,

your tendency to speak your mind. I like having you out
of the bed as much as I do having you in it."

She wondered if he noticed the jump in her pulse at
his words. It would be so much simpler for them both
if he wanted only sex. Why did she have to feel so glad
that he enjoyed more? He could so easily break her heart.
She might even bruise his. Better if their hearts weren't
involved, but God help her, she wanted something deep,
lasting, and true with him. She wanted to be worthy of
the ring he'd placed on her finger, a gorgeous gold band of
emeralds and diamonds that symbolized an undying love.
Not that she expected to ever have his love, but whatever
he felt for her would surely die if he ever learned the truth.

Tilting her head down slightly, he brushed his lips
lightly over hers, as softly as a butterfly landing on a
petal. Tenderness was so much more devastating than the
rapid possession he'd exhibited earlier. Gentleness could
undo her, could fill her with so many regrets.

"Portia," he whispered, pressing a kiss to the corner of
her mouth. "Portia." His lips touched the corner near her
eye. "Portia." His breath skimmed over her temple.

"Killian," she breathed out on a soft sigh as her eyes
closed and she began to melt down into the pillows, the
mattress.

His mouth returned to hers, a bit more demanding.
She parted her lips, welcomed the slow, sure stroke of his
tongue over hers. Threading her fingers through his hair,
she pressed—

The rapid tapping on the door startled her. "M'lord?"

"Damnation," Locksley growled. "Gilbert has the
worst timing in the world."

"At least I'm still decently covered."

"I'll remedy that as soon as I've chased him off." He
shoved himself from the bed. When he returned, she'd

remove the shirt and trousers he'd donned before Cullie had arrived with their tray of food.

He swung open the door. "What is it, Gilbert?"

"His Lordship is in the dining room waiting on you."

"My father is in the dining room?"

"Aye. He won't let us begin serving him until you and Lady Locksley are there."

"Did you tell him we're dining in our bedchamber this evening?"

"I couldn't tell him that, m'lord. It might put images in his head of other things going on in here. A decent sort doesn't discuss bedchambers."

Her husband heaved a great sigh. "I'll be down in a moment." He closed the door, pressed his forehead against it.

"It seems we're dining again," Portia offered.

Turning, he started buttoning his shirt. "No need for you to go down. I'll keep him company."

"Don't be ridiculous. I'll ring for Cullie. It'll take me a while, but you go ahead and join your father."

He dropped into a chair and began tugging on his boots. "I've no idea why he decided to dine with us to-night."

"Lonely, I suspect. Maybe he wanted your company for more than an hour as I play music."

"If anything, it's your company he craves. I think you remind him of how things were before my mother died."

"And how is that?"

"Full of life."

$\mathcal{A}$s Locke made his way toward the dining room, he had never been more grateful for an interruption in his life. He'd been on the verge of confessing that he more than liked Portia; he held genuine affection for her.

Once those words were spoken there would be no going back on them.

In the library, he'd voiced all the things he didn't want as though that would stop her from delivering them. As though it were within her nature not to care, not to give. She returned the blasted allowance, offered to reduce her staff, was concerned with his welfare.

Of course she was, he chastised himself. Until she provided an heir, she was in danger of losing all this. But the argument ran hollow and untrue. She had shown herself that first day. But not her complete self. She was comprised of myriad facets, complex and intriguing. He could spend a lifetime striving to unravel the mysteries of Portia Gadstone St. John.

Damn it all to hell if he didn't want that lifetime with her. He wanted her in his life until his hair turned silver and his sight faded. He wanted her when his body was stiff and bent. He'd married her expecting to want no more from her than the nights. More the fool was he because now he wanted every second of every day.

He strode into the dining room. His father, sitting at the head of table, leaned over slightly as though he wished to see around Locke.

"Portia is still readying herself," he told his father as he drew out the chair at the foot of the table. "Forgive our tardiness. We weren't expecting you to dine with us."

"I decided I wanted conversation as much as listening to music. She's changing things, Locke. More swiftly than I expected."

Locke turned to the butler. "For God's sake, Gilbert, pour us some wine."

"Yes, m'lord."

Once the wine was poured, Locke took hold of the

stem of his glass, swirled the burgundy contents. "I can tell her to stop, to leave things be."

"Does she do what you tell her?"

Locke couldn't stop the smile from spreading over his face. "Not usually, no."

"You married her because you thought she'd run roughshod over me."

"I deduced she might take advantage, yes. I assumed I'd be better able to keep her in line. Odd thing is, I like that she's fiercely independent."

His father nodded with satisfaction. "I knew you would."

"You garnered her nature from her letters?"

The marquess shrugged. "I believed so, yes. So far, she is very much as I expected, taking the bull by the horns, making this place hers. Do you know when I leave my bedchamber and walk into the hallway, I smell jasmine rather than oranges? Your mother always smelled of oranges. I thought if I allowed nothing to change, my memories of her would remain strong. Odd thing is, since Portia arrived, my memories of your mother are stronger than ever. And speaking of the angel—" His father shoved back his chair and stood.

Locke glanced back halfway expecting to see his mother standing there. But it was his wife in a pale green gown. He did wish he'd taken more care with the blue. And he wondered if his father would consider her an angel if he knew how Portia enticed Locke into doing the most wicked things with her, if his father knew that she could hold her own in a bedchamber. If she'd married his father, the Marquess of Marsden would have been dead by dawn of his first night with his new wife.

Truly Locke had saved his father by stepping in.

"Sorry I'm a bit late," Portia said as she took the chair Locke held out for her.

"Nonsense, my dear." His father sat. "I should have alerted you that I had decided to begin joining you for dinner."

Portia's gaze swung between Locke as he settled into his place and his father. "So this is to become a regular occurrence?"

"If you don't mind."

"Of course not, although we tend to dine a bit earlier."

His father's brow furrowed. "Have you already eaten then?"

"Only some cheese and fruit," Locke assured him. "I'm famished now." He signaled to Gilbert, who immediately left to no doubt order the footmen about.

"So tell me, my dear," his father began, "which room are you tidying now?"

"I believe it's a morning room or perhaps a marchioness's library. It has some bookshelves. The sofas and chairs are covered in yellow fabric with flowers embroidered into it."

"Ah, yes, my Linnie liked to read in that room in the afternoons. Looking through the windows, she could see me returning from the mines. Once I walked into that room to discover her stark naked and waiting for me. God, how she laughed at the look on my face. She had a contagious laugh. I couldn't hear it without laughing back."

Locke cleared his throat. "Portia, I believe we need to have all the furniture in the residence reupholstered if not completely replaced."

"Don't be a prude, Locke," his father said.

"I think it's wonderful that you enjoyed each other so much," Portia said.

Good God, had neither of them any shame? He'd considered himself to be a libertine, but his exploits were tame compared to his father's.

"If I'd known our time together would be so short, I'd have never spent a moment away from her."

"You might not have enjoyed your time as much, because you'd have been distracted by the thought of losing her," Portia said.

"There is that. I suppose not knowing is a gift."

Thank God the servants arrived with the first course. Surely now his father would go on to more appropriate conversation.

"By the by," his father said, "Ashe and Edward will be arriving in a fortnight with their families. Might want to tidy up the billiards room."

"Do not tell us you took my mother on the billiards table," Locke stated succinctly.

His father winked at Portia. "As you wish. I won't tell you."

She had the audacity to laugh. A cold chill skittered through Locke with the realization that if she were no longer here, he would still hear her laughter echoing within the rooms.

Chapter 17

As Portia stared at her reflection in the mirror of her dressing table, she was somewhat nervous about the arrival of the marquess's wards this afternoon. It was one thing to be paraded about the village as the viscount's wife. It was quite another to socialize with respectable ladies who were well above her not only in station but in reproach when it came to behavior. After all, one was married to a duke, the other to her second earl. While the countess's second marriage and the early arrival of her son had created quite the scandal, it didn't change the fact that she had noble blood coursing through her veins.

"If I didn't know better, I'd think you were dreading today," Locke said.

She glanced over to where he'd sat to tug on his boots. Finished with the task, he leaned forward, his elbows resting on his thighs. So remarkably handsome, so self-assured. He had no plans to go to the mines today. She suspected he wouldn't frequent them until after their guests left. "I'm simply trying to decide which gown to wear." Swinging around on the bench, she faced him squarely. "I don't want to embarrass you or behave in a manner I ought not."

Narrowing his eyes, he scrutinized her. "Surely when

you answered my father's advert, you expected to entertain nobility."

"To be quite honest, no. I knew him to be a recluse and rather thought that my time would be spent with him and him alone." She waved a hand. "Oh, I thought you might be here on occasion, but I suspected you wouldn't want to have anything to do with me."

"If you never expected to entertain, why the devil are you tidying the rooms?"

The billiards room had not been high on her list to be set to rights, although in hindsight, she supposed it should have been. It would bring pleasure to her husband. When she'd first walked through it, she'd seen evidence of footprints left by young boys. Over the years, the dust had covered them but it hadn't filled them in. She could well imagine the excitement that had thrummed through them when they'd discovered the contents of that room on one of their midnight excursions.

"Because it seemed a shame for a residence as magnificent as this one to be uncared for. Surely you want your children to treasure their heritage. How can they if we leave it all to rot?"

She'd also cleaned up the nursery. The marquess had sat in the chamber and watched while she and the servants saw to that task. He wore a soft smile as though envisioning his grandchildren sleeping and playing in there. The guilt had taken hold and she'd been unable to shake it off completely. Women were so much more intuitive than men. Perhaps that was what she feared: that the ladies would see right through her, would recognize the reasons behind her desperation, would figure her out.

As for the rooms for their guests, she'd discovered that Ashebury and Greyling both had bedchambers down the hall. They'd merely needed to be tidied.

She didn't like that her husband held his tongue and continued to study her as though he was beginning to realize the truth about her.

"I'm a commoner, Locksley," she felt compelled to remind him.

"So is Minerva."

The Duke of Ashebury's wife. "Her mother is nobility, so she has some blue blood in her veins. Regardless, she grew up among the aristocracy. Her father is wealthy enough that a king would have asked for her hand."

"Read that in the gossip sheets, did you?"

Gossip shared by a couple of women she knew, silly women like her who had thought they were headed for better things only to find themselves in a far worse predicament. "I'm afraid I might set a foot wrong and they'll think you a fool for taking me as your wife."

After unfolding that tall, lean body of his that only an hour earlier had her screaming his name, he walked over to her, crouched, and brushed stray strands of her hair back from her face. "You may have been born a commoner, Portia, but you are now a lady. As such, you will be afforded respect and nothing you do will be questioned—least of all by those who are arriving today. The Marquess of Marsden is the closest thing to a father that Ashe and Edward have had for nearly a quarter of a century now. From the moment they arrived, they became my brothers. Think of them as family. As for their wives, they're extraordinary women. I assure you that they'll not sit in judgment. But if they do, they'll find you remarkable."

Her lips parting slightly, she stared at him, surprised by his compliment, so rarely did he offer her praise. As though embarrassed, he shot to his feet and headed for the door. "Wear the lavender gown."

With that, he was gone.

Things between them were changing—slowly, irrevocably. He was coming to truly care for her. She was rather certain of it. She wouldn't feel guilty about it, would not wish that she wasn't coming to care for him as well. Instead she would merely pray that he never learned the truth.

*H*AVING spotted the coaches from an upstairs window, Locke had escorted Portia outside so they could welcome their guests. He wasn't surprised that the four coaches arrived at the same time, two bearing the Ashebury crest and the others bearing the Greyling crest. He'd assumed that his friends would meet up so they could arrive together in order to receive the same first impression of his wife.

He didn't know why Portia's nervousness called to his protective nature. Perhaps because since she'd come to Havisham Hall she'd been so fiercely independent, stood toe to toe with him, that he'd assumed she never doubted, never wavered, never had second thoughts. He didn't like her appearing vulnerable, susceptible to hurt. Had he opened his door to see the worry in her eyes and the number of times she licked her lips while waiting for the coaches to draw to a halt, he might have taken more pity on her that first day. He still wouldn't have allowed her to marry his father, but things between them might have started out on a different foot.

"You have nothing to prove to them," he said quietly, and she snapped her head around to stare at him. He disliked the moments when she appeared so young, so vulnerable. "They didn't ask me to approve their selection in wives. I'm not going to ask them to approve mine."

"Do they know how our marriage came about?"

"I'm not sure what my father may have told them. I merely wrote that I'd taken a wife—just a bit of information in case they visited. Show them the backbone you showed me that first day and you'll do fine."

"It was easier then as I didn't care whether or not you liked me."

He laughed. "I didn't care if you liked me either."

"I didn't. I thought you a pompous ass."

He grinned. "Imagine them the same way then."

"I'd prefer they fancy me a bit."

They were going to adore her. He stiffened with the thought that had sprung forth so easily, with such surety. If they felt that way toward her, how could he not? Except he refused to allow anything other than his head to rule him and his emotions. It was merely practical to like her, as it made things between them more pleasant and enjoyable. He wasn't going to confuse practicality with love. Thank goodness the coaches finally drew to a halt. He needed to turn his attention to matters other than striving to explain his ludicrous thoughts. Before he even realized what he was doing, his hand was on Portia's waist, giving a gentle squeeze. "Let's introduce them to Lady Locksley."

PORTIA was determined to be a good hostess. Her parents had entertained frequently enough that she'd learned early on how to make someone feel comfortable. On occasion they'd even welcomed nobility into their home.

But none of their guests had been as important on a personal level as those who were pouring out of the coaches were to Locksley. She not only wanted to make him proud, she wanted him to be pleased with her efforts. Remaining where she was, she watched as servants and children spilled out of the last two coaches while her husband greeted with a handshake and a clap on a shoulder the man who agilely leaped out of the first coach bearing a ducal crest. The Duke of Ashebury. They were of equal height, the duke's hair not quite as black as Locksley's. Beside Ashebury, her husband appeared darker, more dangerous, more forbidden. He looked to be the sort her mother would have warned her against.

Yet he was the one who'd saved her.

She shook off that thought as the duke turned back and assisted from the coach a woman with hair that appeared at once both dark and red, depending on how the sun played over it. The former Miss Minerva Dodger, now the Duchess of Ashebury. Her smile was bright as she gave Locksley a hug. Portia was taken aback by the sharp stab of jealousy that pierced her chest. The woman was married to a dashing duke. She wasn't going to seek a dalliance with the viscount, although her easy manner told Portia that she would be as comfortable greeting a prince or a king. But then according to the gossip sheets, Minerva's dowry had equaled the treasury of some small countries. Portia assumed when one was graced with so much money, one was relaxed around a good many people.

A wheat-haired gentleman and dark-haired lady had exited the earl's coach and now approached Locksley. He hugged the woman, pressed a kiss to her cheek. The Countess of Greyling, who had won the hearts of two earls. Then Locksley was shaking hands with Greyling. They exchanged a few words, a grin, a chuckle.

Watching the camaraderie shared between the group, Portia had never felt so isolated or alone. Instinctually, she knew they'd never abandon each other, regardless of foolish mistakes or errors in judgment. She'd have traded her soul for such loyalty in friends or family.

Locksley turned to her and held out his hand. Taking a deep, shuddering breath, she walked to him, placed her palm against his, and welcomed his fingers closing firmly around hers. "Allow me the honor of introducing my wife, Portia."

"According to your letter I expected her to be a toad," Ashebury said. "Pleasantly surprised to discover she's not."

"I didn't describe her in my letter."

"Exactly."

"Don't speak of her in the third person as though she's not here," Minerva said, slapping her husband playfully on the arm, before turning to Portia. "Ashe is a photographer. He spends a great deal of time noticing how things appear and trying to capture the truth about them through the lens of his camera."

Then Portia was determined to never sit for him, because she didn't need him uncovering her truth. "It's a pleasure to meet you, Your Graces."

"Oh, please, let's not be quite so formal. I'm Minerva. This is Julia." She indicated the dark-haired woman. "And Grey."

"I prefer Edward," Greyling said, taking Portia's hand and pressing a kiss to her knuckles.

"He's not yet quite comfortable with the title," Julia said, moving in and bussing a light kiss over Portia's cheek. "Welcome to the family."

"Thank you. I hope you'll find the accommodations to your liking, but if there is anything—"

"What are you up to, sweetheart?" Edward asked, and Portia looked over to see him reaching down to a small girl less than three who was holding on to his trouser leg and peering around it. He hefted her up into his arms. "Say hello, Lady Allie."

She buried her face against his shoulder. "My brother's daughter is a bit shy among strangers."

"A hellion, though, once she gets used to you," Ashe assured Portia.

She received only a quick introduction to the Ashebury and Greyling heirs, held by their nannies, before Locksley was whisking them all to the terrace where the marquess was waiting for them.

The affection that both couples and their children felt for Marsden was obvious and heartwarming. It was also apparent that he adored the children, no doubt part of the reason that he'd taken matters into his own hands to acquire an heir. Tears threatened to well up as she imagined the love he would shower upon her child. All of London might think him mad but she thought when it came to love he could very well prove to be the sanest person she'd ever met.

"That wasn't so bad, was it?" Locksley asked near her ear, standing slightly behind her.

She shook her head. "I rather like them. Your father is wonderful with the children." She watched as the marquess took Lady Allie's hand and began walking with her through the weeds. Portia sighed. "I need to get to work on the garden."

"Not today," he groused.

She laughed. "Not today." But soon. If Marsden didn't object. Perhaps she'd plant his wife's favorite flowers. Watching him, watching his wards and their wives, watching the children, all made her long for the warmth of family she'd never had, for the love she knew her husband would never shower upon her.

"So how did you meet her?" Edward asked. "She's not familiar."

He, Ashe, and Locke were sitting in chairs near the fireplace in the library, glasses of scotch in hand. Portia had taken the women to the morning room for a spot of tea. His father had claimed to be in need of a nap, although Locke suspected he was playing with the children in the nursery. He would not feel guilty because his father seemed to take such delight in the little ones and Locke had yet to provide him with an heir. "Know every woman in London, do you?"

"Quite a few, yes."

As a bachelor, Edward had been the most promiscuous among them, but as the second in line to the title, he'd never expected to marry. Then he'd fallen in love with his brother's widow and that was that.

"So she's from London?" Ashe asked.

"She traveled from London. Her family lives in York-shire." He gave Edward a pointed look. "Gadstone?"

"Not familiar with the name."

Locke grimaced. "Actually Gadstone is her married name. I don't know her family name."

"Bit odd that," Ashe mused.

"My father arranged to marry her. Until she arrived for the wedding I'd never met her."

Ashe and Edward exchanged glances before Ashe said, "I beg your pardon?"

"It's a long story, but my father took out an advert for a wife. She answered it. Except I didn't trust her."

"So you married her?" Edward asked incredulously.

"Better me than my father." The whole thing sounded ludicrous and made him come across as a fool. "He signed a damned contract stating that the girl would marry when she arrived. It was either him or me."

Edward burst out laughing. "The clever bugger. I'd wager that all along he planned for it to be you."

"You'd win that wager. I figured it out a bit late. Not that I have any complaints. She's comely enough and quite talented in areas where I appreciate talent."

"Good in bed then?" Ashe asked boldly.

"Marvelous in bed."

"Your father had been after you to take a wife," Edward pointed out.

"He never much liked us not obeying him, did he?"

"He seems . . ." Ashe's voice trailed off as he studied his scotch. "*Happier* I suppose is the word I'm looking for. More at ease."

"Portia has changed things around here a bit. They're not quite so gloomy." Understatement. Not all the changes she'd made were visible. He expected at any minute for the clocks to simply start ticking on their own. "It's been a while since my father was out chasing wraiths over the moors."

"You don't suppose he's upstairs filling the children's heads with tales of ghosts snatching them in the night, do you?" Edward asked, clear concern in his voice.

"They're too young to fully comprehend what he may be spouting," Ashe assured him.

"Allie's not. She's sharp as a whip, that one. Took after her father. If I don't finish with a bedtime story, she'll remind me the next night exactly where I left off. Uncanny the things she comprehends and recalls."

"Is it difficult raising your brother's daughter?" Locke asked.

Edward shook his head. "Not a day goes by that I don't wish Albert were still here, but having Allie in my life is no hardship, even if I'm not the one who sired her. I see a good deal of Albert in her."

Which meant he saw a good deal of himself. Although Locke had never had difficulty telling the twins apart, some people had.

"Do you suppose we have time before dinner for a quick ride over the moors?" Ashe asked.

"Thought you'd never ask," Locke said.

"*I* COULD stay in this room all day," Minerva mused on a soft sigh.

Portia had brought them to the morning room to enjoy their tea and biscuits. They were sitting in the area near the windows that would be jutting out into a garden if they possessed one. It would no doubt be next year before she had flowers blooming.

"Whenever we visited," Julia began, "I was curious about the rooms hidden behind closed doors, but was always afraid I'd find a ghost lurking about."

"No, only spiders," Portia assured her.

Julia visibly shuddered. "You are courageous."

"Hardly. It just made me sad to think of everything being left to ruin."

"This house has needed a woman's touch for a good many years," Julia said. "I'm glad you're here. It feels different already, more welcoming, less frightening. And the marquess seems quite content."

"He's anticipating an heir."

"Are you with child?" Minerva asked.

Portia quickly shook her head. "It's too soon."

Minerva smiled. "Not really. It can happen the first time as easily as any other time. Of course I am assuming that Locksley has exercised his husbandly rights."

Portia wondered if she'd suddenly landed in the middle of summer. Her skin was clammy and warm. "Fervently and rather often," she said, her voice low. She'd discussed men quite frankly and openly with a couple of other women when she lived in London. She didn't know why she was uncomfortable with these two. Perhaps because they were ladies, and she'd always assumed the upper-crust females never carried on conversations about what went on behind closed doors.

"Honestly, Minerva, leave off," Julia said, making Portia grateful for the rebuke. "Poor Portia is turning as red as an apple. Not everyone is as comfortable as you discussing such intimate topics."

"But we should be. There should be no shame in our bodies or the way they function. It's part of life, to be celebrated really."

"Would you care for more tea?" Portia asked, ready to move on to something less personal.

"I hope I didn't offend," Minerva offered.

"No, not at all."

"Oh, there they go," Julia said.

Portia looked to the window where her guest was gazing out. She saw Locksley and the others galloping off over the moors. "You say that as though you expected it."

Turning back to her, Julia smiled softly. "They usually ride out shortly after we arrive. I think it reminds them of when they were young and wild, although I suspect back then they were hoping to sight a ghost."

"Julia knows them better than anyone," Minerva said. "Well, I know my husband better than she does, of course, but she's known them longer."

"I've been in the family longer," Julia conceded. "Although they may not be related by blood, they are a family. Albert and Edward were only seven when their parents died. Ashe was eight. Locke was six when they moved here."

Portia eased up to the edge of her chair. "It must have been strange for him. He told me that he was alone before they arrived, had no other children with whom to play, not even from the village."

"As I understand it, yes, he was quite isolated here. The marquess was still in the depths of his despair over the loss of his wife, even though it had been years since her death. He never abused them, though. You won't hear a one of them say a bad word about him."

Still, she tried to imagine what it had been like for Locksley. Perhaps he climbed walls to gain his father's attention. "What was he like when you met him?"

Julia laughed. "Younger than he is now. I suppose it's been eight years or so since I met him. He was always more contemplative than the others. Quieter. Not one to engage in idle conversation. Not that the ladies seemed to mind. As long as he danced with them, they didn't care if he didn't speak at all. Although actually he seldom attended a ball." She shook her head. "To be quite honest, he hardly ever spent any time in London. I think he prefers the solitude and barrenness of this place."

"Although I daresay there probably isn't quite as much solitude now that you're here," Minerva said. "By the by, how did you manage to capture his attention and lure him into marriage?"

Portia released a deep sigh. She didn't really want to go into the details. "The marquess arranged it. I required security; he required an heir. Locksley obliged. I don't think you'll find a marriage in all of Britain that is based on more convenience than ours."

"But you love him," Minerva said.

Portia felt as though Minerva had slammed her balled fist into the soft area just below her sternum. She was no longer a young, naïve girl foolish enough to fall in love with a man who would never truly love her. "No."

She did wish the word rang truer, sounded more firm.

"You do realize he cares for you," Julia offered.

Once again, Portia was feeling warm, almost dizzy. She forced out the words. "I assure you that he holds no deep affection for me."

Julia and Minerva exchanged a knowing glance.

"My dear, I believe you're wrong there," Minerva said. "Based on the way Locksley looks at you, I'd say he was besotted."

She shook her head. He couldn't love her. It would make things more difficult if he did. She'd married him because she'd known he'd never love her. It was so much easier when he wanted from her only one thing, when he viewed her as merely a bedmate, a body to be used. That her silly heart might long for his love was merely wishful thinking. It wasn't practical, and her head knew it to be a terrible notion.

"You're wrong," Portia insisted. "He has sworn to never love."

"She has a point, Minerva," Julia said. "It is his favorite mantra to repeat."

"He can repeat it all he likes. The heart hardly ever listens to what we tell it. It has a tendency to go its own way. He might not be madly in love but I'd wager my entire fortune that his heart is not locked up as tightly as he might wish."

Contrary to what Minerva might believe, Portia knew that did not bode well for her future.

LOCKE couldn't remember ever being with a woman who made his chest swell with pride. He'd certainly not expected it of Portia when he'd married her, but then nothing about his marriage to her was as he'd predicted. Well, except for what passed in the bedchamber. He'd judged her abilities correctly there.

But he hadn't anticipated that she'd be an outstanding hostess. During dinner, the fare had been splendid, the wine excellent, the conversation pleasant. It didn't matter who was discussed, Portia was familiar with them—not personally but based on their exploits captured in the gossip sheets. She'd mentioned before that she read them, but now he was beginning to think the woman devoured them. He made a mental note to begin having some delivered to Havisham Hall from London.

He also needed to order some more recent music sheets. The ones his wife now used to entertain them in the music room were remnants from his mother. Portia seemed perfectly content with them, but he did wonder what sort of music she would prefer to play. He found himself pondering a good deal about her, even as he cautioned himself against the curiosity.

Ashe and Edward seemed to like her. The women obviously did. Although she was a commoner, she fit in nicely with the aristocracy, could hold her own. A chameleon. Which gave him pause. Where had she learned to be comfortable around all walks of life?

Ashe leaned over. "She's delightful, deserving of better than a man who claims to have no heart."

"Her performance is deserving of silence," Locke shot back quietly.

Ashe had the audacity to merely chuckle.

The marquess had joined them for dinner, and now he sat with his eyes closed, his face relaxed. Locke imagined he was traveling back to a time when another woman played the piano for him. He'd spent a good deal of his life not asking questions about his mother, not wanting to bring forth memories that might upset his father. Only now was he beginning to realize that by curtailing his inquisitiveness, he may have been allowing his father to remain lost in his grief. Although to be honest, neither had he wanted to know what his mother's death had denied him: a ruffling of his hair at bedtime, a soft smile when his lessons were completed satisfactorily, a gentle laugh when he presented her with a handful of plucked wildflowers.

His life would have been different had his mother not died. He'd never truly wanted to acknowledge that fact. He'd opted for pragmatism and accepted life as it was.

Portia made him long for more. She made him want to embrace life with unyielding passion. For all her claims to be a commoner, there was nothing common about her.

The final chords she'd struck lingered, like memories reluctant to fade away. Everyone clapped. She ducked her head, blushed. It always amazed him that a woman as bold as she would blush. It made her all the more endearing, which wasn't what he particularly wanted—and yet Ashe was correct. She deserved a man willing to open his heart to her.

"Would anyone else care to play?" she asked.

"I never mastered the piano," Minerva said.

"Which is odd, considering how nimble your fingers are when it comes to cheating at cards," Ashe responded with far too much pride reflected in his voice.

"You cheat at cards?" Portia repeated.

"On occasion, if I need to win. It depends on the stakes. I can teach you if you like."

"I don't think that will be necessary," Locke said, although he couldn't recall a single time when his wife had followed his edicts. If she wanted to learn to cheat, she'd find a way—just as she'd tidied rooms he'd forbidden to be tidied, showed him the possibilities so he couldn't object. She was clever that way. Never asking for permission but risking his wrath and managing to avoid it when all was said and done.

"To be quite honest, I'm rather exhausted," Julia said. "It's been a long day, with the traveling and all. I believe I'm going to have to turn in."

"We both shall, shall we?" Edward asked, coming to his feet and assisting his wife.

Locke didn't know if he'd ever grow accustomed to Edward being so solicitous to her. For years, Edward had claimed to abhor the woman and she despised him. How odd it was now to see them so deeply in love.

His father shoved himself up out of the chair, walked to the window, and gazed out. "Linnie appreciated seeing you all here tonight."

Locke exchanged glances with Ashe and Edward. In spite of all the changes that Portia had heralded, some things remained untouched.

"It is rather late," Locke admitted. "We should no doubt all retire."

His father turned. "When the time comes you're to bury me beside her."

As though Locke would ever consider anything else. "Yes, well, the time isn't going to come for a good long while yet."

"I suppose you're right. Still much to be done, although you're the one who needs to be doing it. An heir, Locke, you need an heir."

"Working on it, Father." Every night. Not that he found the task daunting or unpleasant. Characterizing it as work was inaccurate.

"Then we should all get to bed and let you get back to it," his father said.

Locke couldn't stifle his groan. Honestly, the man didn't think before he spoke. He'd have a time of it if he ever decided to return to London and polite society. His father began ushering them out as though they were children again. Perhaps in his mind they were. It was difficult to tell sometimes when his father slipped into the past.

In the hallway of bedchambers, Locke bade their guests good night while Portia offered them sweet dreams. Only after they closed their doors, leaving Locke, Portia, and his father in the corridor, did he turn to the marquess. "Sometimes you say the most inappropriate things."

"I'm old enough not to care. Time is short. I must be direct." He winked at Portia. "You were a marvelous hostess, my dear. I knew you would be."

"It's easy when our company is so pleasant."

"You look tired."

"It's been a long day."

His father studied her as though searching for something before finally nodding. "I suppose it has. I'll see you both in the morning." He wandered into his room. Locke turned the key in the door.

"I do wish you didn't have to do that," she said.

He wished it as well. "A lot of memories stirred up today. He'll be wandering the moors if I don't."

"He seemed so content tonight."

Locke almost turned the key the other way. "Because he believes my mother was gazing in through the window. Don't make me feel guilty about my desire to keep him safe."

"You're right, of course. I'm sorry."

He offered his arm, led her into their bedchamber, fighting to ignore the stirrings he heard in the chambers they passed. It seemed his friends were a randy lot. Not that he blamed them. Something about the isolation out here called to one's baser instincts. In London, during any of his travels, he'd never been as desperate to possess a woman as he was to have Portia. If he wasn't striving to maintain a bit of decorum and distance, he'd have taken her hand and dashed to their room.

Closing the door behind them, he pivoted around to find her waiting in the center of the room, her back to him. His unlacing her gown had become a nightly ritual. After shrugging out of his jacket, he tossed it onto a nearby chair. His waistcoat and neck cloth joined it before he approached her. He pressed his lips to the nape of her neck. On a soft sigh, she dropped back her head.

"Father was correct. You are an exceptional hostess."

"The additional servants helped."

Why was she always so reluctant to take credit for her achievements? That first day, modesty was not something he'd expected of her. He went to work unlacing her gown. "You'll have to hire more as you continue cleaning out the residence."

"I thought I would cease with those efforts until the mines are paying off again."

His fingers stilled at the small of her back. He wished she didn't know the truth of the mines. "No need. We're not beggars, Portia." Not yet, anyway.

He eased her gown down to floor. After she stepped out of it, she faced him. "Will you discuss the mining situation with Ashebury and Greyling?" she asked.

"No. They know naught about mining." He cradled her cheek. "You are an incredible lady of the manor. Let me pamper you."

Once he had all her clothes removed and her hair unpinned, he lifted her into his arms and carried her to the bed. Another ritual. He didn't know why he enjoyed it so much when she could just as easily walk those remaining few feet. But he liked that he dictated the pace, that he determined if they went slowly or quickly.

"Roll over onto your stomach," he ordered. She didn't object. She never did, and for the first time, he wondered if she would tell him if there was something she didn't like. Ashe and Edward were more in tune with their wives. It had been evident all night. They would have no doubt known if their wife was exhausted long before they retired to the bedchamber. It wasn't that he didn't pay attention. He simply didn't know Portia as well as his friends knew their wives.

But then they'd known their wives a good deal longer than he'd known his. However, even as he sought the excuse, he knew the truth was that he'd had no desire to truly know her.

Opening a drawer in the table beside the bed, he reached in and removed a vial.

"What's that?" she asked.

"A musk-scented oil I purchased during one of my travels. The seller assured me it would bring heightened pleasure. I thought to test it on you."

"If the pleasure you bring me is heightened any further, I'm likely to expire on the spot."

It was a good thing he'd removed his waistcoat. The buttons might have popped off with the swelling of his pride. He'd never doubted that he brought her pleasure. He couldn't explain why he wanted to bring her so much more. Nor did he know why a shiver of foreboding went through him at the thought of her dying. "Let's give it a try, shall we?" he asked, brushing her hair aside until it all pooled on her pillow.

She came up on her elbows. "With company about? I don't need to be screaming tonight."

"Bite down on the sheet." He rolled up the sleeves on his shirt, loosened the buttons at his throat. He removed the stopper from the vial, poured some cool oil into his palm, and rubbed his hands briskly together to warm the liquid. He pressed his hands to the small of her back. With a moan, she flattened herself against the mattress and closed her eyes.

He took long leisurely strokes up and down either side

of her spine, well aware of her going limpid beneath his touch. "What is your father's name?"

The tightness instantaneously returned. "Why are you asking?"

"When I was talking with Ashe and Edward earlier, in the library, they had questions to which I had no answers. It made me curious."

"He's no longer in my life so his name is of no concern."

He moved his fingers in circles over her shoulders. She'd told him that before, but it suddenly seemed important that he know, if not that, at least something about her. "Share with me a memory from your childhood."

She sighed long and softly. "I'm too tired."

So her defenses were down and he was the worst sort of scoundrel to take advantage, but then a hellion must live up to his reputation. "You're very good at entertaining. Did you learn that skill at home?"

"Yes, we often had visitors and were expected to put on a good show."

Furrowing his brow, he caressed the length of her back, kneaded her enticing bottom. "What sort of show?"

"That we were a happy family. That my father was a good man."

"Wasn't he?"

She rolled onto her back. He gave her a devilish smile. "Are you ready for me to massage your front?"

"I'm ready for you to cease with the questions. Who I was, how things were—they don't affect now. Us. What is or is not between us. I left all that behind."

"All what?"

She shook her head. "It doesn't matter. You married me without it mattering. It can't matter now."

"Did he hurt you?"

With a grimace, she closed her eyes. "He didn't believe in sparing the rod. I'll say that much."

He wondered if memories of the bite of the rod had caused her grimace. She had no scars, but one could inflict pain without breaking skin.

She opened her eyes. "Please leave the past in the past."

Words he'd often muttered in connection with his father. If he'd heeded them perhaps Locke would have held a different attitude toward love, perhaps he wouldn't now be married to Portia or dribbling fragrant oil on her chest, watching it pool in the hollow between her breasts. Setting the vial aside, he splayed his fingers wide, gathered up some of the oil on his thumbs and began spreading it over her skin, up to her collarbone, down to her hips. He shouldn't be concerned by the fact that Ashe and Edward knew the smallest of details about their wives while he knew not the largest one about his.

He knew what mattered. She wasn't averse to working. She considered herself superior to no one. She was an excellent hostess, kind to his father, and worried about the mines not because of what their failure might deny her but what it might deny the estate.

Reaching up, she combed her fingers through his hair, cradling her palm around the back of his head, and drawing him down until his lips met hers. She never only took. He should have known she wouldn't tonight, no matter how exhausted she claimed to be.

He took her slowly, gently. With no rush, no blistering needs, no fury. When the passion rose and she was on the cusp, he covered her mouth, swallowed her screams, relished her body tightening around him, unleashing sensations that threatened to tear him apart even as they made him feel more powerful, invincible.

Panting, still trembling in the aftermath of the explosive release, he rolled to his side, drew her in close, flicked the sheets over them both. She was correct. The past didn't matter, but damned if he didn't wish he'd met her when she was a young girl so now he would know everything about her.

Chapter 18

Since they had guests, apparently Portia had instructed Mrs. Dorset to prepare a variety of breakfast offerings to be set on the sideboard so everyone could take whatever they fancied. Locke couldn't fault the variety, finding it rather nice not to be saddled with the cook's plated offering based on her mood.

Everyone was here, including his father; everyone except Portia. Her absence surprised him, because he'd expected her to be the first at the table to ensure everything met her expectations and to greet their guests. On the other hand, he hadn't been able to resist having her again this morning before preparing for the day. After assisting him with dressing, she'd returned to the bed as she always did "for just a few more minutes." He'd no doubt worn her out. As a husband, he was a cad. Not that she seemed to mind.

"How long are you all staying?" he asked now, trying not to think of the mines and how he was anxious to get back to them.

"Only until tomorrow," Ashe said. "We wanted to welcome your wife into the family, but can't tarry. Will you be coming to London for the Season?"

"I'm considering it." He might actually anticipate attending balls, having the opportunity to dance with Portia, to walk in with her on his arm. Only he wanted people to see that she was more than grace and beauty. He wanted them to see all that she was capable of accomplishing. He wanted them to see her as a hostess, the lady of the manor. Was he actually considering asking her to arrange a ball in his London residence?

Because his father had never returned to London after his wife died, the residence in town had never been abandoned—although neither was it truly alive. Portia would change that. She would whisk down the hallways and through the rooms, brightening them with her presence alone. She would—

Cullie entered the room at a rather fast clip, but then the girl tended to move quickly no matter what she was doing, a trait she'd no doubt adopted from her mistress. Once reaching him, she bent down.

"Her Ladyship's not feeling quite up to snuff this morning," she said quietly, yet her voice still seemed to carry as everyone perked up. "She won't be joining you for breakfast. She wanted you to know so you could carry on with your day and not be waiting about for her."

He was on his feet before he'd even realized he'd tossed down his napkin. Portia never became ill—or so she'd claimed, too smugly for it not to be true. So what the devil was wrong with her and why was his heart hammering and his stomach roiling as though he were the one who was ill? She'd been fine this morning. She'd buttoned him up and knotted his neck cloth as she did each day. That she'd wanted to return to bed for a few minutes had been no cause for alarm.

"We'll see to her," Minerva offered as both she and Julia pushed back their chairs and stood. Ashe, Edward, and his father were quick to follow.

"She won't want to interrupt your breakfast," he insisted.

"If it's what I think it is—a lady's condition—I doubt she'll want you charging in there either."

A lady's condition? The meaning of those words slammed into him. Of course. Her menses. He'd given no thought to the fact that they'd been together for nearly a month now and he'd been able to enjoy her every night. Minerva was correct. Avoiding this aspect of marriage was appealing, as he'd not considered that marriage meant being with a woman during her time. "All right. Yes. I'd appreciate you seeing to her."

"Very good." Minerva gave her attention to Cullie. "Bring some tea with honey and some crackers to her Ladyship's bedchamber."

The ladies disappeared through the doorway. The gentlemen retook their chairs.

"You looked a bit ill yourself there for a moment," Edward said.

"She doesn't get ill, so I was a concerned."

"You're beginning to care for her," his father said, his smile nearly a gloat.

"Don't be ridiculous. She serves a purpose, nothing more." He reached for his coffee, noticed his fingers trembling, and returned his hand to his lap. His reaction had nothing to do with any warm feelings he might have toward her, but merely the inconvenient timing of the situation. Still as the others began talking, he couldn't stop looking at the archway and wishing that he'd been the one to go to her.

"WHY didn't you tell him what you truly suspect?" Julia asked as they headed up the stairs.

"Because it's not my place to tell him, but based on

your question, I'm assuming you think the same thing." Minerva had suspected it from the moment she'd been introduced to Portia. One of the reasons that she was so very skilled at cheating was that she was so very good at reading people and situations. Portia had a glow to her that had nothing to do with marital bliss.

When they reached the last door, she rapped briskly on the wood, waited until Portia bade them to come in, then turned the knob. They entered to find their hostess curled in a fetal position, her face pale, her eyes dull.

"Oh, I thought you were Cullie," she said, pushing herself up.

"Don't get up," Minerva said, rushing over and pressing her back down. "We only wanted to check on you, not disturb you. Your maid said you're not feeling well."

"When I'm moving about I get a bit nauseous. I thought resting for a while might help."

Minerva beamed at Julia, who nodded.

"My incapacitation is hardly worth grinning over," Portia said somewhat grumpily.

"We're smiling because you're exhibiting signs of being with child," Minerva told her.

Portia shook her head. "It's too soon."

Julia moved around the bed, lowered herself to the mattress, and took Portia's hand. "When was your last menses?"

Minerva had never known anyone who looked so reluctant to answer a question, but then some ladies were embarrassed by their bodies' needs and functions. She, herself, had never been particularly shy, but she understood their prying might not be particularly welcomed, in spite of its good intentions.

"I can't remember." Portia blinked several times, pressed her lips together, as though she was striving to solve a difficult answer on a quiz. "Sometime before I arrived here."

"And you've been married for a month," Julia said softly. "I would say there is a good chance you are with child, wouldn't you, Minerva?"

"I would, yes." She, too, sat on the edge of the bed and clasped Portia's hand. The new viscountess looked positively frightened, as though she'd been caught doing something she ought not.

"But the nausea . . . isn't it too soon?"

"I was nearly two months along when I began to feel ill but I think all women are different," Julia said. "What about you, Minerva?"

"I agree, we're all different."

Julia laughed. "No, I mean when did you experience nausea?"

"Nearly right from the start. Have you had any other signs, Portia?"

"I have been tired of late, but I just thought it was because I was working so hard to get things ready."

"There you are then," Minerva said. "I'd say Marsden is going to get the grandchild he craves."

*H*E'D waited as long as he could. When the ladies didn't return straightaway to inform him that all was well, he headed upstairs and barged into his bedchamber without bothering to knock. That Minerva and Julia were sitting on either side of Portia, holding her hands, caused cold dread to wash over him. While he'd never witnessed a deathbed scene, what he saw was exactly how he imagined it would be. Portia's cheeks held no rosy hue. Her eyes didn't light up with challenge at his arrival. His father liked Portia immensely. He didn't know if his sire would survive losing her if she were to succumb to an illness and become another woman who had died too young within this residence.

"I'll send for a physician," he barked, despising that he seemed unable to react with any sort of rational thought.

"I don't think that's necessary," Minerva said, rising to her feet, smiling softly.

The smile unmanned him. "What's wrong with her then?"

"We'll let her tell you."

As Minerva and Julia walked out, he tried to take solace in the fact that neither of them seemed particularly worried. Yet he seemed unable to get his heart to stop its thundering within his chest. As he began striding toward the bed, his wife pushed herself up. He quickened his pace, getting to her in time to help fluff up the pillows behind her back. Straightening, he stood stiffly before her. "So what illness has befallen you?"

Her lips turned up ever so slightly. "I'm not certain I'm ill. Rather there may be a chance that I'm with child."

If he hadn't braced his legs, locked his knees, he might have stumbled back. Instead, he merely stared at her, wondering why there was suddenly no air to draw into his lungs. He didn't want a child cutting his time with her short, didn't want to consider that like his mother she might die in childbirth. It had taken his father three years to get his marchioness with child. Locke suddenly realized he wanted at least that long with Portia. More. "So soon?"

She flinched, lowered her gaze to her lap, and plucked at a thread on the duvet. "I thought the same thing but it has been pointed out to me—by you yourself come to think of it—that it could have happened as early as the first time we came together." She lifted her eyes to his. "I did admit to being fertile, after all."

The tartness in her tone set his world back to rights. She wasn't his mother. And she'd already survived bringing one child into the world. He leaned against the post at the foot of the bed, crossed his arms over his chest, wishing the damn tremors cascading through him would cease. "So you did."

But still he hadn't thought she'd be *this* fertile.

She tilted up her chin. "I do hope your father is happier about it than you seem to be."

"He will be." He grimaced. "It's not that I'm not happy; it's just sooner than I expected."

"Which is quite stupid on your part considering how many times you've spilled your seed into me."

He couldn't help grinning. He hadn't liked seeing her so vulnerable, but she was returning to herself, and as she did, so the tightness in his chest eased. He was no doubt worrying for nothing. "I don't recall your objecting."

"Arrogant—" Suddenly she blanched, tossed back the covers, scrambled out of the bed, and made a mad dash across the room.

Alarmed he shoved himself away from the bedstead. "Portia?"

She came to a stop at the washstand and bent her head over the bowl. Cautiously he approached, well aware of her not moving, but breathing in short gasps. "Portia?"

Shaking her head, she held up a hand. He placed his on her back and began moving it in slow circles. "Relax. It'll be all right."

"My stomach . . . keeps lurching, but nothing comes."

"This is how you know you're with child?"

"That and I haven't had my menses."

He was well aware of that fact as he'd been able to have his way with her every night. Damn. His seed probably had taken root the first time.

She closed her fingers into a fist; her breathing became easier.

"I'm sorry you're not feeling well," he murmured.

"This is nothing compared with what's to come."

He didn't want to contemplate what she would endure to bring his child into the world, the risk she was taking to give him a bloody heir. He rather wished he'd kept his trousers buttoned. "Was it very painful bringing your first child into the world?"

Beneath his fingers, she stiffened. "Whatever a woman suffers is worth it."

He doubted that his mother would agree.

A knock sounded on the door.

"What?" he barked, not welcoming the intrusion.

The door opened and Cullie peered in. "I brought the tea and crackers for her Ladyship. The duchess thinks it'll help settle her stomach."

"Right. Put the tray on the table beside the bed."

With a rapid patter of heels over wood, Cullie rushed across the room, set down the tray, and made a hasty exit.

"Does she always move about so quickly?" Locke asked.

"I think your brusque tone unnerves her."

"I was merely trying to discourage anyone from disturbing you."

With a deep sigh, she straightened. "I think you accomplished that. I'm going to give the tea a try."

She wandered back to the bed, climbed into it, and took the china teacup from the tray. He returned to his position leaning against the bedpost and watched as she blew lightly over the tea. His body reacted as though she were blowing lightly over him. At a time such as this, he was an absolute cad.

"How long will you be feeling under the weather?" he asked.

"Difficult to say. The nausea shouldn't last much longer, I shouldn't think. I'm already feeling better. It may return tomorrow and any number of days after that. I suppose it's my body adjusting to carrying life."

Christ. Life. A life they'd created together. Even knowing the entire purpose behind this ludicrous arrangement had been to provide the next heir, Locke had never truly contemplated the responsibility of it.

"You don't seem very happy by the prospect of a child," she said quietly before sipping her tea, her eyes never leaving him.

"It seems ridiculous to say it, but I hadn't given you getting with child a great deal of thought. I'm not unhappy about it."

She blinked coquettishly. "Well, that makes me feel loads better."

"Portia." What could he say? He hadn't expected his seed to be so competent; although to be honest he'd never before tested his own fertility. Before her, he'd always sheathed himself when with a woman. "I'm . . . delighted with the prospect of an heir—"

"Could be a girl."

He was taken aback by how much the possibility of a daughter pleased him. One with Portia's vibrant red hair and whiskey eyes. One who would live out her life as a spinster because he wouldn't let a man get within three feet of her. "I would like that."

Her eyes searching his face, she lowered her cup. "Would you?"

"I would." He cleared his throat, searching for a way to reassure her that he was not dissatisfied by the developments. "I'd be equally pleased with a boy. As long as the child is healthy and you—" *Survive* flashed through his mind. He realized that worry over her was tamping any sort of joy he should feel at this moment. "And you don't find the experience too much of an ordeal."

"You're thinking of your mother," she said tenderly.

Why was it that she seemed to know him far better than he knew her?

"I'm strong and healthy." But her words offered no assurance because as far as he knew his mother had been strong and healthy as well. "I won't die."

Pushing himself away from the post, he moved up, leaned over her, and bussed his lips over hers. "I'll hold you to that promise."

Then he strode out before he said something sentimental that he'd come to regret. He was not opening his heart to the woman. He just wished he wasn't filled with a sense of foreboding that threatened to remove any ray of sunshine from his life.

THE marquess's reaction was exactly the sort that any woman would want. He was ecstatic. Portia was certain that if he had his clothes as well tailored to fitting his body as his son did, then his buttons would have popped off his waistcoat when Locksley announced in the music room that evening following dinner that she was with child.

She was surprised everyone had held the news to themselves, but she supposed they wanted a wonderful moment for Marsden.

"Bravo!" he exclaimed, lifting his glass of scotch. "I knew it wouldn't take you long, my dear."

She'd been noticing changes for some time now, lacking energy in the afternoons, her stomach feeling a bit queasy in the mornings, but she'd kept it all to herself because it felt far too early to announce a baby was on the way. Even now, she wasn't quite comfortable with it, but Minerva and Julia had forced her hand.

She was most surprised by Locksley's reaction. His mother's death had obviously affected him more than she'd realized, no doubt more than anyone thought. She had sensed his worry that morning when he learned of her condition and it had tempered any excitement he might have felt at the possibility of acquiring his heir. Although she truly wanted this child to be a girl. A sweet little girl whom she could shower with the love and affection that had been denied her.

"We'll have our heir here before the year is out," Marsden said, grinning broadly.

"It might be a girl," she told him.

"Maybe." He tapped two fingers to his chest. "But in here, I know it to be a boy."

"Regardless, Father, you'll welcome the child," Locksley said.

"Naturally." He gave her a secretive wink as though he had no doubts at all that she was carrying a boy.

"Shall I play something on the pianoforte?" she asked, hoping to move the discussion away from her pregnancy.

"You should rest this evening," Locksley said.

"It's not as though I'm incapacitated. I feel perfectly fine now. And I'm not planning to just sit around for . . . well, however many months are left."

His brow furrowed. "Eight I should think."

"Sometimes babies come early. I did. Several weeks early, as a matter of fact. All of my siblings came early."

"So did Locke," Marsden said.

Her husband snapped his attention to his father. "I did?"

Marsden nodded, studying the scotch remaining in his

glass as though he wished he hadn't spoken. "Two weeks I think. Or perhaps the physician miscalculated. It's not as though it's an exact science. One can only guess as to when conception truly took place."

"Speaking of physicians, we'll want to bring a new one to the village," Locksley said.

"But Findley's been here forever."

"He was here when I was born, wasn't he?"

"Yes."

"Then we want a different one."

A wealth of sadness in his eyes, Marsden studied his son. "He couldn't have saved your mother."

He shot up out of his chair and strode to the table of decanters. If she didn't know better, she'd think he was agitated, concerned for her health. "He's going to say that, isn't he? Or perhaps we'll go to London as Portia's time nears."

She didn't want to be anywhere near London. "The babe should be born here, at the estate."

"She's right," Marsden said. "We'll find a new physician."

Locksley filled his glass and returned to his chair, hardly appearing appeased. "Good. I'll place an advert in the *Times*."

"Announce your marriage while you're at it."

Portia's stomach knotted up at that command, but she could hardly object without raising suspicions. Besides, realistically, her marriage to Locksley couldn't remain a secret forever. Best to just get it done and hope for the best.

"I know there is precedent for your concern," Edward said quietly, "but both Julia and Minerva have delivered babes and survived."

"And doctors know so much more now, don't they?"

Julia added. "I daresay, medicine as a whole is vastly improving."

"Not to mention that Portia gave birth before with no ill effects," the marquess said.

The eyes of their guests landed on her with an almost audible thud.

"You had a child?" Minerva asked, sadness and sorrow clearly reflected in her voice.

"He died." She shook her head. "My present condition is supposed to be a cause for celebration and joy, not melancholy. I believe I *shall* play."

Before anyone could object, she rose to her feet, walked quickly to the pianoforte, sat, and struck a hard, deep chord. Moving into a lighter, face-paced tune, she allowed the music to wash over her, through her, calming her nerves. She wouldn't contemplate that she might not live to see this child grow up. The earl was correct. Women survived all the time. She wasn't going to spend the next few months worrying. All would be well. It had to be. After everything she'd done, it had to be.

WITH the first whisper of dawn easing in through the windows, Locke watched as his wife slept. Normally, he would have slowly awoken her with kisses on her bared shoulder and gentle nudges, but he couldn't quite bring himself to disturb her slumber this morning. Not when it might hasten the roiling of her stomach.

Last night he'd taken her three times before she'd contentedly drifted off to sleep. While he'd spent much of the time staring into the darkness, listening to her rhythmic breathing, inhaling her jasmine fragrance. He was hoarding the most insignificant of memories as though she would be snatched away from him. It was ludicrous that he should worry so much when other matters were pressing in on him: ensuring his heir inherited an estate that was worthy of him with an income that would sustain him.

In a single day, everything had changed; everything seemed more urgent. He needed to spend more time at the mines, needed the men to work with more perseverance. It was more imperative than ever that they find an ore-rich vein soon. He would double his efforts, lengthen the hours they toiled. But even as he contemplated longer hours, time spent away from Portia, something within him rebelled. He wanted more hours, more days, more months with her.

Why did his seed have to be so damned potent?

Her eyes fluttered open. Her lips curled up into a soft smile. "Lost interest in me now that I'm with child?"

He loved her voice first thing in the morning, when it was raspy from sleep, hoarse from disuse. It added a sultry element to her cries of pleasure that always caused his body to tighten all the more. "Last night should have convinced you otherwise."

"Why haven't you woken me then?"

His gaze drifted down to her stomach, and he wondered when it would begin to round, when he would look at her and see the evidence of his child growing within her. "After yesterday I wasn't certain you'd be up for it."

She scraped her fingers through his hair, drawing his attention back to her eyes. "The nausea didn't hit me until later."

"Still, we haven't much time with our guests leaving soon. I should probably—"

She sat up, the sheet slipping down to her waist, leaving those lovely breasts of hers exposed. Pushing on his shoulder, she forced him back down to the mattress before swinging a leg over him and straddling his hips. Leaning down, she nibbled on his lips. "I'm not fragile."

The woman's appetite was as insatiable as his. He'd never known anyone like her. Nor could he resist her.

Three hours later, after a lazy coupling and a leisurely breakfast, he was standing on the drive between Portia and his father, watching as the coaches carrying his childhood friends and their families disappeared down the lane.

"It's good to see them doing so well," his father said. "They're happy. That's what matters most. And they have their heirs." He patted Locke's shoulder. "You will, too, soon."

He began to wander off, not in the direction of the manor, but toward the area where the marchioness had been laid to rest. Locke had little doubt that he was going to spend some time talking to his mother's headstone.

"He'll be disappointed if it's a girl," Portia said quietly.

"I doubt it," he assured her. "Did you not see the attention he gave Allie?"

She looked up at him. "Will you be disappointed?"

As long as she didn't die, he'd be pleased. "Why would I be disappointed when it means we'd just have to try all the harder?"

She smiled as a blush crept up her cheeks. "Will you be going to the mines?"

"How are you feeling?"

She seemed surprised by his question. He'd noticed during breakfast that she merely nibbled on a piece of toast and sipped her tea.

"The queasiness comes and goes, although I think I shall lie down for a while."

"I can stay—"

"No. No sense in that when there's nothing you can do. I'm not ill, Locksley. This will all pass."

He was torn between wishing her pregnancy would pass quickly and that it would take forever. The distraction of the mines would be welcomed, would occupy his thoughts so he could ward off all the worst-case scenarios that fought to intrude on his peace of mind.

Chapter 19

May arrived with weather warmer than usual. Portia couldn't bear the thought of cleaning rooms when she could enjoy the sun warming her face. Kneeling, inhaling deeply, she took satisfaction in the fragrance of freshly turned earth. Except for a brief respite for lunch, she'd spent the day working on bringing the garden back to life. The next time they had guests, she wanted to be able to invite them for tea on the terrace. So earlier that morning, once Locksley left for the mines, she had gone into the village, visited with those who had gorgeous flowers blooming, and asked for some cuttings from their favorite plants. She'd never been the beneficiary of such generosity from strangers, and she'd left feeling as though she were accepted by the villagers, as though she truly belonged here. Then when she returned to Havisham she set the servants to work.

The footmen and stable boys were making great progress hacking at the brambles and overgrowth. The maids were pulling up the unwanted vegetation. The marquess, bless him, was turning over the soil with a shovel, creating a narrow path that lined the terrace. She was following along behind him, on her knees, using a trowel to prepare a place for each cutting and potted plant, carefully setting it into its new home, and gently filling in the hole. She did hope they would survive.

"How do you know about gardening?" Marsden asked, taking a break from his toils and resting an elbow on the shovel.

"My mother. The only time she ever seemed truly happy was when she was in the garden. Sometimes she would let me help when she was planting or pruning."

"My Linnie loved flowers."

Although she wore a wide-brimmed straw hat to shade her face, she raised her hand to shield her eyes from the sun as she glanced up at him. "Based upon what you've told me of her, I'm not surprised. I imagine these gardens were beautiful once."

He crouched beside her. "They were. I shouldn't have let them go. She'll be pleased to see you're bringing them back. But we must hire a gardener. This area is massive. We can't have you doing all the work, and those servants are going to grumble about these labors if you keep them at it too long."

"Maybe once the plants are flourishing we'll hire someone."

"No need to wait. It's not as though we can't afford it."

She wasn't quite certain his words were true. It had been a few weeks since she'd learned the truth, since she watched Locksley return in the evenings and noted the dejected slump of his shoulders. His bath always seemed to refresh him, and there was never any evidence of his worry when he joined her for the evening. He assured her that they weren't beggars but she suspected they'd find themselves in a spot of bother if they didn't watch their spending. "I'll discuss it with Locksley," she said, hoping to steer Marsden away from the topic of their finances.

"I like that the two of you talk things over. Linnie and

I decided everything together. She was my partner in all ways. She would—"

Bells began pealing.

"Christ," Marsden muttered, shooting to his feet with a speed that astonished Portia.

"What is it?" she asked.

The maids lifted their skirts and began running away from the manor in the direction that Locksley went each morning. The footmen, still holding on to their shovels, followed on their heels. Trepidation sliced through Portia and she pushed herself up. "What is it?"

"John, ready a carriage!" Marsden shouted at the coachman.

Portia grabbed the marquess's arm and asked again, more forcefully, "What is it? What's happened?"

"There's been an accident at the mines."

RIDING in the carriage with the marquess at the reins, Portia arrived at the mines to discover her worse fear realized: Locksley was one of the ones trapped when a ceiling collapsed.

The marquess had charged into the fray—into the mine—to assist, which terrified her, although she understood his need to be of service. She could do little more than offer water to the workers who periodically emerged to rest for a bit while others, refreshed, took their place. She paced alongside the other women, wrung her hands, and whenever gruesome thoughts of the worst possible outcome hovered at the back of her mind, she fervently squashed them.

Locksley had traveled the world, had no doubt been in far more dangerous situations and emerged unscathed. He would survive this.

"Not to worry, m'lady," Cullie said, standing beside

her. "The workers wouldn't still be in the tunnel if there was no hope."

"It could collapse further, taking them all."

"Aye, but we mustn't think like that, and I've never known you to see the dark side of things. Shall I go in and see if I can determine what sort of progress has been made?"

She shook her head. "No need to put more people at risk. Besides, those coming out would surely share news if there was news to share."

"They're a stoic lot, not wanting to raise or dash hopes, so they keep their thoughts to themselves. But if I was to prod them—"

"No, let them concentrate on their tasks."

"This waiting drives me blooming crazy, though."

Portia released a small laugh. "Me as well."

"You shouldn't be here, m'lady, not in your condition."

"I'm not doing anything other than standing around. At the residence I'd merely pace and wear a hole in the carpeting." And worry all the more. She didn't know why she felt that being here would somehow alter the outcome. Perhaps that was the reason Locksley worked in the mines. It was much easier to be present and involved than merely waiting at a distance for word of success.

A commotion at the mouth of the tunnel caught her attention. A group of men, covered in filth and grime, barely identifiable, staggered out. Yet she recognized one of them by the breadth of his shoulders, the way he held himself. He might be shoveling dirt with the best of them, but every pore of his body screamed noble birth.

Before she'd given it any thought, she was racing to him. He turned and those green eyes landed on her. Then he grinned, his smile white and bright in that dirt-covered face. He held out his arms and she leaped at him. He caught her and spun her around.

"You're alive! You're safe," she cried.

"We found more tin, Portia. More tin." Then his mouth was on hers, hungry and greedy, passionate and so full of life. He smelled of the earth, rich and dark.

When he pulled back, she plowed her hands through his hair, watching as dirt scattered on the wind. "I thought there was an accident."

"There was, but we found the vein just before the collapse. We know it's there now. We'll know where to go after it."

"Isn't that dangerous?"

"We'll buttress it better." Then he was kissing her again.

LOCKE sank down into the hot water. Trapped inside the mine, surrounded by darkness, thoughts of Portia had provided a light for his soul as he'd encouraged the other five men entombed with him to work to dig themselves out. He'd never contemplated not finding freedom, never considered death as an avenue for escape, because it would have kept him from her. When he'd come out of the mine and seen her rushing toward him, the joy that had spiraled through him had been unsettling. She was coming to mean too much, and yet he couldn't quite push back the emotions, no matter how dangerous or risky to his sanity they might be.

Now hearing the door open, he glanced back over his shoulder. He shouldn't be so grateful for Portia's arrival, but damn if he wasn't.

"I thought you could use a drink," she said as she handed him a glass filled with amber liquid.

"Indeed I could." He swallowed a good portion of it, welcomed the burning in his chest.

Kneeling beside him, she took a cloth, dipped it in the water, rubbed soap over it.

"Are you going to wash me?" he asked.

She gave him a saucy smile. "I thought I might. Were you scared?"

"Terrified."

Her eyes widened, and all he wanted was to drink them in. "Were you really?" she asked.

Sighing, he wasn't certain how to explain it. "I wasn't afraid. To be honest, I was more disappointed in myself because I realized that if I didn't make it out, I'd be leaving a great deal undone."

"I would have been so frightened."

"No, you wouldn't have." He trailed his finger around her face. "You would have been encouraging the others, leading them toward digging you out."

"You give me too much credit." She began wiping the cloth over his chest.

"I want to take you to London."

Her hand stilled, near his heart, and he wondered if she could hear it pounding. "Why?"

"To introduce you into Society."

"That's not necessary."

"You're my wife. Surely you understood that we would go to London for the Season."

"You haven't gone in years."

"Which is the reason we need to go. To reestablish ourselves, especially now that a child is on the way."

She began scrubbing his shoulders, his neck. "Can't we wait until next year?"

Most women adored London and the Season. He didn't understand her reluctance. "What's wrong with this year?"

"I don't know all the etiquette. I need to learn it."

"I'm certain you know enough to get by." His friends' visit had shown him that.

"You have far more faith in me than I have in myself."

He did have an inordinate amount of confidence in her ability to handle herself among the upper crust. "I want to show you off," he admitted.

Leaning up, he kissed the corner of her mouth. "Now remove your clothes and join me in the tub."

Chapter 20

A MONTH later, as the coach rolled into London, Portia fought to keep her apprehension hidden. Long, slow, deep breaths had been the order of the journey. As well as a mantra commanding herself to relax. It was highly unlikely that she would cross paths with Montie, that he would discover she'd returned. And if he did, it was possible that he wouldn't care after all these months. He'd no doubt forgotten all about her, moved on to someone else.

He'd never been one to do without and he liked nothing more than a woman's company. In order not to forgo pleasure, he'd have replaced Portia quickly enough. She was rather certain of that fact, as she no longer had any delusions regarding what she'd meant to him: nothing particularly special. In truth, Locksley made her feel more treasured than Montie ever had.

"Where did you live?"

At the unexpected question disturbing the quiet, she jerked her attention to her husband, who sat across from her. They'd spoken very little during the journey, which had suited her, as she'd used her time to mentally prepare for what awaited her here in the city. "Pardon?"

"When you were in London where did you live?"

"I never said I lived in London."

"But you traveled from London."

She'd forgotten how guarded she'd been with him when they first met, weighing every word, fearful she'd give too much away. It felt wrong now to revert to old habits. "Yes. But I didn't live in London proper. I resided in a house on the outskirts. The lease ran out just before I moved to Havisham."

"Would you like us to drive by it?"

"I have no desire to revisit old memories." To risk being spotted by anyone who might know or recognize her.

"Did you keep nothing from the residence?"

"Not a thing." Nothing had been hers to keep. "It's all in the past, Locksley, which is where I prefer for it to remain. Naught is to be gained hashing over the situation or my silliness in taking a husband who would not see to my welfare in case of his death."

He sighed, glanced out the window. "After all this time, Portia, it seems you should call me Locke."

"It would imply an intimacy we do not share."

His gaze came to bear on her. "I put a child in your belly. A couple doesn't get much more intimate than that."

She folded her hands over that belly, which was rounding. The new physician who had moved to the village speculated, based on her size, that twins were a possibility. "We might be physically intimate but we are not emotionally so. I think we can both agree to that."

Calling him Locke would make her feel closer to him, and she was striving to protect her heart.

"People will find it odd," he said.

"When have you ever cared what people think?"

He grinned. "Is that something you read in your gossip sheets?"

She smiled at him. "I'm fairly certain I did. Will we see many people?"

"I suspect so. Once word gets round that we're in town, we're certain to receive all manner of invitations. People will be anxious to meet my wife."

They would be. Everyone had a perverse curiosity regarding the Hellions, and the fact that Locksley hadn't been to London in a good long while made people all the more inquisitive about him. "They're certain to ask how we met. What will we say?"

"That my father arranged the introduction and I couldn't resist marrying you."

She laughed. "Clever. Not quite a lie."

"Not a lie at all. You tempted me the moment I opened the door."

He'd enticed her as well. As London shops passed by the window, she considered that she really should have gone after the mail coach. She wouldn't be back in London if she had. Marsden never would have brought her here. She'd have remained safe at Havisham.

"And how could I resist the charms of your set-downs?" he asked.

How quickly the months had passed since that day. Had she known then how much she would come to care for him she'd have never married him. While her stomach tightened each time she thought of being in London, she wanted to make him proud, glad to have her at his side. Even as she prayed that being in the city wouldn't provide the opportunity for him to discover the facts surrounding her, to come to despise her with every fiber of his being.

Learning the truth would destroy him and the fragile bond between them. It would devastate her as well because she'd done the unthinkable. She'd come to love him.

 $\mathcal{A}$s the coach pulled through the gates and onto the drive that circled in front of a large residence, Portia realized she'd walked past the manor when she'd first come to London. She'd taken a tour of the nicer areas because she'd expected to be living in one of them shortly after her arrival in the city. What a silly young girl she'd been then. And how odd that her hopes had come to pass, just not in the manner or during the time in which she'd expected.

The lawn was beautifully manicured; colorful flowers edged the pebbled drive lined by towering elms. The manor itself was tall and wide, lacking the turrets and spires that characterized Havisham.

"It looks well maintained," she said.

"More so than Havisham. I don't usually open all the rooms when I'm here but they've not been left to fall into disrepair. You'll find the staff is small, only enough servants to see after the most minimal needs whether I'm away or here. You may, of course, hire additional staff."

"We'll make do with a small staff."

"Portia—"

She gave him a pointed look, cutting him off. "A small staff suits just fine. I don't see the need to open everything up if we're not going to be entertaining."

"We might."

Her stomach felt as though it had tumbled to the ground, but it was only the coach swaying to a stop. "What sort of entertaining?"

"We'll decide later, but for the babe's sake, we need to ensure you are accepted by all of London."

Her world could not seem to stop spinning. "It seems a bit soon to be worrying about what we must do for the babe's sake." The irony of her words didn't escape her, as it was something she worried about constantly, ever since she'd realized she was with child.

"It's never too early to put one's best foot forward."

He was correct, of course. She pushed the overwhelming thoughts bombarding her aside. She'd won over his friends. What were a few hundred more?

The door opened and a footman she didn't recognize offered his hand to her while saying to Locksley, "Welcome home, my lord."

He handed her down. Locksley disembarked, extended his arm toward her. She closed her fingers around his sturdiness, grateful for it, knowing she'd be relying on it in the days and nights ahead. Oh, she should have given more thought to the fact that marriage to a younger man would mean returning to London and being part of Society.

"At some point you'll be introduced to the queen," he said casually.

She halted, her stomach roiling as it hadn't in weeks now. "Why?"

He studied her as though she'd sprouted wings and was on the verge of taking flight. "Because you're a viscountess."

"I'm a commoner."

"By birth, but by marriage you are now a lady. My lady."

For how long? For how long would she be his lady if everything unraveled? She had married him because of the protection he would provide. He didn't have to offer it himself. She merely needed to use the threat of him to ensure no harm befell her. He was correct. She was a lady now. She couldn't be treated as though she was worthy of nothing. And if she were to make a favorable impression on the queen—well, that sort of alliance could serve her very well indeed. With a perfunctory nod, she said, "I shall need a new gown."

He grinned, the wide satisfied one that he always bestowed upon her whenever he thought he'd won his way, the one that made her sometimes willing to relent simply to see it appear. "Replace the blue while you're at it."

It was a frivolity, and yet she couldn't quite bring herself to object when she considered the pleasure it would bring him. Such a simply request really. There were times when she was astounded that she could please him so easily.

He led her up the steps and through a doorway where another footman stood holding the door open. Walking into this residence was nothing at all like walking into Havisham. It smelled of roses and lilies, as an assortment was arranged in various vases throughout the grand entryway. On either side were rooms, doors open, draperies drawn aside so sunlight could spill through the clear windows. She doubted she'd find a single cobweb or spider in the place. Farther down, wide stairs swept up to the next level.

A stately man approached and bowed his head. "Welcome home, my lord."

Locksley placed his hand over hers where it rested on his arm. "Lady Locksley, allow me to introduce Burns."

"It's a pleasure," she said.

"The pleasure is all ours, my lady. I've assembled the staff."

As she made her way along the line of servants, each greeted her with a curtsy or a bow and a reverent welcome. No one here was going to challenge her if she wanted the keys.

Just as she finished meeting the last servant—the scullery maid—the footmen walked in, carrying their trunks. Cullie followed them, her eyes growing wide as she took in her surroundings. After Portia introduced her to Burns, who ordered another servant to show Cullie to the bedchambers so she could unpack her Ladyship's trunk, Locksley took Portia on a tour of the residence.

The rooms not in use were shrouded in white but they didn't carry the scent of disuse or musty dust. With very little effort, merely the yanking away of sheets, the rooms would be ready for guests.

When they reached the library, she wasn't at all surprised to find the furniture uncovered, fresh flowers on a credenza by the window, and books filling shelves. Nor was she astonished when her husband separated himself from her and strode over to a table housing an assortment of crystal decanters.

While he poured himself some scotch, she wandered over to a window that looked out onto a gorgeous garden. "Do you think the gardener would let me take some cuttings back to Havisham?"

"The gardener will let you do anything you desire." Locksley pressed a shoulder to the window casing, glanced out, took a swallow of his scotch. "What do you think of the place?"

"It's not too shabby."

He chuckled low, his eyes glittering when they met hers. "I wouldn't be surprised to discover you'd scouted it out before you responded to my father's advertisement."

It would have been the wise thing to do, but she hadn't cared about any London holdings. She'd been concerned only with moving away from the city as quickly and secretly as possible. Still, his suspicions caused a heaviness to settle in her chest. After all this time, why did he still think she was after the wealth, the power, the prestige? Would he ever see her character as it truly was? Although with her past it was nothing to brag about.

"To be quite honest, I was under the impression your father never came to London, so I assumed there was no residence."

He lifted his glass so the sun could shine through it.

"Quite right. He hasn't been to London since my mother died."

"Is this your residence then?"

"No, it's his. I'll inherit it, of course, but since he never came here, there was never an edict that nothing be touched."

She glanced toward the mantel. "The clock isn't ticking but the hour doesn't match the one at Havisham."

"My father didn't stop them. I did. They drove me mad the first night I stayed here."

"So you stopped it"—she narrowed her eyes, focusing on the hands—"at two fifteen. In the morning, I presume."

"Charged through the entire blasted place like a madman, shouting at the servants to get up and stop the infernal ticking. I swore I could hear the tick-tock in distant corners of the residence, even though my rational self knows that can't be the case."

"Once you get accustomed to the sound, you don't really notice it. I hear the absence of clocks more than their presence. Which I suppose makes no sense either."

"Maybe with you here, I won't notice the echoing so much." He turned his attention back to the garden, swallowed more scotch.

He could live here with the beautiful gardens and fresh fragrances and rooms readied in the blink of an eye. Instead he'd opted to live at gloomy Havisham—because his father and the mines needed him.

"Do you like London?" she asked.

"I've never come to know it very well. I don't stay long. Compared to Havisham it's ungodly noisy and crowded."

She smiled. "It is that. I always enjoyed the hustle and the bustle."

"Yet you made the decision to marry a man who would keep you from it."

"I discovered other aspects of the city weren't to my taste."

She really wished they hadn't come to town, that he hadn't faced her squarely, hadn't begun to slowly run his gaze over her as though he sought out the flawed facets of her existence.

His eyes narrowed. "You were running from something."

"Poverty," she answered, twirling toward the center of the room. "I should probably check on Cullie, make certain—"

"It was more than that," he said quietly. "You're beautiful enough, clever enough, resourceful enough that you could have enticed any man with means into marrying you if you set your mind to it. You could have stayed in London."

"All that required work and effort. Answering your father's advert was the simplest solution."

"You're not one to take the uncomplicated route. I also suspect there was nothing at all easy in deciding to marry an aged man rumored to be mad."

She swung back around. She should deny it or, better yet, press her body against his and distract him from this line of reasoning. But she was so weary of constantly raising her guard. "Not all my memories here are pleasant. Even now I'm struggling to keep at bay my reasons for leaving."

He set aside his glass, approached her, and cradled her face between his strong hands. Hands that wielded pick and shovel. Hands that caressed to command pleasure. "Why did you leave, Portia? Why did you come to Havisham?"

She should tell him now, not risk his finding out

through some accidental or careless word. Yet she'd come so far, worked so hard to put everything behind her. "We agreed to leave the past in the past."

"I don't think it was the power, the money, or the prestige. I've seen you on your hands and knees, cleaning. You don't shower yourself with gifts or clothing. You don't flaunt your position. You speak to people as though they are your equals. All the things you gained by marrying a peer, you haven't embraced. So why marry a peer?"

"Security. I told you that."

"Why marry an aging one?"

"It was expedient. Honestly, Locksley, I don't know why we're discussing this."

"I want to understand you, Portia."

"There is nothing to understand." She considered breaking away, pulling back, but he held her with such insistence, not so much with his hands as with his eyes.

"When I married you, I cared about only knowing you in bed. Now much to my consternation, I want to know everything about you."

No, you don't. Not really.

Finally, he released his hold on her, turned away. She balled up her fists to stop herself from reaching for him, apologizing, begging him to forgive her.

"I thought about going to the club tonight," he said as he perched himself on the corner of his desk. "But that's not exactly the place where I want to introduce my wife to Society."

If he was thinking of taking her with him, then he was referring to the Twin Dragons, an exclusive club for men and women. She'd never been inside although she'd once seen it from the outside. Montie had never been one for taking her places, but she knew he frequented the establishment. She had no desire to run into him there. "I agree that a gambling den won't make the best impression. You should go without me."

"Leaving you alone our first night in London hardly seems gentlemanly."

"To be quite honest, I'm rather weary from the journey and was considering retiring early." Stepping forward, she trailed her hands up his chest, over his shoulders. "Perhaps you'd be willing to undress me before you go."

Grinning, he drew her in close. "Delighted to do so, but you know I won't stop there."

She nipped playfully at his chin. "I'm counting on it."

$\mathcal{L}$OCKE had always enjoyed spending time at the Twin Dragons, especially after the owner, Drake Darling, opened the place up to women. The establishment offered gambling, a ballroom, a dining room, a gathering room for all members, and an assortment of areas designated for only men or only women. So one could mix with the fairer sex if one was of a mind or seek less exciting company. He'd opted for the less exciting company. More than that, he'd opted for a less exciting activity: sitting in the gentlemen's room and indulging in scotch. He could have done the same in his library.

He'd given a game of cards a go, but had quickly become bored with the task. Generally he relished pitting his skills against others' talents, but he found himself constantly wishing that Portia were sitting beside him. With her ability not to give anything away, he suspected she'd come away with a good portion of the winnings.

It was the fact that she was so good at not revealing herself that made him know something was amiss in London. He'd felt the tension begin radiating off her as they'd neared the city. It had been so prevalent that he'd have not been surprised if she'd suddenly leaped out of the coach and begun a mad dash back to Havisham.

London made her anxious. Because her husband had died here? Because he'd broken her heart? He could not help but believe there was more to it than that. The woman who had boldly come to Havisham, not backed out of marriage when offered an alternative spouse, was not one to get unsettled, and yet—

"Evening, Locksley."

Locke glanced up at the slender man who had interrupted his musings. He'd always thought him far too handsome and charming for his own good. Women tended to flock around him. "Beaumont."

"Mind if I join you?"

The Earl of Beaumont, only a couple of years older and a couple of inches shorter than Locke, had inherited his title a few months shy of reaching his majority. Their paths crossed from time to time, mostly here at the Dragons. They were more acquaintances than friends, but he might offer some interesting conversation that would prevent Locke from returning home a mere two hours after leaving. He didn't want Portia thinking he couldn't abide being away from her. "Not at all."

While waving two fingers at a passing footman, Beaumont dropped into the chair across from Locke. He still had a boyish look to his features as though he'd secured an elixir that would prevent him from aging. "I understand congratulations on a marriage are in order," he said to Locke as a footman set a tumbler of whiskey on the table. Footmen memorized the members' drinking preference. Beaumont raised his glass. "I wish you well."

Locke lifted his own glass. "Thank you." The sip didn't satisfy as much as it might if Portia were here with him. He seemed to enjoy everything more when she was about.

"I'm trying to recall her name. It was in the paper . . . uh, Peony?"

"Portia."

"Unusual name."

"She's an unusual woman."

"I look forward to meeting her." He glanced around as though he might spy her in a room reserved for only gentlemen. "Did you bring her here tonight?"

"No, she's at the residence resting. The journey tired her out."

"I can well imagine. Quite a trek from Havisham." Although no one, other than Ashe and Edward, visited Havisham, most were familiar with it if for no other reason than to spread the tales that it was haunted. "How did you make her acquaintance?"

"Through my father."

Beaumont's brown eyes widened. "I was under the impression he never left the estate."

"Living as a recluse doesn't mean one is isolated from the world. He has his ways."

He chuckled low. "No doubt. My father always spoke fondly of him, regretted that he'd stopped coming to London or visiting our estate for the annual ball my mother so enjoyed putting on."

Locke had attended a couple of the balls. The Countess of Beaumont's affairs were legendary. Although, with her passing, the country parties ceased. Everything changed with the death of the matriarch. As a bachelor, Beaumont certainly wasn't going to be arranging parties at his estate or here in London.

"What of you, Beaumont? You should be looking to marry soon, I should think." Dear God, could he sound any more established and old? He felt ancient. Where he'd once embraced gambling, drinking, and seeking out women, at the moment he wanted nothing more than to be at home sitting before a lazy fire, listening as Portia enthralled him with tales of her day. It didn't matter how mundane or unexciting her adventures, he still took pleasure in them, in the way her eyes would light up when she reported on the progress made in readying a room.

"I have set my sights on a couple of ladies, to be sure. I shall probably settle on one of them before the Season is done, get on with it, as it were. Like you, I do require an heir."

Settle on one of them? It sounded atrocious and terribly unfair to the girl, and yet hadn't Locke thought the same thing when he'd decided to take Portia as his wife? He'd considered her perfect, *settled* on her, because he'd thought he could never love her. Christ, she deserved better than that.

He shot to his feet.

"Off somewhere?" Beaumont asked.

"I must apologize for my abrupt departure, but there is a matter that requires my attention."

Not a matter, but a lady, one who it seemed was coming perilously close to holding the key to his heart—no matter how much he wished it otherwise.

While Locksley had left her sated, Portia had been unable to fall asleep after he left. She'd rung for Cullie and dressed for dinner, although she hadn't much liked dining alone. Now feeling rather like a wraith, she wandered through the hallways striving to get a better sense of the place. The difference between this residence and Havisham Hall was striking. Not a single door was locked. She didn't need keys to access anything. Every room, even the ones not in use, held flowers. But they didn't hold what she was truly searching for: company.

She missed Locksley, damn it all. Something about the night made her all the more lonely and bereft, made her question if she should be here—not so much in London, but with him.

While living in London, she'd harbored so many dreams of love. Once she left, she thought she'd given up on them, but they were working hard to surface. The love of her child would be enough to sustain her, or so she hoped, because she was finding herself yearning for the love of a man.

She made her way to her bedchamber—hers and hers alone. She didn't like that Locksley's was beside hers, even if only a door separated them. How silly she'd been that first day to be forlorn because she wouldn't have a room of her own. She doubted she'd be able to sleep without his arms around her. Perhaps she'd simply read until she heard him return and then slip into his bed and seduce him.

She rang for Cullie, grateful to get out of her confining clothes. She was going to have to do away with a corset very soon, should probably visit a seamstress while they were in town to acquire some better-fitting frocks. It seemed every aspect of her was changing. Even her shoes were beginning to feel tight.

"Will there be anything else, m'lady?" Cullie asked once she'd finished brushing out and braiding Portia's hair.

"No. I'll see you in the morning."

"It's exciting being in London."

Portia didn't share her enthusiasm. She wished to be anywhere else. "After you help me dress in the morning, you can take the day off, go exploring."

"Truly?"

"I'll get you some pin money from his Lordship."

Cullie smiled brightly. "Thank you, m'lady."

"Have one of the footmen escort you around. There are some bad elements in this town. You'll want to avoid them."

"Aye, I will." She bobbed a quick curtsy. "Good night, m'lady."

With a smile, Portia shook her head and wandered to the window. She didn't know if she'd ever convince Havisham's newest female servants that they didn't have to curtsy to her all the time. Looking out, she could see the fog rolling in, the streetlamps eerily glowing through the mist. Holding herself, she rubbed her hands up and down her arms, trying to shake off a sense of foreboding.

As she began to turn away, she caught sight of a coach drawing up in the drive. Her husband leaped out before it fully stopped. Alarm raced through her. Something was wrong, she was quite sure of it. Had he somehow discovered the truth? Or had word of something dire come from Havisham?

She dashed into the hallway, was halfway to the stairs, when he suddenly appeared on the landing. "What's wrong? What's happened?" she asked.

His long strides ate up the distance between them. "I've discovered I don't like to go places without you."

The joy at his words hit her just as he swept her up into his arms. Laughing, she tightened her hold on his neck. "It was so lonely here without you."

"Lonely." He carried her into the room, set her next to the bed. "Before you, I didn't even know what the word meant."

"Surely there were others at the club to keep you company."

"Boring people who spoke of new farming methods,

the scourge of new wealth, their fascination with American heiresses, and tennis tournaments at Wimbledon."

"I've never played tennis."

He was kissing her neck while loosening the buttons of her nightdress. "I'll teach you, but for now, I have another sport in mind, one in which you excel."

Heat rushed through her body at his compliment. She knew they were well matched between the sheets but she liked having the confirmation that she pleased him. The soft cotton shimmered along her skin, pooling on the floor.

He attacked his own clothes as though they were an enemy to be vanquished. She brushed his hands aside. "We're going to have to hire a valet just to maintain your clothing. I spend half my day sewing your buttons back on."

"Give the chore to one of the maids."

"I like doing it." When he was away in the mines, it made her feel closer to him. She'd done what she'd promised herself she'd never again do: she'd fallen for someone, for him, even knowing that he had the power to destroy her.

When his clothes were piled in an untidy heap, he lifted her onto the bed and joined her there, hovering over her, looking down on her, holding her gaze as though seeing her for the first time. Lowering himself to his elbows, he grazed his knuckles over her cheeks, then he claimed her mouth as though he owned it.

She was his.

He almost said aloud the words that reverberated through his soul. She belonged to him in the same manner that clouds belonged to the sky and leaves to the trees and ore to the earth, part and parcel, a piece of the whole. He was not one for poetry, yet for her he wished he had the ability to write sonnets. He wished he'd met her at a ball, had courted her—properly with flowers, strolls, and rides in the park. But romantic gestures were as foreign to him as love.

He'd never wanted emotional entanglements, yet he couldn't deny that she had the ability to tie him up in knots.

Sliding his mouth from hers, he grazed his lips along the underside of her chin, relishing her soft moan. She was so quick to burn. He loved that about her. From the beginning she'd never played hard to get in the bedchamber. She'd welcomed him, responded, given back.

Was it possible to love things about a person without loving the person?

So many things about her brought him pleasure. The way she laughed. The way her eyes smoldered when he kissed her. The way she smelled after she left her bath. The fragrance she carried on her after he pleasured her.

Bracketing his hands on either side of her ribs, he scooted down until he could easily take the tip of her breast into his mouth. With an urgent whimper, she lifted her hips, pressing her womanhood against his abdomen. He'd never been one to boast of his exploits or to rank his encounters with women. He accepted that each would be different, not better or worse, simply different, and he always found enjoyment in the differences.

He could have a lifetime of bedding her and never grow bored. But tonight he didn't want to bed her; he wanted to make love to her. He wanted to kiss every inch of her, stroke every line and curve, taste every aspect of her. He wanted her scent, heated with passion, filling his lungs. He wanted her cries filling his ears.

He wanted to begin anew, exploring her as though she were a novel discovery.

Dragging his tongue from the tip of one breast to the other, he was aware of her thighs pressing against his hips as though she feared she would fly away if she weren't secured.

"You're so beautiful," he rasped, easing himself lower, planting light kisses along each of her ribs.

"You make me feel beautiful."

He wanted to give her so many gifts: the gift of touch, the gift of pleasure, the gift of a shattering orgasm. He wanted her falling apart in his arms, wanted to hold her afterward as she came back together. For her, he wished he were a romantic, wished he knew the fine art of wooing.

But he'd never planned to court any woman, had always planned to be practical about his selection of a wife. That first day he'd been practical about her. He'd seen a woman whom he could never love.

Only now did he realize that he hadn't seen at all. He'd been blind.

SOMETHING was decidedly different tonight. She wasn't certain exactly what it was. The need was more intense, deeper. He kissed and licked his way down to her toes, so slowly, so provocatively, almost as though he were worshipping her, as though she were a goddess deserving of his adoration.

He moved back up, lingering at her thigh, teasing her with a promise that he wouldn't stop there, that he had no intention of halting until she was writhing and begging.

"Don't torment me."

He licked her, nipped her. "I like how hoarse your voice gets when you're on the brink of pleasure."

"What else do you like?"

His mouth stayed on her thigh, but he lifted his smoldering gaze to her. She didn't know if he'd ever looked more dangerous or more appealing. "I like the way you taste."

Then he was tasting . . . the honeyed spot between her thighs, and she was no longer on the brink of pleasure but had fallen into its vortex, arching her back, clutching the sheets, feeling as though every nerve ending had come alive. He made her feel things she'd never felt before, experience sensations that had only hovered, had never been fully realized. He carried her to levels she'd not known existed; he caused her to soar.

Her cries echoed around her as she took flight. She was still ascending when he plunged into her deep and sure. Wrapping her legs around him, she scraped her fingernails along his buttocks, relishing his growl as he arched his back and pumped into her, faster, harder—

His deep groan, his shuddering body told her that he, too, was soaring. She couldn't help it. She laughed, a quick burst of pure, unadulterated joy.

His responding laughter was quieter, lower, as he pressed his forehead to hers. "Don't let this go to your head, but I have never enjoyed being with a woman so much."

"It's a sin how much I enjoy what we do."

"Don't be ridiculous. We're married, which makes it all legal in heaven and on earth."

"But we do such wicked things."

"Mmm. All the better."

Rolling off her, he brought her up against his side and slowly trailed his fingers along her arm. With her head nestled in the nook of his shoulder, she relished the beat of his heart, wondering if it were possible that he might unlock it just a little bit.

Chapter 21

$\mathcal{P}$ORTIA should have made an excuse so she could have avoided coming to London, but the truth was that sooner or later she'd have to return and confront her demons. Sooner was better, get it behind her.

She'd had the coachman take her to a dressmaker's—one of the more posh establishments that catered to ladies of nobility, according to the gossip rags—and told him to return for her in four hours. Once she'd been fitted for a lilac ball gown and another blue gown, she'd walked out and hired a hansom to bring her to the outskirts of London.

She regretted that the blue gown wouldn't look exactly as the one before it, but what she had described to the seamstress didn't look quite right when she'd finished sketching it out. Still, Portia couldn't risk going to Lola, the woman she'd used before, couldn't take a chance on someone recognizing her, spreading the word that she was here, and the truth of her past coming to light. Lola's clients didn't include noble ladies, but those for whom she did sew clothing kept quite a few aristocratic men company.

Which begged the question: What the devil was Portia doing slowly walking through her old neighborhood, strolling by her prior residence? She couldn't linger, couldn't stand on the corner and watch, hoping to catch sight of a new resident now. But she thought if she walked by she might be able to determine if someone else lived there, if Montie had moved on. If he'd replaced her, it was quite possible that even if he spotted her, he wouldn't care. He'd ignore her. His pride would force him to.

He had so damned much pride. As much as her father. She'd thought all men were the same until Locksley. It would be so much easier if she hadn't come to care for him. While she knew it had been wrong to marry him, he'd been so unpleasant when they'd first met that she convinced herself he deserved what he got: a woman of sin who had once belonged to another.

But now . . .

Dear God, she would sell her soul to Satan and gladly spend eternity burning in hell for the chance to go back in time, to have folded up that contract when he tossed it back into her lap, to have walked out of the residence, out of his life. She'd never expected him to want to appear in public—in London, among his peers—with her at his side. She'd stupidly thought he'd relegate her to the bed-chamber as Montie had. That he'd keep her sequestered at Havisham Hall. That she would be his dirty little secret.

As she neared the townhome where she had lived for two years, memories assailed her. The joy, the happiness, the sadness, the heartbreak. She had grown up here in the presence of a man far more brutal than her father. Her father had struck at her flesh. Montie had struck at her young, vulnerable heart.

She'd thought it would forever remain shattered, but it had somehow pieced itself together and had fallen once more.

A door opened, in the townhome next to what had

been hers. Portia froze, not even daring to breathe, as she watched the young woman exiting. Sophie. Portia didn't know her last name. In this part of London, on this street in particular, women did not own up to their surnames.

Portia turned before she could be spotted and began walking in the other direction. The action shamed her. She'd once enjoyed tea with Sophie on numerous occasions. They'd pretended to be ladies of quality delicately sipping Darjeeling while chatting about tawdry things that ladies of quality would never discuss. Through Sophie—who had a reputation for being incredibly knowledgeable in the ways of men—Portia had learned the skills necessary to please a man, to act coy, to hold his interest. Although in hindsight, she had to admit she'd learned a great deal more from Locksley, yearned to please him more than she'd ever wanted to please Montie. It was a strange path she'd traveled to get where she was today. Sophie had been instrumental in helping her escape, and here Portia was running away from the only person she'd been able to call friend since the day she learned that her family refused to acknowledge her.

And here she was secretly snubbing that person for fear that she'd again be judged, that the one person she had trusted might betray her. She was stronger than this, better than this. Abruptly, she spun around.

But Sophie was nowhere to be seen. She hated the relief that swamped her. She was safe, her secret was safe. For now.

She wanted to wait here and see if anyone emerged from her former dwelling, but her curiosity, her possible peace of mind, wasn't worth the risk. Besides, Montie's possibly moving on didn't guarantee that he would leave her alone. All she could do was hope that her plans weren't on the verge of coming unraveled.

"*I* LIKE your new blue gown."

Tugging on her gloves at her dressing table, Portia glanced over to her husband standing in the doorway that joined the two bedchambers. Dressed in his evening finery that included a black swallow-tailed coat and waistcoat, pristine white shirt and a light gray cravat, he was no doubt the most handsome man she'd ever laid eyes on.

"It's not exactly like the one before it," she said, wondering how it was that after all these months he managed to take away her breath.

"Close enough. A shame your previous seamstress closed up shop."

A small lie she'd told to explain why she was going to a different dressmaker. "I like the new one I've found."

"Good." His stride was slow, lazy, as he approached. "Also a shame you must wear gloves."

"It's a proper ball. A proper lady wears proper gloves to a proper ball." As though to demonstrate, she gave a gentle tug on the end of each glove where it rested just above her elbow.

They'd been in London for a little over a week, not attending any social functions because he didn't deem any of them grand enough for the unveiling of his wife. But tonight's ball—hosted by the Duke and Duchess of Lovingdon—was certain to be well attended, as they were one of the most beloved couples in all of London. Thanks to the gossip sheets, Portia knew all about them. The affair would be a mad crush of people. While she might be introduced to everyone who was anyone, it was also possible that she might be able to avoid running into anyone she didn't wish to encounter. She rose. "Let me just get my wrap."

She was in the process of taking a step and turning when he placed a hand on her bared shoulder. "Wait."

He had yet to put on his gloves, and the warmth of his skin on hers caused her to melt just a little. How was she going to make it through the evening without giving away how badly she wanted him whenever he touched her? "Do we really need to go out?" she asked, offering her most sultry look and placing a gloved hand so it rested partway on his waistcoat, partway on his shirt.

"Introducing you to Society was one of the reasons we came to London."

"I thought you came here because you had matters to see to."

"I did, and one of those matters involves tonight. I've been fending off questions about you since we arrived. At the Lovingdon ball, the curious will be appeased."

"I worry that I'll embarrass you."

"Good God, Portia, where's the woman to whom I opened the door, the one who mistook me for a footman?"

That woman hadn't cared about him, hadn't wanted to make him proud, had cared only about her own needs. She angled her chin. "I was under the impression that you weren't too keen on me that day."

He trailed his finger along her collarbone. "Still, you managed to win me over, didn't you?"

Her heart slammed against her ribs. As much as she craved his love, she could think of nothing worse than obtaining it.

"Here, a little something to commemorate the night."

Glancing down, she saw the black velvet box he extended toward her. Where had that come from? A jacket pocket obviously. Her emotions were already raw, her nerves frayed. A gift from him would only fill her with more regrets. She shook her head. "You've given me enough. A new gown, a dressing table, the piano tuned—"

"Let's not argue about this."

"But it's jewelry, isn't it? It's too much, too personal."

"You're my wife."

"Not because you wanted me to be."

"I want you to be tonight." With his free hand, he cradled her cheek. "Tonight you'll be the most beautiful woman there, the most generous, the most mysterious, the cleverest, the boldest. And the only one without a piece of jewelry."

Her stomach loosened. "So this is for you, so your wife doesn't appear to be a pauper."

"We'll say that's the case if it'll allow you to take it."

Which meant it wasn't the case. "Was it your mother's?"

"No. I purchased it this week. It occurred to me that I've never seen you wear jewelry."

"I wear a ring."

"Then wear this as well." He took her hand and closed it around the velvet. "One is always supposed to be grateful for a gift."

"I've never known one not to come without strings."

"No strings, Portia. You're the wife of a lord and as such, you should wear jewelry."

So it was his pride. Easier to accept knowing that. But when she opened the case, when she saw the beautiful pearl necklace and matching bracelet, she couldn't refrain from releasing a sigh of pleasure.

"You like it?"

It was strange to hear the doubt in his voice, to know her opinion mattered.

"It's perfect. Simple yet elegant. I didn't realize you had such good taste."

"I married—" He stopped, cleared his throat and took the velvet box from her.

She could only surmise that he'd been about to say that he'd married her as a sign of his good taste, and then thought better of it. It showed his bad taste whether he knew it or not. Taking the necklace, he moved in behind her and secured it at her throat.

Gazing at her reflection in the mirror, she couldn't believe how the small pearls transformed her, at least providing the illusion she was a lady. He placed her bracelet at her wrist.

She touched his jaw. "I don't deserve you, and you certainly deserve better than me."

"I'm not so certain then that we're not well matched if we both think the other deserves better."

She was devastated with the realization that he thought she deserved better than him. All she could do was ensure that she was worthy of him. She touched her fingers to the cool pearls at her throat. "I'm the luckiest woman in all of London to have you as my husband."

Placing his hands on her shoulders, pressing his lips to the curve of her neck, he held her gaze in the reflection. "After we return home, I'm removing everything from you except the pearls. When I'm done with you, I promise you will consider yourself the luckiest woman in all of Great Britain."

WHILE a husband had the right to sit beside his wife in the coach, Locke preferred sitting across from his because it afforded him the opportunity to gaze on her more fully, to watch her more closely. Every now and then the light from the streetlamps they passed would reflect off the pearls. He'd bought them because he wanted to lavish her with gifts, wanted her to have everything she'd ever desired.

It was crushing him to realize how much he cared for her.

She was gorgeous in the blue. Whenever she looked at him, there was always a sultriness to her gaze that caused his body to react as though she'd stripped herself bare. But it was more than the sex that appealed to him. It was her generosity of spirit, the way she was uncomfortable accepting something as simple as pearls.

Those who met her tonight would be captivated. She could hold her own. Of that he had no doubt.

"It didn't occur to me to ask if you danced," he said.

Her lips curled up into a soft smile. "I attended a country dance or two. And I'm quite adept at following."

"I hadn't noticed you being quite so docile as all that."

"You wouldn't care for me much if I were docile."

"No, I wouldn't." He liked that she was strong, knew her own mind, went after what she wanted—even if it had brought her to his father's door.

"Are you friends with the Duke and Duchess of Lovingdon?" she asked.

"I know them relatively well. You'll like them, and they'll like you. I chose their ball because the duchess is particularly kind when it comes to easing people into Society. Neither of them have any prejudice against commoners since a good many of their close relatives aren't nobility by birth."

"I don't think the aristocracy is what it once was."

"I fear you're right. I suppose it goes without saying that you're not to discuss my role at the mines."

"Work is nothing of which to be ashamed."

"I'm not ashamed—" Except maybe he was. He hadn't told Ashe or Edward that he'd taken to digging alongside the miners. "I simply prefer that my business remain private."

"I'm proud of you, you know. Proud to be your wife."

She glanced quickly out the window as though she'd revealed too much.

He was grateful that she was absorbed in the passing scenery rather than the shock and relief that had no doubt crossed his features. He was usually so good at keeping his thoughts, his feelings to himself, but she somehow always managed to unman him.

"It takes a great deal of courage to do what one must when it goes against the grain." She peered over at him. "I know you'd rather not be working the mines."

"All gentlemen prefer a life of leisure."

"Only you've never had one, not really. It can't have been easy growing up without a mother. Then all the traveling you've done. You went on expeditions that pushed you to your limits. You returned home to care for your father, the estates. Nothing easy in that. I've come to admire you, Locksley. I wish . . ."

Her voice trailed off, her attention went back to the window.

"You wish what?" he asked.

She shook her head.

"Portia?"

"I wish we'd met under different circumstances."

Under different circumstances, the moment he'd have deduced she was a woman he might come to like or admire, he'd have walked away in order to protect his heart and his sanity. "Is there any other situation under which we might have met?"

A sad, hollow burst of laughter echoed throughout the coach. "Not anything particularly ideal, I'm sure."

The coach slowed, stopped. She leaned closer to the window. "It appears we're here. There's quite a queue of vehicles."

"It tends to move quickly. Shouldn't take us long to get to the front."

Portia bobbed her head, released a long sigh, and touched her fingers to the pearls, torn between wishing to get all of this over with and hoping the ball might have ended by the time they arrived. But Locksley was correct. The coach pulled to a stop in the curved drive sooner than she'd expected. A footman leaped into action, opening the door, handing her down. Once she was standing on the drive, she could see that they weren't unloading a single carriage at a time but were unloading several so they could make way for the next group.

So many people dressed in glorious finery were climbing up the wide steps that led to the open door.

"Try not to gawk," Locksley said, offering his arm.

"It's an incredibly large residence."

"It's just a residence."

"That's rather like saying the queen is just a woman."

"To Albert, she probably was."

"It is said she ruled his heart. Do you think he could forget that she ruled an empire as well?"

"I should think love would demand it, but then it's not my area of expertise."

They walked into the foyer and Portia was struck not only by its magnificence but by the sense that it was truly a home. Love resided here.

They were guided into the front parlor where they deposited her wrap, his hat, and his cane. Then they followed the line up the stairs. Locksley acknowledged those standing nearest to them, introduced her, but she was too in awe of her surroundings to remember names.

She'd once dreamed of this, of attending an affair such as this one. She'd thought when she'd left Fairings Cross that this was her future, only she'd anticipated standing beside a different man, one who loved her, one whom she loved. She'd finally arrived but not at all as she expected.

They walked through a doorway and onto a landing. A gentleman was announcing guests, who would then descend into the ballroom. The mirrors glistened; the chandeliers sparkled. She imagined the ballroom at Havisham would have held its own against this one.

One couple was before them. She was keenly aware of Locksley leaning down, brushing his lips over her ear. "I'm equally proud to have you at my side this evening, Portia."

Gratitude washed through her, even as guilt pricked at her conscience. Before she could utter so much as a syllable, he'd straightened, stepped forward, and handed the invitation to the majordomo.

"Lord and Lady Locksley!" he announced.

Then her husband was escorting her down the stairs that would lead her into either heaven or hell.

Chapter 22

DURING the entire journey down the interminable flight of stairs, Portia not only saw but felt all the eyes coming to bear on them and feared someone would discern the truth and yell out, "Fake, liar, deceiver!"

But she heard only quiet murmurings, spotted an eyebrow or two raised in curiosity. She straightened her spine, lifted her chin. She'd spent a good deal of her life playing a role. No reason to stop now.

As she stepped onto the floor, Locksley led her over to the Duke and Duchess of Lovingdon, who were greeting their guests. They were a handsome couple, the duke as dark haired as her own husband, the duchess with hair a much more pleasant shade of red than her own. She'd always felt hers was too fiery, too harsh—perhaps because her father had thought it a sign that she was possessed of the devil.

"It's such a pleasure to meet you," the duchess said with a kind smile.

"I'm honored," Portia said, dipping into a deep curtsy.

"Where did you find such a treasure, Locksley?" the duke asked.

"My father introduced us. I could not resist marrying her."

Portia held back the grimace at the words that she had little doubt he would be repeating throughout the evening.

"How is the marquess?" Lovingdon asked.

"Quite well. Not up to traveling but holding his own."

"Having lost my father at an early age, I envy you somewhat having yours still about."

"On most days I'm grateful for his presence, although there are times when he gets up to some mischief with which I'd rather not have to deal." His smile was self-deprecating and when he winked at her, she understood clearly that she was the mischief to which he was referring.

"We must get together for tea sometime," the duchess said to her.

"I look forward to it." Portia meant the words more than she thought possible. She had no doubt that the duchess would prove a strong ally should one ever be needed.

As Locksley led her away, she fought to shake off her awe that she was walking among the nobility and being treated as though she was one of them. They hadn't gone far before they were surrounded by a mad crush of people. She'd known her husband was a darling of Society, easily forgiven any transgression, but it was a revelation to witness how he was genuinely welcomed and adored—and their acceptance of him was transferred to her. As though she was worthy simply because he'd taken her to wife.

The array of introductions was dizzying. She wanted to make him proud but it was all so overwhelming as she struggled to associate names she recognized with faces she didn't. Then there were those she'd never heard of, older couples who might have been gossiped about in their youth, but were now settled into mediocrity. Locksley seemed to know them all, was comfortable with them. She kept her posture perfect, took the appropriate curtsies when necessary, expressed delight at making their acquaintance, and was quick to pose a question before one was asked of her, a little trick her mother had taught her. When one had something to hide, it was better to be the one listening than the one talking.

People always welcomed an opportunity to speak about themselves, and her interest in them flattered them. Her mother's attentiveness had always been feigned. Portia's wasn't. For as long as she could remember the aristocracy had enamored her. That tiny captivation had led to her downfall, if she were honest about it. Odd that her disgrace had led her to be where she had once thought to socialize.

"I must beg your forgiveness," Locksley said, "but Lady Locksley's favorite tune is starting up and I promised her a dance. If you'll excuse us . . ."

Before she even knew what was happening, his hand was at her waist and he was expertly wending them around couples, causing them to part with no more than a dashing smile and an occasional word. Then he was sweeping her over the dance floor, and for the first time since their arrival, she finally felt as though she could breathe.

"I'm not familiar with this song," she confessed.

"They'd have never let us go if we told them that. You held up rather well under the circumstances."

"They all love you."

"I wouldn't go that far. But my tragic life has made them more willing to make exceptions for me than they might for others."

"I suspect a good many of the single ladies were hoping to drag you to the altar one day. Was there one you fancied?" She didn't know why she'd never thought to ask before—perhaps because his popularity on paper had seemed distant—but having finally witnessed it in person, she found it impossible to ignore. He could have had anyone.

"Bit late to be asking that."

He had sworn to never love but that didn't mean that he hadn't liked. She angled her chin. "You're right. I daresay you couldn't have cared for her very much if you were willing to give her up so easily and quickly for me."

He grinned darkly, wickedly. "Trying to ease your conscience?"

"I possess no conscience to ease."

"I don't believe that. And no. There was no one I fancied enough to want to marry, and if I did fancy a lady, I walked in the opposite direction."

Faced with the reality of his lack of interest in love, she found it rather sad. "Would you have really chosen someone you could never love?"

He arched a brow, gave her a pointed look.

"I don't count. You didn't choose me. I was forced on you. I simply can't imagine you purposely seeking out someone who would make you miserable."

"Marrying someone I loved would have made me miserable, worrying that I might lose her, might follow my father's path toward lunacy."

"You can't judge love by your father's experience. Or maybe you can. I believe while your mother lived that they had an incredibly happy life."

"And when she died, he went mad."

"I'm not so certain. He misses her, imagines she's still with him. Is that so awful?"

"You had love in your first marriage and chose to give it up for the second go-round. What you sought for a second marriage isn't so different from what I sought in my first. I was simply pragmatic and recognized the value of a loveless marriage sooner than you did."

The final strains of the song lingered on the air as he brought them to a stop. "Ready to face the hordes again?"

She released a long sigh. "I suppose."

"I'm not."

The music started up and she again found herself in the circle of his arms, held tighter and nearer this time. She tossed back her head and laughed. "You'll have people speculating that you're madly in love with your wife, that you can't stand the notion of giving her up."

He didn't respond, merely studied her intently, his green eyes boring into hers. "You enjoy dancing."

"I love dancing."

"Tonight others are going to want to dance with you."

"I'll politely decline."

He shook his head. "No need on my account. I shall dance with other ladies. Out of politeness only, of course. As our arrangement requires that we show respect toward and for each other, especially in public."

Their arrangement. She wanted their arrangement to go to the devil. But she had accepted the terms. The gift of the jewelry, the pride with which he introduced her, had caused her to think that perhaps he had begun to love her. How would the ladies of London feel to know he was a man with no heart? No, he had a heart. He just refused to open it to the possibility of love.

"If I dance with anyone else, it will be only out of politeness as well." She moved the hand that rested on his shoulder slightly, just enough so she could skim her gloved finger along his jaw. "But I'll save the last dance for you."

And until she was in his arms again, she knew she'd be miserable.

H<small>E</small> wasn't jealous. He'd known men would want to dance with her and had encouraged her to dance with other partners. So this irrational need coursing through him to rip off limbs whenever a man took her in his arms was not jealousy. He didn't know what it was other than dark and irritating.

"Here, drink this," Ashe ordered. "You look as though you are on the verge of murdering someone."

Locke glanced over at the glass containing amber liquid, took it, and enjoyed a long swallow. "Where did you find that?"

"Card room. So who has earned your ire?"

He didn't know if the man had earned it. "Sheridan."

"Ah, dancing with Portia, I see."

And before Sheridan, it had been Avendale, who everyone knew was madly in love with his wife. No danger there of his seeking a dalliance with Portia, and even if he did, she would decline. If there was one thing regarding his wife of which he was absolutely convinced, it was her loyalty.

"You made quite the splash with your arrival. You had to know men were going to want to dance with her," Ashe said.

"They don't have to hold her so close or look so beguiled."

"She's beguiling."

Locke glared at his longtime friend.

Ashe held up a hand. "Not to me, of course. Minerva is the only woman who interests me. Good God, if I didn't know better I'd say you were jealous, but that would require that you care for her."

"I care that she is my wife. Those randy swells should respect that."

Ashe had the audacity to chuckle low. "We didn't when we were bachelors."

"We engaged in harmless flirtation."

"So are they."

Only it didn't look harmless. It looked bloody irritating.

"Come play a hand of cards."

"No, I'm claiming the next dance." And the one after that. Christ, what was wrong with him? They were just dancing—in the middle of a crowded dance floor, chandeliers glowing, mirrors capturing their reflection. It was impossible for anything untoward to occur without all of London witnessing it. She wouldn't engage in such unconscionable behavior. She wouldn't embarrass him.

"I think you have come to care for her," Ashe said, a fissure of glee in his tone.

"You talk too damned much." How long was this stupid tune? He should simply cut in.

"Growing up under the care of your father, I convinced myself that love was to be avoided. I was wrong. Loving Minerva has enriched my life beyond all imagining."

"I don't love Portia." The words were delivered succinctly, flatly.

Ashe patted him on the shoulder. "Keep telling yourself that."

Thank God his friend finally walked away, leaving him to brood in peace. He didn't love her, he couldn't love her, he wouldn't love her. But the fact remained that of late, he was at peace when he was with her. She calmed his soul, made the future seem less bleak. She wore optimism like a spring cloak. She looked at a decaying room and saw possibilities.

His heart was as decaying as those rooms: never touched, never visited, never opened. She made him want to take a chance, made him want to offer what she so richly deserved. Only now she carried his child and the possibility of her death hovered. Standing here, he was likely to do something he'd come to regret if he didn't drive himself mad first. Ashe was right. He needed a distraction. A hand or two of cards. Then when he no longer felt like killing someone he'd dance with his wife.

He was halfway up the stairs when the music stopped, reached the landing when he realized that he had no desire whatsoever to play cards. He wanted to be with Portia, to take her on a walk about the garden, kiss her in the shadows. The very last thing any man should want from a woman he could kiss anytime night or day, but he yearned for it with an unsettling fierceness.

Spinning around, he caught sight of her slipping out through the open doors that led onto the terrace. He didn't blame her for needing some fresh air. Instead of standing around disliking that she had the attention of so many men, he should have rescued her from her many admirers.

He headed back down the stairs.

$\mathcal{A}$s Portia stepped onto the terrace, she welcomed the cool night air brushing over her skin. Had she known she'd be dancing so much, she'd have brought a second pair of slippers. She wasn't certain how much longer the ones she was wearing would last, the soles already worn incredibly thin.

The terrace was remarkably absent of guests lingering about, most opting to walk through the gardens. The paths were lined with gaslights, which provided a soft glow that left the couples unidentifiable. She longed for a walk but deemed it would be improper without her husband to escort her, so she moved off to the far side of the tiled veranda where the shadows were thicker, and wrapped her gloved fingers around the wrought-iron railing. Inhaling deeply, she couldn't help but feel that the night had been a success. The only thing that would have made it more enjoyable was if Locksley had been her constant dance partner. No one else moved as smoothly as he did. With no one else did she feel as comfortable or as in tuned. With no one else—

"Hello, Portia."

Her thoughts skittered to a stop, her lungs ceased to function. For two hours, as she'd danced, she'd worried that the Earl of Beaumont would cross paths with her, but when he'd failed to materialize, she'd begun to believe that he wasn't in attendance. Regaining her wits, knowing how dangerous it was to have her back to him, she spun around, her skirts brushing against his legs because he stood so near, angled her chin haughtily, and looked down on him as much as she was able considering he stood several inches over her. She hated that he was as handsome as ever, the slight breeze toying with his blond curls as she once had. "Montie."

His hand, gloveless, bracketed her cheek, held her with a firmness that promised he'd make a scene if she tried to break free. He leaned in, inhaled sharply. "I've missed your fragrance."

"Unhand me. I'm married now, a viscountess—"

Rather than obey her, he merely wrapped his other hand around her upper arm. "Yes, I saw the announcement in the paper." So had she. Soon after the marquess had ordered his son to send their marriage news to the *Times*. Beaumont had known there was a possibility of running into her at a ball, had no doubt been keeping an eye out once the gossip sheets announced that Viscount Locksley and his new bride were in London. Her former paramour drew back, his dark eyes glittering, his lips twisted into a sneer. "Does your husband know about us?"

He jerked her closer until she could feel his breath on her cheek. Why had she ever thought she could escape him?

"No?" he asked mockingly. "I thought not. Otherwise,

why would he have married you? How did you manage to snag the last Hellion?"

"I need to return to the ballroom before he misses me."

"To miss you, he'd have to care about you. I know him well enough to know he's not a man who would give his heart. Unlike me, who loved you then and loves you still."

"You never loved me. Not really. If you did, you'd have not broken all your promises. You'd have married me."

"One does not marry for love; one marries for gain. Isn't that the reason you married Locksley? Because of what you would gain through him? A title. Position. But you are still mine. I want you to come to me tonight."

"No."

"I'll tell him everything."

She slammed her eyes closed. How had she ever thought she would be safe? And if he told Locksley the truth, what then? What recourse would he have except to toss her out on her ear? And she wouldn't blame him one whit.

"Take your hands off my wife."

Portia's eyes flew open at the quietly spoken words that echoed with warning and the promise of retribution. Even in the shadows, she could see Beaumont's victorious smile as he released her and slowly turned to the man whose face reflected a mask of fury that caused her own breath to back up painfully in her lungs.

"Locksley. I was just congratulating my former mistress on her recent marriage."

The rage remained as Locksley's gaze shifted from Beaumont to her. She could have sworn that for the briefest of moments she saw something else reflected in his eyes: pain. She wanted to die, wanted to beg his forgiveness, wanted to punch Beaumont until that handsome face of his was no longer handsome.

"Did she not tell you?" Beaumont asked cockily. "Two years—"

"Montie, don't," she whispered, despising her pleading tone.

"Oh, my dear, nothing good comes from secrets in a relationship. He deserves to know." His gaze never left Locksley. "For two years she warmed my bed—"

"Take her advice and hold your tongue," Locksley said.

Beaumont had the audacity to chuckle. "Surely you're curious."

"Get the hell out of here."

"As you wish. Farewell, sweet Portia. I wish you every happiness."

As though she could have that now. He'd ruined everything. How had she ever loved him?

He'd taken two steps forward, stopped when he stood even with her husband. "I can also see that other congratulations will soon be in order. Still I'd carefully count the months if I were you, Locksley."

Locksley's fist smashed into Beaumont's face. She heard bone cracking. Based on Beaumont's yelp, the way he was cradling his chin and rolling back and forth on the tiled floor, she assumed Locke had broken the man's jaw. She hoped so. She dearly did. She also prayed Locke had not damaged his hand.

Standing over Beaumont, Locksley pressed his foot to her former lover's chest, stopping his rocking from side to side. "Touch her again, and I'll slice off your hands. Speak to her again, and I'll cut out your tongue. Look at her again, and I'll pluck out your eyes. And if I hear any rumors regarding Portia's past or the paternity of the child she carries, I will destroy you."

He must have pressed his foot down harder because Beaumont grunted. When Locksley stepped back, the man rolled to his side and whimpered. Her husband held out his hand to her. "Let's be off, Portia."

She put her hand in his, trying to draw comfort from the closing of his fingers around hers, but there was nothing tender or gentle in his touch. He pulled her forward and she skirted around the moaning Beaumont.

"I can explain," she said quietly.

"Not now. We're leaving."

He spoke not a word as he led her around the side of the residence as though she were now something of which to be ashamed. When they reached the front, he sent one footman scurrying off to alert his driver they were ready to depart and another to fetch their things from the parlor. His face was expressionless except for the hard set of his jaw.

"You're hurting my hand," she said softly.

He immediately relinquished his hold, when all she'd wanted was for him to loosen his grip. When the footman arrived with their things, Locksley draped her wrap over her shoulders. After the coach arrived, he handed her inside before joining her and taking the seat across from her.

"Locksley—"

"Don't say anything, Portia."

His firm tone forced her to press her lips together to keep from speaking. She wanted to tell him everything, to explain it all, to help him to understand. Her desperation, her fears, her lack of options.

She held herself close. She was cold, so very cold. She didn't know if she'd ever feel warm again.

Once the coach pulled to a stop in front of the residence, he leaped out and waited as the footman assisted her, as though he could no longer bear to touch her. Into the house they went, in silence. Up the stairs. At her bedchamber, he shoved open the door and waited as she preceded him inside. With the door banging closed, she jumped, turned, and faced him.

"Were you with child on the day we wed?" His words sliced through the air, sliced into her heart.

She held out a hand imploringly. "Lock—"

"It's a simple question, Portia. Yes or no. Were you with child on the day we wed?"

She swallowed hard, wanted to lie, wanted the truth to be anything other than what it was. "Yes."

The way his blistering gaze slowly traveled over her as though he were only just seeing the true her for the first time made her want to weep. She stepped toward him. "It was never supposed to be you. I wasn't supposed to marry you. I was supposed to marry Marsden. And what would he care?" She flung out her arm. "He had his heir. You would marry and provide your heir. All I wanted was to protect this child, to give it a chance to survive, to thrive—"

"But it *was* me, Portia," he said quietly and yet his voice reverberated like the boom of thunder.

Turning on his heel, he strode from the room, slamming the door in his wake. She wanted to run after him, wanted to explain, but what more was to be said? How could she explain the inexplicable? Staggering back until her knees hit the chair, she crumpled and curled into a ball as the sobs had their way with her, causing her shoulders to shake, and her chest to ache, her throat to tighten. Devastation swept through her. She'd hurt him, deceived him, and in doing so, she'd destroyed that last bit of goodness she possessed.

Chapter 23

HE couldn't stomach the thought of being in the residence with her, considered going to the club, but he couldn't abide the notion of inflicting his foul mood on others or dealing with the possibility of running into Beaumont. He might truly kill the man if their paths ever again crossed.

So he sequestered himself in the library, with the door locked so no one could disturb him, and drank straight from a bottle of whiskey as though he were a barbarian. Everything made sense now. Why she'd answered his father's advert. Why she refused to speak of the past. Why her family wanted nothing to do with her.

She'd been a man's mistress.

He slung the bottle toward the fireplace, taking no solace as it shattered in the hearth, glass flying, whiskey splashing. He should be grateful there were no flames to catch the liquid alight, but at the moment he was hard-pressed to be thankful for anything. He stalked to the liquor cabinet, retrieved another bottle, and downed half the whiskey before coming up for air.

Damn her! Damn her! Damn her!

She'd made him care for her. He dropped into a chair and fought the excruciating anguish that threatened to bring him to his knees. He'd trusted her, enjoyed her company, made love to her. With her, it was more than sex. While he'd never left a lover wanting, he'd given more of himself to her than he'd ever given anyone.

Damn it all to hell if her betrayal didn't hurt more now for it. Had only a week passed since his damned meeting with Beaumont when he'd rushed home to be with her and had almost spouted that he loved her?

She made him want to recite poetry, enticed him into smiling, laughing. She lured him into looking forward to the day and anticipating the night. She calmed his demons and brought solace.

She'd made him believe that she carried his child. Acknowledging that deception very nearly doubled him over. Instead he gulped down what remained in the bottle, anything to dull the agony that threatened to rip him apart. He'd been right to shelter his heart all those years, to close it off to the mere hint of love.

Love was not something to be sought, heralded, or admired. It was merely a false mask for cruelty and disappointment.

He'd wanted a woman he couldn't possibly love. He'd certainly succeeded in that regard. Before dawn, he intended to wipe clear any kind thought, any joyful memory, any speck of caring where she was concerned. He would feel nothing toward her, nothing at all.

$\mathcal{P}$ORTIA had wept until exhaustion overtook her and she fell asleep fully clothed, lying on the floor. She didn't stir until the door opened and Cullie walked in.

"M'lady!" The young girl rushed over and knelt beside her.

"I'm all right," Portia assured her as she pushed herself up. She ached inside and out, but the inner pain was so much worse. Had she known Locksley then as she knew him now, she wouldn't have married him. But she'd thought him a man with no heart, who would never care for her, never care for their children. A man ruled by obligation.

A man she hadn't liked and didn't care if she deceived. But then Beaumont had taught her to trust no man. That every man cared about only his own selfish needs. So what was wrong with a woman doing the same?

So much, she realized now. So much was wrong with it. How would she ever live with herself?

"Here, m'lady, let me help you up."

She moaned as Cullie assisted her in standing. Her neck popped as she twisted it one way, then the other. Arching, she rubbed the small of her back. What a silly woman she'd been not to rouse herself and crawl into bed.

"You do look a fright, m'lady, but I think we can get a quick bath in if you like before we leave."

It seemed Portia's mind was as sluggish as her body. "Leave? What are you talking about?"

"We're returning to Havisham. His Lordship has ordered us to be packed and ready to depart within the hour."

But they were planning to stay until the end of the Season. She slammed her eyes closed. How could they after last night's revelation? "Where is Lord Locksley?"

"In the library."

"Do prepare a bath." She felt incredibly soiled, should have washed off Beaumont's touch from the night before, but she'd been too devastated by Locksley's reaction and words to do much of anything except wallow in regret. "I'll return momentarily." First she had to speak with her husband.

He was in the library just as Cullie had informed her. Sitting behind his desk, he looked as ghastly as she felt, shadows beneath his eyes, unshaven, his jacket, waistcoat, and neck cloth absent. With her arrival, he didn't bother to rise. Merely handed two envelopes to the waiting butler. "See that those are dispatched in the post today."

"Yes, m'lord." Burns pivoted sharply and headed for the door. He bowed his head slightly as he neared her. "M'lady."

"Burns." She waited until he was gone to approach the desk where Locksley had returned to scribbling pen over parchment, totally ignoring her. "I thought we were staying until the end of the Season, that you had business to attend to."

"Introducing you to Society was the business. Anything else I can handle from Havisham." He tossed down his pen, leaned back, and held her gaze, his green eyes revealing nothing, completely emotionless. "After last night, London has left a sour taste in my mouth."

"Will you let me explain?"

"What is there to explain, Portia? You were Beaumont's mistress. He got you with child and no doubt refused to marry you. For some reason, after living in sin for two years, you drew the line at bringing a bastard into the world. I suppose I should admire that you had a line you wouldn't cross when it came to improper behavior, but I'm hard-pressed under the circumstances to admire anything at all regarding you. You sought marriage to my father, taking advantage of a gentleman who isn't quite right. When I stepped in to protect him, you accepted me as a substitute knowing full well that another man's child"—he shoved back the chair and pushed himself to his feet—"could *bloody well be my heir!*"

She didn't know if she preferred the coldness of his gaze or the fury that now burned within the green depths. He was entitled to his anger. She wouldn't hold it against him nor would she turn away even as each second under his harsh glare flayed her heart.

"Have I the right of it?" he demanded.

"I've been praying for a daughter."

He laughed harshly. "Then let's bloody well hope that God answers that prayer, shall we? Between us, our child would have either red hair or black. How were you going to explain presenting me with a blond-haired child?"

"My father is blond, as I told you. It's possible—"

"You conniving tart, you have an answer for everything, don't you?"

His words were as hurtful as physical blows. She'd walk out if she weren't keenly aware that she deserved the unkindness he threw at her. Swallowing hard, she took a step nearer. "If you want to divorce me, I'm willing to publicly acknowledge that I was unfaithful." It would destroy her, but she had to make this right.

"Ah, yes, let's have all of London question my foolishness in marrying. There will be no divorce, as I suspect it will do no good, since that babe is coming at least two months early, isn't he? No matter how insistently either of us deny it, the law will make him mine. Even if I disowned him, even if I went to Parliament and admitted to being a fool—"

"You're not a fool."

"Of course I am. No, there will be no divorce." He moved around the desk and began to stalk toward her. "You will remain my wife."

She backed up. He advanced.

"But I want no more from you than I wanted the day we wed: for you to warm my bed when the need strikes."

She came to a halt so abrupt that he nearly slammed into her. "I will not be your whore."

"You were his."

The crack of her palm making contact with his cheek echoed through the room. "I was not his whore," she stated with utter conviction. His mistress, yes. The woman who had foolishly loved him, yes. But she'd never given herself to Beaumont for gain.

Locksley's gaze burned into hers. She could see the bright red hue of where she'd smacked him. His face had to be stinging as much as her hand.

"You'd do well to eat breakfast before we leave." He spun on his heel, presenting her with his back, walking away from her. "Our sojourn to Havisham will not be leisurely. We'll be stopping only at night."

At that moment, she realized she'd been mistaken when she believed Beaumont had broken her heart. He'd merely bruised it. Only Locksley had the power to shatter it, and he'd done it with remarkable ease.

*H*E had chosen to ride his horse rather than travel in the coach with her. Whenever they rounded a curve, she would look out the window and see him trotting ahead, such a lonely figure, the sight of which caused an ache in her chest. Although even from this distance, she could sense the anger roiling off him. He sat so stiffly in the saddle. Even when the dark clouds rolled in and the rain started, he didn't seek shelter within the confines of the vehicle. She should have welcomed his absence. Instead she mourned it.

Reaching into the wicker basket that the cook had presented to her before leaving, she removed a block of cheese, took a bite, and slowly chewed. There had to be some way to make this situation right. She didn't expect him to ever forgive her, wasn't certain she'd ever forgive herself. At the time, she'd had no choice, no options—or at least not any that she could see. In hindsight—

A light fluttering just below her waist caused everything within her to still. She dared not breathe, but simply waited for it to come again. Detecting the tiniest flickering, she placed her hand on her slightly rounded stomach and slowly released the air she'd been holding. Her babe. Tears stung her eyes. Her little one. How was it possible to love someone so much when she had yet to meet her— or him?

She'd burn in hell for the path she'd chosen to save this child. But at that particular moment she didn't care about her own welfare. She cared only that she knew beyond any doubt that no matter how furious Locksley may be at her, he'd not do what Beaumont had threatened: he'd not have the baby killed.

LOCKE had driven them hard all day. It wasn't that he was particularly anxious to return to Havisham, but he wanted to put as much distance between him and London as possible. Although he wasn't willing to kill the horses, so when the Peacock Inn had come into view he'd called for them to stop for the night.

He'd secured rooms, escorted his wife to hers, arranged for a tray to be taken to her, then settled at a table in the corner of the tavern. In need of a bath and shave, he more closely resembled a highwayman than a lord. But he hadn't the aspiration to see to either. He was beginning to understand why his father paid so little attention to his own appearance.

When one had been betrayed—whether by death or deception—the will to carry on shriveled into nothing. The depth of his despondency astounded him.

He'd thought of the child Portia carried as his, had believed it was his, had anticipated its arrival more than he'd thought possible. Then to discover that another man had planted the seed—

Every time he considered that moment on the terrace and the words Beaumont had flung at him, he wanted to put his fist through a wall—or better yet, through the blighter's handsome mug. When he contemplated the earl touching Portia, gliding his hands over her, kissing, suckling, thrusting—

God help him, he thought he would go mad.

It made no sense. He'd known when he married her that she'd been with another man, but he'd viewed him as an abstract shadow, given him very little thought. Besides, he'd believed him to be dead. Knowing the man was very much alive made everything repugnant. That she had willingly given herself—

His dark laughter had those sitting nearby turning their heads to stare at him. He finished off his ale and slammed the tankard on the table, getting the barmaid's attention. Not even a minute passed before he was gulping down a fresh pint.

He'd bedded women who weren't married to him, weren't married at all, and he'd never been disgusted by them. On the contrary, he'd considered them adventurous and fun. If he had met Portia under other circumstances, at a ball or a dinner or a garden party, he couldn't claim with certainty that he wouldn't have tried to seduce her. He'd wanted her the moment he'd opened the damned door to her. He'd have reveled in taking her, enjoyed every moment, and never once would he have blamed her or been put off by the fact that they weren't married.

I was never his whore.

Because she had loved the fellow. That portion of her story was true.

I've known love, my lord. It provided little security. Now I am in want of security.

He couldn't reconcile the fact that Beaumont had possessed her love and had tossed it away. Not that Locke had ever had any desire to possess her love or even wanted it—

"I've had a bath prepared for you."

He jerked his gaze up to Portia, who, by the looks of her, had bathed. Her cheeks were rosy, her hair was pinned up, and her traveling frock showed nary a wrinkle. "I'm not in need of a bath."

"I daresay even from here I can dispute that claim. Think of your poor horse. You wouldn't want him to expire from the fumes."

She was not going to make him smile or lessen his anger. "Return to your room, madam."

Instead of obeying him, she had the audacity to pull out the chair opposite him and take a seat. "Our arrangement was that we would at least be respectful to each other."

"That was before I knew you to be capable of horrendous deception."

"Once we married, I never lied to you."

"But you were certainly full of deceit before we married."

At least she had the good graces to flinch. "Will you not at least let me explain?"

"No."

"But if I—"

"No!" Once again, he garnered the unwanted attention of the tavern customers. "Do you not understand that I can barely stomach the sight of you? Why the devil do you think I'd prefer riding in the rain to traveling in a well-sprung conveyance?"

The woman who had stood up to him so many times blanched. Tears welled in her eyes. He wouldn't soften toward her. Ever. "I thought you a cold bastard."

"Even a cold bastard should have the choice of serving as father to another man's leavings."

"Would you have married me if you'd known?"

"No."

"Would you have allowed me to marry your father?"

"No."

"So you'd be out ten thousand quid."

"It would have been money well spent." But even as he spit out the words, he wasn't certain he spoke the truth. He wanted to hurt her as he'd been hurt, his agony making no sense. How was it that she had the power to decimate him?

"It must be a wonderful thing indeed to have never felt powerless, to have never been frightened, to have never been completely alone, abandoned by all those whom you thought had loved you. To experience the overwhelming responsibility of knowing an innocent child was completely dependent on you for survival." She pushed back the chair and stood. "I don't regret my actions, not a single one. I do regret that I seemed to have hurt you when I thought you were a man immune to hurt, to caring, to love."

"I don't love you."

"That's obvious. Good night, my lord."

She walked away. He ordered more ale, intending to drink himself into oblivion so he could forget, at least for a few hours, that never in his life had he been as content as he'd been with her before he walked out onto the terrace, that he'd begun to believe his father had given him a treasured gift when he'd brought Portia into his life.

He recalled the horror on her face when he'd announced that he would marry her. It had pricked his pride that she'd been so adamantly opposed to the notion. He was a good catch for any woman, but especially for a commoner who didn't move about in aristocratic circles. He understood now that she hadn't objected because she didn't want him; she'd objected because she didn't want to burden him with the child she carried.

She was correct that for his father it wouldn't have mattered. Locke fully intended to provide a son someday. To his father, the child would have merely been a welcome addition to the family. If only she'd told them the truth—

Locke would have scoffed and declared the contract voided.

What of the child she'd claimed had died? It would have been a bastard. Why not give the same care to it as she had to the second? Unless there had been no first child, unless she'd lied about its existence as a way to prove her fertility because she'd known an announcement she was with child would come shortly after they were wed. No wonder she'd been so concerned with consummating the marriage. If he hadn't been so randy, he would have messed up her plans. Instead he'd played right into her hands, taking her so often that it would be impossible to believe he hadn't gotten her with child.

Little wonder she hadn't been thrilled with the prospect of going to London and facing the possibility of running into Beaumont. Before Locke had interrupted their little tryst on the terrace, he'd seen her face marred with disgust, had heard her order him to unhand her. Had heard Beaumont's veiled threat that she come to him—no doubt because he'd tell Locke everything if she didn't.

He'd told him anyway, and Locke had seen the devastation crumple her face. But in his fury, he'd ignored it. He hadn't wanted to comfort her; he'd bloody well wanted to strangle her for playing him for a fool.

Why shouldn't she? He'd claimed to never love. He'd been forthright that he wanted only one thing from her:

her body. She'd no doubt seen the scapegrace Beaumont in Locke; only Locke was offering what Beaumont wouldn't: marriage.

Why shouldn't she have grabbed it with both hands?

Sitting here with far too much drink coursing through his veins, a thousand questions swirled through his mind, a thousand things he should have asked her. He should have pressed her regarding her reasons for responding to the damned advert, but he'd wanted to fill his palms with her breasts and fill her with his cock. He hadn't gone in search of the truth because he'd feared that it would prevent him from tasting her fully.

Perhaps he was no better than Beaumont. Perhaps he deserved her deception. He'd acted as a barbarian. Why should she have cared about the cost he would pay when he'd treated her no better than a whore?

PORTIA lay on her side beneath the covers, staring at the pale moonlight filtering in through the windows. Her life had been a series of escapes, of running away, each one leading to something worse than what had come before. Reading the gossip sheets, she'd never considered the nobility to be very noble. The men were womanizers; the ladies were silly chits who cared only about gowns, fans, and dance partners. None of them had real troubles or concerns. Through Montie, she'd learned they were a selfish lot concerned only with their own wants and needs.

The other mistresses she'd known had seen the upper crust as a means to an end. Nice residence, fancy clothes, fine jewelry. And if it meant giving up one's good name and reputation, they thought it worth it for all they gained to be spoiled and pampered, even if it meant indulging the whims of a specific gentleman anytime day or night.

To be his bird in a gilded cage, to sing when prompted, to keep silent otherwise.

Mistresses mistakenly believed they had some prestige, some power that eluded those silly shopgirls. Portia would have preferred to be a shopgirl.

She hadn't followed Beaumont to London to become his mistress. She'd followed him to become his wife.

Although she doubted Locksley would understand. She wished she hadn't been so quick to discourage any talk of their pasts. She'd been so worried that he'd figure her out that she hadn't given him a real opportunity to get to know her. Perhaps if she had, he'd have been more understanding when he learned the truth. Perhaps if she'd known him better, she'd have grasped how to tell him before Beaumont could toss out his hateful rejoinder.

She'd made such a mess of things, handled everything poorly. But knowing what Beaumont had planned for this child—*his* offspring—she'd seen no other choice in order to ensure the child's safety as well as her own. She'd needed someone who could stand up to the earl. Could a farmer or a shopkeeper or a blacksmith have taken Beaumont to task? Could any of them have struck him and not found themselves brought before a magistrate? Could any of them have threatened him with ruination and carried through on it if it came to that?

Locksley could. Locksley had and when his fist had struck Beaumont, at that moment, she loved him more than she thought it possible to love.

Hearing a key scraping in a lock, she bolted upright and reached over to increase the flame in the lamp. The door burst open. Locksley charged in, slammed it behind him, and stood there, his fists clenched at his sides, his eyes those of a madman. She'd seen him angry before, but he was always controlled. At that moment, it appeared he was barely holding on to a strained tether, that he was contemplating murder.

As she scrambled out of bed, he staggered across the room, stumbled, grabbed the post at the foot of the bed, and glared at her. "How did you come to be his mistress?" he demanded, revulsion hardening his voice.

She wanted to explain, to confess all, to tell him everything, but not when he was in this condition. "You're foxed." She didn't bother to hide her disgust at seeing him in this unkempt and repulsive state.

"At least three sheets to the wind, if not more." He wavered, tightened his grip on the post until his knuckles turned white. "Answer me, *my lady*. How the devil did you come to be his mistress?"

"Do you really want to do this here, where people might hear through the walls?"

"Bloody well explain to me what possessed you to crawl into his bed."

"I never crawled, damn you. I loved him. I thought he was going to marry me. I gave myself to him because I believed he loved me as well." Tears stung her eyes.

"For two years?"

She laughed bitterly, hollowly. "Where does a woman go once she is ruined? Once her family has washed their hands of her, declared she is dead to them? I loved him," she repeated. "I thought he would marry me. He never said he wouldn't. He only said it took a while. For the first time in my life I was happy. I felt cherished and appreciated. I don't expect you to understand, you who has an aversion to love, but having his cherished regard made me so much more than I was. I was so glad to have him in my life I would have done anything to keep him there, did do anything."

Breathing heavily, he closed his eyes, widened them

as though he struggled to stay focused on her. "How did you meet him?"

Clutching her hands together, she realized it all sounded so stupid now. What a silly chit she was. "His estate is near the village where my father serves as vicar. There was a fall festival. I was always forbidden from attending at night when the bonfires were flaring and the music played and people were laughing and dancing. But I could hear the festivities, the joviality. I was all of nineteen, and I decided I was missing out on life. So I slipped out through my bedchamber window, climbed down a tree, and ran off into the night like some wanton, experiencing my initial taste of freedom. He was there. He danced with me and spoke with me and strolled with me. Just before dawn he kissed me. It was so gentle and sweet."

Not like the first time Locksley had kissed her: demanding, devouring, determined.

"So you ran off to London with him."

She hated that he sounded so blasted judgmental. It wasn't as though he'd led the life of a saint. She'd actually returned home to an existence that involved hours on her knees, at her father's command, praying that the devil would not have his way with her. Whenever she could, she would sneak off to be with Beaumont. For a year it was picnics and rowing and strolling and innocent kisses. But Locksley was too drunk to care about all that. "Not right away. My father discovered what we were about. He insisted that I was sinning with a lord even though our time together wasn't carnal, but Father was determined I wouldn't bring him shame. He arranged for me to marry a farmer."

"A farmer when you wanted a lord," he sneered.

She was growing weary of his thinking the worst of her. "I wasn't opposed to marrying a farmer but he was three times my age."

"A bit of irony there in you answering my father's advert."

"One does what one must. Beaumont asked me to come to London with him, promised he would always take care of me, that he loved me with all his heart. I assumed he meant to marry me. So I ran off with him. He was exciting, young, handsome, and a lord. What woman could want for more?"

Releasing his hold on the bedpost, Locksley bounded forward and wrapped his fingers around the post nearer to her as though he still needed the support to keep himself upright. "And when you got to London?"

The truth stared her in the face but she refused to see it. "He set me up in a house on a street commonly known as Mistress Row. Several lords lease townhomes there for their fallen women. At the time, I thought it temporary. Still, I was so pleased to be away from Fairings Cross and my father and marriage to an old man that when Beaumont kissed me with a bit more urgency and claimed he'd die if he didn't have me, I didn't resist. After all, we were going to marry."

"But you didn't marry."

"No. I was silly enough to believe we would until I got with child. Before that, he put me off by saying that we had to wait until he was established within the aristocracy, until he was respected enough by everyone that he would be forgiven for marrying a commoner. Otherwise life for me would be unpleasant. He was trying to protect me, you see? Or so he said. And why shouldn't I believe him when he loved me and I loved him?"

"Then you got with child and realized he was a scoundrel."

She held his gaze. "I realized he was much worse than that. He told me that we would farm the baby out and someone else would take care of it. I was devastated. I wanted to care for the child, hire a nanny. But he assured me that wasn't the way the aristocracy handled matters. Are you familiar with baby farming?"

He blinked, released his hold on the bedpost, and leaned his shoulder against it. "No."

"The upper class's dirty little secret. Sophie lived in the townhome next to mine. Lord Sheridan's mistress."

"You danced with him at the ball."

She released a burst of laughter. "Indeed, and it curdled my stomach." Fortunately he'd never met her although she'd spied him on occasion entering Sophie's residence.

"You didn't seem displeased by his attentions."

"When you serve as a man's mistress, you learn to disguise your feelings. Without the lessons I learned from Beaumont, I'd have never made it through my first day at Havisham. You'd have figured me out in a flash.

"Anyway, I was having afternoon tea with Sophie and mentioned my disappointment that someone else would raise my child, that my son or daughter would grow up away from me, and that I had no idea how often I might be allowed to visit my little one." Clasping her hands tightly before her, she forced herself to plow through. "Sophie explained that when Beaumont said that someone would take care of my child, he didn't mean that person would nurture and *care* for it. Rather he meant that she would kill it."

THE silence that descended over the room was nearly deafening. Portia wanted Locksley to say something, anything, but she quite understood his inability to speak. After Sophie had hit her with the truth, she'd stared at her teacup for long minutes striving to deal with the horrendous reality of her child's future.

"He had a mistress before you, you know?" Sophie had said.

She hadn't known.

"She lived in the same residence as you. I came to know her rather well. She, too, got with child and he farmed out the babe. He took the bairn from her within minutes of her giving birth, when she was too weak to stop him."

Her heart clutched and tears welled. "That's awful."

"She never forgave him. When she was strong enough, she tried to find the babe. But it was too late, of course. She became so despondent that he simply cast her out."

Portia had never felt so ill in her life. Every tender feeling she'd ever held for Beaumont had withered at his heartlessness and cruelty.

"I suppose you confronted him," Locksley said now.

Slowly she shook her head. "No, he'd made his position clear, and I learned that he handled the babe of his mistress before me in the same manner. It was her child I described when you asked me about my fertility. Where Beaumont was concerned I decided it better to pretend ignorance until I determined a course of action. They advertise, these baby farmers. It's usually a widow, offering to take on a sickly babe for a certain amount per week with the option of paying a larger amount and being done with it." Looking at Locksley, she took some comfort in the horror etched on his face. "People are actually wagering on how long the child will live. Is it cheaper to pay by the week or more advantageous to hand over the higher single fee? I didn't believe Sophie at first. No one could be so cruel as to neglect a child until it dies. But I scoured the papers for the advertisements, found a couple and while I was at it, I spied your father's. I saw his as a way to save my child."

"Surely you had other options."

"I wrote my parents, telling them that I'd gotten into a bit of trouble and wanted to come back home. My father informed me that I was dead to them. Beaumont never gave me an allowance. I never thought to ask for one. He provided everything I required. So I had no coins of my own. He gave me several pieces of jewelry but he kept them in a safe, to be worn only when he saw fit. I didn't know how to access it. I considered pawning off some of his possessions, but I feared I'd find myself charged with being a thief. A man who had no qualms about killing his own child would surely have no regrets when it came to making his mistress suffer for disappointing him. Marriage to your father seemed my only salvation. A woman in my position is vilified. I'd have not been able to find employment, not even in service. So tell me, my lord, how was I to survive and keep my child alive?"

"There had to be another way."

The impertinence of him thinking that she hadn't exhausted all her options irritated her beyond reason. "Yes, well, when you think of it be sure to let me know. Meanwhile, it's late and I'm tired. I'm going back to sleep." She turned for the bed.

His arm whipped out. He grabbed her, hauled her up against him. The fury was still burning in his eyes, but she saw something else there, something that almost looked like unimaginable pain.

"You should have told me," he ground out.

While the guilt surged through her because she hadn't, she couldn't escape the truth of where that path would have led. "What difference would it have made? I fully understand what I am: a disgrace, a loose woman with no morals. If I'd told you before we were married, would you have still married me? No? Allowed me to marry your father as I'd planned? I seriously doubt it. Given me a house, an allowance, vowed to care for me and my child anyway? Or sent me on my way? If I'd told you after we were married, would you be any happier than you are now?"

He plowed one of his hands into her hair. "I might want to throttle you less. Do you have any idea how much restraint it took on my part not to murder Beaumont on the veranda? That's why you hesitated to go to London. You knew the truth would come out."

"I knew there was a chance. I prayed my secret would remain hidden, but it seems of late my prayers are not being answered." Which meant in all likelihood, she would give birth to a son.

"You could have warned me before we went to London."

Only she'd known she'd lose him. She'd wanted to hold on to him a bit longer. She shook her head as tears burned her eyes. "I couldn't. I knew the truth would cause you to hate me and I'd made the ghastly mistake of falling in love with you."

He gave a caustic laugh. "You seem to fall quite easily."

Anger fissured through her. "I will not stand here and suffer through your unkind regard."

She made to move past him, but he grabbed her arm, swung her around to face him. "I was raised by a man who gave his heart only once. You gave yours to Beaumont. You think that feeling the same for me is some sort of honor when I know what a scapegrace he is?"

Had his pride been pricked? Or was it that he didn't believe her? Why should he believe her after all the lies she'd told him? "What I feel for you, I never felt for him. Not this intense, not this huge, not this terrifying. I would give anything for this child to be yours. The one thing that I don't regret about the past two years is that it provided me with the opportunity to come to know you."

"Damn you, Portia. Damn you for getting under my skin, for burrowing so deeply that the very thought of extricating you makes me even angrier."

Was that his way of saying he cared for her, that she had disappointed him, ruined his life? She released a bitter laugh. "Oh, I have no doubt that I am damned."

"We're both damned. We might as well enjoy our time in hell." His mouth landed on hers with a sureness and a purpose to which she no doubt should have objected, but she couldn't turn him away, not when she wanted him so much, not when she felt raw and exposed and so terribly alone.

She could draw strength from him, from his desire for her. He might not love her—at that moment, he no doubt despised her—but they could revel in their bodies coming together. Besides, she wanted him as she'd wanted very little in her life.

Looking back, she could see now that she'd held affection for Beaumont, but it hadn't been soul-deep, hadn't absorbed her very essence. Otherwise, she'd not have been able to walk away so easily, without a backward glance, without any regrets. The same could not be said of Locksley. What she felt for him defied description. Under normal circumstances they'd have never met, but if they had he certainly would have never married her. And yet, despite the agony of losing him, she couldn't quite regret it.

He dragged his mouth along her throat and she dropped her head back to grant him easier access. It had been torment to sleep alone, to have not had him in her bed after Beaumont's cutting words.

"I'm drunk," he growled. "Send me away."

If he were sober he wouldn't be here. If she were the good and decent girl her father had tried to bend her into being, she wouldn't be here. But she was neither good nor decent, and if drunk was the only way she could have him, she'd take him drunk. "No," she breathed on a raspy sigh.

They tumbled onto the bed, and he went still, completely still. She heard a sonorous snore. For the best. In the morning, he wasn't going to remember a thing about tonight. Lying on her side, she pressed her back against his chest, drawing comfort from his nearness, knowing she might never have it again. He draped his arm over her, his splayed fingers coming to rest against her swollen belly. The child moved, his hand flinched, before he pressed it more firmly against her.

"I wish it were mine," he murmured.

Her heart nearly broke. Things between them would never be the same, never be right again, because he now possessed the knowledge about something that couldn't be undone, that could never be overlooked or forgotten.

She wished it was his as well, but it wasn't. It never would be. She'd been wrong to believe it ever could be.

Chapter 24

LOCKE awoke with his head feeling as heavy as his heart. He rather wished that he hadn't asked Portia about her history with Beaumont, because he had a strong need to return to London and pummel the man to within an inch of his life. He'd caught glimpses of her innocence when she killed spiders, fell into the arms of a waiting footman and laughed, danced her fingers over the piano keys. He wished he'd known her before Beaumont had torn away her guilelessness, although he recognized that he'd have considered her too pure for the likes of him, would have given her little thought because she would have been likeable and the last thing he'd wanted was a woman he could fancy.

How ironic then that he'd ended up with one he could love.

He shouldn't have come to her, should have resisted, but where she was concerned he'd had no resistance from the moment he opened the door to her. He cursed her for bringing a loneliness to his life that he'd never before experienced. He'd never had any trouble sleeping alone, and now he despised doing so. He missed her, damn it, and with enough spirits coursing through him, his determination to avoid her had weakened. Not that he needed the spirits as an excuse. She occupied his thoughts every minute of every hour. And yet she'd placed him in an unconscionable position: choosing between duty and desire, between happiness and misery, between forgiveness and pride.

Between journeying back to Havisham and lying in this bed all day, pretending that London had never happened.

Reaching for her, he encountered naught but rumpled sheets. Squinting, he lifted a hand to shield his eyes from the blindingly bright sunlight streaming in through the window, light that caused not only his eyes but his head to ache. God, what time was it? How long had they slept?

It seemed the gods wanted them to have a day without reality crashing in on them. He'd take it.

With a groan, he shoved himself up. His skull revolted, threatening to split in two if he didn't move slowly. He wondered if it were possible that Portia was bringing him some strong black coffee and something to eat. His stomach probably wouldn't like it, but he needed to get himself straightened out so he could think more clearly. Surely this situation had a solution. He doubted it would be very tidy, but he'd spent his youth living in an untidy residence. Neatness was overrated, as far as he was concerned.

He sat on the edge of the bed for what seemed like forever, waiting for Portia to return. It was in her nature to care for people, for things. Surely she recognized that he'd be suffering upon awakening. On the other hand, she wasn't prone to drinking and she'd never seen him in such a state. Perhaps she hadn't a clue regarding how miserable too much drink could make a man.

Gingerly, slowly, he pushed himself to his feet. A quick look in the mirror caused him to grimace. He was far

from being at his best. He'd feel better after tidying himself up and joining his wife for a quick bite.

Only he determined quite quickly that she wasn't sitting at any of the tables, because the tavern was fairly
empty.

"Afternoon, m'lord," the proprietress squawked, her
voice reminding him of the harsh cry of an irritating bird
he'd run across during his travels.

Afternoon was it? Good Lord, he had slept in.
"Mrs. Tandy, might I have some coffee?"

"Absolutely, m'lord. I'll fetch it straightaway." She
turned to go.

"By the by, have you seen Lady Locksley?"

She spun back around and looked at him as though he
were some strange new species of insect. "Aye, m'lord. I
saw her first thing this morning, bright and early."

Speaking with her was like carrying on a conversation with the servants at Havisham. Sometimes they took
questions far too literally. "Do you happen to know where
I would find her now?"

"Well, let's see. It's been about six, nearly seven hours,
so I'd say close to two hundred miles away if she just kept
on going."

Staring at her, he realized he really needed the damned
coffee. "I beg your pardon? Two hundred miles away?
Are you saying my coaches have already left?" It didn't
matter, as he was riding his horse, but it made no sense.

"No, m'lord. I'm saying she hopped on a mail coach."

He rushed outside for no good reason, as though he
expected to see the offending vehicle on the horizon. Of
course he couldn't. He saw his coaches waiting to have
horses harnessed to them, and one of his coachmen leaning against the building, speaking with a serving girl. As
Locke approached him, the coachman looked guilty as

hell. No doubt because he'd been caught flirting. "Did you see Lady Locksley leave this morning?"

His eyes rounded, his mouth dropped. "No, m'lord. How could she leave? The coaches are still here."

He wasn't going to get into it with the man. "Have you seen Cullie?"

"At breakfast. She went back to her room to await her Ladyship's need of her."

Damn it all to hell. Why hadn't he noticed that his wife had packed up and left? Because her things were still there. He might be feeling rotten but he wasn't blind. So where was she going and how was she going to make her way?

He dashed back into the tavern, up the stairs, and into the room they'd shared. Like a madman, he began tearing through her belongings.

"M'lord?"

He spun around at the sound of Cullie's voice. She appeared horrified by his actions, was going to be even more horrified when she learned the truth of the situation. "I'm searching for Lady Locksley's pearls. Where did you pack them?"

"She was carrying them in her reticule."

It would be left out in the open but was nowhere to be seen. He slammed his eyes closed. She could take them to a fence, trade them for coins. Not enough to get her far, but enough to see her through for a bit. But where would she go? How would she manage? What the devil was she thinking?

And with her gone from his life, why did he suddenly feel as though he might go mad?

I⊤ was the very worst place she could come, but she had nowhere else to go. Knocking on the servants' door, she held her breath, striving not to think about what might have gone through Locksley's head—other than a great deal of pain considering how much he'd imbibed—when he awoke this morning to find her gone. Would he have even cared or would he have thought good riddance?

A footman opened the door, blinked at her, furrowed his brow, and she knew he was trying to place her. "I'm here to see Miss Sophie."

"What is the nature of your business?"

"It's personal." In her reticule, she had several calling cards that Locksley had given her when they'd arrived in London in the event she made morning calls. He'd had such faith in her garnering the love and respect of Society, of being welcomed, of being accepted as his wife. Instead, she'd merely managed to ruin his life. And she'd ruin it further if she handed over a calling card and anyone discovered that Lady Locksley was very familiar with Mistress Row. "Just inform her that Portia has come to call."

"Come in."

Grateful for the opportunity to get beyond the sight of anyone peering out a window in a neighboring residence, she stepped over the threshold and into the small area where the butler, housekeeper, or cook usually spoke with vendors who weren't allowed into the residence proper. She knew her place. That she had tried to step out of it marked her as a very foolish girl.

She'd arrived in London before dark, but had waited until night fell to make her way here, hoping to avoid suspicious gazes and lessen her chances of being discovered. With Locksley snuggled against her, his hand on her belly, she'd been unable to sleep, and had simply lain there considering the unfairness of her actions. Well aware of the ramifications if this child were a boy, she should have walked away, should never have married Locksley. Exhausted, frightened, and desperate did not excuse her actions, did not justify her tainting a bloodline. She simply hadn't truly understood the pride in their lineage that the aristocracy held on to.

The rapid patter of footsteps had her straightening her spine, forcing a smile. Sophie rounded the corner in a pink silk dressing gown, her black hair flowing down her back, over her shoulders. She didn't stop until her arms were around Portia and she was hugging her tightly. "What are you doing here?"

Portia leaned back, fought not to look so worried. "I'm in a bit of bother again."

Sophie glanced over her shoulder. "Sheridan could arrive at any time." She returned her gaze to Portia. "You can stay in a back bedroom, but you must remain quiet. He's not keen on my having company."

"I shan't make a peep."

"Are you hungry?"

"Starving."

Sophie showed her to a bedchamber and had a tray brought up. Portia felt like an absolute glutton as she sat in a chair before the fireplace and dug into the beef and potatoes.

"When was the last time you ate?" Sophie asked, settling into a nearby chair, watching her fondly. She was the sister Portia had never had, so different and accepting, while her true sisters had taken after their father and constantly found fault with her.

"Breakfast."

"That can't be good for the bairn."

Portia laughed. "He didn't half let me know about it." He'd kicked several times during day. She licked her lips. "Did Beaumont bother you when he discovered me gone?"

Sophie rolled her eyes. "He was like a raging bull, wanting to know where you were. But as you didn't tell me where you were going, I couldn't tell him no matter how dire his threats."

"He didn't hurt you, did he?"

With a scoff, Sophie shrugged and laughed. "Sheridan would have killed him if he touched me and well he knew it. But recently I saw the announcement about your marriage in the paper. You married a lord!"

"And now I must divorce him."

Clear concern mirrored in her expression, Sophie leaned toward her. "Why? You have a title, money, position. You have everything we ever dreamed of having, whenever we talked. Portia, why give it all up?"

Gently, she placed her hand on her belly. "What if it's a boy? I can't do that to him. I thought I could, but I can't. His titles and estates should go to a son who carries his blood."

"Oh, Lord, why?" Sophie hopped up and began to pace. "They don't care about us. They're spoiled and rotten. They think nothing of taking advantage because they consider us below them." Spinning around, she grabbed the back of the chair. "We don't owe them anything."

"Nor do they owe us. He didn't put this babe in my belly. It's not his responsibility."

"And how are you going to care for it?"

"I haven't worked out the particulars yet. All of this came about rather suddenly." Lifting her shoulders, she smiled self-consciously. "I'm very good at cleaning houses."

With an exaggerated sigh, Sophie dropped back down into the chair. "It would be less exertion and far better benefits to find another lord to take you on."

She shook her head. "That wouldn't work for me."

Sophie stared at her. "Oh, my God. You fell in love with him."

"I did."

"Well, that was a rather silly thing to do. That's why you want a divorce."

She couldn't help but laugh. "Ironic, yes? I'm leaving him because I love him. I love him so much, Sophie. Ten, twenty . . . a hundred times more than I ever loved Beaumont. He married me to protect his father. He's a good man."

A knock sounded on the door, and a maid poked her head in. "His Lordship's here, miss."

Nodding, Sophie rose to her feet. "Thank you. Tell him I'll be down in a moment." Once the maid left, she looked at Portia. "I'm wanted." Only she wasn't, not really, not in the way Portia had felt wanted by Locksley. "Make yourself comfortable, get some rest, and we'll talk more tomorrow."

"Thank you, Sophie. I shan't linger."

"You can stay as long as Sheridan doesn't know you're here. Good night."

After she was gone, Portia set the tray aside, walked over to the bed, and stretched out on it. She should have packed some clothes, but she'd been worried about waking Locksley, and traveling with a trunk would have made it more difficult to move about quickly and unnoticed.

She'd ridden in a mail coach going north. At the first village, she'd disembarked and waited for a mail coach headed to London. She'd known the proprietress of the Peacock Inn had seen her climb into the mail coach, so she'd wanted to leave a confusing trail, just in case Locksley awoke early and searched for her. He'd either slept late or hadn't come after her. Probably the latter, which was just as well. It would make things so much easier going forward.

Unfortunately, it wouldn't ease the pain of her broken heart.

Chapter 25

$\mathcal{H}$E'D ridden like a madman all through the day and into the night in order to catch up with the mail coach. When he finally did reach it, he discovered she'd disembarked in the first village at which it had stopped. Naturally by the time he returned there, she was nowhere to be found.

So where the bloody hell had she gone?

She wasn't going to return to Havisham. Of that he was fairly certain. In no mood to explain the situation to his father, he'd sent the coaches and servants back to London while he carried on to Fairings Cross. He thought it unlikely that she would seek out her parents for help, but he was hopeful they could shed some light on where she might seek refuge.

Having attended a couple of balls at Beaumont's country estate, Locke was familiar with the area and sought out the parsonage near the church. After knocking on the door, he glanced around, his chest tightening as he studied the towering oak that brushed up against a window on the uppermost level. He imagined Portia—bold, brave, undeterred by the dangers—clambering down it. He did hope that wherever she was now, she was exercising more caution. When he caught up with her, he was going to sit her down and ask her a thousand questions so he knew every damned thing about her and she could never again elude him. He needed to know how she thought, where she might go, what she hoped to accomplish.

The door opened and a young maid looked up at him. "Yes, sir?"

He handed over a card. "Viscount Locksley to see Reverend Gadstone."

"Yes, m'lord. Please come in."

He stepped through into an austere entryway and was led to an equally Spartan front parlor. Except for the roses, which reminded him of Portia. She so enjoyed her flowers. At least he knew that much about her.

Everything here was clean and tidy. She must have been appalled when he took her on her first tour of Havisham. No, she'd merely looked at everything and seen the potential. He wondered if she'd recognized the potential in him, if she'd known she could open him up as easily as she did the house. She could swipe away the cobwebs surrounding his heart and bring in the light.

Turning at the clip of footfalls, he wasn't surprised by the stiffness of the man who entered or the grim expression of the woman beside him. Neither of them appeared to be the sort who ever laughed.

"My lord, I'm Reverend Gadstone and this is my wife. How might I be of service?"

"I'm looking for your daughter."

He tilted his head to the side like a confused dog. "Florence or Louisa?"

"Portia."

His wife gave a small gasp, while the reverend merely hardened his features into an uncompromising mask. "We have no daughter named Portia."

"So I've heard. Is there anyone in the family who might not have judged her as harshly as you?"

His chin came up in a manner similar to Portia's, yet Locke didn't find it anywhere near as adorable or charming. Rather he had an urge to introduce it to his fist.

"She is a sinner, bringing a bastard into this world. Is it yours? Did you fornicate with her?"

"You'll watch your tongue when you speak of my wife."

Their eyes widened and both their heads snapped back as though he'd punched them.

"She's your wife?" Mrs. Gadstone asked, clearly flummoxed by the notion.

He considered how any other woman who might have married him would have come here, draped in silk and jewels, arriving in a well-sprung coach, and lorded her newly obtained position over them, would have insisted they bow before her, address her by her title, and acknowledge that they were beneath her. But not his Portia, because gaining a title had not been her goal, had meant nothing to her. He'd come to realize that fact about her, but having it reconfirmed now only emphasized how badly he'd misjudged her. How he'd misjudged his own value. She'd needed someone to protect her and her child. Even if he possessed no title, no estates, he had it within him to shield her from the harshness of life. "She is. For some months now. She and I had a bit of a row. I'm striving to determine where she might have gone."

"I'm not the least bit surprised that she ran away from you because things weren't quite to her liking," the reverend said. "She was always scampering off, hiding when she knew it was time for the switch, never willing to take her responsibilities, accept her due."

"You took a switch to her?" Those who knew him were aware that his low tenor spoke of warning, of menace, yet Gadstone didn't have the foresight to realize he was treading on dangerous ground.

"Often. She had the devil in her. Never sitting still in church. Never properly memorizing the Bible passages I gave her. Hiking up her skirts to chase after butterflies. She was incorrigible, refused to bend to my will."

Jolly good for her hung on the tip of his tongue, but he kept his thoughts to himself. Little wonder she'd seen Beaumont as her salvation. It wouldn't have taken much kindness on his part to win her over. "Has she any friends in the village?"

"None that would acknowledge her now. She's a fallen woman, a disgrace. They would neither associate with her nor help her. They all know what she is," he sneered.

She'd told him that she had no one, but still he'd had a difficult time believing she was completely, absolutely alone and without resources. Although since he'd judged her poorly when he met her, was he any better than these horrid people? He gave a quick impatient tug to his gloves. "What she is, sir, is a viscountess who shall one day be a marchioness. Yes, I can see why they might not wish to be seen in her shadow. I thank you for your assistance."

"Pray you don't find her, my lord. She will be your downfall."

The need to hit Portia's father had his muscles quivering with his restraint, but one did not strike a man of God. He walked past him—

To hell with it. He swung around and landed a good solid punch to that self-righteous chin. The blow had the man landing on the floor in a sprawl and his wife screaming. Locke bent low over him. "She is the most remarkable woman I have ever known. I will find her. If it takes me to the end of my days, I will find her."

He strode out, mounted his horse, and began riding hard back to London. He'd known coming here would probably be a wild goose chase, but a part of him had wanted to see where she grew up, to meet her parents. That she had turned out to be so giving and kind was a miracle. That she was strong, not so much. She'd had to be to survive. They could have killed her spirit, but they hadn't. He admired her all the more for not succumbing to their dictates. He would find her.

THE Earl of Beaumont had never had as much luck playing cards as he was having this evening at the Twin Dragons. From the moment he'd sat down half an hour earlier, he'd taken every hand. This latest would be no exception. Fortune was smiling so brightly on him—

"I need a word."

Christ, he nearly jumped out of his skin at the low rasp near his ear. He recognized the owner's tone as one that didn't bode well. He snapped his head around, his gaze slamming into Locksley's, the green eyes indicating a high price would be paid for any disobedience. But he was known for his stubbornness.

"I'm otherwise occupied." Did he have to sound as though his heart was lodged in his throat?

Locksley grabbed his cards, tossed them down. "He's out."

"See here—"

The viscount swung back around to glare at him. There was a tenseness, a danger, to him that had no doubt led to his surviving his treks into the wilds. Not even the king of the jungle would want to tangle with a man who looked as though he'd take great delight in devouring his prey for dinner.

"Outside."

One word. A command. But Beaumont wasn't a complete fool. He needed to be certain there were plenty of witnesses so he didn't suddenly disappear from the face of the earth. "The library."

A curt nod, and the viscount stepped back. Regaining his composure, Beaumont glanced around the table. "I shall return." He hoped, prayed. "Hold my winnings for me."

The Dragons might be a club of vice, but it was an honest one. Reluctantly he followed Locksley to the library, remembering the night when he'd joined him here in hopes of learning more about his marriage to Portia, of striving to determine when he might see her.

Not surprisingly, Locksley chose a seating area in a back corner of the room, away from everyone else. When they'd settled in, he did little more than study Beaumont with an intense stare until a footman delivered their drinks. Beaumont hated that his hand shook as he lifted his glass, took a fortifying swallow, and leaned forward. "Look, I haven't said a word regarding Portia's past—"

"Where is she?" Locksley was curt, to the point, except Beaumont didn't know what the point was.

Leaning back, he glanced around. "Who?"

"Portia."

"How the devil should I know?" Then the point came to him, sharp, clear, and ever so satisfying. He couldn't help but grin like a lunatic. "She ran off."

It boosted Beaumont's pride to know he wasn't the only one she'd left. Locksley narrowed his eyes until they resembled the finely honed edge of a sword. Beaumont's smile dwindled and he fought the urge to scurry away. "She didn't come to me."

But dear God, he wished she had. He missed her more than he thought it possible to miss anyone. He'd handled things poorly on the terrace. Instead of ordering her about, he should have wooed her as he had in the beginning. He could have won her back with the proper approach.

"Where was her residence?"

With the viscount's obvious need of his assistance, suddenly he was feeling quite superior. "You nearly broke my jaw. It still aches." The bruise was an embarrassment, but worse was the fact that he had to cut his food into tiny pieces because he could barely widen his mouth.

"If you don't tell me where she lived, the next blow will surely break it, then."

He sighed. "You're not going to punch me here."

The stony look he gave said he would indeed. Beaumont sipped his scotch, studied his glass. "She's not there. My current mistress is the jealous sort. She'd have not welcomed her."

"It didn't take you long to replace her."

"A man has needs," he said indignantly. "Besides, no one could replace her. I loved her, you know."

"You had a strange way of showing it."

"She brought neither coin nor position to a marriage. I'm in need of both."

"You were going to have the child she carried killed," he hissed.

"Wives don't like having bastards running around. My father took care of his in the same manner. Anyway, I can't afford to take care of a passel of children."

"But you can afford a mistress."

"As I stated, a man has needs. One must prioritize."

"I have an overwhelming need to punch you again. You're spared only because I have no wish to touch you."

He hated that this man who was beneath him in station was commanding him about and lording over him. "Well, at least my father wasn't a nutter."

Locksley struck so fast that Beaumont didn't even see it coming, but the pain that shot through his face told him that his nose, at least, was broken. His eyes watered as he dug his handkerchief out of his pocket to collect the blood pouring down.

"Where did she live?"

Through clenched teeth, he ground out the address. "But as I said you won't find her there."

"I'm well aware. Keep this conversation and your past relationship with her to yourself, or I shall see you ruined. Ashebury and Greyling will help me see to it."

As though he wished to tangle with the Hellions. One was bad enough. All three would ensure he was never again welcomed in polite Society. "The threat is unnecessary. Believe it or not, I want her to be happy. But if you hurt her—"

He had no chance to complete his threat, as Locksley was already gone. It was an odd moment to realize that he had never envied a man more.

SHE'D hated parting with the pearls, but she didn't have any other choice. Unfortunately they didn't bring in as much money as she'd hoped, but it had been enough that she had felt confident going to her solicitor, that she could pay his fee. As it turned out, he didn't charge her for his advice, as there was nothing he could do for her.

"I can't divorce him." Portia paced in front of the fireplace in her temporary bedchamber.

"I thought infidelity was a justifiable reason for getting a divorce," Sophie said.

"Yes, but I can't divorce *him* because *I* committed adultery. Only *he* can divorce me for my transgressions."

"You can divorce him if he commits adultery, so say he did."

Shaking her head, she stopped pacing. "No. I'll not have some woman he might wish to marry questioning his faithfulness. He is loyal. Besides, it's not enough for him to be an adulterer. He must desert me for two years. Yet I don't have to desert him. There are different laws applied to men than to women, which makes it near impossible for a woman to get out of an unwelcomed marriage. In truth it makes everything hard for a woman." Not that hers had been unwelcomed. It had been wonderful and exquisite.

"Well, the law always has, hasn't it? Made it difficult for women."

"Sophie, I don't know how to make this right." She dropped into the chair. "I could write a letter to the *Times*, explaining I was unfaithful. Once published it would leave him with no choice except to divorce me. Although he would hate me all the more."

"What does it matter how much he hates you?"

She nodded, fighting back the desolation and tears. "You're right. What matters is that Beaumont's child not become Locksley's heir."

"And when you are free of Locksley?"

Her throat and chest tightened. She couldn't have swallowed if she needed to. "I'm going to find a family—a proper family who will love and care for this babe as though he were their own. I should never have been so selfish as to want to keep him."

"Or her."

She laughed. "Or her." Although of late, it seemed she could envision herself with a son, one with coal-black hair and green eyes.

"But how will you support yourself?"

"Go into service, I suppose." Without an illegitimate child to mark her as a fallen woman, it would be easier to find employment. But how she would miss having someone to love her unconditionally.

A sharp rap had her turning toward the door as the

maid opened it and strolled in. "A gentleman caller," she said, handing Sophie a card.

Her friend read it, her eyebrows lifted. "Well, I daresay, I don't think he's here for me." She extended the card.

Portia took it, her eyes glancing over what she'd feared she might see. Her heart galloped as though it needed to leave the room, the residence, London. "What the devil is he doing here?"

"He's come to fetch you back," a deep familiar voice said from the doorway.

She shot up out of the chair, took two steps back, and grabbed the fireplace mantel to steady herself. He looked marvelous. Every single hair in place, his face freshly shaven, his clothes immaculate. So different from the last time she'd seen him wander into a bedchamber, the last time she'd gazed on him sprawled over a bed.

Gracefully, Sophie rose to her feet and began ushering out the maid.

"Where are you going?" Portia demanded.

"To leave you two to it."

As she neared Locksley, he said, "You must be Miss Sophie."

Of course she'd told him about Sophie, blast her. That knowledge had no doubt aided him in finding her.

"I am indeed, m'lord."

He took her hand, bowed over it, and pressed a kiss to her fingers. "Thank you for being her friend."

"We loose women must stick together." She glanced back over her shoulder at Portia. "He's quite the charmer. I approve, for what it's worth."

Only her approval carried no weight, could not undo the horrendous wrong. As soon as Sophie was out of sight, he closed the door and leaned against it, never taking his gaze from Portia. She was not going to fall into the depths of green; she was not going to let him deter her from her path. "I'm glad you're here," she stated succinctly.

"No, you're not."

She bit down on the inside of her cheek. "No, I'm not, but as you appear to be somewhat sober—"

"I am completely sober."

"You might be more open to my plan."

"And what plan is that?"

Did he have to stand there so calmly, sound so reasonable? She released her hold on the mantel because her fingers were going numb, and clutched her hands just above her waist, above where her child was growing. "We shall fake my death."

His flummoxed expression gave her a bit of satisfaction. Knowing she could take him as off guard as his appearance had so easily done to her was rewarding.

"I beg your pardon?" he asked.

"You will tell people that I died—in childbirth if need be—and I will quietly slip away so you can marry again."

He shoved himself away from the door. "So you'd have me be a bigamist? None of the children my second wife gave me would be legitimate."

"No one need know that. However to ensure their legitimacy we'll get a divorce first, but a quiet one, so you don't have to suffer through the humiliation—"

He began walking toward her. "There is no such thing as a quiet divorce. Besides, it would be a matter of public record."

"No one is going to go looking for it," she said impatiently. He was too near now. She could smell his sandalwood-and-orange scent, wanted to inhale it into her lungs and hold it there forever. How would she ever eat an orange without thinking of him?

"Have you not learned that secrets never remain secrets? Besides, I've told you before, there will be no divorce."

She didn't back up this time because she knew he'd only advance, so she stood her ground until he came to a halt in front of her. Only then did she notice the dark circles beneath his eyes, the new creases at the corners. "Locksley, be reasonable. If I'm carrying a boy—"

"Then he will be my heir."

"Precisely. Which is the very reason that you must rid yourself of me as quickly as possible. If there is a way to annul—"

"There will be no annulment."

"Will you stop interrupting me? It irritates the devil out of me when you interrupt. I will tell whatever lies are necessary—"

"No more lies, Portia."

He'd done it again, interrupted her, but before she could object, he cradled her face between his hands. So warm, so familiar. She wanted a lifetime of him touching her.

"Listen to me, carefully," he said slowly as though she were dimwitted. "We will not get divorced, and it has nothing to do with public embarrassment, or ridicule, or shame. I don't give a fig what people think about me. My God, I grew up among whispers about my mad father and our haunted estate. Do you really think that getting a divorce would bring me to my knees?"

"Then why not do it? If you're willing to endure the shame of it, why not divorce me?"

"Because I am not willing to give you up. For you see, my little vixen, I've fallen quite madly in love with you."

It was as though he'd closed his fist around her heart. Tears stung, filled her eyes, rolled over onto her cheeks. Beaumont had told her he loved her but the delivery had never been so heart-felt, so soul crushing. Nor so uplifting as to make her feel as though she were soaring. "But your bloodline."

"I don't care about my bloodline. I care only about you." He glanced down. "And this child that means so much to you." He raised his eyes to hers. "As I said earlier, if you are carrying a boy, he will be my heir and I shall recognize him as such. He will know me and no other as his father. My own set a good example for me. He raised two other men's sons as if they were his. I think he would be the first to agree that family is not determined by blood."

"Will you tell him the truth about this child?"

"He already knows it. It's our child."

Her sob was the most awful sound she'd ever made, but then to her best recollection, she'd never cried other than the night he'd learned the truth. She'd always been stoic, strong, and determined to carry on. But this soul-wrenching blubbering shook her shoulders. As his arms closed around her, she pressed her cheek against his chest, heard the steady pounding of his heart. "I love you, Killian. So much and for so long. I don't know why I ever thought I'd loved another."

"For what it's worth, he did love you."

In surprise, she jerked her head back, met his gaze. Slowly, she slid her hand up his cheek, around to the back of his head. "But not enough. You love me enough."

She brought his head down, opening her mouth to him, her heart fully, her soul. He took, with no apologies, no excuses. Yet for all the kisses that had come before, this one was different, unguarded. He was no longer shielding his heart; it was no longer locked to her.

She owned him, just as he owned her. Heart, body,

and soul. At long last, someone was accepting her, frailty, warts, and all. She had made mistakes, taken wrong turns, but she couldn't regret a single one when they had led her to him. It stunned her that she could love him so much, that he could love her without conditions.

Lifting his mouth from hers, he stroked his thumb over her swollen lips before glancing around the room. "Let's go home."

"You should know that Beaumont never took me out in public, never introduced me to anyone in the nobility, so it is unlikely—as long as he holds his tongue—that my past will haunt us."

"He gains nothing by hurting you, except his own ruination. He knows that. He was also an idiot for not appreciating what he had."

"I'm rather glad he didn't." Otherwise, she might not have Locksley, and she was so much happier with him.

She grabbed her traveling frock and pelisse. Downstairs, she found Sophie in the parlor. "We're leaving."

"Of course you are," Sophie said as she rose from the chair and came over to give her a hug.

"I'll send back your dress tomorrow."

"Keep it. It never fit me properly anyway. Be happy, Portia."

"I will be."

The front door suddenly opened and Lord Sheridan strode in. He came up short. "Locksley, what the devil are you doing here?"

"My wife and I were just visiting with her friend."

"Her friend? Sophie, what's going on?"

"As he said, I was simply catching up with an old friend. They're on their way out now."

Portia leaned in, kissed Sophie's cheek, and whispered, "If you ever want another life, you know where to come."

Lifting a shoulder, Sophie gave her a sad smile. "I love the sod."

Portia found it odd that love could break and mend hearts. Joining Locksley in the entryway, she wrapped her hand around his arm and let him lead her out of the house and away from her past.

Chapter 26

*A*s soon as the coach took off, Locke dragged her to his lap, latched his mouth onto the soft skin at her throat, suckled, nipped, journeyed up and down the long column, while she moaned, dropped her head back, gasped short breaths. "If you ever leave me again, without so much as a word of warning—"

"You'll what? Spank me? Lock me in my room? There is little point in running away if you warn the person ahead of time or leave a message stating where you are."

Threading his fingers through her hair, he brought her head level with his, held her gaze. "Never leave me again."

"I did it for you. To spare you—"

"The agony of losing you nearly killed me." Something he'd never admit to another soul, but to her he suddenly felt that he could admit anything.

"How did you find me?"

"Not as easily or as quickly as I should have. I went to see your parents."

Her eyes widened. Wanting to drink in the whiskey, he wished it wasn't dark, that they weren't ensconced in shadows. "I told you I was dead to them."

"Since you'd lied about other things, I thought perhaps you'd lied about that. Or maybe I was merely hoping that you had, that they wouldn't have it within them to turn you out. I punched your father, by the way."

Her eyes growing more circular, she covered with her hand that mouth he was about to kiss. "You did not."

"I didn't like him. He was the reason you hid in trees."

She nodded, remembering how she'd recklessly revealed that information the first night. "Yes. I could never do anything right. He made me spend hours on my knees praying for my soul. It only made me want to rebel more."

"They know you're a viscountess now. Should you ever wish to invite them to Havisham, I shall strive to behave, but I can't promise I won't strike him again."

"I might invite them just to see you smack him." She shook her head. "No, I'll never invite them. I will not have them ruin Havisham for me as they ruined Fairings Cross. But they wouldn't have known where I was, so how could they help you?"

He skimmed his fingers over her face, her brow, her cheek, her chin. He couldn't get enough of touching her. "They didn't, but then I remembered you mentioning Sophie, so I had a talk with Beaumont. He now has a broken nose."

Laughing, she pressed her face to his shoulder, angling herself so she could kiss the underside of his chin. "I had no idea you were so violent."

"He called my father a nutter, a disparaging term for a madman. He may not be totally sane but he is still a marquess and entitled to respect."

"I'm glad you hit him."

He grinned. "You're a bit bloodthirsty yourself."

"Your father is a kind, sweet man. He misses his wife. Nothing wrong in that."

Months before, Locke was convinced his father missed her too much, but that was before he knew what it was to lose someone he loved—and he'd only lost her temporarily. He'd known she was alive and he would locate her whereabouts, reclaim her. For his father, there was no hope of finding his wife again. At least not until he died.

But Locke didn't want to ponder that, consider the fact that his father was mortal. He wanted to think only about Portia. He returned his mouth to her neck, nibbling his way along until he neared her lips.

She placed her hand on his shoulder, pushing him back slightly. "You're distracting me, and I still have questions. Beaumont didn't know where I was, so how did he help?"

"He knew where you'd lived and you told me about a neighbor you visited. Once I knew which was your residence, I had only to knock on doors until I found the correct one. Fortunately I found her on the second try."

"How far would you have gone?"

"Down the entire blasted street." He cradled her face. "Portia, do you not understand that I was lost without you?"

"I didn't want to leave." She knocked her head against his shoulder. "I sold the pearls."

"They're replaceable. You're not."

Straightening, she met his gaze. "I like you very much when you're in love."

"You're going to like me a good deal more before the night is done."

She was still laughing when the coach drew to a stop outside the London residence. A footman opened the door. Locke leaped out, turned back, and handed Portia down. As soon as her feet hit the pebbled path, he lifted her into his arms.

"I can walk," she stated.

"You need to conserve your energy."

He carried her up the front steps, into the residence,

barely acknowledging the butler before bounding up the stairs to their bedchamber. Word would make the rounds that Lady Locksley had returned. Her maid would be alerted but he trusted that the girl was smart enough to know she wouldn't be needed until morning.

He set Portia on her feet. Because the frock wasn't hers, because it was an atrocious fit, because he'd overheard that she didn't need to return it, he ripped it from her, taking satisfaction in the rending of material. Other than the evening when she'd worn no undergarments, he didn't know if he'd ever divested her of her clothing so quickly.

It had only been a few nights since he'd last seen her naked, but it seemed as though her body had changed, or perhaps he'd just not looked as closely. But her breasts were larger, her stomach more swollen. Now that he knew she was further along than he'd realized, he supposed changes would be happening more quickly.

Filling his hands with her delightful orbs, he pressed a kiss to the valley between them. Scraping her fingers through his hair, she dropped her head back on a moan. Then to ensure she understood his dedication to her, he dropped to his knees and kissed her belly.

"Locksley," she whispered on ragged breath.

He looked up at her gazing down on him. "I love you, Portia. Every aspect of you, every part of you. And I shall love this child if for no other reason than because some part of it is you."

"I don't deserve you."

"You've told me on numerous occasions that I'm an ass. I don't think you're getting any great prize here."

"You're wrong there. I'm getting the greatest prize of all: love."

He shot to his feet. "Take off my clothes."

She gave him a seductive and wicked grin. "Gladly."

He'd always loved that about her, how comfortable she was with the body, with sex. He didn't know if it came from her being a mistress or the devil in her, as her father claimed. It wasn't important. He was coming to realize that a good many things he'd worried over didn't matter. With her at his side, he was going to have everything he'd ever wanted, ever needed.

She took her sweet time disrobing him, tormenting him, slowly rubbing skin that became visible, licking it, taking it between her teeth, nipping. When he was completely nude, he moved to take her in his arms and she stopped him with a hand pressed to his chest. Her eyes, her intoxicating whiskey eyes, held his for two heartbeats before she went to her knees.

"Portia, you don't have—"

"I've always wanted to do this. I've heard about it, but I've never done it. I never wanted to and Beaumont didn't force me. But I want to now."

His mouth had gone so dry that he doubted he could have spoken had the residence caught on fire and he needed to warn people. He merely nodded.

The rough edge of her tongue traced the length of him, up and down, over and over. His groan echoed through the room, and he thought she would be the death of him. Then her lips were taunting and teasing. He'd never known such exquisite torture. He fully intended to return the favor.

"Ah, my little vixen. You have the power to bring me to my knees."

"It would make it more difficult to do this."

He couldn't believe he was chuckling. Before her, he never laughed when bedding a woman, although he realized it had been a good long time since he'd thought of himself as bedding her. Sometime between the moment that he married her and now, he'd begun to think of himself as making love to her.

Her mouth enveloped a good part of him, heated silk against velvet, her tongue swirling over him. He plowed his hands into her hair because he had to touch her, had to complete a circle. Christ, he was beginning to think like a poet. The next thing he knew he'd be spouting rhymes.

Although for her, he'd spout anything she wanted. With each sweep of her tongue, the pleasure spiraled through him, with each stroke of her mouth sensations set his nerve endings afire. She was innocence and vixen, daring yet unschooled, and he loved her all the more for it. Reaching down, he slipped his hands beneath her arms and brought her to her feet. Her mouth was wet, swollen, and he took it, tasting the saltiness of his skin on her tongue.

He backed her up until the backs of her knees hit the bed. Then he lifted her up and placed her gently on the mattress so he could feast on her.

SHE'D not yet had her fill of him, but she'd sensed his tension, his quivering need. She'd been driving him to the brink of madness. She'd understood that well enough as he did it to her far too often and easily.

Spreading her thighs, he skimmed his mouth up one leg and down the other. Up again and down. Up again . . . and hovering there. Blowing on her curls, using his fingers to open her up as though she were a rose that needed help unfurling. Then just as she'd tormented him, he tormented her with long slow licks, knowing exactly when to apply pressure and when to recede. He came at her like the waves of an ocean, undulating, forceful, retreating but leaving dampness behind. Burying her fingers in his hair, she wondered if he truly understood the power he held over her. She would do anything he asked, even remain his wife.

He loved her. She was still humbled by the notion, and yet she'd also never felt more victorious. He was hers. Completely. He'd given her a portion of himself that he'd never given to anyone. No other woman had ever held his heart, and while she could not determine what she'd done to acquire it, she certainly wasn't fool enough to argue with him.

She loved him too much, and she would love him until the day she died.

The pleasure cascaded through her, ebbing and flowing, taking her breath, taking her strength, taking her will. With so little effort he could possess her, control her, rule her. Yet he never pushed to own her. He gifted her with his touch, his tongue, his fingers. Kisses and licks, strokes and nibbles. She could so easily come undone, but tonight was a new beginning; tonight was one of lovemaking, of unselfishness, of giving and taking equally.

"Killian," she breathed, hovering on the edge. "I want you inside me. Now."

He took one last stroke, one last swipe with his tongue, before moving up and flopping onto his back. "Straddle me."

Rising up, she rolled over until her legs were on either side of his hips. Plowing his hands into her hair, he held her still.

"Tell me you love me," he ordered.

"I love you."

"I love you, too, and the thought of losing you terrifies me. I understand now why my father went mad."

"You'll not lose me." She said the words with conviction even though she knew it was a promise she shouldn't make. No one knew what the future would bring, but she had to believe that for them it held years of being together, years of knowing each other's love.

"I'll hold you to that," he said before grasping her hips and lowering her, filling her.

She began to rock against him, controlling the rhythm, the tempo, running her hands over his chest, across his shoulders, dipping down to take his mouth, to circle her tongue around his nipple. His groans filled the air; his growls incited her passions.

Had she truly thought she could leave him, leave this? Perhaps her father was correct. She was a wanton, sinful creature. But dear God, wantonness felt so grand, sin so rewarding, especially when shared with a man who knew his way well around a woman's body.

A man who was hers.

Moving his hands back to her hips, he guided her movements, helping her to move faster as the tension built. The sensations danced in frenzied gratification, sweet and torturous, from her toes to the top of her head.

"Look at me," he demanded. "Look at me."

She locked her gaze onto the green. This position gave her an advantage. She controlled the tempo, the pressure, the pulsating between her thighs. She watched as he tightened his jaw, shortened his breath—

"Don't you close your eyes," she commanded.

"You are a witch."

"Your witch."

Then it was all too much. The ecstasy ripped through her, hard, fast, intense. She couldn't hold back her scream as he pounded into her, his feral growl echoing around her. Totally spent, she collapsed on his chest, aware of his final deep thrust as he tensed below her. He clamped his arms around her, held her tightly.

"Welcome home, Lady Locksley."

Laughing, she pressed a kiss to the center of his chest before lifting her head and looking down on him. "Welcome to love, Lord Locksley."

Chapter 27

THEY stayed in London until the end of the Season. No rumors about her past circulated. Occasionally she caught a glimpse of Beaumont, but he kept his distance. It seemed to her that he always looked rather sad. She did hope that happiness was in his future.

It was certainly in her present. She was glad to be back at Havisham. Sitting on the terrace with the marquess, sipping her afternoon tea while he drank scotch, she didn't know why she'd ever thought the place desolate. "I love it here," she said on a sigh.

"It's not for everyone," he told her.

She looked over at him. "It's for me, though." And it would be for her children. Here they would know only happiness. They might climb trees but it wouldn't be because they were afraid of receiving an unjust punishment.

She knew her husband would be returning soon. He was spending less time at the mines these days. He still went down into them—he couldn't seem to refrain from accepting the challenge of it. But he didn't go as often—or so he told her. She had no cause to doubt him. They were coming to know each other so very well. She'd confessed that she wasn't afraid of horses, but had been afraid that riding one would cause her to lose the babe, so she'd created an excuse to avoid them. Locksley had promised her hours of riding after the child was born. She'd also revealed that she enjoyed wine and brandy, but again, she hadn't believed it would be good for the child she carried.

"I look forward to a lifetime of discovering everything about you," he'd said.

She was looking forward to the same, still occasionally pinched herself to make certain she wasn't dreaming, that life could be so marvelous and good.

"I believe I shall take a walk to visit with Linnie," Marsden said. "Care to join me?"

"My legs could use a bit of a stretch." As she stood up, the pain seized her. She couldn't hold back her moan as she pressed a hand to the table as though that would lessen the impact.

"What is it, my dear?" Marsden asked, concern clearly written on his face.

Straightening, she took a deep breath as the discomfort subsided. "Oh." Another deep breath, in through her nose, out through her mouth. "I've just been having occasional twinges since last night."

"That was more than a twinge."

She nodded. "It was a rather harsh one."

Calmly he pushed back his chair and stood. "We're not going for a walk. We're getting you upstairs. Then we're sending for the physician and Locke."

"It's too soon for the babe to come." She hated lying to him, especially as it wasn't too soon. If anything it was a bit later than she'd expected, but she didn't want him questioning the paternity of this child. Oh, God, now that the moment was upon her, the guilt she'd so effectively buried surfaced. *Please, please, please be a girl.*

"Perhaps I'm mistaken," he said, "but let's take precautions just in case I know what I'm talking about."

Offering his arm, he escorted her indoors, where he shouted at one footman to fetch Locksley and another to fetch the village physician. He called out for Cullie and Mrs. Barnaby. Suddenly she was very much aware of the sound of rushing feet as people hurried to do his bidding.

Halfway up the stairs, she had to stop as pain again ratcheted through her. She clung to the railing and his arm, hoping she wasn't bruising him. The pain went longer and was sharper than the one that came before. When it finally dissipated, she offered him a fragile smile. "I believe you might be right."

"I'm right about most things."

An odd moment to realize where Locksley had gotten his arrogance. She might have laughed if she didn't want to get to her bedchamber as quickly as possible.

He continued to lend her support as she made her way to the landing and carried on down the hallway. In her bedchamber, he led her over to a chair, helped her sit.

"Your maid should be here at any moment." He turned to go, stopped, walked over to her dressing table, and skimmed his fingers along one of its intricately carved edges. "You have Linnie's vanity."

"It was at the furniture maker's. Locksley didn't think you'd mind."

"I used to love to watch her get ready." He faced her. "I'm glad it's being used."

"It's the most beautiful piece of furniture I've ever seen."

"When the time comes, pass it on to your eldest daughter from her grandfather. I want her to know how precious she is to me."

She might be bringing her eldest daughter into this world at any moment, a girl who would not be carrying his blood. She'd thought a daughter would ease her guilt, but it seemed there would always be an aspect to what she'd done that would trouble her.

Cullie rushed in. "Oh, m'lady. This isn't good. It's too soon."

"Don't be worrying your mistress with dire words such as that," Marsden said. "Babies come when they're meant to come."

Bending over he kissed Portia's forehead. "I shall be downstairs, awaiting the news."

He shuffled out. Cullie closed the door and returned to her side. "We need to get you out of your clothes."

Portia could only nod and pray that Marsden would never learn the truth regarding her child. She couldn't bear the thought of facing his disappointment.

LOCKE paced in front of the large windows in the music room. He'd chosen this room because it was Portia's favorite and he felt closest to her here. By the time he'd gotten back from the mines, she was well into her labor, and the physician wouldn't allow him into the room to see her, claiming his presence would upset her and delay the child's arrival. But it was now long past midnight and another one of his wife's screams rent through the stillness and the quiet.

"Damn it! How long does this take?"

"She's going to die," his father murmured quietly.

The words couldn't have hit Locke harder if they'd been delivered with a sledgehammer. He spun around to glare at his father, who sat in his favorite chair, looking older and frailer than he had in months. "Why do you say that?"

His father lifted tired eyes to Locke. "Your mother screamed like that. The physician assured me nothing was out of the ordinary, but still your mother perished. I never felt so powerless in my entire life."

"Portia is young and strong—"

"So was your mother."

"Portia will not dare leave this child—"

"Your mother had no desire to leave you, but when death is hovering in the shadows, it will not be denied."

"To hell with that nonsense." Death would not have its way this time. Locke was striding from the room before he even realized he had a destination, barely remembered charging up the stairs, or bursting into his bedchamber. Every memory of every moment spent in here with Portia rushed through his mind like a kaleidoscope continually being turned so light could illuminate the pieces in a variety of ways, and he saw her in all those different facets. Haughty, bold, gentle, kind. He heard her laughter, her music, her voice whispering in his ear.

He saw her now, exhausted, damp with sweat, her eyes glazed over but the spark not diminished, never diminished. She would fight until the end to protect this child. She would do whatever necessary to protect anyone she loved, this child, him, his father. But who protected her?

"My lord, you should leave," the doctor said, standing at the foot of the bed as though he had little more to do than survey the contents of the room.

Only he couldn't, not now that he'd seen her. Quickly, he rushed over to her, took her hand, felt her fingers closing around his. "I tried to see you earlier but they wouldn't let me."

"I know." Reaching up with a limp hand, she brushed at his hair. "Don't look so worried. I'm just tired."

"It's taking so long." Too long, too damned long. He could see how much the ordeal had weakened her. His father might be right. He might lose her. Never in his life had he known such terror—and he'd faced wild animals, harsh storms, treacherous terrains. He knew what it was to have his heart pumping with fear, but all he felt now was cold, frigid fright skittering through him. He lowered his head until his cheek touched hers and his lips rested near her ear. "Portia, I know you're weak and weary, but you must find the strength to carry on. If you die, I shall run mad."

"I shan't die. I'm sorry I keep scream—"

"Scream all you want."

"Don't interrupt."

He lifted up, gazed down on her, smiled. "There's my tough girl with her tart tongue."

She rolled her head from side to side. "You should want to be rid of me."

Damn her parents, damn Beaumont for making her ever doubt her worth. "I love you so much. You've fought so long for this child, Portia. Don't stop fighting now. Fight for it. Fight for me."

"I want to, but I can't seem to find any strength."

He squeezed her hand. "I'll stay and lend you mine, shall I? We can do this together, you and I. We can do anything as long as we're together."

Nodding, she began gasping.

"I need her to push, m'lord."

"Push, Portia," he urged. "Push."

She not only pushed, but she screamed for another hour. In between her cries, he murmured over and over how much he loved her, how special she was.

When her child—their child—finally came into the world, he'd never known such relief or such joy.

"It's a girl," the physician announced.

"I want to see her," Portia said.

Locke took the squalling infant and placed her in Portia's arms. Then he ran his fingers over the soft fuzz covering her tiny scalp. "She has red hair."

"She's so small." Portia looked up at him. "Thank you."

"You did all the work."

"But you were here."

"I'll always be here for you, Portia. Always."

LOCKE found his father in the library, sitting before the fire, drink in hand. He went to the side table of decanters and reached for the scotch. "It's a girl."

His father released a deep breath. "Good."

Stilling, Locke slowly looked over at his sire. "You're not disappointed?"

He waved his hand dismissively. "The next one can be a boy."

After pouring his drink, Locke dropped into the chair opposite his father's and studied him, the way he didn't hold his gaze but kept shifting his attention to the fire. He didn't want to tell his father anything he might not know, but his reaction was incredibly strange for a man who had been so insistent upon gaining an heir.

"How is Portia faring?" the marquess asked.

"Tired and weak, but the physician says that's to be expected. She's sleeping now."

"I've heard it's easier with the next one."

But Locke was still bothered by his earlier reaction, was rather certain he understood the reason for it. "When did you realize the truth about her child?"

His father had the good graces to look uncomfortable. "Shortly after we learned she was with babe. She was showing too soon, increasing too fast."

"Yet you held your silence."

"I didn't want to interfere with your developing relationship. When did you realize it?"

"While we were in London."

"Do you know who the father is?"

"I'm the father."

The older man smiled. "Jolly good for you."

Locke leaned forward, his elbows on his thighs, his glass clasped between his hands. "You wanted an heir. Why didn't you say something?"

"I wanted you to find love. Gaining my heir was an excuse."

"And if she'd had a boy?"

"Love is more important. Which I think you came to realize."

He'd come to realize it was the only thing.

PORTIA opened her eyes, striving to ignore the aches and discomfort. It had all been worth it.

"You're awake."

Glancing in the direction of Locksley's voice, she saw him sitting in the chair by the window, cradling their daughter bundled in swaddling in his arms. "How is she?"

"As beautiful as her mother."

At that moment, she suspected she looked quite a fright, nowhere near beautiful. He rose, approached, and without her saying a word, placed the child in her waiting arms. The joy that swept through her with the weight of the small body nestled to her breast nearly made her weep. "How can she be so small yet cause so much trouble?"

"You're not particularly large."

"Are you claiming I cause trouble?"

"An abundance of it." His smile was warm. "How are you feeling?"

"Tired, but happy. I want to name her Madeline. I thought it would please your father, but you know the truth of her, and if it would upset you or not be a proper homage to your mother, I'll call her something else."

"The truth of her, Portia, is that she is yours, and therefore she is mine. That is the only truth that matters. To name her after my mother will please my father . . . and me as well." He tipped his head to the side, gave his lips an ironic twist. "And my mother's ghost, no doubt."

"We could call her Maddie."

Leaning down, he bussed a quick kiss over her lips. "We shall do that." Straightening, he studied her and she had the sense that something was troubling him.

"What's wrong?"

"Nothing's wrong, but you should be aware that he knows. My father. He figured out that it wasn't I who planted the seed, but I'm not going to tell him who did as it's not important."

"Does he hate me?"

"Not in the least. He loves you, Portia. And he will love her as I do."

"You love her already?"

"It is an odd thing, love. Once you open yourself up to it, it has its way with you. I could no more not love her than I could not love you."

"I will give you an heir, I promise."

"I would welcome an heir, but know this, Portia—with or without an heir, my love for you will not lessen."

"Every time I think I can love you no more than I do, you say or do something that proves me wrong—and I find myself loving you a little more deeply."

"Then I shall look forward to a lifetime of proving you wrong."

Epilogue

Havisham Hall
Christmas Eve, 1887

STANDING on the landing at the top of the stairs with her husband behind her, his arms circling her just below her breasts, and the marquess beside her, Portia could not have been more pleased. "What do you think, Father?" she asked.

"Beautiful, my dear. It's just as it was the last time that Linnie and I held a Christmas ball here. Of course, we had an abundance of guests then."

She'd saved the tidying of the ballroom for last, and this was her gift to Marsden. Every room in the manor was now absent cobwebs and dust; every room had been set to rights.

"Will you host a ball here?" he asked.

"We thought in the new year, if you've no objections."

"You're the lady of the manor. It's your decision."

"If you're not comfortable with so many people—"

"It'll be good to see old friends. Will you dance with me now?"

She smiled at him. "We don't have an orchestra."

He patted his chest. "The music is here. You don't mind, do you, son?"

"Not as long as I get the last dance."

"Will you dance with me, Papa?" Maddie asked from her crouched position where she was peering through the railings.

"Absolutely," Locksley said, lifting his daughter into his arms as she squealed.

It always touched Portia deeply to see the love he showered on their daughter. She was truly his, no doubt about it.

"And me?" their three-year-old son asked, his mop of black hair unruly, his green eyes filled with mischief.

"And you." He scooped his heir up with his free arm before jogging down the stairs, the children clinging to his neck and laughing.

"He's a good father," Marsden said as he escorted Portia to the dance area.

"You set a good example." She squeezed his arm, leaned against him. "Thank you."

His white bushy eyebrows shot up. "For what, my dear?"

"For giving him to me."

"All I did was place the advert. You answered it."

"Thinking I was to marry you."

"But I told you it would be better if you married him."

"Indeed you did."

When they reached the center of the room, he took her in his arms and swept her over the floor with an ease that she imagined had characterized his moves in his youth. While she couldn't hear the music, it was obvious that he did, a tune that had no doubt played when he danced with his beloved.

"Thank you for my heir," he said quietly, smiling.

"You've thanked me enough."

"I shall thank you as often as I want. I love both those children. They've been a great gift. Although you must watch the boy carefully. I caught him climbing shelves in the library the other day."

Since Maddie's birth, Marsden had begun to spend less time in his bedchamber. He was a more active part of their lives, especially the children's. It had been years since Locksley had turned the key in the door to his father's bedchamber. None of the rooms in the residence were locked any longer.

Portia smiled brightly. "He is his father's son."

Marsden grinned. "He is that."

The patter of running feet had them stopping, and just in time. Both children slammed into Marsden's legs.

"Grandpapa, will you read to us?" Maddie asked.

"I will, but only one story." He leaned down. "Father Christmas is coming tonight." Taking their hands, he began leading them from the room.

Watching them go, Portia felt a joyful ache in her chest. Her children knew love, so much love.

"Dance with me."

Turning into her husband's arms, she found herself gliding once more over the floor.

"You've made him very happy," Locksley said.

"I think the children do that."

"You, the children, the way the manor is once again bright. I love you, Portia."

"Good, because I love you, too."

He lifted her into his arms.

"What are you doing?" she asked.

"After all these years, you still have to ask? I'm taking you to bed."

"Not until the children are asleep."

"Father will see to them. I told him I was planning to give you another child for Christmas."

Laughing, she pressed her head to his shoulder. "That must have made him happy."

"It made him ecstatic."

"Wait until you see what I'm giving you for Christmas."

"What would that be, my little vixen?"

"I think it's high time I taught you how to take me upside down."

$\mathcal{L}$OCKE awoke to see the barest hint of dawn easing in through the windows. He could see gently falling snow. The children would be delighted. His father would no doubt take them outside to build a snowman.

Snuggling up against his wife's warm body, he buried his nose in the curve of her shoulder, inhaling her jasmine scent. After all this time, it still had the power to incite his desires. If she hadn't worn him out the night before—

Suddenly he became aware of two things. The howling wind was not the high-pitched shrieking he was accustomed to, which was odd, as it was always worse in winter.

And a ticking clock.

Alarmed, he shot straight up in bed, threw back the covers, and rolled to his feet, crossing over to the mantel. The time showed twenty minutes past seven.

"What is it?" Portia asked sleepily.

"The clock is ticking and the time"—he looked toward the window—"the time could be accurate."

He crossed the room, snatched up his clothes from the floor, and began to don them.

"Killian, what's going on?"

"Go back to sleep. I just need to check on something."

"Your father."

He stilled. Deep down in his heart, he knew what he was going to find. "Something's not right."

"I'll come with you."

He wanted to argue with her, urge her to stay in bed, where it was toasty warm, but if he was correct, he was going to need her. When they were both dressed, they went down the hallway to his father's room. The door was open, the room empty.

"I think he's gone to her," he said quietly.

"He could be downstairs playing Father Christmas."

He shook his head. "No, he's gone to her, for the last time. That's why the clocks are ticking. He started them up before he left."

He headed back to the bedchamber, grabbed his coat and her pelisse, and held it out to her. "You don't have to come with me if you don't want to."

"I'm not going to let you face this alone." She turned and he draped the heavy cape over her shoulders.

They went down the stairs. In the foyer, the grandfather clock gonged the half hour. Taking Portia's hand, he led her outside. The wind and falling snow whipped around them as they trudged toward the ancient oak tree and his mother's grave.

And there was his father, lying prone over the mound of earth, one hand resting against the headstone as though he'd been caressing it. He was covered in a light dusting of snow. He hadn't been here long, not long enough for the cold to have done him in.

Crouching beside the body, Locke pressed his fingers against his father's throat. There was still a hint of warmth, but no pulse. "I think his heart gave out."

"Do you think he knew it was time?" she asked softly. "Was his starting up the clocks a parting gift to us?"

"Perhaps."

She knelt beside him and leaned against his shoulder. "I'm so sorry. I know this is hard. No matter a person's age . . ." She tightened her grip on his arm. "Killian, look at his cheek. It looks as though he was kissed by an angel."

On his father's cheek was a spot where the snow was not quite as thick, a spot whose shape very much resembled the outline of a mouth. "It's a paw print."

"There are no others on him or around him. I think it's as he always said. Your mother was waiting for him."

"Ghosts don't exist." Although he couldn't deny that the wind was quieter than he'd ever heard it.

"If I were to die before you, I wouldn't leave. Believe it is the mark of an animal if you wish. I choose to believe it was your mother welcoming him back into her arms."

Turning to her, he wanted to believe in a love that strong, a love that could transcend death. Out of the corner of his eye, a movement caught his attention, a shadowy image, two people holding each other close, walking away. Only when he looked squarely in that direction, he saw nothing at all. No distinct shadows, no footprints.

"What is it, Killian?" Portia asked softly.

It wasn't possible. Ghosts didn't exist. They were merely figments created by grief, a profound grief that was now washing through him, that had washed through his father for years.

Locke had been a babe when his mother died, too young to even understand loss, to weep for her, but he bowed his head now and let the tears flow, for a man he had loved and a woman he'd come to love through his father. Portia closed her arms around him, and they rocked while the wind wailed and the snow fell and at the residence the clocks ticked.

"IT'S odd to hear the clocks keeping time," Edward announced.

They were seated near the fireplace in the music room—the Marquess of Marsden's sons and their wives. His funeral had been a grand affair. Locke had been unprepared for the number of people who came: royalty, nobility, villagers, servants, miners. People coming to pay their last respects to a man who many of them remembered with fondness. Apparently his father had spent a good deal of time corresponding over the years, letters offering advice, counsel, and opinions. His father may have been a recluse but he hadn't been completely withdrawn from Society.

Fortunately, Portia had anticipated the crowd that descended on Havisham. Not that Locke was surprised. The daughter of a vicar certainly knew how to manage a funeral. His father now rested in a grave beside his mother.

"I'm growing accustomed to them," Locke said.

"I remember the day we arrived," Ashe said. "I never wanted to leave someplace so badly in all my life."

"That's understandable," Portia said. "You'd just lost your parents."

"It was more than that. It was the desolation, the wind, the silence of the clocks. And the way Marsden looked so lost. But that night after we'd gone to bed, he came to me and shared a story about a prank my father played at school. And he told me that it was okay to cry when I missed them, that for a year after he lost his wife he cried every night. 'The pain will never go away,' he said, 'but you will learn to live with it. And I will show you how.' Damned if he didn't." He raised his glass. "To the Marquess of Marsden and the privilege we had of knowing him better than most."

"Hear! Hear!" they all said, lifting their glasses in a salute.

$\mathcal{I}$T was sometime later that Portia found her husband standing out on the terrace that led from the ballroom, the place where he had first kissed her, no doubt hoping to run her off. She ambled up beside him. "Are you looking for your mother's ghost?"

"And my father's."

His words caught her by surprise. "I didn't think you believed in ghosts."

"The morning we found my father, I thought I saw something. I want to believe I did. My father and mother together."

"Then you should believe it."

"It makes me sound like a lunatic."

"It makes you sound like a man who can believe in the impossible."

He sighed. "When I was a lad, I awoke one night because I felt something brushing over my brow. But no one was there. I lay as still as death, afraid I was going insane, afraid I wasn't."

"You thought it was your mother touching you."

He nodded brusquely. "I may have done my father a disservice, believing he was mad."

"You never locked him away in an asylum. You cared for him. And he loved you. It was obvious in the letters he wrote me."

He studied her for a moment. "I often wonder how he knew you were the one for me. What did you say in your letters?"

"Didn't he let you read them?"

"No, he said I needed to ask my own questions. But I'm curious as to what questions he deemed important, what he asked of you."

Wedging herself between him and the railing, she placed her hands on his shoulders. "He only asked two things of me."

"Two? But he said you corresponded quite a bit."

"We did. In his first letter, he asked me to describe myself and to explain why I felt I met the requirements he sought. You heard those answers on the first day."

"And the second question?"

"Came in the last 'interview' letter he wrote to me. He asked if I believed in love."

"And you said yes."

She shook her head. "I said, 'Not any longer, but your letters make me wish I did.' I thought he would dismiss me at that point, but he wrote back, 'You're perfect.' And we began corresponding concerning our terms."

"Between the first and last interview letter, if he wasn't asking you questions, what was he telling you?"

She smiled softly, with sweet memories. "He told me all about the woman he loved and how he came to love her."

"I should like to read them."

"I thought you might, although I should warn you, he does tend to get a bit explicit sometimes."

"Oh, dear God, don't tell me he wrote about the piano."

"All right, I won't tell you."

His laughter echoed out over the gardens, where come spring an assortment of flowers would bloom. Then he crushed her to him and took her mouth with the same fever and passion he had the first time here on the terrace.

If he hadn't kissed her, she might have been able to walk away that day. Instead he'd sealed their fates. And she was ever so glad he had.

Author's Note

Baby farming was an actual Victorian practice. In this day and time, sometimes it's difficult to comprehend how disgraceful and damning it was to give birth to a child out of wedlock. It is my hope that I portrayed Portia's desperation in relation to the times in which she lived. Obviously, it is very unlikely that a woman in her position would have married an aristocrat—but then I do write fiction.

And this series isn't quite over. I want to share with you the love story that started it all. In early 2017, look for *Making Merry with the Marquess*, featuring the Marquess of Marsden and his Linnie in an e-novella with a very special happily ever after from Avon Impulse.

My best always,

Lorraine